When Love is not Enough

Wade Kelly

Dreamspinner Press

Published by
Dreamspinner Press
382 NE 191st Street #88329
Miami, FL 33179-3899, USA
http://www.dreamspinnerpress.com/

When Love Is Not Enough
Copyright © 2011 by Wade Kelly

Cover Art by Paul Richmond   http://www.paulrichmondstudio.com

ISBN: 978-1-61581-984-3

Printed in the United States of America
First Edition
August 2011

eBook edition available
eBook ISBN: 978-1-61581-985-0

For my friend Mark Bowne.
He was a true and dear friend to all!

Also for Anna and Jason.
Mom, Dad, and Nick.
And Meike

Thank you for your love
and support and encouragement.
Without you, this book
would not have been written.

Prologue

September 25, 2010

I NEVER thought life could fuck me in the ass this hard. What a shitty week!

I never expected to feel so much pain. Not at the age of twenty-one.

I wanted to shove my fist through the wall…

I was frozen to the spot as every muscle went limp…

… when I heard the words "he's dead," but as I clenched my fists I discovered all my strength was draining right out of my fingers.

… and the strength drained out of me.

I couldn't breathe.

I couldn't breathe. The glass of water I was holding slipped from my fingers seconds before I hurled all over my mother's pink carpet.

Harsh reality seized all logical thinking, pushing my mind beyond its capacity to grasp the truth. I sank to my knees and stared at the wooden floorboards, wondering why the fuck there was a small piece of blue shag carpet still sticking out from the shoe molding. My dad tore that carpet out years ago when he refinished the hardwood. Nothing made sense. My hands shook— my hands never shake—and I tried in vain to block the images flashing before my eyes: images of Jamie.

My hands shook as I swatted the images in front of my face…

I know Darian must have been feeling the same horror and disbelief I was.

… trying desperately to rid my mind of what I saw before me: images of Jamie, dead. Somehow, I know Matt shared what I was feeling right then.

It had to be.

It had to be.

Of course, I didn't know about Darian then.

I'd never met Matt before, not before the viewing.

It's so fucking odd, sitting in Jamie's room. The air's stale, and the bed's made up like a hotel suite. Darian should be here with me, but he lacks the balls. I don't blame him. His pain is worse than mine, in so many ways. I feel like he knew a different person than I did, and in a sense that was true. Darian knew a side of Jamie I will never know.

I can't bear being away from Matt, but I can't face Jamie's empty room. I have to trust Matt knows what he's doing by going in there. I have to trust he'll find the answers we're all looking for.

EVERYONE stared at me before the funeral. Whether they were conscious of the fact or not, their eyes darted in my direction with a certain loathing. As if I'd known he was going to do this and I had the power to stop him. *How could I know?* I'd known him my entire life, but I never knew Jamie was contemplating suicide.

The wake, if you call it that, was at my mom's after the "mourners" visited the gravesite. Everyone sat around gossiping about how shocking it was to hear the news. They whispered things like, "How could Jimmy Miller possibly have been so depressed? He was such a nice boy. He was such a pleasant boy. It must have been the strange friends he had. It must have been the music he listened to. It must have been the pressure he was under to succeed where his father failed in life." It must have been blah, blah, blah….

No one really knew the answer. Not even me.

I stood in his sterilized room, poking around, wondering where to begin my search for clues. All his things were tidied. I know who did it. Why his mother thought his death would be made easier by straightening up the piles of papers and CDs and photographs that cluttered his dresser and desk is beyond me. Jamie had *just* died; couldn't she leave his fucking stuff the way it was for more than six fucking days?

I looked in a few drawers before my brain clicked. *Behind Jamie's bed!* I snapped my fingers when I remembered the hole I put into the drywall the time we moved the furniture around and used his room as a mock battlefield. We stole two swords from his stepfather's collection of Elizabethan broadswords, and I swung mine too wide, missing Jamie's midsection. *Lucky for Jamie.* Jamie then added to the faux pas by slicing a neat square around the hole. He added hinges and a handle and everything, creating a door to stash his private things inside the wall.

If there were answers related to his death, they'd be in there!

I shoved the bed aside, removed the soccer poster from the wall, and opened up his secret compartment. In there I found his journals. Six in total, one for each school year, starting with 2004-2005 when our school's counselor came up with the idea he *write* instead of fight. He started at the end of sophomore year 2004, around March or April, I think. He never let me read them, but one time he told me he'd read me parts of the entries if I were "a good little boy." *Comedian!* He never did, though.

"I wonder if Darian read these?" I mumbled as I sat cross-legged on the floor and hurriedly flipped through each one until I found 2010. I needed to read the end. What was his last thought? Who did he write about? Did he think about slitting his wrists and OD'ing ahead of time? I had to know.

As my leafing neared the last few pages, an envelope fell out. It had my name on it. I couldn't blink as the curves of Jamie's handwriting held my eyelids open, my eyes fixated on the last piece of mail I would ever receive from him. I tore it open.

Dearest Matt,

Don't let Darian read this book. Burn it. Burn all of them. Take my secrets to the grave and let my pain end here. I couldn't be the person I wanted to be, the person you would want. I'm sorry. Know that I loved you more than the stars have power to kiss the night sky.

~Jamie

He loved me? Of course I knew he did, but he'd never stated it openly in all these years. I dropped the note and frantically found the last entry. What I saw was nothing like I expected to read. I'm not sure *what* I was looking to find, but this wasn't it!

I started crying, like my little sister had when our dog died, as I thought back on the moments he and I shared. I knew he had a lot going on. I knew he was under pressure and how much he tried to please everyone. No matter how hateful the words were, why would one comment push him over the edge? Knowing the end wasn't enough. I had to know what was going on in his head from the beginning.

I picked up 2004 and thought to myself, "Who the hell was Jamie Miller?"

1

April 16, 2004

    I punched Joey Taylor for calling my dad a loser. I got suspended, and now I have to write down my feeellliiings. FUCK!!! I'd rather punch something.

May 21, 2004

    I don't know why I have to write down my fucking thoughts. What if I don't have any thoughts?

June 10th

    School's out. Fucking Hallelujah!

July something

    My dad says he has to move again. I feel bad for him. My mom tells me I can't visit until he gets his house shit figured out. That totally blows. I miss my dad.

August 14, 2004

    Happy fucking birthday to me!

    I thought turning sixteen would be a big deal for me. Like maybe my mom would view it as some sort of rite of passage and she'd treat me different. I guess that only applies to girls, or to moms who give a shit. Obviously my mom couldn't care less. She sent me to my dad's this weekend: no presents, no cake.

I don't know why I feel so angry about it. I normally jump at the chance to see my dad. I miss him like hell most of the time. I only get to visit one weekend a month since my mom kicked him out and filed for divorce. I guess I should have started this fucking journal talking about the divorce and shit, but oh well.

My mom is such a bitch. What did my dad ever do to her? Seems to me he worked his ass off so we could afford to live in that big house she wanted. But what the fuck do I know? I'm just some dumb kid who gets in the way.

"HEY, Jimbo."

Jimmy looked up at the sound of his dad's voice. He grinned and closed his notebook.

"What you got there, buddy?" Dan Miller asked as he walked through the small kitchen and poured himself a cup of coffee. "Thanks for making my coffee, by the way." He smiled pleasantly as he added creamer to his mug.

"No problem." Jimmy shrugged. "It's a journal," he explained, keeping his eyes on the table in front of him. "The school's counselor suggested I keep one after the fight I had with Joey Taylor back in May."

"Did she say why?" he asked, concerned, dumping copious amounts of sugar into his coffee.

Jimmy pushed the crumbs around on the table. It wasn't like keeping the journal was a big deal. He just didn't know how his dad was going to react to the reason. "Um, she thinks I have anger issues over the divorce."

Mr. Miller paused. "Oh, I see."

Jimmy knew his dad was not an irrational sort of man. He always held his tongue in lieu of saying the wrong thing. Jimmy witnessed his behavior time and time again when his parents were still together—fighting, but still together. His mom would blow up, and his dad would stop midsentence and bite back his response. Seeing him go quiet now made Jimmy wonder what he was thinking. He just stood there, stirring his coffee incessantly.

"Dad, it's no big deal, really. She suggested if I write down my feelings instead of slugging people, I might learn how to control my temper. So far it's been fine." He rose and walked over to his dad. "Joey was the last bloody nose I dealt out."

His dad finally smirked. "Okay, as long as it's fine by you. I don't want you to feel obligated to express your feelings like a girl. Your mom never understood that boys show their emotions different than girls. I was proud you kicked that boy's behind." He winked and reassuringly squeezed Jimmy's shoulder. "But I also know fighting excessively spells more detention. I see the counselor's point. If writing in that thing helps, go for it. School starts in about two weeks. I'm hoping it'll be a better year for you."

"Thanks, Dad. Me too."

"Now," Dan turned his attention to the bread lying on the counter, "I need to make myself something to eat and get to work. I'm sorry I couldn't take off, but I didn't expect you for another two weekends. Your mom made my *lack* of visitation rights very clear to the lawyers. I'm hoping she'll bend a bit and give me every three weeks instead of once a month." He sighed, "Oh well. This isn't a great birthday, is it?"

Jimmy sighed also. "No, but I don't care. At least I'm not stuck at home with her."

"Hey," he said, pointing a finger at his son. "Don't disrespect your mother." He stopped threatening with his finger and turned back around, continuing the conversation with his back to Jimmy. "Do you want me to drop you at the mall? I could leave you there for a few hours and pick you up when I'm done with my shift at Walmart?"

"Nah, I'm gonna go exploring around here. Since you moved into this farmhouse, I haven't had time to look around. The summer flew by, what with you moving twice and Mom giving me all kinds of chores to do. I want to see if there are any good places to mess around." Jimmy picked up his notebook and headed toward the steps.

"Sounds good. And Jimmy...."

"Yeah, Dad?" He stopped with one foot on the step.

"Be careful. Some farmers around here don't like trespassers. They'll shoot first and ask questions later."

"Dad," he objected, sticking up one eyebrow, "this isn't the hills of West Virginia. I'll be fine."

"I'm merely letting you know."

Jimmy shook his head and walked up the steps.

The farmhouse was small, with only two bedrooms and a bath on the second floor. Jimmy brushed his teeth and stared into the mirror. His tired green eyes stared back. "I should go back to bed," he whispered. With a huff and a sigh he trudged out of the bathroom, grabbed his journal, and headed out the front door.

There had to be something interesting to do around here.

JIMMY walked down the country lane, looking at the surrounding fields and farms. A lot of corn was planted here. The state was known for sweet corn. He liked corn. It was great on the grill with barbecued chicken, or better yet—crabs! He loved steamed crabs the way the little shop around the corner made them. Loads of Old Bay made anything taste good. He remembered eating crabs in Massachusetts once, when he was a kid. The restaurant boiled them. Yuck! No flavor at all. Blue crabs were awesome steamed with Old Bay, a little vinegar, and sometimes beer. He licked his lips, thinking how yummy they would taste right now. If he only had a couple of bucks. His pocket produced lint upon inspection, so he kicked a rock and just kept walking.

He turned left onto the next crossroad and followed its winding path through the trees and cornfields. As he passed a dirt driveway on his left, Jimmy paused. Dirt driveways sometimes led to abandoned houses or hunting shacks. His eyebrow shot up. He was feeling rather inquisitive and decided to check it out.

The driveway was rutted and obviously rarely used. Grass grew in the center, at least a foot tall. No one could have driven up here lately unless they had four-wheel drive. The forest on both sides got thicker, obscuring his view. The birds in the trees were singing and chirping happily, so Jimmy wasn't bothered to be so completely isolated. Quiet always accompanied danger in the woods, like a precursor. Silent birds meant something was wrong. It was the same as growling dogs in the house at night. He felt safe when the dog was sleeping soundly, and now while the birds were chirping.

Something glinted through the hemlocks and oaks, and Jimmy stopped. *Water?* He could swear it was sun reflecting off of a pond. What a great place to explore! A few more feet and he noticed an overgrown path heading in that direction. He took it, and in five minutes Jimmy found the path opened up to reveal a hidden paradise. "Paradise" because it felt like it was solely his. It was a huge pond, surrounded by hemlocks and sycamores, a willow tree and a few redbuds, with just enough grass to lie back and enjoy the view of blue skies above.

He was about to walk to the water's edge when a voice from his right stayed him. "Who are you?"

Jimmy jumped. He looked to the person seated on the grass and stuttered, "Um, I, m-my name's J-Jim."

"This is private property, you know," the boy said, glaring at Jimmy from underneath his shaggy black hair.

"Oh, I'm s-sorry. I didn't mean to trespass." His dad's warning flashed through his mind. *Did this guy have a gun? He certainly looked scary.*

The kid, dressed all in black, got up and walked over to Jimmy. "I don't care." He shrugged. "It's not my property. I'm here illegally too. Got a light?" He took out a cigarette and tapped the butt on the pack.

"No." Jimmy shook his head. "I don't smoke."

"You're better off. I wish I never stole my mom's cigs when I was eleven. It's a bad habit to get into." The kid's expression lightened and Jimmy felt much less threatened. "So, what's your name again?"

"Jim. I don't mean to bother you. I can leave."

He gave Jimmy the once-over. "No, it's okay. You look all right." The boy tucked his cigarettes back into his tight black jeans and stuck out his hand. "My name's Darian. Darian Weston. I live up the road. I was just messing with you about the private property shit. I mean, it *is* privately owned, but the owner hasn't been around for years. My mom says he's trying to sell this land, but no one wants to pay the asking price. Whatever. I come here to be alone."

Jimmy shifted his weight from one foot to the other. "Are you sure it's okay if I stay? I mean… you don't even know me."

"No, but most people won't even talk to me. So, if you aren't afraid, and you aren't gonna beat the shit out of me, then I'm glad for the company." He pointed to Jimmy's notebook. "You write? Or draw?"

Jimmy looked down and lifted his notebook. "This? I write."

"Cool. I draw. You write poetry, or what?"

Jimmy chuckled. "Poetry? Um, no." It finally clicked; this kid must be emo. Or goth? *What was the difference again?* He unquestionably had the look of some high-school clique. Black T-shirt, black jeans, abnormally black hair, purple nail polish, pierced eyebrow, and Jimmy even noticed black eyeliner under his long lashes. Most assuredly emo and possibly gay, Darian was no longer a threatening presence. Jimmy felt his insides relax. "I write… stuff," he answered ambiguously. "Whatever comes to mind. Kind of a project my school's counselor suggested."

"What? You got emotional issues?" Darian asked bluntly.

"Something like that," he answered with a shrug. Maybe he wasn't vague enough.

"Me too." Darian bent down and picked up a stone. He skipped it sideways into the pond; five hops and then it sank. "I was cutting last year. My gym teacher freaked when he noticed the marks. I had to sit through weeks of bullshit." He held out his arm, removing the leather wrist cuff. "See. I still have three scar lines."

Jimmy swallowed a lump in his throat. "Fuck." He'd never thought of cutting before. Sure, he was upset a lot, but he never thought of hurting himself by dragging a blade across his skin. Mostly his frustration came out in the form of fistfights. Darian didn't even seem to mind showing him. Jimmy wasn't sure if he was proud of the scars or just didn't care about them at all. "What school do you go to?"

"Winter's Mill. You?"

"Westminster High School."

"Ah, Heroin High. Too bad. How come you go there when you live out here?"

Jimmy sat in the grass and set his book down. "I'm just visiting my dad this weekend. Most of the time I live with my mom on Larson Court. I used to live practically across the street from the high school, but we had to move after the divorce."

Darian's eyebrows shot up. "To the richie-rich part of town!"

"Not really," he said defensively.

"It's cool. I'm not judging." Darian picked up and threw another stone. "I live with my mom as well. Never knew my dad. My mom has a different boyfriend all the time. Got four siblings, all from different sperm donors."

Jimmy's eyes went wide. "Damn!"

"Yeah, we're a fucked-up family. Do you have brothers and sisters?"

"Two stepsisters and a half brother. Tommy is six months old. My mom only seems to have time for him, lately."

Darian came over and sat in the grass next to Jimmy. "And let me guess, you get left out of everything?"

"Yup." Jimmy grinned, looking at this very congenial fellow. *How could people not like him?* Jimmy's normally reticent personality took a back seat in light of Darian's charm. It wasn't so much the things Darian said that drew him in as the way Darian's eyes lit up when he looked at Jimmy. He found himself asking, "You got a book of drawings I might get to see sometime?"

Darian smiled and nodded. "Sure, I'll see what I can find." He lay back in the grass and closed his eyes, folding one arm behind his head and the other across his stomach.

Jimmy grinned and did the same.

The clouds floated by and drained away every care Jimmy had in the world. He closed his eyes. His ears picked up a blue jay, off in the distance. He heard a bullfrog. He heard rustling in the leaves, somewhere behind his head. *A squirrel, maybe?* It didn't matter. The birds were chirping, and he felt safe.

Jimmy also heard Darian breathing, slow and steady, as if he were sleeping. Jimmy knew he wasn't. The boy was just lying there listening to the sounds of nature and enjoying the quiet. Jimmy's insides fluttered. As he lay there with Darian, listening to the smallest of sounds and sharing the most peaceful moment of his life, Jimmy knew meeting Darian Weston was going to be one of the best birthday presents of all time. He took a deep breath and relaxed more fully than he had in years.

2

September 3, 2004

Labor Day weekend starts tomorrow. I can't wait. I get to be at my dad's for three whole days. I know he has to work, because it's a holiday and all, but I don't care. When he's not working maybe we can go hiking or something. Ooooh, or fishing at that pond I found a few weeks ago.

I wonder if Darian likes to fish? Hmmm... I'll have to ask.

School is going good so far. Nobody's said anything to me about my parents or how my dad moved or how my mom put the house up for sale when she finally married Mr. Mustache Man. No jokes yet, but I won't hold my breath. I think Joey was about to say something in PE, but Matt glared at him for me.

I've been grateful for Matt. If it wasn't for him looking out for me, I think I'da been in a lot more fistfights. I guess it pays off for him to work out all the time and build up his muscles. No one messes with him. Well, come to think of it, no one messed with him before. I remember him being a scrawny-ass little guy in middle school, and no one seemed to care. They liked him anyhow. Who wouldn't? Matt's the perfect friend.

I think he's....

Something hard smacked Jimmy on the back of the head and stopped his thoughts dead in their tracks. He stopped writing but kept his head down. He really didn't want to turn around and see who threw the dinner roll that came with the school lunch. He waited. *No more fights,* he whispered to himself.

"Hey, Miller. Your stupid dad get a job yet? I hear they fired his ass from Big Lots." Snickering ensued.

Jimmy closed his eyes. He knew that voice and those snickers. Joey Taylor was not the guy he wanted to deal with right now. He was controlling his anger. Right? Control. He took a few deep breaths and sat stock-still. A juice box hit him in the back of the head. Jimmy turned quickly in his seat at the lunch table.

"Now, now, Joey Taylor…." Matt happened by at the most convenient of times. "I thought you were due in Mrs. Monroe's room for academic support?" He winked at Jimmy before peering confidently at Joey.

Joey scrunched up his eyes and scratched his head, mussing up his unruly red curls. "Yeah, so? I don't see how it's any of your business, Dixon."

"It's not." Matt shrugged. "I was simply dropping off some textbooks in her office and overheard her talking to another teacher. She said something about 'wondering where you were' and having to talk to your mom, that's all."

Matt's cool tone almost made Jimmy snort juice out through his nose. He choked back laughter. *Damn, Matt's good!*

"Aw, shit!" Joey cursed, grabbing his books and dashing off through the lunchroom doors.

"Did you really hear Mrs. Monroe saying that?" another boy asked.

Jimmy piped up and answered for his friend. "Rob, you know Matt wouldn't lie about something like that."

"Nah, I guess not." Satisfied, the boy went back to eating. Joey was forgotten. So was Jimmy.

Matt smiled at Jimmy, sauntered over and sat down. "Joey's such a schmoe. He'll never learn to leave you alone."

"I know."

Matt's eyes flickered over to Jimmy's notebook. "You still writing?"

"Yup."

"It working?"

"I guess. I didn't chuck my lunch tray back at him."

Both boys chuckled. Matt nudged Jimmy with his elbow and shook his head. "You really going to your dad's this weekend?"

"Yeah."

"Bummer. I was hoping we could shoot some hoops. It's been a real drag since you moved. I can't crawl into your window whenever I want and talk about my problems."

Jimmy rolled his eyes. "What problems do you have? You have the perfect family. Your dad is perfect. Your brother and sister aren't pestering you all the time. And your mom never screams at you for anything."

"That's only because she doesn't know anything." Matt lifted an eyebrow and tilted his head toward his friend. "It's all in how you play your cards, young Padawan."

"Padawan!" He slapped the table. "That reminds me… I can't wait to show you the sword collection that Mustache Man—I mean, my stepdad—has in our living room. It is so cool. He has broadswords and chainmail, even a whole suit of armor! Maybe we could do a mock battle or something when my parents aren't home?"

Matt's mouth hung open. "And *this* is the year your parents decide to split up and move? That sucks. We could be reenacting the Battle for Middle-earth this weekend."

Jimmy grinned. Matt might sound irritated, but he knew his friend was all growl with no fangs. He knew Matt was as unhappy about the move as he was, but there was no way around the situation. It wasn't like he'd moved far—they still went to the same school—it was the unwanted inconvenience of *not* walking to school every morning and hanging out every afternoon. Matt walked from Tall Pines Drive, and Jimmy took a bus.

"We can reenact it, just not over winter break. I think there's a wine-tasting thing in… February. Maybe you could spend the night! My parents will be gone all day, and you can pretend to be Legolas all you want. As long as we don't break any of my mom's stuff."

"Sounds good. We'll hang out in your room. I don't want to set foot near your mom's mini art museum anyway. Too risky."

Jimmy rolled his eyes. "You got that right."

Matt stood up at the sound of the bell. "Come on, you can't be late for Mr. Reeves' class."

"You're not kidding. My mom shit a brick when I got a 91 percent on the review quiz we took Wednesday." Jimmy picked up his tray and his books and walked with Matt to the door. He deposited his trash in the bin as they left the cafeteria.

"Why'd you tell her about the quiz? It was only for review."

Kids crowded the halls, but to Matt and Jimmy the noise faded into nothing when they were together.

"I didn't." Jimmy shrugged. "It fell out of my backpack, and she picked it up for me. I thought she was going to hit me. She had that look in her eyes. You know the one."

"Shit. Sorry, man. I'll help you study for the next one."

"Thanks. I really wish I still lived next door." Jimmy's shoulders drooped.

Matt picked up on his gloominess and placed his arm across Jimmy's shoulders. "Cheer up, man, things'll get better. I've had my license for a few weeks now—finally passed the stupid parallel parking. Dad said I can borrow the Jeep whenever I want—*as long as I keep my grades up*—so I'll be over all the time. He might even buy an Outback and *give* me the Jeep. We'll get together often, you'll see. It just takes more planning than popping through a window."

"Yeah." Jimmy was not bouncing back so easily, even if Matt was practically hugging him. "Maybe when you come to my new house, you can come through the window for old time's sake?"

"Yeah, okay." Matt laughed, casually removing his arm from Jimmy's shoulders. He shifted his books as they stopped at his locker.

Jimmy leaned on the locker next to his. "So, are the new neighbors nice?"

"They're fine." Matt placed his physics book in his locker and took out calculus.

"Will you be climbing through my old window to chat with the new kid?"

Matt shook his head. "No, I don't think so. That kid is wound too tight. I think he'd probably rat on me if I crossed the yard through the flowerbed, let alone crawled through the window instead of using the front door."

Jimmy chuckled. "Ah, but is he cute?"

Matt's eyes bulged. "Dude!" He looked around nervously. "We're in school."

Jimmy looked down, ashamed for forgetting himself. "Sorry."

Matt scanned the immediate surroundings. "It's okay, Jamie." He gripped Jimmy's shoulder. "I know it's hard to keep all my secrets to yourself, every second of the day."

"But I do!" he stressed.

Matt smiled. "I know. You're the bestest friend ever." Matt closed his locker and leaned closer to his friend. "And *yes*… he is. But it doesn't change rule number one."

"The proximity rule?" They started down the hallway and picked up the pace as they both noticed how few students were left meandering.

"Exactly! I'm not fucking a guy within fifty miles of my house. I may even up it to seventy-five. The last hook-up was sixty miles away, and it made me think that's still too close. I seriously don't want to see that dude again. Way too clingy."

"What was his name?"

"I'm not sure. Something with a 'P', I think. Peter or Patrick, Paul or Penelope?"

"Penelope's a girl's name."

"Oh, yeah, then it *definitely* wasn't Penelope! Here's my class. I'll see you later."

"And *why* do you never bother to catch a name, again?"

"Jamie! Fuck and run, I keep telling you. I'm seventeen fucking years old, for goodness sake, and I'm a senior. I don't need to be tied down and deal with relationship crap. As soon as I cum, I'm done. I don't need anything else."

Jimmy nodded. "Right." He'd heard the explanation before, but deep in his gut he hoped the reason would change. He hoped Matt would change. His lifestyle seemed meaningless, and Jimmy worried Matt would waste his youth chasing after the next piece of ass. "See ya later."

"Yeah, see ya, Jamie!"

Jimmy heard the bell and knew he was late for class. He really didn't want to go. Suddenly he longed for a serious rewind of his life, back to the times when things were simpler. Back to when it was just him and Matt, and they were too young to think about life beyond *Star Wars* and *Lord of the Rings*.

3

September 22, 2010
3:38 p.m.

MATTHIAS DIXON fingered the rim of the wooden casket with distant fascination. It wasn't as if he'd never attended a viewing before, but this one… this one sucked all the sorrow right out of him, until he felt as if he were nothing more than a hollow shell. The real Matt, the one who truly cared about people and expressed emotion and sadness at appropriate times, was somewhere on holiday. The Matt who stood in Haight Funeral Home this afternoon was a wraith, a disembodied spirit, a mindless zombie version of his true self.

His arm fell limply to his side. *Why the fuck'd they pick blue satin?* Matt scoffed. *He wouldn't like blue satin. Black, or even white, but never baby blue! Pft!*

Okay, perhaps *all* his emotions were not drained from his body. Right now he felt cynical. His eyes wandered to the spray of flowers on top of the casket. "Stupid roses," he mumbled. *Didn't they know he hated roses? Ever since the summer of '05 when he worked for Larson's Lawn and Garden Service, and his arms got all ripped up on Mrs. Buckman's Pink Promise roses. Why would someone choose those?*

His eyes caught the card. "James, I'll always love you. Mother." Matt fussed and rolled his eyes. "Figures! Nobody called him James but you."

Matt heard someone sniffling behind him, so he stepped aside politely. He recognized the woman—short brown hair, angular face—it was Mr. Miller's cousin Maggie. Her eyes were red, and tears flowed freely down her cheeks. She clutched a sodden tissue to her nose as she looked at the body. Matt studied the bouquet on a stand next to the casket, which displayed "Beloved Son" across the front of carnations and alstroemeria, in an attempt to keep from staring at Maggie. That would be rude. She was obviously devastated, judging by the way her shoulders bobbed up and down in time with her loud sobs.

Matt didn't want to make Maggie feel self-conscious—she wasn't normally a weepy woman—and so he looked at the flowers instead. He would move away altogether, except he hadn't actually worked up the nerve to look his best friend in the face. He knew what he'd see, but four attempts later and Matt still hadn't looked into the embalmed face of the person he'd laughed with for the last twenty-two years.

A small vase of red gerbera daisies caught the corner of his eye, and he stepped over to read the card. "*I'll miss you, Jamie. ~D.W.*"

Matt was taken aback. "Jamie?" He sneered at the accuracy. "Who knew him as Jamie besides me?" *And gerbera daisies?* Matt wondered how the hell D.W. knew Jamie liked those. "Who the fuck is D.W. anyway?"

Matt voiced his discontent a little too loudly and was shushed by a blue-haired lady with angry eyes. "Sorry," he whispered back. She stuck her nose in the air and moved away.

He went back to staring at the card. "D.W.… D.W." He could not stop repeating those initials. It was as if he craved some epiphany to occur like a resounding crescendo and enlighten him to the owner of said initials. He waited. Nothing happened. Several minutes went by, and Matt could not come up with one friend of Jamie's whose initials were D.W. He didn't have that many friends.

Cousin Maggie was still sobbing her goodbyes as she walked away, allowing Matt another opportunity. He couldn't do it. Now he was suddenly obsessed with the initials D.W. and how Jamie had a friend he knew nothing about. *How could he have a friend I knew nothing about?* He knew everything about Jamie!

At least he thought he did.

He knew Jamie liked gerbera daisies because a girl in school wrote a poem about them, and it almost made him cry. He loved

Mounds Bars, and his favorite color was red. People stupidly assumed it was because red was the color of blood, and Jamie was pretty depressing and scary-looking when he went through his goth stage in eighth grade, but blood had nothing to do with it. Jamie liked red because it reminded him of the red crocheted quilt his grandmother used to cover him up with when he spent the night at her house, when he was little. She died in '98, and Jamie said the color helped him remember her.

Jamie Miller liked Mustangs, black widows, and the smell of smoke after the fireworks on the Fourth of July. Matt knew Jamie. He was the only guy Matt could say anything to and never feel embarrassed, judged, or ashamed.

They grew up together on Tall Pines Drive in a small development across from Westminster High School. Matt remembered kickball in the middle of the street and tree forts built in the narrow strip of trees across from Jamie's house before the county extended Hook Road and cut down the trees.

Matt was the one to call Jimmy "Jamie" in the first place! *He was like, nine, I think... yeah, nine...*

... Matt crawled up the tree outside Jimmy's window. He could hear Jimmy's parents fighting in the living room, and he *knew* his buddy was stuck upstairs having to hear every word. "Jim," he called. Nothing. He leaned closer to the window. "Jimmy?" he said in a louder voice, but hopefully not loud enough to be heard downstairs.

Nothing. He broke a twig off and flung it at the windowpane. A moment later, Jimmy peeked out. He looked awful. His puffy eyelids spoke volumes, and Matt knew he needed to get him out of there. He waved him to come out.

Jimmy opened the window. "What?" he asked weakly.

"Come on, you know you can't stay in there when they do this."

Jimmy hesitated but climbed out onto the porch roof as asked and reached for the branch. Lucky for the both of them, the Millers had not taken the time to trim the tree limbs away from the house. The two boys climbed down the tree and scampered off to the Dixon residence.

The two-story colonial sat just next door, modest yet spacious enough for three children and a dog. The Dixons had lived there two months longer than the Millers had lived in their home. Matt opened the front door and walked right in.

"Where're you boys going?" asked Mr. Dixon from his comfortable recliner.

"Up to my room," Matt answered and kept on walking.

Once upstairs, Matt shut the door and turned on the stereo, quiet enough not to get in trouble, but loud enough to cover their conversation.

"Why do you have lipstick on your floor?"

Matt turned around to see Jimmy picking up a gold tube off the shag carpet. He snatched it away from him. "I don't know. Maybe Mom dropped it." He tossed it on top of the dresser and flopped onto the bed. "Sorry your parents were fighting again. Must be pretty tough to listen to them bickering all the time."

"Yup," Jimmy answered.

Matt watched his expression change from indifferent to frustrated to full-on sad in a matter of seconds. Jimmy could not fight the tears. His shoulders slumped, and he covered his face with his hands.

"Crap," Jimmy uttered.

Matt reached out and pulled him to his side. They both sat there on the edge of the bed. Jimmy cried, and Matt kept one arm draped over his friend's shoulders. Matt didn't know what to say. His own parents hardly ever fought. Jimmy leaned closer to him, laying his head on his shoulder. He was crying harder, so Matt gave Jimmy's shoulder a consoling rub.

Just then, some '80s rock tune came on. Van Halen, maybe? He didn't know the words, but he had heard the song enough. His dad played '70s and '80s rock all the time. *Something, something, she wants to send him a letter, something.* But he knew the chorus: *oh, whoa, whoa, Jamie's cryin'.*

Matt could not stop his mouth from singing along. "Oh, whoa, whoa, Jamie's cryin'...." Jimmy tilted his head and glared at him. Matt repeated, "Something, something, oh, whoa, whoa, Jamie's cryin'...."

Jimmy shoved Matt's arm away from his shoulders and snapped, "Shut up!"

Matt sang louder, "Oh, whoa, whoa, Jamie's cryin'...."

Jimmy clenched his fists by his sides. "I said shut up!"

Jimmy wasn't crying anymore. He actually seemed to be on the verge of laughing, so Matt kept it up. He butchered the words and stood up and did a little dance. "She's gonna write a letter and make herself feel better. Oh, whoa, whoa, Jamie's cryin'." Matt twirled around and wiggled his posterior at Jimmy.

Jimmy rolled away from him. "Stoooopppp!"

Matt turned around triumphantly and smiled. "I knew I could get you laughing again! Jay-*me*."

"*Ha, Ha*! Quit it." Jimmy was not laughing.

"No seriously. I'm calling you Jamie from now on. Then every time you get upset, you can remember tonight and how I can make you laugh, even when you're crying like a girl."

"You jerk," Jimmy fussed and threw Matt's pillow at him.

Matt giggled. His friend lunged at him, tackling him and pinning him to the floor. Matt smirked. "You know I'm stronger." He flipped Jimmy over and straddled his waist, tickling his ribs.

"Stop, stop, stop!" Jimmy wrestled to get free.

Matt got off Jimmy and offered him a hand to stand up. Jimmy glared but took it. Matt patted his shoulder. "I can't fix your parents, but I can keep you laughin'... Jamie."

This time Jimmy didn't argue. "Thanks," he replied with a thin smile. "You're the bestest friend I've ever had."

Matt felt the same but couldn't bring himself to be all sentimental about it. "And don't you forget it!" He gloated instead...

... Ever since, the nickname stuck. Jamie called Matt the bestest friend he ever had, and the two of them were inseparable. Matt walked back over and fingered that stupid little card attached to the vase of red gerbera daisies one more time. "So how the hell does D.W. rate 'Jamie'?" Matt swore, feeling somehow betrayed.

4

October… what the fuck day is it? 2004

> *There are times when I wake up and forget we moved. I push back the covers and wander over to my window, and that's when it hits me: Matt's window is no longer opposite mine.*

"PARENTS are getting a divorce, huh? That sucks." Matt turned the top tuning peg on his guitar and plucked the string again.

"Totally. But that's not the worst part." Jimmy shifted on Matt's bed to face his friend, who was leaning against the windowsill. "The worst part is we're moving."

"What!" Matt's shock made him drop his cigarette from the corner of his mouth. "Shit," he snapped as he hurriedly picked up the burning butt before it singed the carpet. "When?"

"Not sure. Dad said it depends on the market and how fast the house sells. Mom says she and… Kevin, are keeping it. I don't know who to believe," Jimmy said. "You should really quit those."

"Yeah, easier said than done." Matt put the cigarette out and went back to tuning. "So, you *might* be moving—that blows. We just got a routine down where you make breakfast and I do your Spanish homework. That totally sucks! Where am I gonna eat in the morning?"

"Shut the fuck up, man. You can eat at your own fucking house. Let's focus on the bigger picture—me, leaving the neighborhood. *Me*— living far away from *you*. Whose window do I crawl into when I'm thinking of killing myself?" He got off the bed and paced the cluttered room.

"Jamie, you wouldn't do that."

"No." Jimmy stopped and rubbed the back of his neck. "But I might kill my mom. I saw that in a movie, I think. Ooooh,"—he snapped his fingers—"I could *make* the movie. A repressed kid picks up a cleaver one day and hacks his mom into little bits when she's asleep, all because she grounded him for getting a B- on a science quiz." Jimmy paused for effect and added whimsically, "Then he goes into the kitchen to make himself a ham sandwich."

Matt rolled his eyes. "More proof it will never happen. You get straight A's. Plus, deep down you love your mom."

"Did you know she's pregnant?"

"What? No way!" Matt laid the guitar flat on his lap.

"Yup. One month. They think I don't know, but they yell pretty loud sometimes."

"Is it your dad's?"

Jimmy glared. "No! Would you sleep with her the way she treats my dad?"

"You can't expect me to answer that. It's apples and oranges."

"Sorry…. Your orientation aside, would you ever think about sleeping with my mom?"

"No. She's too moody." Matt strummed and grinned, happy with the adjusted pitch.

Jimmy flopped back onto the mattress and stared at the ceiling. "Exactly."

I miss being able to talk to Matt whenever I want. He's really the only person in the world who understands me. I don't know why life is so fucking complicated. I liked it before all the change. Well… not really…. If I'm totally honest, things were not great for years.

It was awful when the fights started between my mom and dad. I sat in my room and tried in vain to drown them out with loud music, but it never worked. They'd punish my ass with more chores for being a bother when they—the friggin' parents—were trying to have a discussion. Yeah, right!?! I don't know how Dad put up with her for as long as he did. She was never happy then, and she's never happy now.

She wants straight A's; I get straight A's. She ranted about me wearing black; I bought a red shirt. Nothing makes her like me any better. Now she keeps telling me Matt's a bad influence. SINCE WHEN? I've known him my whole life, and now he's a bad influence? She grumbled about his use of guns and killing small animals. Whatever! I know hunting can't be the real issue, since she said I could go with him sometime. Something else is bothering her, and she's using hunting as the excuse.

All I know is that she better not tell me I can't see Matt. I think I'd rather die. He keeps me together, ya know?

Matt....

JIMMY tapped the side of the pencil on his forehead.

Where is Matt today? I hope he's not out doing some nameless dude behind a Tevco. He's going to get hurt one of these days.

Jimmy pushed his chair back from his desk and picked up his cell phone. He flipped it open and sent a text: *Dude, Where U @? Can I call?*

He got a quick reply: *I'm @ Target w/ my mom. Sure, call...*

He hit the speed dial and listened as it rang. Once.

"Hey, Jamie, what's up?"

Jimmy liked the sound of that voice. "Missing you."

"What?"

Matt genuinely sounded as if he didn't hear Jimmy's comment. Knowing he sounded pathetic, Jimmy quickly got to his point. "Nothing. Are you really going deer hunting this weekend? Because I think I'd like to go."

"Oh, good golly. Jamie, buddy, my dearest friend, there is no way you're going deer hunting, especially during bow season. I'd be afraid of you hitting *me*!"

"Ha, ha, ha," he exaggerated his mock laughter. Jimmy plopped down on the edge of his bed. "You don't know that. I bet I could hit something."

"Something? Yes. But a deer? No. I thought your mom loathed hunting anyway?"

"She does this week, but she likes getting steaks from your dad. I asked if I could go, and she said okay. I gotta make sure my chores are done and my homework is all caught up, and I need a ride from you. She can't be bothered to drive me to your house." Jimmy huffed. His mother's rules were exhausting to remember.

"No problem. I'll come get you. Better yet, spend the night. We have to leave at like four o'clock in the morning and shit."

"I'll ask and call you back."

"Okay."

Jimmy flipped his phone shut and went downstairs to find his mom in the kitchen, making dinner. He took a deep breath and steadied his nerves. "Mom?"

"Yes, James?"

It irked him that she didn't even give him the courtesy of looking up. She just kept chopping carrots with her back turned. "Mom, can I spend the night at Matt's this Friday?"

She stopped chopping and looked up. "Matt?" To Jimmy it sounded like an accusation rather than a question.

"Yeah, Matt. Remember? You said I could go hunting with him if I did all my chores and stuff. He's going deer hunting this weekend with his dad and suggested I spend the night since they'll leave real early in the morning."

She took a breath and appeared to be mulling it over. He hated when she looked like that, because normally the answer was *no*. "Fine. But you better make sure the laundry is done, because I don't have time to do your chores and take care of the baby and make dinner and—"

"Mom, I will!" he insisted. "I've been doing a load a day just to make sure I don't get behind. I even ironed Kevin's, I mean Dad's, favorite work shirt."

She smiled. "Well, that's a good boy. It's nice to see you listening for a change."

I listen all the time, but you never take the time to notice. "So I can go?"

"Yes. Against my better judgment." She resumed her dinner preparations.

"Mom, Matt is a great guy. I don't know why you think—"

"James, Matt is one of those Bible-thumping Christians. We lived next to his parents for fifteen years, don't you forget. They belong to that Bible church on the hill and go around evangelizing the whole town." Joan Smithers shook her head in disgust. "I just wonder about their ethics if they condone killing animals."

Jimmy had never seen her act this way. Why did she suddenly loathe Christians? *And killing animals? What the fuck?*

"Mom," Jimmy felt the need to defend his friend's honor, "Matt's family never tried to shove their religion on us. They didn't knock on our door every summer like the Mormons or Jehovah's Witnesses. They invited us to church activities sometimes, big deal. They were always nice, even when you continually turned them down. And you never minded the hunting when Mr. Dixon gave you deer steaks."

Joan gave him a stern glare. "I don't appreciate being reprimanded by my own son."

Jimmy quickly changed his tune, almost begging but without the "falling prostrate" part. "Mom, I'm not. I'm sorry. I didn't mean anything by—"

Joan dropped what she was doing and thrust the knife handle toward her son. "Since you are so full of time and energy, you can finish chopping these vegetables and put them in the pot. Make sure you set the stove to simmer."

"But Mom, I still have homework to do."

"You should have thought of that before you back-talked me. You can finish your homework after you're finished doing the vegetables." She turned on her heel and left Jimmy gaping at her back.

His phone buzzed.

Jimmy made sure she wasn't about to walk back in before he flipped it open.

A text from Matt: *Long convo, man. U in for Fri?*

He texted back: *Yeah, I'll spend the night. I'm just gonna go through hell between now and then.*

K. See ya!

See ya :-]

Jimmy resumed chopping and hoped he had enough time after dinner to finish his homework *and* get some sleep before school tomorrow.

5

November 6, 2004

"YOU really went hunting? Wow."

Jimmy looked at Darian. "Yeah."

He was sitting on the floor in Darian's room, leaning against the side of the bed. Visiting his emo friend was fast becoming a permanent activity on the weekends he spent with his dad. In truth, ever since they'd first met, Jimmy enjoyed seeing Darian just as much as he enjoyed spending time with his dad. Dan Miller always had to work at least one or two shifts on the weekend, so during the hours his dad was at Walmart, Jimmy hung out with Darian.

It wasn't so bad missing time with his dad if he could fill those hours getting to know someone new. He liked Darian. He was interesting. Unusual. And a little rebellious. Jimmy liked the edgy vibe he got from Darian. He was confident in a different way than Matt. Matt dripped with self-assurance. Matt was tall and strong and popular. He practically walked on water at their school, and Jimmy felt completely safe in his presence.

Darian made Jimmy feel just as content, but for different reasons.

Darian wasn't strong. Jimmy could see that in his body structure. The boy was a bag of bones. His skintight clothes clung to him, and Jimmy could see there was no real definition to his chest or his arms. Still, Darian didn't carry himself like a coward or a weakling.

Jimmy also gleaned from conversation that Darian was not popular. His comments suggested he was ridiculed for being different, yet Darian did not seem to cave to the status quo. He wore what he wanted, painted his nails, and shrugged off slander by saying, "I can't make people like me by pretending to be something I'm not. Then they'll end up liking whatever I become just to be accepted. I'd rather be hated for who I am than liked for who I'm not."

Jimmy longed for that kind of strength.

"Can I look yet?" he asked, leaning forward.

Darian protectively pulled the sketchpad against his chest. "No. I told you, 'when I'm done'. Just sit there and try not to move." He resumed drawing when Jimmy sat back against the bed.

Jimmy's eyes drifted over the room as he waited for his portrait to be completed. Darian was undeniably an artist! He had all kinds of pictures pinned to his black walls.

My mom would never let me paint my room black.

There were watercolor paintings and charcoal sketches. Jimmy even noticed a few scribbles in crayon, which were obviously done when Darian was younger. Even using crayons, Darian's talent showed through. His attention to detail in things like a cat's face or a water pitcher was just about the best Jimmy had ever seen. He marveled at the shading and definition Darian put into each of his creations.

Jimmy realized Darian's art was the reason his books and clothes were all over the floor. His walls had no space for shelves. They were covered ceiling to floor with art. Sure, there were spaces in between the paper and canvases, but even those areas had something "arty" pinned there. Jimmy noticed scraps of magazine photos and labels from beer bottles. There was a plastic Baggie hanging near the light switch, containing bottle caps. There was even a decorative mosaic tile trivet hung among the agglomeration.

Is there no limit to his talent?

"Done," Darian announced.

"Finally," Jimmy groaned. "I think my butt fell asleep waiting. We've been sitting on this floor for hours." He arched and stretched his back. "So let me see."

Darian hesitated.

"What?" Jimmy asked. "Why do you look so concerned? Is it that bad?"

"No, I just… I've never sketched someone before. More precisely, I never sketched someone I know and then showed it to them. Please don't laugh."

Jimmy didn't know why he was acting so worried all of a sudden. He was very talented. *Surely he knows that?* Judging by all the stuff hanging in his room, Darian could become a professional artist or an art professor. What made him so self-conscious? "Come on, show me. I promise I won't laugh."

Darian slowly turned the sketchpad around, and Jimmy's jaw dropped.

It was him. Of course he knew it would be! When the two of them had sat on the floor, hours ago, Darian had asked if Jimmy would mind if he drew his portrait. Jimmy had shrugged and said, "Go ahead." Jimmy was not prepared, however, for the amount of detail and care his friend would devote to creating something so lifelike it was as if the picture would move any second.

The sketch was done in pencil and layered over in chalk. Darian had captured Jimmy perfectly, from the deep color of his dark green eyes to the tiny scar through his right eyebrow. It was like looking into a mirror. The portrait's brown hair was exactly his shade—and longer than he remembered.

Maybe I do need to get it trimmed, like Mom said?

Darian's depiction showed Jimmy slumped forward, arms draped over his knees, leaning back against the mattress and peering sideways at the artist through his unkempt hair. Darian had captured the folds in Jimmy's black T-shirt and the holes in his high-top Chucks. Even the silver cross hanging around his neck—the one Matt had picked up when he was on a mission trip to St. Petersburg a few years ago—had not been missed by Darian's trained eye. This was Jimmy, through and through, and suddenly he was at a loss for words to express his approval to Darian.

"Darian, I… wow, this is…." The words stumbled through his lips. "Wait!" Jimmy scooted closer. "What's this?" Jimmy pointed at the portrait and furrowed his brow. "I don't have a lip ring!"

Darian shrugged sheepishly. "I know. I just thought it'd look cool."

Jimmy grinned and tugged the sketchpad free from his friend's clutching fingers. He looked it over a few more minutes. "It does look pretty cool, but my mom would never let me get my lip pierced."

"Too bad. Mine doesn't care. Or at least she never says. So, you really like it?"

Jimmy looked up. "Yeah, totally! This is the best drawing I've ever seen. I can't believe you drew me so well."

Darian took the portrait back and ran his chalk-covered thumb along the edge. "It's all about how you perceive the subject and allowing your emotion to drain out through your fingertips. A good artist draws what he feels, like a good musician plays from his heart."

Jimmy felt a flush of heat go through his body. *Is Darian hitting on me?* He wasn't sure what he meant by that statement, but if Darian truly let his emotions fuel his artistic direction, then *shit*, that would explain why the likeness came out so beautifully.

"Here." Darian gave it back to Jimmy. "You can keep it." He uncrossed his legs and stood up, moving across the room. He stood at the window looking out, his back to Jimmy.

Jimmy flipped the cover of the sketchpad back over the top to protect the chalk from smearing. He could not help but notice Darian's mood change. Suddenly things felt awkward. *Why? Did I say something wrong?* Jimmy didn't like the sudden quiet. He wanted Darian to smile at him again. "Um, so, you think a lip ring would be cool? How come you don't have one?" He got off the floor and sat on the edge of the bed.

Darian turned around. "I haven't gotten around to it. I'm only allowed one piercing a year, or I have to pay. And I don't have any money."

Jimmy lifted an eyebrow. "Say what?"

Darian chuckled. "I guess I didn't tell you. I have this tradition of getting something pierced for my birthday ever since my mom dated a tattoo artist—one who also does piercings. Even after she stopped seeing him, he told me he'd still pierce something for free every birthday. This year I'm getting my tongue done."

"You're crazy. How many piercings do you have?" He wondered because he'd only counted two.

"Three. I got the first one done when I was thirteen. Madd Max pierced my cartilage. See?" He moved his black hair away from his right ear and exposed the hoop hanging at the top.

"I remember seeing that one. And you got the eyebrow done at fourteen?"

"Yup. Next week I turn sixteen, so I thought I'd get Max to do my tongue."

"Won't that hurt?" Jimmy asked, feeling a shiver run down his spine as he thought of how someone might pierce a tongue.

Darian gave Jimmy an I-don't-care shrug. "Nothing could hurt as bad as this." He lifted his purple leopard-print T-shirt and exposed his last piercing. "Getting my nipple pierced was about the most painful thing I've ever done. I nearly blacked out. Hurt so bad I broke into an instant sweat and had a hard time breathing for almost ten minutes."

Jimmy swallowed hard and stared at the brown nubbin growing hard in the cool air of the bedroom.

"That's why I only got the left one done. I think I would've lost my lunch if he even moved toward the right one… Jim?"

"What?" Jimmy's eyes snapped back up, and he immediately shook off the daze he'd fallen into. "I was just…. Shit! You got your nipple pierced! Dude! I could never do that." It sounded way too painful. Although it also looked completely hot, but Jimmy was not about to point that out.

"To each his own." Darian looked down and ran his fingers over the small gold hoop. "I like it." He let his shirt hem down and looked back up.

Something odd caught Jimmy's attention, and he reached out to stop the shirt from covering Darian's abdomen. "Wait a second." Jimmy lifted the side and exposed a purple bruise. "What happened here?"

Darian pulled the shirt from Jimmy's hand and walked across the floor. "Nothing. I fell."

Jimmy crossed his arms over his chest. "You also can't lie worth shit. Did someone punch you?"

"No…. Yes. John Divers, a senior, got pissed when he caught me eyeballing his tattoo." Darian let a breath of frustration escape his lungs, and then he flopped down on his bed, staring at the ceiling. "I've thought about getting inked, and his design was unique."

"Why would he care if you were admiring it? Isn't that the point of getting a tattoo? To show it off?" Jimmy didn't see why taking a peek would instigate a beating. He sat down next to Darian and waited for an answer.

"It wasn't as much the admiring as it was the timing. We were in the locker-room showers, and the tattoo was on his hip."

"Oh." *That does change things.* "So he thought you were looking at him? So what? He still shouldn't have hit you."

Darian sat up, which brought him very close to his seated friend. "You *do* know I'm gay, right? Half the county does." Darian looked bemused.

Darian squinted at Jimmy like he was blond and clueless and somehow found Jimmy's naivety endearing. That irked Jimmy. "Yeah!" Jimmy was quick to say, except the shrillness in his voice gave away his timidity. He sighed and relaxed his shoulders. "I mean…. Yes, I kind of thought you were gay the day we met. But it's not like I go around thinking 'Darian's gay' every time we're together. You're just you, and I still think John whatever-his-name-is shouldn't have hit you."

"You're an awesome friend, you know that?"

Darian smiled a very warm smile, and Jimmy was instantly drawn to the light in his rich brown eyes. The quiet of the room surrounded them, and Jimmy felt Darian's finger graze his wrist and glide over the back of his hand. Then his stomach flipped, and his mouth went dry. He could swear Darian was leaning forward.

A door slamming on the floor below broke the magic, causing Jimmy to jump.

Darian reluctantly got off the bed and headed to the door. "That's probably Devin." He pursed his lips. "Or is it Derrick? It's something with a 'D'."

"You *did* say your mom has a lot of boyfriends." Jimmy got up to follow him.

"Yup, one for every day of the week." He opened the bedroom door. "Go for a walk?"

"Absolutely. You think I could get a drink?"

Darian smirked. "Sure."

Fuck, do I look that nervous?

Jimmy grabbed his jacket and slipped into the hallway behind Darian, hoping the conversation would shift to something other than what *might* have happened just then. Jimmy was not ready to deal with the hungry look he'd noticed in Darian's eyes.

It doesn't bother me that Darian's gay. Matt is, after all. And I guess it helps me to sort out some of the things Darian says and does. It's just… when we were sitting there in that second before Donny—that was his name—slammed the door, I was feeling things I never thought I'd feel before. My stomach was doing all kinds of flips when Darian touched my wrist. I felt nauseous. I think he was going to kiss me. I'm not sure how I feel about that.

I never gave a thought to my sexuality, one way or the other. Matt's been gay forever, but his decision didn't sway me over the years. I just never thought about it before. I've liked some girls. I've liked some boys. When do I know what I'm feeling is what makes me gay or straight?

I just don't know.

And, crap, what's Darian feeling?

Another "I don't know."

I feel more complications coming on.

6

September 22, 2010

3:46 p.m.

DARIAN threw up once more before he regained enough composure to face "that room." On the way to the funeral home, he'd pulled his car over six times to heave his guts on the side of the road. By now, there was nothing left. He flushed the toilet and left the stall. His reflection in the mirror reminded him of how little sleep he'd had in the last few nights, as well as just how much he'd cried. He splashed cold water on his face and fingered through the long layers of his hair.

"I can do this. I can do this," he muttered to his reflection.

His shoulders sagged. He was lying to himself. "Jamie's right, I can't lie worth shit." He leaned on the sink with both hands and rested his forehead against the mirror. His stomach flipped again, but instead of dashing to the toilet he panted in short breaths, like a pregnant woman trying to make it through contractions.

"I can do this." His mantra for the day gave him enough resolve to leave the restroom and plod down the hall.

Darian looked up when he reached the dreaded doorway. A little sign protruded from the top corner: "J. Miller." Just *seeing* those letters caused the tears to stream down his face. This was a living nightmare, and no matter what he tried, Darian could not wake up from the horror. His Jamie was gone, and no amount of prayers or wishful thinking was going to bring him back. He wiped the tears from his eyes and stepped over the threshold.

He could see the casket against the far wall of the room, miles away, with a sea of people he didn't know between him and the body of the only person he'd ever loved in his life. Jamie. Somehow he had to say goodbye, only there were no words to express how a soul could let go of its other half.

He recognized Jamie's cousin Maggie. He'd met her at a family reunion in 2008. Jamie really liked her, and so did he. She was even more of a mess than Darian, and he wanted to reach out to her as she stumbled away from the casket. As she was just about to pass him, someone called her name, and she waved away their offered hand and swiftly exited the room.

Darian couldn't blame her. He'd have been blubbering violently as well if he wasn't a guy and stereotypically expected to suppress all emotion, or in his case, stereotypically expected to overdramatize every situation, simply because he was gay. Darian refused to give in to either pigeonholed reaction and strove to display something in the middle. The result: lots of vomiting in the last forty-eight hours.

Another couple walked up to the casket, so Darian took the opportunity to look at the flowers as he inched his way in that direction. Step by step, he moved along the perimeter, reading the cards attached to the bouquets of flower arrangements. He read phrases like "In loving memory" and "We're sorry for your loss," and it occurred to him how little most of the people here knew Jamie. They knew his name, but they didn't know *him*. He stepped a few feet closer.

Do people actually think flowers convey condolence? he thought as he casually inspected more of the obligatory bouquets.

Sneering at the perfunctory action of sending flowers to a funeral was a welcome distraction for Darian. It helped strengthen his courage. He and Jamie had often talked about "Hallmark holidays" and the conspiracy of card companies to create more holidays, just to get people to spend money and send cards. People die, and what was everyone supposed to do? Send flowers and a card. It was a rote response.

Of course, he was a lemming himself. Everyone did it, and Darian went right along with the masses. He grinned when he saw the next arrangement, because he knew it must be the one he'd sent: red gerbera daisies in a black vase. He liked the addition of the Mounds Bar on a stick jutting out from the middle, but he didn't recall mentioning it to the florist. He fingered the smooth petals and glanced at the card.

"*Even in death, you're still a part of me. ~Matt.*"

Darian's fingers brushed the edges of the card, and he whispered, "Matt." A nervous sensation coursed through his body when the thought finally registered that he was going to get to meet the larger-than-life Matt Dixon. His stomach flipped again, and it was all he could do to rush from the room and back to the bathroom stall before vomiting again. …

…"Who's this?" Darian asked as he picked up a picture off of Jimmy's cluttered desk.

Jimmy looked up from tying his shoelaces and asked, "Who's who?"

Darian held it out. "This picture of you and some kid covered in mud."

Jimmy finished tying and took the photograph from Darian's fingers. "That's my best friend, Matt." He laughed. "This was taken at the creek when he and I covered ourselves in mud and walked around like mud monsters, trying to scare his little sister and her friends."

Darian smiled. "That sounds so fun. How old were you? You look young."

"Ten, but Matt's a year older. His mom was so mad. She threatened to make us walk home." He handed the picture back to Darian. "You'll meet him eventually. He's a great guy."

"Cute too, even covered in mud," Darian muttered as he placed the picture back where he found it.

"Huh?"

"Um, nothing." He quickly turned around, expecting to be scrutinized for a phrase he was sure Jimmy heard, but instead he found him rummaging through a stack of books. "What are you looking for?"

"Another picture of Matt." Jimmy shrugged. "I know I stuck it over here someplace. I don't really have a system yet, and most of my stuff is still in boxes or over at my mom's, since I live there most of the time."

"Yeah, that sucks. I wish I lived closer to you," he said, leaning against Jimmy's desk and trying unsuccessfully to keep his eyes from lingering on Jimmy's oh-so-squeezable posterior.

"That would be cool."

"Seeing you once a month is a pain, but I guess I understand if your mom and dad hate each other."

"My mom hates my dad, but not the other way around. Dad just hates how it affects me."

"Oh."

Jimmy shifted his position, and Darian grabbed a magazine off the desk and kept his eyes glued to the pages. Jimmy had acted weird and uncomfortable months ago on the afternoon when Darian drew his portrait, and he did *not* want to bring about the same awkwardness again. If Donny hadn't come home when he did, Darian was sure he would have worked up the nerve to lean forward and kiss Jimmy when they were sitting on his bed sharing a very pleasant gaze into each other's eyes.

"Here it is!" Jimmy held up the photo and promptly dropped it.

Darian swallowed the lump in his throat as he stole one more glance at Jimmy's rear. *You're killing me!* he thought, wiping the drool from his chin.

"This is Matt." He presented the picture with a beaming smile.

Darian felt another buzz zing through him as he gazed at the photo. Different than the one he felt when Jimmy bent over just then. This zing was stronger. He hoped his friend would look away for a moment, so he could adjust himself without being noticed. He *soooo* did not want to try and explain how his breath got caught in his throat, and his dick leapt to attention after just one glance at Matt's picture.

Jimmy's friend Matt was *hot*! Decked out in camouflage, he was holding a gun like an Army sergeant. Even though he had curly hair as high as a white man's Afro, Darian would gladly clean his barrel any day. He cleared his throat. "Um, so, Matt's your hunter friend, right?"

State the obvious, Dare, real smooth.

Jamie nodded. "Yup. He's really good too. Perfect aim. Makes his dad jealous. When we went bow hunting in October, he downed a five-pointer with one shot—right through the heart. And when he took me squirrel hunting, he shot six. I couldn't believe it. Those things are fast and so small! He said I was his good-luck charm. His dad looked pissed because he only got one. I nearly peed my pants trying not to laugh. It was so cool."

"Sounds like it." Darian noted the brightness in Jimmy's eyes and the pitch of his voice. Darian subconsciously started taking note of the way Jimmy talked about Matt. "He's pretty great, eh?"

"The best! Matt's the nicest person I know. He's funny and considerate, smart, clever, athletic..."

And gay, please tell me Matt's gay. Darian silently pleaded, but the list went on without including that particular adjective.

"... and mischievous, but in a fun sort of way. He can always make me laugh, even at my worst moments."

"Sounds like he's perfect."

"He is."

Darian analyzed what was going on. Jimmy knew *he* was gay—they'd already had that conversation—but what about Jimmy himself? Was he gay? Normally, Darian was very confident in his ability to spot other homosexuals—gaydar, they called it—but he didn't get that vibe off Jimmy at all. Jimmy had such an appealing spirit. Darian was sure he'd want to be close to him, whether he was gay or not. Of course, hoping for something more was always a bonus.

Still, the way he went on and on about his friend Matt made Darian think there was something going on that Jimmy wasn't sharing.

"Did I tell you he got four deer last season? The one antlered buck and three does. He even showed me how to clean and dress one. *That* I could have done without. It was disgusting, so much blood. Bleck! Although he told me it was nothing compared to cutting into the bowels by accident. He said the stench could kill you. I believe him. He knows everything there is to know about deer hunting. He said he'd take me with him again this fall since I didn't shoot him in the foot or anything when we went the last time." Jimmy stopped his rambling and looked at Darian. "What? Why are you looking at me like that?"

Darian smirked and took a stab. "How long have you been in love with your best friend?"

Jimmy's eyes popped wide open. "What? In love? No way! I'm not… Matt's just… he's my best friend. We've known each other forever. I'm not in… whatever… forget it." Jimmy turned away and placed the picture on the table by his bed.

Shit! No bonus if he's mad at you, Dare!

Darian realized he'd made a huge mistake. If he thought the awkwardness between them was bad when they were sitting on his bed, moments from kissing, *this* was going to be intolerable. He had to backpedal. And quick!

"Jimmy, I'm sorry. Please, don't be pissed at me. I was just making a stupid observation, and I was wrong." Darian walked over and stood behind him. Jimmy remained silent and facing the table. "I just noticed you talk about Matt differently then you talk about anyone else. I'm glad you have a best friend like Matt. I wish I did. I think you're the closest friend I've ever had, and I *seeeriously* don't want to screw this up. Please, Jimmy, don't be mad at me."

When Jimmy didn't respond, Darian tentatively reached up and touched Jimmy on the center of his back. He gingerly stroked his fingers up and down. It was the only soothing gesture he could think of. "Jimmy? Talk to me." He kept on touching Jimmy, glad his friend did not pull away.

Darian stepped closer. He could smell Jimmy's sweat. He liked it. His nose was inches from Jimmy's neck, and his palms were dying to slide over Jimmy's hips and pull him back against his chest and groin, but he dared not push his luck. Darian was torn. He was anxious over saying just the right thing but also extremely attracted to Jimmy. Months of hanging out and playing video games and such were fun, but he wanted so much more than that. Keeping his libido in check was so fucking hard. *Literally.* He wanted Jimmy, but he wasn't stupid. Jimmy was a virgin, whether they spoke about it or not. Darian could tell. And whether Jimmy liked girls or guys, Darian was sure he had to take things slow, or he'd scare Jimmy away. He stopped caressing his friend's back and stepped away.

"Jimmy," he whispered with enough urgency to convey how much he needed a reply.

"Jamie," came a hushed response.

"Huh?" Darian was confused.

Jimmy turned around slowly. "I like to be called Jamie." Then Jimmy smiled at him, and the weirdness of seconds ago was definitely gone.

Darian had to ask. "You introduced yourself to me as *Jim*. And your dad calls you *Jimmy* or *Jimbo*. Where'd *Jamie* come from?"

"Matt started it, years ago," Jimmy glared at Darian and blurted, "And don't give me that look again! I'm not in love with Matt! He just… Matt made me feel special, giving me a nickname, and he's the only one allowed to call me Jamie."

"Then why me?" Darian asked.

Jimmy looked down but could not hide his blushing cheeks. "Because… because you make me feel special too." His eyes slowly made their way back up.

Darian's stomach quivered. *Is he flirting with me?* Darian could not believe his ears. His heart started racing. *Was Jimm—Jamie—really giving him a sign this could be something more than friendship?* He reached up cautiously and ghosted his fingers across Jamie's cheek. Jamie closed his eyes. Darian's heart raced faster, and he felt as if time was zeroed to a halt, instantly locking them in the moment.

Dan Miller's voice boomed up the steps. "Hey, Jimbo, you upstairs?" Time ticked again.

"Yeah," Jimmy called back. Frozen moment sufficiently thawed.

Fuck, Darian cursed in silence as Jimmy stepped away. …

…"I can't do it," Darian sobbed. "I can't go in there." He sat on the tile floor and muttered his lament. "Whatever we had… I can't measure up to Matt. I can't look at Jamie's face and wonder who he loved more."

He had to get out of there.

Darian scrambled to his feet and stumbled his way out of the bathroom and through the front door of the funeral home. He'd parked down the side street. Maybe after sitting in his car for a while longer, he could work up his nerve to try again later. Viewing hours were 3:00–5:00 p.m. and again from 7:00–9:00 p.m. If he could not make it into that room by five, he would still have a chance to make it by nine. Or, if his nerves were really frozen, there was another slot tomorrow from 7:00–9:00 p.m. One way or another, he would force his body into the viewing room before the funeral service on Friday. He had to, just not now.

He made his way across the parking lot toward the side street and completely forgot about his jacket hanging on the rack inside the foyer of the funeral home.

7

December 27, 2004
Christmas sucked.

January 10th
If Joey looks at me again, I'm gonna punch him.

Um, March... 2005
I think I've missed the point of these journals. I totally forgot to write down shit. I think I've been thinking too much. Not sure. Or maybe my brain's been on vacation. It's one or the other.

School's fine. Matt's helping me to pass the classes that are just not up to "Mom's standards," and she hasn't bitched about my grades for weeks. Hallelujah! I don't know what I'll do when he graduates.

I miss Darian. Is that wrong?

March 20, 2005
I gotta get Darian's cell number. Maybe we can text. I hate not knowing what he's doing.

April 11, 2005
I'm so confused.
I think I'm gay.
Oh God, just writing the word "gay" makes me think it sounds weird. For Matt to be gay feels normal. I've known about him since he

was eleven. For Darian to be gay sounds normal. He's gay and very "emo." I like the way his piercings, shaggy black hair, and nail polish fit in with his gayness. (Is it okay to say "gayness?") It's fine with me that Darian's gay. It's ME I'm worried about. I don't know how I feel about ME being gay.

I see the way Matt is. I don't want to be like that. He'll fuck anything. Or at least I think he does. He rarely talks about his Internet hook-ups. I just know he has them, because I'm his alibi most of the time. Luckily his mom is overly naive and trusting, so she never questions him.

Anyway....

Then there's Darian. I wouldn't mind being like him, but I don't like the way he gets treated. He's out, unlike Matt, and he gets beaten up for it at school. I don't want to get beaten up for being gay. I'M the one who does the beating up on people! Although I'm supposed to be keeping it to a minimum if I want to stay in school.

I don't know what to do.

Darian and I keep getting closer. He texts often, and it makes me smile. I wish I could spend more than a few hours a month with him, but it's just not possible. I NEED A FUCKING CAR!!! I swear there were a few times in the last couple of months when we almost kissed. I thought my insides would explode. Does that mean I'm gay? Because I was excited to almost kiss another guy?

I lay in bed at night thinking about him sometimes. I can't get the image of his nipple ring out of my head. All I could think about at the time was leaning in and running my tongue over it. Does that make me gay?

And does just one kiss mean you are, or do you have to go all the way?

I know my mom'll freak if I tell her I'm gay. At least I think she will. She's not very tolerant of the other homosexuals we've come across when we go shopping and stuff. She's downright rude. She won't even let me go into American Eagle just because one time she saw a gay couple walking out of the one store. Bitch.

Maybe I can talk to my dad about it. I see him in two weeks.

JIMMY walked into his dad's kitchen and plopped down heavily into the chair. "Dad, can I ask you something?"

"Sure, Jimbo, anything." Dan was standing at the sink, washing the dishes from breakfast.

"How do you know when you like someone?"

His dad turned his head to look at his son and arched his brow. "Jim, you can't be seriously asking me how you know you like someone? You like 'em, you like 'em; ya don't, you don't."

Jimmy huffed. "That's not what I mean. How do you know if you like the person more than as a friend?"

Mr. Miller finished rinsing the cup he was holding and set it in the dish drain. "Well, I guess it depends on how much time you spend thinking about this person. Do you think about them all the time or just occasionally?" He turned off the water and dried his hands.

"All the time." Jimmy sagged onto the table, leaning his head on his arm.

"Okay." Dan walked over and took a seat across the table. "When you think about this person, does it make you happy or indifferent?"

"Happy." Jimmy smiled.

"Do you think up scenarios where you meet or talk?"

"Sometimes."

Dan shifted in his seat. He leaned forward and hesitated before asking the next question. "Do you... think about this person when you're in the shower?"

Jimmy jumped back and sat up straight. "Dad!" He was aghast.

Dan grinned. "Son, I'm just trying to help you figure out the seriousness of this crush. I *was* your age at one point, ya know? As I see it, if you really, really like someone, you tend to think about them when you're alone. Like when you're in bed at night or in the shower."

Jimmy just sat there silently, letting his dad keep going, even though the embarrassment factor was creeping up to hazardous levels.

"I know we don't normally have these types of conversations, but I'm flattered you brought it up. I'm glad you trust me like this."

"I do." Jimmy relaxed. His face reverted back to its former display of inner turmoil. "I just… oh, Dad, I'm so confused." He put his face in his hands briefly. "I think I'm scared of how I feel."

Dan reached across the table and patted the back of Jimmy's hand. "It's normal to be confused. Is this the first time you've felt this strong of an attraction?"

"Yeah."

Dan cautiously added, "Do you… touch yourself thinking about her?"

Aghast? How about mortified! "Dad! I'm not answering that!" He jumped up from the chair. Thoughts raced through his mind. *Yes, yes I have. Last night. Oh God… Dad, I kept picturing his hands on me. Down* there*! I came and nearly yelled out his name.* Jimmy thought it, but was *far* from telling his father everything!

"Except… Dad…." Jimmy paced the limited floor space, rubbing the back of his neck. This was the part he dreaded bringing up. He stopped, looked his dad in the face, and got it off his chest. "Dad, it's not a *girl* I keep thinking about."

Mr. Miller sat back in the chair. "Oh."

Judgment was all Jimmy could think about. His dad was thinking the worst, and he hadn't done anything… yet. "Dad, please don't sit all quiet like you used to do with Mom. Say something. Anything. But don't assume you know everything, because you don't. I haven't done anything. I don't understand what it means. Most of all," he took a deep breath, "I'm scared to think I'm… gay."

His dad pushed the chair back and walked over to his son.

Jimmy froze, not knowing what was going to happen. He heard about some dads beating the crap out of their gay sons. He didn't think *his* dad would hit him, but Jimmy still froze in fear. His dad placed his hands on Jimmy's shoulders, smiled at him, and then pulled him into a strong hug. Jimmy was shocked at first but quickly squeezed his dad in return.

"Oh, Jimmy," Dan sighed. "I love you, son." He rubbed Jimmy's back and kissed his hair. When he released him and stepped back, he looked him in the eyes. "Being gay is not an easy thing in this day and age. You don't see very many people openly admitting it, especially where we live."

"I know. Kids get beat up over it."

"Jimmy," he mused, "boys have been beating up other boys for being gay since the beginning of time. It never mattered if it was true or not. Boys your age are cruel. I'm sure you know this."

He thought about it. "Yeah, I guess you're right."

"Now, if *you're* gay then you have to think about the repercussions of acting out on it. For one, your mother may not approve."

"Tell me about it."

"Number two, promiscuous sex with random boys can be dangerous, especially if you go for older guys who don't care so much about your feelings. You could get seriously hurt." He moved back to the table and motioned for Jimmy to take a seat.

Jimmy did. This was going way smoother than he thought it would. And rather clinical.

"Three… and I do not intend this to sound at all as if I think you're stupid… make sure you use protection."

"Daaaad," he whined.

"Jimmy, if you're thinking about this guy in the shower, it's only a matter of time before you act out on the fantasies going through your mind. Anal *and* oral sex can pass on all kinds of diseases, and I just want to make sure you understand the dangers involved with intercourse. I care about you, boy. I don't want to see you hurt."

His dad's true sincerity shone in his eyes. How could Jimmy feel any more loved? Instead of damning him for his thoughts, his dad brought logic to the table out of love and deep concern. Jimmy could not feel any more proud to have such a great father.

"Thanks, Dad. I'll think about it. Like I said, I don't know how I feel about being gay. I'm afraid. But… but I also like this guy a lot. I don't know what to do about it."

"Then I suggest you take it slow. Spend time with him. Don't rush into sex. Boys do that all too often, gay or straight. You're sixteen. You have plenty of time to have sex. I think you should figure out what you really want and take your time. If it's meant to be, it'll happen. You won't need to force it."

"I'll try to remember that." Jimmy rubbed his eyes.

"Good. One more question." Jimmy looked at his dad again. "Have you kissed this boy?"

"Daaaad. Are you trying to make me regret bringing this up?"

"Son, I'm just trying to gauge the situation."

"Noooo," he huffed, "we haven't kissed."

"Good. I suggest you refrain from kissing until you're sure of your feelings."

"Why?"

"Because a kiss is way more than people think. For girls, it's like a floodgate to their emotions. One kiss and a girl is swimming in a sea of emotions and contemplating your deep connections to her and so on. I imagine it can be the same for boys as well. Generally, I suspect boys don't think on it as much as girls, but a kiss undeniably burns a streak of fire straight to your groin. Even if you think it's safe and a *kiss is just a kiss*; if it's done correctly, you won't be able to think of anything beyond ripping each other's clothes off."

"Dad, I'm not ready for sex."

"You don't have to be. If you kiss the right person, and sometimes the wrong person, a kiss can trigger things you never thought you'd do. Promise me you'll think about it."

"Fine. No kissing." Jimmy sighed. It was a relief to think this conversation might be over.

"Feel better?"

"Yes."

"Good! I was going to suggest we go fishing this afternoon. What do you think? Are you up for it?" Dan got up and walked back over to the sink to finish up the last few items.

"Yeah," Jimmy answered excitedly as he too arose. "Can Darian go?"

Dan gave Jimmy a look. "Is *that* the boy you keep thinking about?"

Jimmy swallowed. *Why do I open my big mouth?* "Yes," he squeaked.

"Mmhmm. I can see why you're confused."

"What does that mean?" He knew it came out harsh, but he couldn't help being defensive.

"Jimbo, I've seen you two together a few times—watching TV and playing video games. Darian is a nice boy, and you're very relaxed around him. I'm so used to the way you act around your mother. I forgot how easygoing you can be. And you smile a lot more. Darian is gay, isn't he?"

"Yeah. How could you tell?"

"The way he looks at you, as if you were the only one in the room."

"He does?"

"Mmhmm. You look the same way back at him. I also noticed the way he touches you, a little bit more than boys tend to touch other boys. And the last time Darian was here, I caught him blatantly checking out your posterior. *That* was a dead giveaway!"

Jimmy blushed.

"I can't blame you for liking him. Without sounding perverted... he's cute. At least from what I gather he would look like without the piercings and eye makeup. Just make sure being with him is what you really want. You won't be able to hide your sexuality if you're involved with someone who doesn't try to hide it in the slightest. Once you're out, you're out!"

"Thanks, Dad. I'll go call Darian."

"Okay."

April 23rd

My dad is so cool. He was more supportive than I ever imagined. The talk we had this morning was awesome. Then when he took us fishing, he acted like nothing happened. Darian had no clue we'd been talking about him.

Fishing was fun. Darian said he'd been before, and I went along with his obvious lie. Darian can't lie worth crap. He caught more bushes than anything else. It was hard not to burst out laughing. What I like the most was how he didn't act embarrassed about it at all. He laughed it off. He even got the hook attached to the back of his shirt and asked for help without one word about being stupid or incompetent. I really like that about him. He doesn't talk down about himself. He likes who he is and doesn't apologize to anyone.

Maybe that's what attracts me to him? His confidence. Darian is secure in his sexuality, and I think I long for the same feeling.

So... am I gay?

Yes.

I think so. No, I know so!

I, James Miller, am gay.

But don't tell anybody yet. I'm not ready to come out.

JIMMY pulled the covers up and turned out the light. The moonlight drifted in through the window. "Darian," he whispered.

He reached down and slid his hand inside his briefs. He felt himself swelling as his fingers gripped a very deprived part of his anatomy. He would have never attempted this at home. Not in his mother's house! She'd know. She always knew. Only lately, the urge to do things she disapproved of overrode his fear of being caught. Jimmy could not remember a time, before meeting Darian, when he touched himself so often. *Not that it was very often at all.* It was a new thing for him—a new thing that was fast becoming a favorite thing. *Funny how seeing Darian and masturbating are synonymous with favorite things?* Jimmy would have chuckled, but he was too consumed with the heat in his groin.

He gripped himself and moved his wrist slowly up and down, all the while imagining purple nail polish on the tips of the fingers gripping him. *Yes.* He could see the mole on Darian's right index finger. He could see the ink marks on his thumb as it rolled over his throbbing head across the piss slit. *Oh, God.*

He shoved his underwear down with his left hand as he picked up the pace of his fantasy.

Darian's hands were on him.

He could clearly see Darian's luscious mouth, inches from touching his most sensitive parts. He looked up, and the lust burning in those beautiful blue eyes was so very....

"Wait," Jimmy stopped mid-stroke. "Darian has brown eyes. Those blue eyes belong to… Matt! Fuck!"

Jimmy extracted his hand and rolled over, wailing into his pillow. "Why? Why is my brain so fucked up? Ahhhhh!"

"Jimbo? You okay?"

Jimmy jerked into a sitting position at the sound of his dad's voice from outside his door. "Yeah, Dad. Fine. Goodnight."

"Goodnight."

He waited, and when his dad moved on to his own room he flopped back down.

"I am so fucking screwed." No one answered his statement. Jimmy fell asleep, uncomfortably turgid, listening to the barred owls hooting in the pine trees across the street.

8

May 13, 2005

School is out in a few weeks. Thank God! It's been really hard to keep from smacking the smirks off Joey's face, but I've been good. I think it's because I'm so distracted about how I feel and who I feel it for that I've been ignoring Joey's comments about most everything. It seems to be working. Joey just shrugs and walks away. Even the one incident in chem class only got me detention after school. Mom didn't even have to know about it.

It's also been a few weeks since I had that talk with my dad. That awful, yet insightful, talk with my dad. I'm glad he let me be so open without criticizing me, but I'm still in the same boat. I don't know what I am feeling. I'm confused.

I'm feeling more okay with being gay. I am. I like guys. Well... not ALL guys, just some. Well, two. I like two guys. My confusion now is over which guy I want more and why I want him.

I cannot believe I was jacking off thinking about Darian, and he morphed into Matt. Shit! I haven't touched myself since. I'm afraid of who it will turn out to be. Maybe Darian was right? Maybe I secretly love Matt? Do I? If I'm honest with myself, I DO think about him all the time. I text him about everything, and I can't wait to see him. Except... I feel like that about Darian too.

Maybe I need to talk to Matt about it.

JIMMY lifted the iron dumbbell and started counting curls. *One, two, three, fou—*

"Twenty pound curls. What? Are you a girl?" Matt scoffed and switched dumbbells, placing another one into Jimmy's hand. "Try fifty."

"Are you trying to kill me?"

"No. I'm trying to bulk you up. Joey won't pick on you so much if he thinks you can kick his ass."

Matt sat on the weight bench, positioning himself to do flies. His defined chest was outlined through his tight, black wife-beater. He knew just the right routine to build all his muscle groups and maximize the definition of every part of his delicious body.

Oh, my gosh, Jimmy thought, *and I have the nerve to question my sexuality? I just called him delicious! I am sooo gay.*

Jimmy watched Matt pull the weights from his sides up over his chest several times before he tried to curl the fifty-pound weight he held in his own hand. It was a struggle, but he could manage. It dawned on him that no one was in hearing range as they worked out at the gym. *Maybe everyone's at dinner or something?*

"Matt, do you ever think about the guyyyirls you date, beyond the next day?" *A+ for the quick save, Jamie!* Jimmy metaphorically patted his back.

Matt stopped, holding the weights straight over his chest. He looked at Jimmy. "No, I do not think about the… *girls* I date. Why?"

"I was just wondering." Why not start a conversation about it? They were open with each other most of the time. Jimmy could do this and make it seem natural. "Do you ever kiss these… *girls?*" Jimmy kept his eyes on the dumbbell in his fist. He thought avoiding eye contact with Matt might make this seem more casual.

"Sometimes. But I try to avoid it if I can." He resumed pumping iron.

"Why?"

Matt stopped and sat up. He leaned forward. "Is there a point to this? You've never expressed such an interest in my exploits before."

"It was just a question. My dad and I had a talk about kissing, and I was just wondering what you thought about it." Jimmy was proud of himself for keeping his cool. Hopefully Matt would not think too much about his inquiry.

Matt studied him a minute but did answer the question. "I think it's too intimate." He repositioned his body flat on the bench and resumed counting flies. "That's why I made it rule number two."

"Too intimate?" It sounded absurd. "More intimate than sticking your dick in someone?"

"Yeah. Like… you can detach yourself from fucking. If you close your eyes you can picture whatever you want."

"Can't you do that when you kiss?"

"I guess, but it never worked for me. The few *girls* I kissed took it to mean a whole lot more than I planned, and even *I* had a hard time separating the orgasm from the ass it happened in. I don't want that kind of connection. So… I don't kiss. I fuck!" Matt finished his answer and sat up, placing the dumbbells on the rack. He moved to the next station and adjusted the machine to do leg presses.

Jimmy got up and followed. He opted for leg extensions since that machine was next to Matt. "Do you…. Do you ever have somebody fuck you?" His interrogation continued.

"A couple times."

"Did it hurt?"

"At first. But it doesn't matter. I'm more of a giver than a taker."

Jimmy nodded, mulling over the answers. It seemed to hold true to what he read on the Internet. Some guys were into being a "top" while others "bottomed." He wasn't sure where he fit in yet. "Would you ever consider dating someone you knew?"

"No. Too risky. I can't have my *church-going family* finding out I'm gay. There'd probably be a scandal or some sort of inquiry into their ability as parents. Like it was their fault I'm gay. Nope. Anonymous fucks, that's what I'm about. Maybe when I'm old, like thirty and shit, I'll decide to go a different route, but for now this works out just fine." He leaned over and moved the pin lower for the next set of reps.

"You never get lonely?"

"Lonely? No. Why would I? I have you to talk to and hang out with. Why do I need to start a relationship with someone who doesn't know anything about me?"

"I don't know." Jimmy stopped working his legs and sat there thinking.

"I'm not worrying about that right now. When I meet the right person, I'll know. It'll just hit me—*bam!*—like lightning!"

Jamie smirked. "You realize you just quoted *The Little Mermaid*."

"Shit. Whatever. You know what I mean. Why are we talking about this anyway? Jamie? Do you have a crush on somebody?"

Damn Matt's intuition! "No."

"Jamie, come on, it's me. Tell me who she is."

Matt's smirk was irritating. Jimmy wanted to wipe it off! The worst part was he assumed it was a girl. "Who says it has to be a girl?"

"Me," he answered with complete conviction. "Jamie, you're not gay."

"What if I am?"

"Jamie, trust me, I know homosexuals, and you're not one of them." As if his was the last say in the matter, Matt started doing one more set of reps.

Jimmy didn't like how Matt was making his decisions. *He was gay! How dare Matt say otherwise?* He could prove it—step right over to Matt and plant a kiss on his lips so passionate they'd both stop breathing, but what would it accomplish? He might end up losing his friendship in the process. Matt was not a kisser. He said so himself. He was also not into dating people he knew. He was also—and this was the deciding factor—not into having a relationship past one night. Jimmy wanted more than that.

He got up and moved to the "crunch machine," as he called it. He fixed the amount of weight and started counting. He got to four, and then his mind left the numbers behind.

What did he want? He wanted sex… well, eventually. What guy didn't? But he didn't want it to be anonymous. Jimmy wanted to know the guy. Jimmy wanted a connection. Jimmy wanted to be intimate with a person he knew, inside and out. He wanted to feel like he was a part of whoever he made love to.

His dad said not to rush into anything. *Don't rush. Let it happen.* He could do that. Somewhere around the eightieth crunch, his brain registered the burn in his abs. He sat back and panted.

"I gotta stop thinking so hard, or I'm gonna kill myself."

MATT pulled up to the curb out front of Jimmy's house and put his mom's Jeep in park. "You all right, man? You've been quiet the entire trip home."

"Fifteen minutes, Matt. It takes fifteen minutes to get to my house from the gym."

"Seventeen, and that's not the point. You're not pissed at me about something, are you?" Matt fidgeted, running his hand over the top of the steering wheel.

Jimmy could see he was worried. "No."

Matt glanced up and then back to the steering column. "Are you sure? I don't want my lifestyle to become bad blood between us."

"Nah, Matt, we're good." Jimmy held up his fist.

Matt grinned and they bumped knuckles. "So, what's up for tonight?"

Jimmy sighed. "English paper. Twenty pages, due Monday."

"Good times!"

"Shut up. I can't wait until this class is over. At least next semester I'm a senior."

"Yeah! Just think—in three weeks I graduate. In two months I turn eighteen! Woohoo! Yeah, baby!" Matt did a little wiggle behind the wheel. "No more high school, no more boring classes I'll never need. I get to start doing what I want to do and not what I'm *told* to do—training as a firefighter! I can't wait."

"Nothing like rubbing it in."

Matt laughed but stopped gloating. "All right. I'll catch you later. You up for a run in the morning?"

"Um, sure, I guess so. I need to be home in time to mow the lawn by two."

"No problem. See you tomorrow."

"Okay." Jimmy stepped out of the Jeep and shut the door. "Bye." He waved and Matt drove away.

As soon as Jimmy walked into the front door of his house, his phone buzzed. He retrieved it from his pocket and flipped it open, fully expecting the text to be from Matt. It was Darian.

Hey, what ya doing?

He texted back: *Got home from the gym. Worked out with Matt. Taking a shower in a sec. Got English to work on. U?*

Nothing. I was hoping you'd be by this weekend.

No. Can't. Sorry. English paper due Monday. Plus it's not Dad's weekend.

Can't you visit even if it's not his turn?

Jimmy got to his room and closed the door. Sitting at his desk, he typed back: *No. Remember, my mom hates my dad and tries to keep me from visiting as much as she possibly can.*

Oh. Well, text when you're bored. Or if you need a break. Or call. I like talking to you... I miss you.

Jimmy sat there looking at the keys on his phone. Some of the numbers were worn off from texting so much. He grinned. *Who do I text? Matt and Darian.* He smiled, knowing he was in constant contact with the two people he cared about most in the world. It made him feel warm inside.

He paused too long. Darian texted again: *Jamie?*

Then another text right after: *Please ignore that last bit. It sounds dumb. Forget it.*

In the last couple of hours, Jimmy had contemplated how he felt. He was trying his hardest to sort things out. Matt wasn't much help, but one thing was for sure: Matt was not going to change anytime soon, and Jimmy was not going to be a one-night stand. He needed to keep his best friend close. So, if Matt was simply going to remain a friend, then Jimmy was free to pursue things with Darian. That is, if Darian was interested. Jimmy needed to take some initiative and ask. He took a deep breath.

Darian.... Will you.... Do you want... argh, this is so hard.... Darian, I like you.

Text back: *:+) I like you too!*

Darian... I want to be your boyfriend, but we need to take things slow.

Really? You want to? I wasn't sure. I was hoping but.... Yes, I'd like that.

R U sure? I mean slow. Like slow, slow. Like in reverse slow. I'm not ready 2 B out & everything. I just know I really like U & I want this 2 B more than friends. Not that friends is bad, I just want more. Ya know? R U OK with that?

Yes! Hell yes! YES YES YES!!!! I want to be your boyfriend, Jamie. We can go as slow as you like. I don't care. I just want to be yours. :+)

:-]

Jimmy smiled as a warm wave traveled up from his toes. This felt good. This felt right.

I have English. If I don't get an A, my mom may never allow me to go to my dad's.

Then go. Get an A. I'm smiling.

Me too.

Good night.

Night.

May 15th

Somehow I finished my paper. Between mowing the lawn, laundry, taking a run with Matt both mornings, and answering all Darian's text messages, I finished it! I think it's "A" worthy.

I am glad I asked Darian to be my boyfriend. It makes me feel all gushy inside, knowing he likes me too. He's such a sweet guy. And like Dad said, he's cute. Really cute. He's funny and gentle. I love the way his hands move when he draws. I am feeling so good right now.

Darian likes me, and I'm walking on air.

9

September 22, 2010

3:55 p.m.

MATT turned away from the daisies. He was angry but couldn't explain why. "Jamie" was his. "Jim" was what everybody else got to use. He clenched his fists and suppressed the urge to chuck the vase across the room. He needed to punch something or yell at the top of his lungs, but neither choice was appropriate in a funeral home.

I need to leave, he thought, *right fucking now!*

Problem solved. He could leave, expel some energy somewhere, and then return for the next viewing time slot. If he hurried, no one would notice he was gone.

Matt tried not to make eye contact with anyone as he slipped from the room. He especially didn't want his dad to notice, or he'd grumble about it. He wove his way around the sniveling guests and groups of relatives steeped in hushed conversations and slipped through the door. Once down the hall and out the front entrance, he took a deep breath of the warm, humid air. Autumn was here, and the trees were changing, but this week was calling for warmer temperatures.

Matt was planning on taking full advantage of these gorgeous days. Soon it would be cold all the time. Maybe he'd wash his truck this weekend? Jamie always liked Matt's Dodge Dakota when it was all shiny.

His gut clenched. Everything he did seemed to produce a thought of his best friend and what he liked and what he'd think. *Would it always be like this?* Would he think of Jamie in every situation and feel his absence? Or would it only happen for a few months and then disappear like the seasons and melt away to the point where his heart would not remember the little things like shiny trucks and Mounds Bars?

Fuck!

Matt hoped that would never happen.

Today was one of the hardest things he'd ever done. Standing in that room was depressing—crushing even—but it was nothing compared to thinking how hard it would be when the funeral came on Friday. He'd promised to say a few words. *But what the hell was he going to say?* Burying his best friend was not something he'd planned on doing for another eighty years, and only then when Jamie was riddled with cancer: not now when he'd been in the prime of his youth and healthy as an ox.

Why do they use that phrase anyway? "Healthy as an ox." Why not stallion or water buffalo? "What? Jamie?" Matt mumbled a pretend conversation. "No, he was healthy as a water buffalo!"

He took another cleansing breath and looked across the front parking lot, where he saw someone walking. A boy dressed in all black shuffled along the side street with his shoulders slumped and his head hung low. He was walking beside the row of parked cars. Matt watched him and felt his groin wake up. He couldn't punch anyone, but maybe Matt could *fuck* someone. Sex would help relieve his tension.

Matt took a step and hesitated.

He couldn't very well assume from this distance that the person was the sort prone to random hook-ups like Matt, but right now he was desperate. He needed to fuck someone bad! Taking a chance couldn't hurt, Matt rationalized. He ditched his suit coat in the lobby and hurried to follow the stranger.

The guy Matt had his eye on looked emo. Maybe. Not every guy dressed in all black was emo, and not every emo guy was into anonymous homosexual activities, but in a few minutes Matt would figure it all out. He trusted his gaydar. He was just so angry right now—angry with Jamie on so many levels—he had to let it out. His mind, and dick, wouldn't accept any other option. This guy was going to be fucked, whether it was a good idea or not!

He hustled across the street and then abruptly slowed to a casual stroll. No need to startle the guy, who was now seated on the curb in front of someone's house. Matt needed this to look casual, spontaneous, and nowhere near stalkerish. There were no cars in the driveway or along the street in front, so Matt got a good look of the guy as he approached.

Definitely emo. Although, was it called emo once a guy got past his teens? Matt didn't know. He'd go with emo for now. Tall and thin, the guy slumped forward with his elbows on his knees and face in his hands. His unnaturally black, collar-length hair obscured his profile. Matt slowly continued to walk right past him, attempting to look like just another guy walking up the street. His steps faltered as he passed by.

Was emo-guy crying?

He could have sworn he noticed the guy's shoulders bob and maybe even heard a faint sob or a sniffle. *Shit!* He couldn't very well fuck a guy who was emotionally troubled, could he? He didn't take advantage of people like that. He took a few more steps and stopped. He pivoted around and meandered back over to his target. Maybe he would feel him out first.

He stopped a few feet away and took out a pack of cigarettes. He tapped the pack on his other hand and asked, "Cigarette?"

Emo-guy barely glanced up. "No, thanks. I quit last year."

Well, at least this guy wasn't freaked out by his approach. "Yeah, I'm trying to quit myself." *Jamie hated my smoking.* Matt put the butt between his lips and fished a lighter out of his pocket. He gave a long drag and blew the smoke out slowly. "You all right? You look pretty upset." His eyes slid over the guy on the curb, and he took another puff. *Jeez, he probably weighs no more than one-thirty, tops.*

"Bad day," emo-guy quietly confessed as he sniffed and wiped his nose on the back of his hand.

Matt drew more smoke into his lungs and nodded. *Okay, here it goes...* "I know something that'll make the pain disappear. If you're interested."

The guy looked up and gave Matt an inquisitive stare.

"Well, for ten minutes, anyway." Matt grinned, trying to alleviate the tension with humor.

He sniffled again. "W-what d-do you have in mind?"

The guy's voice sounded interested. Matt could only hope this stranger was thinking *sex* and not *drugs*. Sometimes one never knew until the zipper came down and the prospective trick freaked out. So, he gave emo-boy the sexiest grin he could muster. He stepped closer and tapped his foot against the guy's shoe. "Come on," Matt urged with a wink, lifting his chin and motioning to the house behind him.

They walked over to the residence Matt indicated and quickly scanned the layout for any possible spots. Next to the house was a wooden shed with Leyland cypress planted next to it. He waved for the guy to follow. "Here's good."

"Won't somebody see?"

Matt liked how he wasn't hesitating. This guy seemed as eager as he was. He stood there eyeing the side of the shed with his hands in his pockets, but he was in no way looking as if he'd bolt. "Not unless they walk between the houses." Matt sucked one last deep breath of smoke through the cigarette and put it out with his shoe. "Come here."

Matt pulled the guy casually into the space between the bush and the house and cornered him there. He forced the shorter emo-guy's back up against the little shed while he ducked his face under his chin, tonguing his Adam's apple and nipping. His fingers did fast work sliding over Emo's thin body, exploring the contours of his ribs, hips, and ass. It was not long before Matt had the boy's shirt untucked and his belt unbuckled, all the while licking and sucking the skin of his neck and nuzzling under his ear. Emo-boy moaned and squeezed Matt's upper arms.

"Fuck, you smell good," Matt rasped. He heard him gasp when he reached into the guy's pants. He whimpered when Matt started palming his erection. Dude was rock hard, and Matt got even more turned on. If that was possible!

Good, he's enjoying this. It's better when they enjoy it.

Not that that ever mattered before. Matt had fucked plenty of guys without giving any thought to their feelings. Jamie was the one over the years who poked and badgered Matt about knowing the guy, about caring and connecting. Matt was about taking what he wanted.

Matt aggressively turned him around to face the wall and shoved his pants and briefs down enough to expose only as much as he needed. "Put your arms up on the wall to cushion your face." The emo-boy complied without complaint, and when Matt moved in close and jacked the guy from behind, he let out another moan. Matt steadily stroked as he undid his own trousers with his free hand. True to his boy-scout motto, he came prepared. He was always prepared. Matt fished a pre-lubed condom from his pocket and ripped it open with his teeth. Sheathed, he slid himself up and down the guy's crack, pulling one cheek wide and spreading the excess lube over his hole.

Just before shoving his way in, Matt whispered in his ear, "You're okay with this, right? I just really need to fuck you." He moved his nose into Emo's hair. It smelled nice and it tickled.

"Yes," the anonymous guy answered breathily. "Just do it."

You're breaking rule number one, his conscience whispered. *Remember the proximity rule?* Matt hesitated briefly. For one thing, he'd never tricked in this town, never in the adjacent one, and only a half-dozen times in the whole fucking state. It just wasn't safe! He didn't want to chance anyone he knew finding out he was gay. Only one person around here was privy to that information, and that one person was dead.

Still, in this moment, when he pushed the head of his cock beyond the tight ring of muscle, Matt forgot all the reasons he didn't do this so close to home. The hot passage surrounding his dick and the breathy moans coming out of the guy he had pinned against the wall made the chance he was taking worth the risk. It felt soooo good. He didn't give the guy much of a chance to adjust to the pressure, and he also didn't apologize for the insufficient amount of lubrication required to maximize pleasure. He took what he wanted. Matt slid in and out slowly at first, creating a steady rhythm that matched the pumping of his wrist on the guy's ample shaft.

Matt nuzzled his nose in the guy's hair again. *He smells so fucking good!* The image of threading his fingers through the black hair played across Matt's mind. *Oh, man, to tug on his hair as he sucked me off....* "Ohhh," Matt moaned. "You have such a sweet ass. So tight."

Matt nuzzled some more and found the soft skin of his neck. He kissed him there and picked up the pace of his thrusts.

"Harder," the boy breathed.

"You sure?" Matt asked, as if he couldn't believe his ears.

"Harder," he pleaded.

Matt complied happily. This boy's firm and eager ass milked him perfectly. It was exactly what he was seeking when he left the funeral home. His body needed release, and this emo guy was just the ticket. Nothing like fucking! Hard. Fast. Anonymous. Matt was getting so close.

He had to admit, the sounds coming from this boy's throat were thrilling. *Had others sounded like that before?* He couldn't remember. Matt wished he could see his face. He barely got a glimpse of it before he shoved him around to face the wall. He suddenly wanted to watch his expression. Matt wanted to see his pleasure flow over his features and darken his eyes, especially when he came. Matt felt the disappointment of anonymity for the first time. "Wh-what's your name?" He had to ask. Deep down, he felt a peculiar need to find out who was giving him such a mind-buzzing experience.

"Dare-Darian," the young man panted.

"Darian," Matt softly repeated.

This inexplicable feeling must be what Jamie had tried to explain to him for years. Random people, random places, never a meaningful relationship. Jamie said these things would eat away at him and leave him feeling empty. Up until now, it'd been fine. Matt fucked whomever he wanted and came home to Jamie. Jamie fulfilled all his emotional and relational needs, and Matt never found a reason to seek those things out in the guys he fucked. Those guys were just that—a fuck. But now, here, in light of the fact that Jamie was not going to be there for him when he came down off his orgasmic high, Matt felt guilty. And yes... empty. This was wrong. He was using this poor guy to work through his issues and frustrations with no regard for his feelings or his obviously fragile state of mind. Matt was taking full advantage of Emo's—Darian's—weakness.

Matt's thrill from the fuck dissolved.

He had to stop.

"Shit!" Matt exclaimed. He ceased moving. "I can't do this," he huffed in Darian's ear. His cock pulsed and begged him to resume, but he held still, panting in Darian's hair.

"Please," Darian pleaded, letting his head fall back onto Matt's shoulder. "I'm so close. Don't stop."

"But I don't even know you. You looked so troubled before, and I don't have the right to take advantage of you like this." He couldn't stop himself from rubbing his chin against the side of Darian's face as he rested his head on Matt's shoulder. For some unknown reason, Matt liked nuzzling this boy. He even let his tongue trace the side of Darian's jawbone. Matt's body wanted Darian, but his brain was in conflict with his testosterone.

"Please," Darian pleaded again, nudging his rear and squeezing his asshole tight around Matt's cock. "Finish me." He brought his hand down and covered Matt's hand, which was still on his throbbing erection.

Matt groaned. The pressure of Darian's tightening muscles was enough to coax him. Matt muttered a curse and resumed thrusting. *He shouldn't be doing this. Jamie would not approve.* He pulled on Darian's erection, and within minutes they both found their release. Darian sagged back onto Matt's chest. Matt let go of his flagging penis and gripped his waist with both hands, splaying his fingers across Darian's belly, under his shirt. He felt his ribs. Matt kissed the side of his neck. Darian was much smaller than him, and Matt entertained the idea of wrapping himself around him, dominating Darian, bending his supple body into multiple positions. Darian's skin was warm and smooth, and Matt wanted to lick and explore every inch of him.

Darian turned his face to look at Matt, and Matt tenderly—and uncharacteristically—leaned in and kissed his lips. Matt's stomach quivered. His fuck-and-run tendency skipped town and left in its wake a deep desire to know more about this guy than just his name. He eased back and held the base of the condom.

"Sorry about your shirt, man." He shrugged casually, masking his inner thoughts. He tied off the condom and placed it in the trashcan on the other side of the shed.

Darian looked down. The bottom of his shirt was wet. "I don't care. I have another one in my car."

Well, thanks. It's been fun.... The words went through Matt's mind, but he didn't have the power to speak them. His normal lines were obsolete. This situation was different somehow. And Darian held more of Matt's interest than any other guy had held before. Matt was drawn to him, and he didn't know why.

He did up his pants and re-tucked his shirt as Darian did the same. Then Matt looked him in the face. Darian's eyes were puffy and red. He *had* been crying! Without thinking about it and what the ramifications would be if he did it, Matt stepped closer and took Darian into his arms. Something in those sad eyes told Matt that his day had been just as bad as Matt's, probably worse. He caressed his cheek, and when Darian leaned into it, Matt smiled. *This guy is adorable* and *submissive. And his eyes are fucking gorgeous!* Matt melted into Darian's deep brown pools of looming sorrow. He could see his hurt. He could see his need.

Suddenly Matt's mind flashed to *Lord of the Rings*. He was clad in armor, standing atop a castle wall. Darian was on the ground before a minion of Mordor and about to be slain. Matt leapt in, thrusting his sword through the warrior's chest. He knelt down and cupped Darian's face with a gauntlet-covered hand.

Matt always wanted to be a knight, the one who rescued and protected the princess. Of course, in his queer version of any given fairytale, the "princess" would ultimately be a minstrel or court jester or some such character who was undeniably *male*. He and Jamie often played role-playing games, and Matt was always the one to rescue the damsel, where Jamie was the supportive character—Gimli or C3PO. Jamie was the one to assist the champion in his tasks of heroism and advise him in the mystifying realms of romance. Matt even remembered a conversation or two where Jamie asked him what his "dream guy" would be like....

..."So what do you look for in a guy?" Jamie asked as he scrubbed his side of Matt's Jeep.

Matt rolled his eyes. "Dude, what teen magazine are you reading? I'm not looking for anybody."

"It's just a question," Jamie huffed.

"I don't see why it matters so much to you." Matt finished detailing the driver's side rim.

Jamie tossed his rag in the bucket of water and stood with his hands on his hips. "It just does. So, you gonna answer me or not?"

Matt could see on Jamie's face it was not a joke. His friend truly wanted to know and was not going to take "no" for an answer. Matt rolled his eyes and shook his head but gave in. He always gave in. He'd give Jamie the world if he asked, but he wasn't going to tell him that! "I guess I'd want someone who needs me. Not necessarily helpless or weak, but someone... vulnerable, who needs protection. I could be his champion or knight in shining armor. I have all these muscles. I guess I'd like to use them for good."

"You make your muscles sound like a 'superpower'." Jamie laughed.

"Well, I don't have a sword like Legolas, and I can't use the Force like Luke Skywalker. My manliness is all I got." Matt proceeded to flex his biceps—first out to the side, and then he brought both arms sweeping down to bulge in front of him like the Hulk. Then Matt looked to the left and winked at no one. He stood up straight and puffed out his chest. He spoke metaphorically to his invisible "princess" in a fake-debonair voice. "That's right, baby, I'll protect you." He kissed his bicep. "You want a piece of this?" Matt rubbed his groin. "You got it. Let me kill a few more Orcs before we ascend the spire steps to your chambers where I can give you a little... poke in the whiskers." Matt wagged his eyebrows and winked again. "Does that sound good to you?"

"Oh, God!" Jamie shook his head and walked back to the other side of the car.

Matt chuckled. He thought he was funny, even if Jamie didn't. He didn't understand why Jamie was all inquisitive one minute and dropping the conversation in the next. He was the one who brought it up! Jamie was moody, and Matt learned over the years to go with it. Whatever. It wasn't like Matt's "princess" was out there anyway....

… Matt shrugged it off at the time, but the conversation sat in the back of his mind for years after. Matt *did* like the thought of protecting someone. And here in this moment, Matt *wanted* to protect this boy, this young man. Whatever made him cry, Matt needed to kiss away his tears and hold him securely to his chest. He knew he could play the part way better than Orlando Bloom!

He didn't even care that he was about to break rule number two.

Matt leaned in and kissed Darian. And then he kissed him again. And again. Tiny kisses at first. Kisses that built anticipation. They coaxed a soft moan from Darian's throat. A quick swipe of his tongue awarded Matt with Darian's willing mouth opening. Matt didn't rush. He slid his tongue inside, set on enjoying every taste and texture of Darian's mouth. They'd already fucked. The urgency was over. This was Matt's first experience with what happened "after," and he was not going to screw it up. It felt nice. Darian felt nice. And Darian's tongue piercing…

Oh, fuck me, he's got a tongue piercing!

… was all she wrote. Matt was done for. The thought of that tongue piercing gliding over other parts of his anatomy heated his groin again. He held the boy's body, snug against him. One hand slid down, groping his rear, and the other clamped around his shoulders. Darian's palms were crushed against his chest. Matt could feel Darian pinching his nipples through his shirt. He groaned into Darian's mouth. He moved one hand up into Darian's hair and tangled his fingers in the long strands. He tugged back, and Darian cried out.

Matt playfully nipped and blazed a trail of hot kisses over his throat and up to his ear. "I want you again, Darian. I need to have you in my bed." He sucked his earlobe into his mouth while ignoring the tiny voice in his mind reminding him about rule number three. "I want you, but not like this. I want to take my time and get to know every part of you. Fuck for hours, and maybe talk after. Ya know?"

Darian froze in Matt's arms. "I… I don't… I can't… I was just in… not ready for…."

Darian's frantic sputtering flooded Matt's heart. The knight in armor flashed before him again. He immediately changed his demeanor from lust and wanting to comfort and gentleness. "Shhh, shhh." He instantly released his hold and cupped Darian's face in both hands, caressing his cheekbones with his thumbs. "It's okay. Shhh. I understand. No pressure."

When Darian's body relaxed, Matt pulled him into a tender hug. Just a hug—no seduction. "Shhh." He softly rubbed his back. "My truck is just up the street. Let me take you back to my aunt's house, and I'll make you something to eat. Or maybe some tea. My aunt always makes chamomile tea. She says it's good for the soul. Will you come with me?" Matt pleaded with his eyes.

Darian's arms squeezed his waist, and he nodded silently.

"Okay?"

Darian nodded again and stepped back.

Matt melted into his forlorn eyes. Darian looked so lost and lonely. Matt *had* to comfort him. He led him by the arm back to the street. "My truck is parked right over there." He pointed. "Are you sure you'll go with me?"

"Yes," he answered weakly.

Matt opened the door and helped him into the seat.

Matt then closed the door and walked around the back of the truck, muttering to himself. "What the fuck are you doing, Matthias Dixon? What the fuck are you doing? Now you're breaking rule number four."

His stomach trembled, his fingers were tingling, and his heart was beating a million times a minute. He was sure if he paused long enough to think about it, he'd surely vomit. This was out of character and completely inexplicable. *Who the fuck is this guy that he's slipped under my skin after one random encounter?* Darian was like a sudden gust of wind out of a clear blue sky, and Matt was shaking in his dress shoes.

He nervously got in his truck and pulled it out of the parking spot. Darian was looking the other way, staring out the window. Part of Matt wanted to pull the boy into his chest for the ride, but that was getting downright ridiculous.

This guy had him all cattywampus.

Where did this nurturing impulse come from?

Jamie!

Fuckin' Jamie and his probing questions! Fuckin' Jamie leaving me with all these... these emotions! Fuck! This is Jamie's fault for filling my head with girly notions of compassion. Why didn't I stick with rule number one?

Matt drove, desperately, trying to rid his mind of all the disturbing touchy-feely crap. It didn't work. No matter what he did, Jamie's ideals had seeped in and stuck, and now Matt was trapped in his own role-playing fantasy!

10

June 14, 2005

I'm waiting for Matt. I'm waiting for Matt, but all I can think of is Darian. We haven't kissed yet, but gosh, I want to. My dad said to think hard about each step and make sure of my feelings first. I think my feelings are clear. I think I love him. I know that sounds silly, but I might. He makes me feel all tingly. I look at Darian, and I feel like I'd die if I looked away. He has the most beautiful eyes. They're such a rich, dark brown. I know people think brown is boring, but I don't. It may be the way his long lashes accent his eyes, but I think they are the prettiest eyes I've ever seen.

I got to hold him, the last time I was at my dad's. I guess it was our "first step." I promised Dad I'd take things slow, and Darian agreed. Dad had to work that morning, and I asked if I could have Darian over to watch TV…

… "And you guys are *just* going to watch television?" his dad asked, as if he could not believe one word Jimmy said.

"Yeah, Dad, we are. I told you I'm not ready to decide anything yet. I told you I'd take things slow. Trust me. Nothing is going to happen." Of course Jimmy hoped something would happen, but he also knew it was best not to push.

As soon as his dad drove off, he grabbed the phone. "Hey, Darian. My dad has to work for a while—do you want to come over and watch a movie?"

"Yeah, sure. I'll be right over."

Jimmy hung up and sprinted up the steps to his room. "Coming right over" still meant walking, which would leave Jimmy about fifteen minutes to get ready. He yanked his shirt off and sniffed. He couldn't tell. Another sniff. Washing his armpits couldn't hurt. He dashed into the bathroom and turned on the sink. After wetting himself and lathering, he rinsed off and grabbed a towel. A little deodorant and….

Jimmy froze as he glimpsed Darian grinning at him from the doorway. "Getting all spiffy for me, are ya?" Darian teased in a silly voice.

"How'd you get here so fast?" Jimmy asked as he finished wiping off.

"I was already on my way over. I knew it was your dad's weekend. I didn't know if you already had plans, but I was willing to take the chance. You *aaare* my boyfriend, after all."

Jimmy felt giddy. He did ask him that two weeks ago. He gave Darian a shy smile. "Yup. I am."

Darian stepped closer and reached out. His finger traced a line down the center of Jimmy's bare chest. "But if you really want to take this slow, I suggest you find a shirt. I'm not going to be able to resist touching you, otherwise."

Jimmy felt his heart skip a beat. He gulped down air. "O-okay." He hastily moved past Darian to get one from his room.

Darian followed him. "How about this one?" Darian asked, standing next to Jimmy as he sifted through his shirt drawer.

"Really?" Jimmy asked. "Not the black one?"

"No, I like the black one too. But this one is light enough that I can see your nipples through the fabric."

Fuck! Jimmy's heart palpitated. He knew he was blushing because his face felt hot. "Darian, you're not making this easy for me."

Darian sighed. "I'm sorry." He reached out and slid his fingers down Jimmy's forearm. "I just can't stop thinking about you. You have no idea how sexy you are."

Sexy? Me? You haven't seen Matt! "Uh, no, but you could tell me." Jimmy was nervous but so completely drawn to the fire in Darian's eyes.

Darian didn't smile, he grinned. His lips curved into a mischievous half smile, full of lust and desire. Jimmy swallowed hard, wondering if he would regret the answer. Darian stepped even closer. "First of all," he started to say as he touched the side of Jimmy's face, "you have the most unusual eyes I've ever seen. They're green, yeah, but they change shade. Most people's eyes change depending on what they're wearing, but yours change depending on what you're thinking."

"I like… I like yours too." Jimmy tentatively lifted his hand and touched Darian's stomach.

Darian continued. "I like the way you laugh, and I like the way you smell, and I like the way you blush when you're looking at me." He slid his fingers down to brush over Jimmy's still-exposed chest. "I like the way you pant when I touch you."

Too much! Alarms were going off in his head. Jimmy backed up. "I'm sorry. I can't. Not yet." He tugged the cream-colored shirt over his head.

"Jamie, I'm sorry."

"I'm not upset. I'm just not ready for all those things I see in your eyes." He took Darian's hand in his and looked at his fingers as he spoke. "I want what you want. I'm not stopping you because I don't. But I promised my dad I'd take things slow."

"You told your dad?" He sounded shocked.

"Yes. The day we went fishing. He knows I like you."

"Really?" His shock pulled Jimmy's attention up to his eyes.

"Really. My dad was so cool when I told him. He didn't judge me. He only told me to be careful and think about my decisions. Once I'm out, I'm out."

"Yeah, pretty much."

"How did your parents take it? I mean… you don't seem like you try to hide that you're gay."

"You're right, I don't. My mom rolled her eyes and hasn't said a word about it since. I got the feeling at the time she thought it was some sort of phase. I don't know. I hardly see her. I never knew my dad."

Jimmy could see it bothered him to talk about it, but he wanted to understand. "What do you mean, you hardly see her? Don't you live with her?"

Darian shrugged. "Technically. She works two full-time jobs to feed us all, so she's rarely home. My older half-sister takes care of the youngest sibling. And the other two come and go as they please."

Sounds depressing. "Jeez, and I thought my family was screwed up."

"I told you I come from a fucked-up family. We just never discussed how bad."

"I'm sorry I brought it up."

Jimmy took Darian by the hand and led him down to the living room. They selected *Ferris Bueller's Day Off* and then took a seat on the couch. This was more difficult than Jimmy thought it would be. He wanted to hold Darian, but sitting side by side was problematic. Shoulder to shoulder wasn't enough contact. He could hold his hand, and Darian could lean his head on Jimmy, but that wasn't what Jimmy was picturing. Darian could lie across his lap, but then he figured he'd just get a hard-on and be embarrassed. After several minutes of shifting positions, Jimmy stood up and looked at Darian.

"This isn't working," he declared.

"What isn't?"

Jimmy sighed heavily. Hands on hips, he scanned the room and came up with a brilliant idea. "Come here," he said, grabbing Darian's hand and hauling him off the sofa. "One sec," he directed, holding up his index finger. Jimmy pulled his dad's big, comfy chair until it was angled how he liked toward the television. He sat down, flipped the leg rest out, and held his arms out for Darian. "Sit here with me."

Darian smiled his mischievous smile again, and Jimmy promised himself he'd be good. Darian crawled onto the cushion and sat back against Jimmy's chest, nestled between his legs. He shifted around until he was comfortable: resting his head on Jimmy's shoulder, back against Jimmy's groin, and arms draped over Jimmy's legs on either side. "I like how you think," he cooed, rubbing his head along Jimmy's jaw.

Jimmy swallowed hard for the hundredth time. Having Darian in his lap in this position was going to give him a boner anyway! Still, he enjoyed having his arms around him. He liked nuzzling his face on the side of Darian's head and smelling his clean hair. He barely remembered watching the movie at all…

… Oh, man, what a day that was! I keep reliving it every night. I wanted to make out with him, but I thought my dad would be disappointed. Luckily Darian didn't say anything about a "goodbye kiss" when he went back home. I may have given in.

Cool, Matt's finally here!!!!

"Dude, where you been?" he asked as Matt came through the front door. Jimmy closed his notebook and jumped off the floor where he'd been sprawled, writing.

"Sorry, Jamie. Mom got a flat and called me. Dad was in a meeting and couldn't help her. She had groceries and my brother and sister. It took a while for me to assemble the jack and put the spare on. Pieces of the jack were scattered all over the trunk. I don't think it's ever been used, so why it wasn't in one piece I'll never know." Matt pointed at Jimmy's notebook. "You still writing in that thing? It's been over a year."

Jimmy nodded. "Yeah. It helps. I find it… therapeutic."

Matt chuckled. "There's a psychotherapist's term if I ever heard one. *Therapeutic*…. Shit! You ready to go to the gym? I thought we'd play some pickup basketball after a workout."

"Sounds good."

JIMMY and Matt spent the day together. They hit the gym first, like Matt suggested, and then found some guys hanging around the basketball court to play a couple games of two-on-two. They were sweaty and exhausted when the sky began getting dark.

"I'm surprised your mom didn't expect you home by five like usual."

Jimmy shook his head as Matt watched the road, driving them back to his house. "Dude, I think my mom is bipolar. Or maybe schizophrenic."

Matt laughed. "Why do you say that? Although I think you're right."

"Well, one week she's all like, 'Matt is a bad influence because he's one of those Christians'," Jimmy explained in a high-pitched mocking tone. "And the next thing I know she's glad I have you to hang out with. I don't get her, man!"

"Oh, my gosh. She wasn't acting weird back in October, was she?" Matt steered onto Jimmy's street.

Jimmy's eyes went wide. "Yes. Do you know something?"

"Only that *my* mom's been acting moody too. She brought Joan up a few times for 'prayer' since October. I heard her telling Dad that your mom stormed out of a ladies' thing back in October because the message included something about divorce being a sin. Your mom got mad and wasn't talking to my mom for weeks." He parked the Jeep and turned to face Jimmy. "Women! They are so fucking emotional. Give me a guy any day!"

Jimmy grinned.

"Hey, I turn eighteen next month. You want to celebrate? Maybe go camping that weekend or something?"

"Nah, I might be at my dad's that weekend. I'm hoping Mom will let me go more often over the summer."

"What do you do over there? Your dad works, doesn't he?"

"Only some of the time. We go fishing. Watch movies. Play video games. Stuff."

"Sounds boring." Matt looked at him skeptically.

"It's not," he replied. "It's quiet. I like being away from my mom."

"I can't fault you for that. I'm gonna be joining the firefighter cadets in July. I can apply right after my birthday."

"Wow, that's cool." He was truly happy for his friend. "You've been talking about being a firefighter for so long."

"Yup. And after I go through the cadet stage, I can start my real training."

"Where is the cadet thing at? I remember you said there wasn't one around here."

"Anne Arundel County."

"Geez, what a haul."

"But it'll be worth it. Dad said it was a great opportunity when Mom griped about the gas."

They both jumped when someone knocked on the window of the Jeep. Jimmy turned and found his stepsister looking at him. He rolled the window down. "What, Emily?"

"Mom wants to know if you're coming in or staying in the Jeep all night with your boyfriend?" Emily snickered.

"Shut up. She didn't say that."

"No, I did." She snickered some more. "You two are always together. I just thought you were boyfriends."

Jimmy was not happy. "Well, we're not. Now go back inside and tell Mom I'll be right in." When Emily walked away he rolled the window back up. "Boyfriends," he scoffed.

"If they only knew, my friend, if they only knew…."

"What's that supposed to mean?" Jimmy asked defensively.

"Just that your mom's not gay-friendly. She'd shit a brick if she found out her perfect little son's best friend is gay."

Matt's reply was innocent enough, but Jimmy still felt irritated. Matt continued to voice his opinion that Jimmy was straight, no matter his protests to the contrary, and now he was calling him the "perfect little son." It had to stop! "I'm not perfect, Matt, and my mom hardly thinks of me that way. And you're *not* the only one who's gay in here."

Matt's head hung to the side, like he couldn't be bothered to hold it up. "We're not back on that again, are we?" he bellyached.

"Ya know what? Forget it." Jimmy opened the door and jumped out. He grabbed his gym bag and shut the door.

He was one step from the front door when his phone buzzed.

Matt texted: *Don't get pissed. If you say you're gay, then you're gay! Come out clubbing with me on my birthday, and we'll see how gay you are.*

Jimmy rolled his eyes and texted back: *I said I'm gay, not a man-slut like you!!!*

That's MR. MAN-SLUT! Get it right! Catch you later, Jamester. ;p

Later :-]

Jimmy showered. Ate. Had some obligatory conversation with his mom and headed up to bed. He was irritated with Matt but couldn't blame him. He blamed himself. He had a boyfriend! So why didn't he say so?

So why didn't I tell Matt about Darian? I don't know. It was the perfect opportunity, and I had evidence. But then again... would that be using Darian to make my point to Matt? I don't like the sound of that. I'm not using Darian. But why didn't I say something?

I think I like having something that's just mine. At least for now. This is the first time I haven't shared something with Matt. I feel like I'm betraying him, but on the other hand, if I share, then Darian becomes "ours," and I've never had a friend that was mine and Matt's at the same time. There's just me and Matt. I guess I have friends, but they're mainly in school and not after the bell rings. I know Matt has friends, but he never ditches me to do stuff with them. And then there's Darian, the enigma in my life.

I think about him all the time, but given the opportunity to brag about him, I cave. Maybe I'm afraid Matt would judge me. He'd say I'm going about it all wrong and guilt me into having sex the very next time I saw Darian. I don't want to be like that. I'm not ready for sex. No matter how much I think about it, I'm not ready.

Matt, the man-slut, be damned!

11

July 15, 2005

    I hate my job at Larson's Garden Center. Fucking roses cut up my arms! I may have to quit. I don't mind mowing lawns with Matt though. The work is easy, and the money is good. It gets me out of the house for a few hours too!

    I'd rather spend more time with Darian than work, but it never seems possible. What's worse is that I just got off the phone with Darian. He's pissed. I can tell. His voice was calm, and he said he wasn't mad, but I could tell he was. This is the first weekend where I ditched my dad's turn and opted to stay home. ALL BECAUSE OF MATT'S BIRTHDAY. Which is the worst part. If it was some family thing, and I told Darian that I'd have to see him another weekend, he would understand. But I told him it was because I was going out with Matt to celebrate his birthday. The drop in his voice just about killed me. I tried to tell him nothing was going to happen between us, but I'm not sure he bought it. The rest of the conversation was way too clipped.

    Fuck! It wouldn't matter to me if I missed the "celebration" or not, but part of me worries about Matt. He's all excited about turning eighteen because now he's "legal." I don't really like the sound of that, but what am I supposed to tell him? He said he wasn't limited to MySpace twinks anymore. Whatever the hell that means. I'm worried he's going to get in over his head one of these days if he starts going for older guys. Like my dad warned: some guys don't give a crap about your feelings.

    I hope he doesn't decide to take a walk on the wilder side while I'm with him Saturday night!

JIMMY walked through the front door of Darian's house on Sunday. It was unlocked, like usual. They didn't have anything worth stealing, so no one bothered to lock the door. He'd opted to drop in unexpectedly and hoped Darian wasn't working.

When school let out, Darian got a job working part time in the deli department of a nearby Super Walmart. The deli wasn't as mind numbing as some positions could be. They kept Darian busy, and he told Jimmy that working it made it easier to be away from him. Plus, he finally had some money!

Jimmy spied Darian's half brothers playing Atari in the living room on their ancient television set. Darian said his mom found the Atari at the Goodwill, and the boys were thrilled it worked! No PSP or Xbox 360 in this house. The boys didn't notice his presence, so he skipped up the steps.

The door to Darian's room was cracked. Jimmy peeked in. The bed was a crumpled pile of blankets with a bare foot hanging off the mattress on one side. Jimmy grinned. He recognized that foot! He opened the door slowly and crept over to the bed. Darian lay there 99 percent buried. Only his foot and some of his hair could be seen. Jimmy knelt down and lifted the corner of the comforter, revealing Darian's lovely face. He lay on his stomach, his arms tucked up to his chest with his hands curled by his cheeks. He was adorable. Jimmy carefully pushed the blankets back so they would not fall forward and then proceeded to lightly stroke his boyfriend's hair. It was so soft. It was getting long too. Jimmy liked it the way it was when they met, when Darian's hair was not quite shoulder length and layered, with slanted, shaggy bangs. Now it was all grown out and edging past his shoulders. Maybe he could urge him to cut it without sounding like he disapproved of his looks. Also, the eyeliner had to go. Jimmy didn't see the need for it. Darian's eyes were captivating.

A few more strokes and Darian began to stir. Here it was one o'clock in the afternoon, and Darian was still asleep! He needed to get up. Jimmy touched the side of his face. A smile curved his lips, and Jimmy knew he was awake, at least slightly. Then Darian sighed and stretched. His hand shot out and pulled Jimmy's into the blanket heap.

Jimmy giggled. He didn't mind being practically in bed with him, as long as his bottom half was kneeling on the floor. He slipped his other arm under as well and caressed Darian's bare shoulder.

"I can't believe you're still asleep," Jimmy said.

"What have I got to motivate me to get out of bed? You said you weren't going to be here this weekend," he grumbled, his face resting on the mattress. "Why are you here?"

"Gee, nice greeting. I guess I'll be calling my stepdad to come pick me up." He tried to extract himself from Darian's grasp but failed. Darian was not letting go of his hand. "Or not. Seems my hand is stuck."

Darian chuckled. "And I'm not letting it go." He opened his eyes and lifted his head to look at Jimmy. "In faaaact...." Darian gave him a wily expression as he lifted his body up on his elbows. He moved back as he pulled Jimmy forward, causing him to stretch across the bed.

"Darian, I don't think this is such a good idea," he protested.

"I'm not ready to get up yet; it's all warm under here. Just lay next to me, I promise not to bite. Although I might nibble." He winked.

Jimmy huffed in protest but climbed in beside Darian. "I still have my shoes on."

"So kick 'em off."

Jimmy did so and pulled the blankets over his fully clothed body. It felt strange. "So, now what do we do?"

Darian snuggled up to him, resting his head on Jimmy's chest. Jimmy pulled him close, enjoying the feel of naked back under his palm. Darian had smooth skin. He was afraid to ask if *all* of him was naked.

"You tell me all about your clubbing adventures with Sir Cums-a-Lot."

"Oh, God. Please don't ever call him that to his face."

"I won't. *If* I even meet him, I will pretend I haven't heard about any of his tawdry affairs. *If* being the pertinent word."

Jimmy could tell his excuses were wearing thin. Darian had asked a number of times when he would meet Matt, but Jimmy was not so willing to make the meeting happen. "I told you. He works a lot. He mows lawns most of the summer. And now he's joined a cadet program for firefighter wannabes. I don't know when we can get together."

"You haven't told him about me, have you?"

Darian's soft question made him feel guilty. "No, I haven't."

"I guess I shouldn't ask why?"

"I don't know, Darian. Every time we're together at the gym or out for a morning run, I clam up. Matt has it in his head that I'm straight. He doesn't think I could possibly like guys if my first thought isn't about sex. He is such a slut; he really is! I'm not sure he'd know the difference between a trick and a possible life partner if his life depended on it. He doesn't see guys as anything more than instant gratification. Last night proved it!"

"Really? Tell me about it," Darian asked. He moved his hand over to Jimmy's buttons and slowly undid his shirt. Jimmy felt what he was doing, but his mind was focused on Matt, so he didn't gripe.

"We were somewhere in DC. That's all I know. We got into some club where Matt knows the bouncer guy, and he let me in with no ID. I had to promise not to drink. Like I would? The place looked like a breeding ground for herpes." Jimmy relayed the story in disgust. "After we were in the front door, Matt took his shirt off and flung it at me. He was gyrating with his crotch crushed up against some huge black guy's leg. It was so vulgar. I can't believe he does things like that all the time."

"I don't know. Sounds like it could be fun. Like if you were the one gyrating up against *my* leg." The buttons undone, Darian opened Jimmy's shirt and caressed his skin softly.

Jimmy shivered at his touch but kept talking. "Yeah, I guess that would be different. But that's what I mean—Matt didn't talk about anything but sex. When we left he didn't know any of their names. He didn't know where any of those guys worked or if they'd be interested in dating. The only information he remembered was how long their dicks were and if they could deep throat him or not. I think I counted seven times he went to the bathroom with a different guy in tow. It was disgusting."

"Seven?"

"Three—whatever," Jimmy gruffly corrected his use of hyperbole.

Darian's hand moved up to his exposed nipple. His finger circled the nub, making it harden. Jimmy heard Darian's sigh of pleasure. The finger disappeared and came back to that spot, slick and cold with saliva. Jimmy's heart rate increased as he sucked in a quick breath. "Darian," he rasped, "what are you doing?"

"Enjoying myself. All the sex talk got me thinking." Darian moved off Jimmy's shoulder and slid down his body a few inches. After opening Jimmy's shirt all the way, he dipped down and started licking Jimmy's other nipple.

Jimmy shuddered. He panted at the pleasure that was rolling through his body. Darian was nibbling with his lips and swirling his tongue around Jimmy's very erect right nipple while his fingers played with the other side. His fingers pinched the nub and made Jimmy whimper. "Dare-Darian… ohhh…" His head was spinning. Darian was doing things that felt so good. It was as if he knew just the right amount of pressure to apply with his teeth for it to be erotic but not too painful.

Darian smoothed his palm over Jimmy's stomach, rubbing almost to the point of tickling, but not quite. He moved his mouth up to lick across Jimmy's throat and kiss his way over to Jimmy's other nipple. Jimmy was helpless to move, arrested by Darian's erotic ambush. He knew he was moaning, but he had no ability to stop himself. Darian's tongue was making him feel so good. Then he felt Darian's palm slide southward. He was rubbing Jimmy's erection through the fabric of his shorts.

"Dare… don't… please… stop…."

Darian nipped his earlobe. "Let me suck you, please?"

Jimmy burned with need. If Darian kept rubbing the front of his shorts he'd blow his wad in a minute. This had to stop. He grabbed Darian's hand under the blanket. "Stop."

Darian did not resist his stilling grip. "You don't sound very convincing."

Jimmy opened his eyes and looked into Darian's questioning gaze. "I know. I want to, but I'm not ready. You sucking me off reminds me of Matt's bathroom appointments. I don't want to think of you in the same context. You're not a slut." Then the statement begged the question. "Are you?"

Darian shook his head.

"You don't *look* very convincing." It was Jimmy's turn to question Darian's conviction.

"I've done some things you'd consider slutty."

"Like?"

"Sucking some guys off in the toilets at school."

"Really?" He was shocked.

"Yeah. I'm not proud of it. Back when I came out, I used to get picked on more. A few times I said I'd suck the guy off if he left me alone. It worked." His expression fell. "Are you disappointed to hear that?"

"No. I guess not. Have you… done it?"

"Done it? Oh, *it!* Once. A baseball jock. He sheathed up and shoved his way in, and it hurt like hell. I didn't even get hard by the time he was done."

"Do you still—"

"No," Darian was quick to answer. "Not since… not since I met you."

"Oh." Jimmy liked hearing that. He smiled.

Darian returned the question, "Have you?"

"Nooooo. You're the first boy I ever kissed."

"Um, Jamie, I hate to inform you like this, but we haven't kissed. We've cuddled. And now I've practically made you cum in your shorts, but we haven't kissed."

"Oh," Jimmy replied. Thinking about it for a nanosecond, he decided to remedy the situation. He flipped Darian gently onto his back and leaned over him. "I can fix that." He closed his eyes as he brought his lips down on Darian's.

The kiss was soft and controlled. He lingered there, moving his mouth around like he saw in the movies, where the guy looks like he's nibbling away at the girl's mouth. No tongue, just lots of relaxed, open-lipped smooching. When he was sure the first-kiss experience was a done deal, he leaned back. "How was that?"

Darian's expression was pure serenity. "Mmmm, perfect. I want more." He lazily opened his glassy eyes.

"Okay. Only go brush your teeth first."

Jimmy's bluntness was embarrassing, and Darian blushed. He rolled over, groaning into the pillow.

Jimmy laughed.

SUMMER weeks were slipping by fast. Jimmy was thoroughly taking pleasure in every visit to his dad's. Somehow he'd managed to convince his mom to consent to every other weekend until school started, which meant two more visits on top of the whole week he got the second week of August! They fished, sometimes with Darian and sometimes alone. His dad showed him how to put up drywall, and the two of them put an addition on the farmhouse. They patched up the rundown areas and laid new linoleum on the floor in the kitchen. Jimmy learned some very useful skills that summer.

He also learned you can have a wonderful time with your boyfriend without having sex. Intellectually speaking.

Jimmy enjoyed every second with Darian, however fleeting those moments were. Between Darian working and Jimmy helping Matt mow lawns, and trying to coordinate trips to his dad's when his mom could drive him, it was still less than he would have wished for. They talked a lot and texted, but nothing compared to holding each other on the comfy chair.

Jimmy also learned he was addicted to Darian's tongue. Man, could that boy kiss! He was incredibly good at swirling that muscle around Jimmy's mouth and pressing the ball of his tongue piercing on parts of Jimmy's skin in the most erotic ways. It didn't take but a few months for Jimmy to reconsider Darian's offer to suck him off.

TWO months into the start of senior year, Jimmy was back to the "one weekend a month" visits to his dad's. Luckily, his dad had made a lady friend over the summer and didn't mind sharing his time with Jimmy one bit. His dad spent time with Cheryl, and Jimmy got to hang out with Darian.

"ARE you sure your mom won't come home?" Jimmy nervously asked one night in November as Darian walked him backward into his room. Darian's arms were locked around his waist, and his lips were attached to Jimmy's neck.

"Nope. She's out with Jerry," Darian answered between kisses.

"Wow, this one's lasted at least three months."

"Yup, they've even mentioned marriage." Darian slid his hands under Jimmy's shirt and pushed it up, finding his nipples and pinching.

Jimmy yelped and then gasped. He pulled his shirt off the rest of the way and tugged on Darian's, who was quick to allow its removal. Once shirtless, the boys pressed their bodies together and kissed hard and long. They fell backward onto the bed. Darian straddled Jimmy and expertly devoured his mouth.

When Darian finally moved his lips to Jimmy's neck, Jimmy asked, "Is your offer still good?"

Darian sucked hard and left a mark. "Offer?" More slurping ensued.

"To suck me off?"

Darian froze. He sat up and looked at Jimmy as if he could not believe his ears. "Are you serious?"

"Yeah. I thought about you doing it for months, and next week is your birthday and everything, and I didn't know what to get you...." He didn't need to continue. Darian was sliding down his body and rapidly undoing his jeans.

"Lay on the bed properly, so I'm not half on the floor," Darian instructed.

"Are you sure no one will come in?" Jimmy asked as he got situated.

"I'll make sure they won't." Darian got up and locked the door. "How's that?"

"Better. Are you sure you want to—"

"*Yes!* Oh, yes. Ever since I met you, in fact. And that weekend we went swimming in the pond, I'm surprised you didn't notice how... *glad...* I was to see you shirtless. I've been dreaming about getting my mouth on you all summer." Darian pulled Jimmy's jeans and briefs down his legs and dropped them on the floor. "Glorious," he mused.

Jimmy wanted to blush as Darian ogled him, but he wasn't embarrassed. He was turned on. The lust in his boyfriend's eyes was for him, only him. Darian got onto the bed and settled between his legs. Jimmy closed his eyes and relished the kisses Darian planted on his legs from his ankles to his inner thighs.

Matt will never understand how awesome it feels to know who it is doing the kissing!

"Ohhh," he moaned as Darian took him in hand. "Ahhh," he whimpered with the first swipe of Darian's tongue. "Holy shit!" he cried out when Darian took him to the back of his throat.

The pressure in his groin was mounting. He tingled and burned all over from the pleasure Darian was giving him. *Why did I wait for this so long?* Jimmy wasn't sure. This was pure heaven. His entire body felt like it was alive with dancing electricity.

No wonder Matt can't stop. This is incredible!

His mind swirled. He was so close. Darian kept moving on him. Jimmy grasped his hair and tugged. He could feel the vibrations from Darian's throat as he chuckled. Jimmy was so close.

Jimmy squeezed his eyes shut as he pushed his hips upward into that beautiful, wet heat. "Ohhh, Matt." The pressure exploded.

Darian jumped back just as Jimmy started spurting. "What did you call me?"

The attitude in Darian's voice was lost on him. "Dare-Darian." Jimmy's body jerked. He was only slightly disappointed that Darian pulled off before he came. This was the best orgasm of his life. He sighed, contented.

"No! You didn't!" Darian picked a shirt up off the floor and pulled it over his head. He unlocked the door and hastily left the room, leaving Jimmy lying naked on his bed.

Jimmy sat up and grabbed the nearest piece of clothing to wipe off his sticky stomach. He found his underwear and pulled them on.

Why the hell is Darian so pissed? He couldn't figure out what went wrong. He felt amazing! *I thought the greatest thing would be to hear his name in the throes of orgasm.... Oh shit!* It finally hit him that he *didn't* gasp Darian's name—he'd said Matt's.

Jimmy snatched up a shirt as he dashed out of Darian's room. He found him in the bathroom, brushing his teeth. Tugging the shirt on, he scrambled to apologize, "Darian, I—"

He was cut off by a death glare. Darian spit into the sink. "Save it." He took a swig of water and rinsed, then spit again. "Just get your clothes and leave." Darian wiped his mouth and left Jimmy standing by the sink.

When he entered Darian's room, Darian thrust his jeans into his hand.

"Darian, please...."

"I said, just leave." He was very stern.

Jimmy pulled his pants on and found his shoes. Guilt squirmed in his gut. What could he do to make this right? He'd made the worst mistake of his life. How could he possibly explain that he didn't mean it? "I didn't mean—"

"Yes, you did!" Darian cut him off again. "I always knew you had a thing for Matt, but I kept hoping anyway." Darian stood defensively, with his arms crossed, facing Jimmy as he finished tying his shoes. "I'm so stupid." He turned away.

Jimmy arose and approached him. He placed his hands on Darian's shoulders and felt him tense up and attempt to pull away. Jimmy turned him. "Darian...."

Darian pushed at his chest. "Stop." He struggled again, but his efforts were weakening. "Go away." His voice cracked. "I want you to leave." Tears pooled in the corners of his eyes.

"Darian." Jimmy's voice was soothing. He knew he was in the wrong. When Darian stopped pushing on his chest, he wrapped his arms around him and kissed his lips. Darian didn't resist long. In seconds he opened to Jimmy's beckoning tongue. Jimmy groaned as he invaded that wonderful mouth and explored. Oh, how he loved that tongue! He kissed and moaned and moved his hands to grip Darian's posterior.

Darian pressed his groin to Jimmy and rocked his hips. Then he pulled back suddenly. "No. I can't. I'm still mad that you said Matt's name. Just go." He hung his head and turned away.

Jimmy complied, heavy hearted.

November 5th

I don't think I've ever done anything so brainless. Damn my stupid mouth! I can't blame Darian for being mad. I'd be too. I only hope he decides to forgive me soon. Christmas is coming up. I was hoping to do something special for his 17th birthday, and I completely blew that! All I can think of right now is trying to make him realize I love him, not Matt.

Fuck! Why didn't I tell him? I am such a twat. Now if I say "I love you," he'll just think I'm trying to get him to forgive me. It won't sound sincere. Shit. I am such an asshole.

12

September 22, 2010

6:50 p.m.

DARIAN WESTON was not prepared to get fucked out of his mind when he numbly agreed to go back to the stranger's house—or rather, to the stranger's aunt's house. He'd been in a daze since he'd gotten the news about Jamie's death. He was weak and tired from lack of sleep and food, as well as from vomiting constantly. He was purely going through the motions of putting one foot in front of the other, hoping to make it through to the funeral on Friday.

Then this guy showed up and suggested he could "make the pain go away." Secretly Darian had been hoping for drugs, but the prospect of sex roped him in just as easily. He'd never been fucked by a random hook-up. (Even the ones in high school weren't exactly random.) He was numb, lonely, and not thinking about what he'd feel afterwards.

As he got into the guy's truck, Darian felt the panic start. *What have I done?* Guilt rose up, screaming in his ear about betraying his only love. How could he do that to Jamie? He had no answer. He wasn't thinking. *There's your answer, Dare, you weren't thinking. You just wanted to escape, run away and hide. He came along at just the right moment and offered you a moment of escape.* Darian knew now he should have refused—hindsight being 20/20 and all.

The promise of warm tea and possibly some comforting conversation—or a stranger's shoulder to cry on—sounded really good as well. Again, he should have refused, but Darian needed comfort. He had no one, no one but Dan. Darian wasn't ready to face Jamie's dad. It would make his death become too real. Darian didn't want real. He wanted escape.

He felt so lost.

Stepping inside the house, it seemed to Darian that the stranger *wanted* to comfort him. He brought the tea he promised. He let Darian cry on his shoulder without asking why. But when that incredibly hot-looking guy started rubbing his back and kissing his hair and face, Darian lost himself again with the need to feel something other than pain.

He whimpered and leaned into the guy's expert touch.

The next thing he knew, they were naked on a bed, and his nipple ring was being tugged on by the man's talented tongue. He writhed beneath him and begged to be fucked. Darian could not recall a time he'd felt so desperate.

At least he'd managed to ask the guy's name between moans and coming for the third time. Matthias. Darian felt a surge of "something" go off in his head, like a warning, but it was dashed aside when Matthias's fingers twisted inside his canal, causing him to moan louder.

That was hours ago.

The naked god next to Darian leaned over and looked at the clock. "Shit! Ten of seven." He rolled back and gazed at him with a totally forlorn expression. "I'm sorry, Darian. I hate to seem so cold, but I've got someplace I need to be."

Darian shrugged as Matthias flung the sheets back and strutted his absolutely gorgeous body into the bathroom. "It's okay. I have to go too," Darian lied. Even if there was a second viewing time today, there was no way in hell he was going to it. It had been hard enough the first time. Maybe he could work up the nerve tomorrow. For now, he just wanted to bask in the after-sex euphoria.

He watched Matthias leaning over the sink, washing his face. He was grateful to have such a nice view from the bed. It gave him all the more reason to stay right where he was for just a few more minutes. Matthias was incredible. Darian had never experienced such mastery in bed before. Jamie had been a wonderful lover, for sure, but this was… this was… well, there wasn't a word for what this had been! Darian could barely feel the lower half of his body. He was completely wasted.

The way this guy could swivel his hips to reach just the right spots inside of Darian was astounding. He knew how to use his fingers and his tongue, everywhere! Darian didn't know such pleasures existed. Discreetly, he pulled the sheet up and stroked himself leisurely, thinking about the things they'd done.

His eyes studied Matthias's perfect butt. It was tight and all muscle, rounded enough to give plenty to squeeze but not so much as to be called a "bubble butt." *Perfect!* He stroked a little harder. His eyes moved from the curve of Matthias's ass to his muscled thighs. *I bet he runs a lot. Legs like that!* Matthias was the epitome of physical perfection.

Darian closed his eyes as he neared orgasm again. One more twisting stroke and… cum shot across his belly. He panted a second and moved to rise off the bed. Matthias was standing right there, watching.

"Niiice. Very hot." He sat on the bed and swiped his finger through the cum on Darian's stomach, then seductively put that finger into his mouth.

Darian groaned. He sat up and forcefully claimed a kiss. Matthias didn't resist. He gave Darian all he wanted. He groaned into his mouth and climbed atop Darian as he pushed him back onto the pillow. Darian felt Matthias's erection slide over his hip. Matthias nudged his legs apart with his knee and positioned them for another round. He broke their kiss and reached for a condom, then froze when he looked at the clock.

"Fuck!" Matthias's head bowed in defeat. "I can't do this right now. I am so, so sorry. As much as I want to be inside you again, I don't have time." He slid away and reached for his underwear. "You are so fucking addicting!"

Darian liked the sound of that. *Me? Addicting?* He never thought of himself like that before. He wanted Matthias to be addicted. Darian needed the high Matthias gave him, the tingling in his body and coherent thought draining away. Soon enough the feeling would fade, and he would be left with pain and self-loathing for what he'd done. If Matthias didn't have to go, he'd be begging again to be pounded breathless.

He watched Matthias get dressed as he slowly gathered his clothing from around the floor. Would Jamie mind? Darian closed his eyes briefly, trying to will away the guilt. *How could I do this to Jamie? I was desperate. I was alone. Jamie left me alone.* Matthias was a rebound fuck, but deep down Darian hoped it would last beyond tonight. He couldn't deal with being completely alone. He longed to be touched, and Matthias was a wonderful diversion. Darian loved the strength in his hands and confidence in his dominance. Darian liked being submissive.

Jamie had never taken advantage of Darian's penchant for submission. He'd liked things simple and routine. Jamie was a gentle lover and partner, except for that one time on the bed at his mother's house. He believed in mutual and reciprocal love. Jamie liked making love with the covers over them and the lights dim, the way he saw it in the movies. But Darian wanted more. Secretly he hoped to work some kink into their relationship as the years progressed. Now Jamie was gone. He'd never get the chance. He didn't regret one day with his former lover, but now that Jamie was gone, should he deny his own needs for fear it was too soon?

Jamie had *just* died. He should be mourning. He *was* mourning. But the electricity that traveled through his body when Matthias touched him was undeniable. He craved how Matthias made him feel. It was all he could do to keep his hands at his sides and not reach for Matthias again right then.

Matthias tucked in his shirt and smiled. "I'll go see if my aunt has bananas or something. I need a bite before I leave. You want one?"

"Sure."

Matthias left the room, and Darian finished dressing. He was missing one shoe. He got down and looked under the bed. *Ah ha!* He walked to the other side and picked up the shoe. Tying it, he could not help but notice the picture lying face down on the nightstand. He remembered seeing Matthias turn it over, but with all the groping and kissing, he'd dismissed it.

Darian reached over and picked it up. He nearly dropped it once he saw who it was.

Darian carried the picture into the kitchen with him, each step an effort as his legs wanted to give out at any moment. "Matt?" he shakily asked.

"Yeah," came the casual reply he expected.

When Matt turned around, he held the picture out to him. "Matt, as in… *Jamie's* Matt?"

Matt's eyes narrowed. "Uh-huh. Where'd you hear that name? Did you know him?"

Darian's stomach seized. Guilt with the strength of an angry lion roared in his ears. "He was my boyfriend." His voice came out like a whisper. "We were going to get married."

Matt's expression was hard to read, but confusion was Darian's guess. "What? Wait," Matt said, holding one hand up and covering his forehead with the other, as if he was overcome with a sudden headache. "Are your initials D. W., by any chance?"

"Yes. Darian Weston."

"Fuck!" Matt cursed, his face going green.

Darian was equally ill at figuring this all out. It was bad enough feeling like he'd betrayed his lover and fiancé by allowing the first guy he happened across to fuck him. Not just a one-time deal behind a shed, mind you, but hours of ecstasy that took Darian to places he'd never dreamed of reaching—places he wanted to soar to again. But the ecstasy was with Jamie's best friend!

His stomach muscles convulsed. Darian crumbled to the floor, and Matt's chamomile tea came back to visit his aunt's linoleum floor. He vomited again and felt Matt's warm hand on his back. He was kneeling beside him, soothing him, telling him, "It's okay. Let it out." Darian wheezed as he tried to catch his breath. He hated throwing up, truly he did, and in the last couple days, he should have become an expert. He hadn't, and breathing and heaving did not mesh well together. He retched one more time, but this was only phlegm. He sat back.

Matt handed him a dishtowel and pulled him to his chest. Darian wiped his mouth and started to cry. He hated how weak he was, but there was no force in hell that could have stopped the tears from flowing. He sobbed heavily and clung to Matt's strong body. He felt

Matt hugging him securely, kissing his head, and massaging his back. Darian let everything out, and Matt allowed him to.

Neither one of them said a word for a long while. When Darian was composed enough to stand, Matt led him to the couch, where the two of them sat nestled together in silence. Darian leaned his face against Matt's neck and laced his fingers through Matt's. He should be angry with himself. He should storm out and be angry with Matt, but he wasn't. Being in Matt's arms was comforting. It felt safe. He could not deny it, no matter *who* Matt was. Darian lacked any strength to pull away.

"We should probably talk about this," Matt said at last.

Darian shook his head and pressed himself closer to Matt's body. He didn't want to talk.

"Darian, we need to."

Why? Why do we have to? This was too hard. Darian couldn't possibly voice the shame he felt.

Matt stroked the hair on his arm and kissed his forehead. "Dare, ignoring this won't make it go away," he urged. "You and I had sex, lots of sex. I can't regret that."

Regret. The word triggered Darian's response. "I'm sorry," he cried. Fresh tears poured from his sore eyes as he clung to Matt, balling Matt's shirt in his fist. "I didn't know. I wasn't thinking. You must think I'm a horrible person for treating Jamie like that. I feel so awful. I couldn't stand the pain. I—"

"Shhh," Matt silenced him, hugging tightly with both arms. "You're not a horrible person. You're not the only one who was in that bed. I couldn't cope either. I am as much to blame, if not more, for what happened between us. When I saw you, I knew you weren't in a stable frame of mind, but I went ahead and pressed you into having sex."

"No, you—" he started to protest. Sitting back, he noticed fresh tears in Matt's eyes.

"Darian, stop, let me finish," Matt insisted. "You were vulnerable, and I took advantage. I was angry and frustrated, and I took it out on you." He grinned and added, "More precisely, on your ass."

Darian gave a thin smile in reply. Matt was really trying to soothe him, and Darian was touched. And seeing Matt cry, even slightly, made his comfort genuine.

Matt wiped his eyes. "This was my fault." He stroked Darian's jaw and looked deeply into his eyes. "I'm the asshole. I also should've noticed you were wearing the cross I gave him." He lifted the chain from Darian's shirt and fingered it. "*And…* this is how *non*-observant I am…." Matt took Darian's wrist and turned it over, exposing the tiny spider tattoo. A black widow. "I should have realized this tattoo matched Jamie's. I'm sorry, Darian."

It made sense. Matt was looking for relief too. But Matt said he didn't regret the sex. Did Darian? He wasn't sure. It was all confusing. Darian sat there, looking into Matt's eyes as if they held the answer.

Matt's fingers closed over his hand. "I don't know what to say. I guess we both screwed up. But as I see it, it was inevitable. Jamie left us both. I can't speak for you, but I'm frustrated as hell, and I have no one to talk to about it."

"Me neither," Darian whispered.

"I can't imagine what you're going through. He was your boyfriend. Holy shit! If I'm not thinking clearly, your brain must be toast!"

Darian could not deny how close to the truth that was. "Pretty much."

"Maybe this doesn't have to be about what went on in there." Matt pointed toward the hallway where the bedroom was. "Maybe it can be about needing each other right now?"

Darian nodded. His head was swirling with possibilities. What should he do? Trust Matt? Maybe they could spend some time together? Maybe Matt would make his pain go away? Maybe Darian would find relief in Matt Dixon's arms? He had to admit the notion seemed appealing.

Wait.

Matt Dixon.

Matt Dixon, Jamie's best friend. Matt, the guy who fucked anything and didn't believe in commitment. Not that Darian was ready for any kind of commitment, but he also wasn't ready to be used and discarded on a whim. Darian slipped off the couch and stood with his back to Matt. "I don't know. Jamie talked about you all the time. I feel like I already know you. We already made one mistake. I don't think I could stand another." Regret roared in his mind. He shouldn't have done this.

Matt's voice was directly behind him, pleading. "Darian, please don't walk away without giving this a chance. I don't think I can go through this alone."

Darian bowed his head. The word "alone" resounded through his mind a hundred times, filling his ears like echoes in a canyon. He didn't want that either, anything but that! He felt Matt's hands on his shoulders. A shiver went down his spine. Being with Matt was like playing with dynamite. Darian's sexual attraction to Matt was strong, and resisting his lips would not be easy. He knew Matt's reputation. He had even nicknamed Matt "Sir Cums-a-Lot," much to Jamie's chagrin. What if he started to really care for Matt? He'd only be setting himself up for more hurt.

In his silence, Darian felt Matt step closer. He could feel the heat of Matt's chest against his back. His fingers massaged Darian's shoulders, and Matt's breath was in his ear. "Darian, I don't pretend to know what you're thinking," he whispered soothingly. "I don't even know what's going on in my own fucking head. You have to believe me, no matter what you heard about me, this is different."

"Yeah," Darian answered sarcastically. "Okay. Different."

"No, it is," Matt stressed, squeezing Darian's shoulders affectionately. "Oh God, I don't know how to convince you."

"I don't know." Darian had more doubts than he could count.

Matt let his arms drop to his sides, like he'd given up. "Darian, I don't know what Jamie told you, but I'm not known for doing a guy twice. I don't kiss, and I never bring a guy back to my place." Darian heard his frustrated huff, but remained still, listening to the rest of Matt's argument. "Hell, Darian, 99 percent of the time I even use a condom when I blow a guy! And I have never, ever, had my tongue in a guy's ass! It's like I became a completely different person with you. I want to get to know you."

Darian turned to face him. Over the years, Jamie told him the very same things, and it encouraged him that Matt would be this honest.

Matt went on before Darian could comment. "Jamie never approved of my lifestyle. He told me I'd lead an empty life, and maybe I have. But until now it didn't matter; I always had Jamie." Matt sighed. "Now he's gone. You're all I have left of him."

"I *do* remember him saying more about you than the one-night stands. He had some nice things to say, too." He smiled, trying to encourage Matt since he looked so dejected. "A lot of nice things."

"Oh, thank God!" Matt looked relieved. He stepped into Darian's personal space and pushed his hair over his ear. "Darian, I don't know what to do." Matt touched his face gently. "I just know I can't leave you like this. Especially knowing you're Jamie's fiancé. I feel horrible for you."

Matt looked deeply troubled. Maybe he really did care? He seemed sincere. Darian didn't understand why all this was happening, but taking refuge in Matt's offered embrace was logical enough. If Darian was Matt's last link to Jamie, surely seeing Matt in the same context made sense. Darian knew how much Jamie cared for Matt.

As he was thinking over his conflicting impulses, first to run and now to stay, Matt leaned in and softly touched his lips to his. "I need to kiss you," Matt said seductively. Darian felt his arms slide around his waist. As was true this whole night, Darian was powerless to resist when Matt's mouth was touching him. He whimpered. Matt swiped his tongue over Darian's lips and pulled back suddenly and smirked. "Okay, maybe not at the moment, since you need to rinse your mouth out."

Darian covered his face from embarrassment. "Oh, sorry." He stepped away. The tender moment was sufficiently squelched.

Matt followed and grasped his chin. "Stop." He kissed him lightly one more time. "Vomit or not, I'm addicted to your lips." He stroked his cheek and winked.

The soft look in Matt's eyes pulled on his heart, and it made this situation even more confusing. He didn't know what to feel. Darian started toward the bathroom but stopped. Turning, he asked, "Are you going back to the funeral home?"

"Yeah, I have to. I don't want the wrath of my family. You going?"

"I don't know. Not sure I can." He felt so weak he leaned on the wall. "But if I muster up the strength, at least I'll have you—" he started to say but caught the panic in Matt's eyes. "But you aren't out. And people seeing us together wouldn't be good."

Matt confirmed his assessment. "I'm sorry. You're right. I can't have people knowing. I also can't have people thinking there may be something between us."

"But we could talk. Right? We both know—knew—Jamie. Everybody talks at viewings, don't they?" Darian asked, hoping to hear that was a possibility. He didn't want to go there alone.

"Sure, I guess that's fine. It would be natural for me to talk to you. You knew Jamie and we are—for all anyone there will know—meeting for the first time. I would naturally have a million questions. I know absolutely nothing about you. Yeah, we could talk the whole time. Why are you looking at me like that?"

Darian's jaw dropped. "You know nothing about me?" The statement hit him hard.

"No," Matt answered simply.

"But… Jamie and I have been together for almost six years." Darian was flabbergasted. "Jamie didn't mention me in all that time?"

Matt walked over to him. "No. In fact, if it hadn't been for the gerbera daisies you sent, I wouldn't have had a clue. I saw you referred to him as Jamie, and I wondered who the fuck knew that nickname besides me. It made me angry."

It was all falling into place. "Angry enough to fuck the first guy you saw," Darian lamented. Just when Darian thought he couldn't feel more despair, more information was added to the crap heap. Matt was angry enough to fuck him, and *he* was desperate enough to be fucked. "Just forget it." He waved Matt off.

"No, Darian, wait…. Yes, that's why I did it, but that was before." Matt tried to refute the facts, but there was nothing to argue. "Look, Darian, I—"

Darian held up his hand. "Don't. Please. I need time. This is just too much." He turned away and walked down the hall into the bathroom, and this time Matt let him go. His head was spinning. *What happened here?* Darian felt sick, but at the same time he was too empty to even think of heaving his guts again.

How could Jamie not have mentioned him to Matt, his best friend, in all these years? Why? Why would he hide that information? *Was he ashamed of me?* Darian hoped that wasn't true. They were going to get married. Jamie had promised to take him to Washington, DC, since the President passed the same-sex marriage law. Jamie had said he was going to finally tell his mother. Jamie had said they could live anywhere Darian wanted. Jamie had promised them a life together. *What went wrong?*

13

December 10, 2005

Darian hasn't talked to me in weeks. Even when I went to my dad's, Darian "conveniently" had shifts at Walmart. I asked dad to drive me to see him, and Darian ignored me. He told me he had to work. I left feeling totally dejected. Calling him Matt was the biggest mistake I could have made. I am so mad at myself, but what can I do? What's done is done.

On another note, I am feeling pretty good about being gay. Saying Matt's name aside, being with Darian that way felt so right. I thought I'd be embarrassed about letting him see me naked. I wasn't. I thought maybe I would regret it later if something like a blowjob happened, but I didn't. Being with a boy, that boy, *was the rightest thing I could have done.*

I'm gay.

See, it feels good saying it!

What kind of "gay" am I? I'm not flamboyant, that's for sure. I don't give a crap about my looks or how I dress. I'm not into fashion, theater, or dinner parties. I definitely don't want to dress up in drag.

Oh God… that reminds me of how I found out about Matt. LOL— that was hilarious. I walked in on him in his mom's room when he was wearing her makeup and a dress. I about died, but so did Matt. He was so embarrassed. But after the initial shock, he realized it was just me, and that I didn't care. He was still my best friend, even if he liked dressing up as a girl.

I wonder if he still does that? I think it was a phase, but you never know. Matt does all kinds of things we don't talk about. Sometimes I get details, but I never push for them.

So, since I'm gay, do I need to define myself? I don't have a definition. I like boys. I like Darian. I love Darian. I would do anything for him. Like right now, I'm giving him space to be mad with me. He better get over it soon, though. I want to give sucking him a try.

December 16th

So much for me convincing myself I don't feel anything for Matt. I dreamt about him last night. This was the most erotic dream I've ever had! Who knew things like that went through my brain? I think I was sleep-blushing. Point being, if things like that are in my head at night, who knows if I would call out "Matt" again when I'm with Darian? Even if we do get back together, I think I'm going slower. I can't risk that happening again.

JIMMY walked into Darian's house like he owned it. No one noticed. It was as disheveled as it normally was, but the smell in the air had changed. It was almost sweet. *Marijuana?* Jimmy didn't know for sure, but he suspected. He climbed the steps to Darian's room. It was vacant. Defeated, he turned to go, and there stood Darian in the doorway.

"What are you doing here on a weekday?" asked Darian.

"Gee, nice greeting. Hi, Darian. How've you been? It's nice to see you," he mocked.

Darian's stern façade softened despite the sarcasm. "It is nice to see you." He came into the room and stood in front of Jimmy.

Jimmy could see Darian was torn between staying angry and caving in. Jimmy thought to give him a nudge and see which way he'd fall. "I've missed you," he whispered.

"I have too," Darian said as he melted into Jimmy's arms, clinging to him.

Jimmy hugged him back and thanked his lucky stars. *Well, at least I know which way he's leaning.* "I can't stop thinking about you. I need you. I want you," Jimmy confessed.

"I want you too." Darian groped Jimmy's backside and kissed his neck. He ground his groin against Jimmy's as he enthusiastically left a mark on his throat.

Jimmy pulled back. "Darian, I need to go slower," he said into Darian's confused face. "I know you said before I had a thing for Matt, and although I really think I don't, I'm not chancing a repeat of November."

"Fair enough," Darian reluctantly agreed. Moving away from Jimmy, he took a seat on the bed. "I'd really end up hating you if all you did was scream out Matt's name when we were having sex."

Jimmy sat next to him. "Exactly. And I've… I've dreamt of him a few times."

"You have? Why are you telling me this?"

"Don't be mad, please? I just want to be completely honest with you."

Darian worked up to a grin. He hesitated, but ended up leaning into Jimmy. "I forgive you," he whispered.

Jimmy hugged him. "I'm glad. I don't want to hurt you. I don't ever want to hurt you." After a few minutes of holding each other, Jimmy said, "I have something for you." Darian sat back. Jimmy dug into his pocket and pulled out a tiny silk bag. "I didn't wrap it, it came like that."

"Okay." He opened the bag and dumped the contents into his hand. It was a purple titanium barbell for his tongue. "Awesome!" He looked to Jimmy, glowing.

"I know you like changing jewelry. I didn't think you had purple."

"I don't, thanks!" Darian threw his arms around Jimmy's neck.

"Merry Christmas."

"It is now!" He squeezed Jimmy one more time and let go. "Let me get yours." Darian jumped up and went to his dresser. He brought back a flat, rectangular gift. "It's not much, but I thought you'd like it."

Jimmy ripped open the paper and stared at a framed chalk portrait of Darian. "It's just like the one you did of me; chalk, I mean."

"Yeah, I know it's lame. Mom's been using more and more of my money for food and the electric bill. I didn't have much left this month."

Jimmy warmed as he looked at the exquisite replica. "I love it. I'll hang it in my room at my dad's, next to the one you did of me."

"You really like it?"

He turned and smiled wide. "Yes, Darian, I love it."

"Cool! Stay here. I'll be right back. I'm gonna put this new one in." Darian dashed out of the room.

Jimmy sat there patiently, looking into the chalk drawing's brown eyes. Darian returned and stuck out his tongue. The ball sat right in the center, an inch or so from the tip. Jimmy felt a shiver run through him, remembering what that ball felt like on his dick. "L-looks good," he squeaked out.

Darian got a sly look. "You like my tongue piercing, don't you?"

Jimmy nodded nervously.

Darian grinned. "You don't have to look so scared. I'm not going to make a move on you. You want slow, we do slow. I'm not reliving the last few weeks again. It was hell. I hate being away from you."

"Me too. I may get to see you more often." He got off the bed and put his arms around Darian. He kissed him softly.

"How do you mean?" Darian lazily kissed back, arms around Jimmy's neck.

"I got a car."

"What!" Darian exclaimed.

"I did. It's an old Ford Taurus, *not* a Mustang, but it runs. As long as I get all my chores done and keep my grades up, I'll be able to drive wherever I want without telling Mom every detail. She's told me that much. That's how I got here tonight."

"Awesome! We could like, maybe, sometime, go out on a date?" Darian wondered out loud.

Jimmy knew they could not hide their relationship forever. They were both seventeen, and come June they would graduate. What came after that? College? Living together? A date would be a logical first step toward those things. "Yup. Okay. I'll take you on a date, but it can't be here. I'll do some research online and see if there are places in the neighboring towns that are more gay friendly, and we'll start there."

"I heard there's a restaurant about thirty minutes south owned by a gay couple. Can we go there?"

"Sure."

Darian squeezed so tight, Jimmy thought his shoulders would crack.

JOEY TAYLOR strutted to the lunchroom table opposite Jimmy. Jimmy felt his blood boil in anticipation of a fight. Joey never looked smug unless he was going to start something. He was looking at his friend Butch, not Jimmy, which was the only positive note to go on.

"Butch, did you hear about that gay kid over at Winter's Mill? My friend Tim told me he got the shit kicked out of him again," Joey reported proudly.

"No, really? Damn! What a way to start the new year. I guess he deserved it. Dumb fuck. What? Did he cop a feel on somebody, or was this a random 'because-you're-gay' shit kicking?" Butch asked.

Jimmy listened intently. His hands were shaking. He only knew of one gay kid at Winter's Mill.

"He was showing his belly button to some girl on the volleyball team, and her boyfriend didn't like it. He called him a little fag and told him to take his piercings someplace else. I think the skinny fag actually tried talking back. That's when Tim said the punching started."

"The fag hit the guy?"

"No, dumbass, the boyfriend clobbered the fag." He shook his head at Butch. "Punched his lights out and kicked him. Serves him right. Stupid fag."

Joey barely had a chance to turn his head before Jimmy was clobbering *him*. His right-hook smashed right into Joey's jaw. Blood splashed the lunch table. Jimmy swung two more times before Butch stepped in, delivering blows.

In seconds, the cafeteria was screaming with teenage boys gathering around the ruckus. Jimmy was swinging, kicking, and biting, but he was outnumbered, five to one. Teachers descended and blew whistles. Other teachers pried the boys apart.

Minutes later, six boys lined up, ragged and bloody, in the principal's office, awaiting their parents.

Jimmy knew he was in a hell of a lot of trouble.

"IT HAD to be today, didn't it?" his mother grilled him. "You *had* to pick today to get into a fight and pull me out of an important meeting. I was promoted today to Branch Manager. This was a big day! I have loads of responsibilities, and here I had to drop everything to pick up my son from school for fighting."

"I'm sorry, Mom." Jimmy hung his head.

She glared daggers. The tires screeched as she made a turn too sharp. Jimmy knew better than to comment on her driving, but her lead foot was scaring him.

"Sorry doesn't cut it, Mister," his mom hissed. "I'm just going to have to make things tougher on you. You obviously have too much time on your hands. Too much time for idle thinking and getting into fights over… what was it all about? Oh, never mind, I don't care what it was about. From now on things are going to change. I've been too lax about letting you do whatever you want. From now on, you are going to church with me."

"Church?" *Since when does my mom go to church?*

"Yes, church! I've been going with Linda Dixon for a few weeks now. I really like it. I think I've found something there that I haven't felt in a long time. Their views on divorce aside, it's a fine church."

"All right. Is that all?" Jimmy wondered.

"No, that's not all, Mr. Smarty-pants!"

Shit, I think I irritated her more.

"You will also give me your keys. There will be no driving for a month!"

"But, mom! I just got the car," he protested.

"Too bad. You should have thought about that when you were beating that poor kid up today. And this is your senior year! You are months from graduating. Did you even think about what this could do to your transcripts?"

"No."

"Of course not!"

Jimmy's stomach got queasy, and it was not purely from his mom's driving. He was remembering why the fight had started. He was beating Joey up for talking about Darian—the gay kid. Darian had gotten beaten up! He needed to go see him right now. *But Mom took my keys.*

They pulled into the driveway and got out. Jimmy's mother kept on talking without skipping a beat. "You're father and I…" *Stepfather,* Jimmy mentally corrected, "… have dinner plans tonight. The girls are already with your Aunt Debbie, and the baby is with Margie. I'm going to go out on a limb and trust you to stay home tonight. No walking over to Matt's. No calling people for a ride somewhere. I will call to check up on you."

"What if I'm in the shower?" he blurted out.

Joan glared. "You'd better not be."

As soon as his parents pulled out, Jimmy went into his room. He pushed his bed over, flipped up the soccer poster, and opened his secret stash hole in the drywall. Jimmy stuck his arm in the small door and fished around for the spare car keys he'd had made. He had to see Darian at all cost!

He drove as fast as he dared. Getting stopped for speeding would only make the trip over to Darian's longer. He tried to think logically, even though his mind was screaming to see his boyfriend.

He entered the house. The smell of marijuana was unmistakable this time. He noticed Darian's mom passed out on the couch and a guy, who he assumed was Jerry, sitting on the floor smoking a bowl. They were too high to notice his presence. Jimmy slipped up the steps and into Darian's room.

"Darian," he said quietly.

No answer. Jimmy crept to the bed. Darian was curled up in his blankets. Jimmy sat on the edge of the bed and touched his hair. He stirred.

"Jamie?" he asked weakly.

"Yeah, it's me. What happened today?"

"Some asshole broke two ribs," he answered.

"What? Oh my gosh. Are you okay?"

"I'm in pain, but Jerry gave me something. He said Percocet was too wimpy. Said he had strong drugs. I like strong drugs." Darian rolled onto his back and smiled stupidly.

Jimmy finally noticed the bruises on his face. In the dim light of the bedside lamp, Jimmy could see the purple patches and stitches on his swollen lip. "Oh, Dare, look at you!" He gingerly touched his face.

"It's okay, Jamie. I'm fine. I just need a few weeks off to rest. Doctor said I'll be fine." He stretched and winced.

"Your ribs hurt, don't they?" Jimmy didn't know what else to say.

"Only a little. I told you Jerry gave me something."

"Yeah, about that. Did you know he's smoking marijuana downstairs right now? And your mom is passed out on the sofa?"

"Yeah, they do that a couple times a week. He let me have a hit last Friday; it felt nice."

"Darian, I don't think it's a good idea. Drugs are bad news." Worry descended upon him like a raptor, claws extended for a death grip. This was not going to be an easy conversation if Darian did not see things the same way.

"Oh, Jim,"—he waved off Jimmy's concern—"don't be so cautious all the time. Jerry said that marijuana can be used medicinally. I need medicinal. I'm in pain. He made the pain go away. It'll be fine. You worry too much."

"And you just called me Jim. You're not thinking clearly. I'm gonna go. Don't take any more of Jerry's drugs. Okay? Please? Take what the doctor prescribed." Jimmy touched the side of Darian's face. "I'm grounded, so I'm not sure when I can sneak back over. You need to rest and heal. Okay?"

"Okay, baby. Anything for you." Darian gave a weak smile.

Jimmy leaned down and kissed his forehead. He was worried, but he couldn't very well do anything about it. Darian lived eighteen miles north of where he lived. He couldn't walk. He could only risk driving over on rare occasions, or his mom might figure out he had another set of keys. He was stuck. He'd have to trust that Darian was going to be fine in his absence.

He caressed his cheek and reluctantly left.

January 11, 2006

This is going to be a hard few weeks. I guess I'm limited to calling often and hoping Darian isn't gonna get hooked on marijuana or whatever else this Jerry guy is giving him to take away the pain. I hate feeling trapped.

JIMMY did not sleep well for days.

14

January 19, 2006

TEXT from Matt: *What the hell, man? Why'd you fuck up Joey again?*

Jimmy huffed as he stared at his phone. *Personal reasons.*

And you did this last week? While I was in New York? Why'd you not tell me?

I dunno.

You were doing so good. I thought you were over fighting. What happened?

Joey said something I didn't like.

Jamie, I can't be there every moment for you, especially now that I'm graduated. You have to think about your actions!

"My actions?" Jimmy said out loud. "How hypocritical of you to say, Mr. Dixon." He said it, but he didn't text it back. Instead he wrote a less cynical response. *You're right. Now I'm grounded for life.*

Shit! Can you come running with me? When are you off suspension?

I'll go back on Monday. No, I can't go running.

OK. This sucks, dude. I heard about all it from Butch's brother's girlfriend's sister. Did you really pop Joey 'cause he dissed a gay kid?

Yes. You know where I stand on that.

There was a long pause. *I guess it's good I wasn't there. I woulda had a hard time holding back. I don't want 2 B out, but I also don't like others taking a beating 4 being gay.*

Me neither. I just snapped. Now my mom is all over my ass. I should have waited until after school. She took my keys.

I thought you made another set?

I DID, but if she finds out or catches me driving then I'm done for.

Good point. I guess lay low. Do what she wants. Suck up big time.

Jimmy grinned. "Thinking alike," he muttered. *I am. Believe me, I am!*

Good. I'm pullin' for ya! We're in this together.

Thanks. She's coming. I gotta go.

Jimmy shut his phone and shoved it into his pocket as soon as the door to his room opened.

"Are you ready?" she asked, hand on hip, as if he knew what he was to be ready for.

"Ready for what?" he asked as sincerely as he could.

"To go see a counselor. I arranged a meeting to talk about your fighting." She walked in and started picking up clothes off the floor and looking around.

"Moooom, I don't need to see a counselor."

"Of course you do. There is certainly some reason for these outbursts."

"But I haven't popped Joey since the end of sophomore year. I was doing good. Besides, he deserved it."

She stood there looking at him as if the cogs were turning and she was conjuring up an even worse plan than seeing a counselor. "True, it has only been the one fight."

Relief washed over him.

"I just worry this is over something… something that we rarely speak about." She placed the stray clothes she'd picked up off the floor onto the desk chair. "Joey's mother's sister works at Target, and she told my friend Rachel the fight was over… homosexuality." She whispered the last word.

"What?"

"You're not… *gay*? Are you? I found a great Christian counselor to talk to you about it."

"No! No, Mom, I'm not… gay. Why would you think that?"

She took a deep breath and sighed noisily. "I don't know, dear. Rachel sometimes gets the facts wrong. She said it was about that gay kid at Winter's Mill. I didn't know what to think." She sat on the bed next to him and patted Jimmy's hand. "I never see you with girls. You're always with Matt. I was just wondering if I should be worried about you. You've always had an angry streak in you."

"No I haven't, Mom."

"James. If you're confused and angry with your father for leaving, that's normal. The counselor I know can talk to you about your issues with a lack of a father figure and how to bond with Kevin in a more meaningful way. You shouldn't doubt your sexuality because your father was a bad example."

"What? Mom, what are you talking about?" Jimmy got off the bed and gawked at his mother. He had no idea where her thoughts were coming from, and it was very hurtful. "Dad has nothing to do with this. Joey was being an ass. I punched him because he thought it was funny that kid got beat up."

"So it *was* over the gay kid?"

"Yes…. No… I mean… Joey made me angry, and it didn't have anything to do with Dad's example of a father figure. I don't know where you come up with that."

"I'm just saying that boys who lack a strong father can become… *confused*. I'm just glad you hang out with such a good boy as Matt. I'm sure he knows some girls you could call. In the meantime, I think seeing Pastor Dennis would help you straighten out your thoughts. He's very good."

"The counselor is a pastor?"

"Yes." She looked very pleased with herself, and Jimmy was not liking where the conversation was going.

"I'll think about it." He turned and rubbed the back of his neck nervously.

Joan got up and placed her hand on his lower back. She leaned in and kissed his cheek. "I'm here for you, James." She patted his back before walking to the door. "Just try to stop fighting. I'm hoping colleges will overlook this one incident. You need to be careful, or you'll lose your chance at a scholarship."

"Thanks, Mom."

"LOOK who's back, the *gaaay* lover." Joey did not miss the opportunity to jump on Jimmy's case as soon as they lined up for gym class. He bounced the basketball across to another student and kept his eyes on Jimmy.

"Shut up, Joey." Jimmy took his turn at a lay-up and stepped to the back of the line.

"What's wrong, Miller? Can't take a little heat? A little jibbing about loving… *the gaaayys?*" Joey gestured with a flip of his flopping wrist and the batting of his eyelashes. Some other boys giggled.

"Shut up. You're only picking on me because Matt's not here to kick your ass. You know you couldn't take the two of us."

Joey hopped backward and covered his mouth with his fingers. "Oh, Matt." He continued in his mock-homosexual flamboyance. "Sthtop it." He faked a lisp and flicked his limp wrist again toward Jimmy. "I bet the problem here is that you *miss* your boyfriend."

"What?" Jimmy stopped dead at the accusation, and the basketball, which was passed to him, bounced off the side of his face. Several boys laughed.

"That's it!" Joey announced proudly. "He misses his big, strong protector, My-thigh-ass Dick-son."

"I hear he's training to be a firefighter," one boy piped in.

"So?" Joey shrugged. He looked back to Jimmy. "Is *that* why the two of you are always together? You're queers. I bet you blow him, don't you? Cock sucker!"

"Stop, Joey." Jimmy was getting hot and more nervous than he was in his public speaking class. Joey was not letting up, and this was *not* a conversation Jimmy wanted to have, especially not in gym class.

"Or what?" he pushed. "You'll go and get your firefighter boyfriend to beat me up? I don't think so." He stepped closer and shoved Jimmy.

"Stop it." Jimmy shoved him back.

"You boys having some trouble shooting lay-ups?" the teacher called from across the gymnasium.

All the boys in Jimmy's group fell automatically in line and started shooting hoops. "No sir, Mr. Greshem," one boy called back.

As soon as the gym teacher looked back to the other group he was instructing, the insults started again.

"I bet Jimmy's dad's gay. Maybe that's why he left Jimmy's hot mom."

"Good one!" Joey high-fived Kenny for his stellar observation.

"My dad is *not* gay," Jimmy replied sternly.

"Is that why he works in the women's underwear department?" a boy asked from Jimmy's left.

"He does not!" Jimmy sneered through gritted teeth.

"Yeah, I bet he tries them on in the break room," another boy threw in from Jimmy's right. Loud guffaws ensued.

At this point, all the boys were jesting and coming up with wild stories about what his dad was doing at Walmart: cross-dressing, sleeping with the owner, Manny Shilhiem, and other things that made Jimmy's blood boil. He was vaguely aware that they'd stopped talking about him and Matt, but their turning onto his dad was not welcome either.

Everyone was laughing, except Jimmy.

"Hey, Miller, maybe your dad could get you a lifetime supply of condoms for when you and Dixon butt fuck each other!" Joey doubled over, laughing at himself. He was clutching his sides and nearly fell off his feet.

Jimmy stepped over and helped him.

Before any of the others realized their mocking had taken a turn for the worst, Jimmy hauled back a fist and brought it down on the side of Joey's head. He went down instantly, and Jimmy dropped to his knees, swinging.

The other six boys' eyes popped out of their skulls before they took the initiative to rush in and stop it. Two boys grabbed Jimmy's arms, and another one got kicked in the face as Jimmy flailed. He wrestled his way free and swung at whoever was close enough to hit. He punched Kenny in the nose and heard a distinct *crack*. Blood poured down the boy's face, but Jimmy didn't care. He swung again at the person who grabbed his shoulder from behind.

Mr. Greshem took a fist to his jaw but wasn't fazed. He grabbed Jimmy's wrist and flipped it painfully behind Jimmy's back. "Okay, Mr. Miller, I think there's been enough punching for one day. Mr. Taylor, you and the rest of your cronies can get dressed and meet me in the office. I think Principal Dell would like to talk to each and every one of you before he calls your parents."

The very capable gym teacher escorted Jimmy from the gymnasium and straight to the principal's office. He was not normally hard on the kids, but he was also not one to take any nonsense. As soon as the principal looked up, Mr. Greshem was explaining things. "Mr. Dell, I think Jimmy needs to spend some more time at home. It seems a few days wasn't enough to straighten him out."

"Thank you, Mr. Greshem." He eyeballed Jimmy. "Mr. Miller, do sit down."

Mr. Greshem left the room, closing the door, and Jimmy felt the doom and gloom approaching as if he was awaiting a jail sentence.

"AGAIN? Really, James, I can't understand what is going on in your head. And this time you hit the teacher!"

"It was an accident! He grabbed me from behind, and I thought Joey was—"

Joan crossed her arms. "I don't care why poor Mr. Greshem got hit. I only care that my son cannot control his outbursts. You obviously have mental issues that need to be addressed, and I am forced to have you see a professional."

"But Mom… Joey said my dad was gay and that he—"

"So we're back to the… *homosexual* talk, are we? I think I'll make an appointment with Pastor Dennis, after all."

It irritated him how she whispered the word *homosexual,* like it was too horrible to speak out loud. "I don't need to talk to him, Mom. I was just mad that Joey would talk bad about my dad."

"Your father has not been a good influence on you, has he? Shacking up with that woman, filling your head with ideas that it's okay to fight in school."

"Mom, he hasn't done anything." Jimmy was trying to defend himself and his father, but his mother's thought process was hard to follow.

"I'm going to make some calls." She waved him off. "Go, go on, off to your room. If you are going to be stuck here for two weeks, I'm going to get you some professionals to talk to who can straighten up that brain of yours. And when it snows in February, you'll be shoveling the neighbors' driveways for free!"

"Free?"

"Yes, as a community service payment for fighting in school. Mr. Dell and I came up with that one."

Jimmy huffed and stomped up to his room. As soon as he flopped onto his bed, his phone buzzed.

Dude! Not again. Katie's friend Andi told me you decked Joey, Kenny, AND the gym teacher. What the fuck?

Jimmy rolled his eyes. Hyperbole in high school gossip was hilarious. Although not so much when it was about him. He texted back: *NO! Just Joey. I broke Kenny's nose, and Mr. Greshem nearly broke my arm when I accidentally clocked him.*

Are you mental?

NO!! Joey was insinuating my dad was gay, and that you and I were boyfriends. He said we butt-fucked each other. I just lost it.

Matt texted right back: *Dude! You have to chill! I can't have people guessing that about me, especially when it's true.*

Jimmy knew he meant "true about being gay" but it was hard to block the mental image of Matt fucking him. What if *that* was the "true" part? Jimmy felt heat roll down his chest and into his groin. *Don't worry. Your secret is safe.*

How can you be sure? You flipped out over the gay shit again. You can't be doing that if you're really considering being gay. This is NOT the time and place to take a stand.

Jimmy keyed in another question. *What do you mean?*

Matt texted back: *This is not New York or San Francisco. If you want to take a stand on what you believe, then wait until you're eighteen and out of your mom's house.*

Jimmy didn't understand what difference that would make. *Huh?*

Wait until you can safely be who you want to be. If you try pushing the boundaries now, you're going to get your ass stuck in counseling.

"You couldn't be more right!" he commented as he texted back what his mom had already threatened. *Mom said I gotta talk to Pastor Dennis about my rage.*

Pastor Dennis? As in the pastor of MY church, Pastor Dennis? Shit! See what I mean? This is NOT good! He knows we're friends. He's gonna ask shit.

So?

SO?! I can't have him prodding you about being gay. You'll cave. I can't be outed, Jamie. I can't!

I'm not gonna say anything.

You better not. I was All State in track. Captain of the basketball team. I'm training to be a firefighter. I am NOT queer in the eyes of all those around me.

Before Jimmy could respond, he got another message: *I don't know any gay firefighters, or maybe this would be different. I don't know what they'd do. I can't be in a burning house and have my fellow firefighters leave me there to burn, just because I'm gay. I don't know if it really happens, but I've heard of cops being left without backup because they were gay. Men die in my chosen profession. I don't want it to be because I choose to sleep with men. I'm not bothering anyone.*

What I do, or any gay man does, behind closed doors is their own fucking business. You gotta be with me, Jamie. Please. Don't out me.

The desperation Matt felt came through even in a text message. Jimmy got it. This was more than just taking a stand for what *he* felt, this was also about taking a stand in light of what *Matt* felt. Matt feared rejection. Matt chose a "closeted life," and Jimmy had to respect that, even if he disagreed. *I'll chill, I promise. No more fighting. No more talk about being gay.*

Thanks. Look, if you're gay and you want to come out, just do me a favor and wait.

Sure.

I'm planning on moving in with my aunt in October. She's fine with my sexuality. If I can just live someplace else and put some distance between me and my folks, maybe you being gay won't come back on me.

Jimmy was starting to get a headache. Was his friend really that self-centered? Was this all about Matt? *Dude, I thought we were talking about me here. I'm the one who's grounded for life. I'm the one who has to talk to your pastor and shovel driveways this winter for free.*

I know. I'm sorry. I was freaking. Sorry. Really.

Okay. Fine. I won't say anything about you. I promise. For some reason, Jimmy felt the need to lie. This would all be easier if he lied. He texted again: *And I'm not gay, so you have nothing to fear about me being out and inadvertently "outing" you.*

Really? You admit it. You're straight?

Yes. "No, I'm not, but it's easier this way," Jimmy grumbled at his phone, wishing he had the balls to tell Matt the truth.

I knew it!

Can we drop it now? There's nothing going on that the pastor will get upset over.

Yeah, sure. I gotta go anyway. Mom's done at the hairdresser's. Talk soon.

K. ttyl

Bye.

Jimmy grabbed his notebook.

January 23, 2006

I don't know why I can't just be myself. Why did I lie to Matt? I guess I just want to make him feel like he'll be okay and that no one will ever know about him. I don't understand why he's so paranoid. Why does it scare him that bad? So what if someone found out? Wouldn't it be easier than trying to live a double life?

Although… I guess Darian would not see his life as any easier to deal with.

The phone buzzed. Jimmy picked it up. A text from Darian: *I miss you.*

Jimmy grinned. *I was just thinking about you. I miss you too. How do you feel?*

Great. Wonderful. Blissful.

Jimmy narrowed his eyes at the phone. *What? No pain? I thought your ribs were broken.*

Jerry made the pain disappear.

Jimmy's stomach clenched. *Jerry is giving you drugs, Dare. You need to stop taking them. They're dangerous.*

Nooooooo. They're fine. Jerry said a little wouldn't hurt. He said the pills would help me heal.

Please stop taking whatever it is he's giving you. Please. For me.

There was a long wait for the next text. *Okay. For you. I love you.*

As much as Jimmy relished hearing that phrase from Darian for the first time, it was anticlimactic. First of all he was texting it, second he was under the influence of some unknown narcotics. Jimmy's heart hurt when he texted back: *I love you too.* This was not the way he'd planned to tell his boyfriend how he felt. He wasn't even sure Darian would remember in the morning.

When the texts stopped coming, Jimmy picked up his notebook again.

I don't know what the hell I am supposed to do. I'm afraid Darian is getting in over his head. Jerry is clearly NOT a good influence. But I'm here and he's there. I can't drive over again, or Mom might catch me. Text is all I have.

Matt is the other problem. I don't want to "out" him. That would be wrong. No one outs someone else; it's rude. I can be careful. I can make this all about my dad, and no one would even bat an eye. Joey has made fun of my dad for over a year, and me beating him up for it would seem normal. I'm not even worried about talking to the pastor. He doesn't know me. And my mom is just weird. She's been all over the board with comments and emotions, so I can use that to my advantage if this "Pastor Dennis" questions me too much. He's bound to know my mom is a little off.

And lying to Matt....

I don't know why I lied. I'm not straight. I have a cute boyfriend!!! Maybe I'm just as afraid as Matt is about being "out." Darian's life is a testimony to the difficulties that can arise. I'm going to wait, like Matt said. I'll be graduating soon. Life will get better. It has to!

15

September 22, 2010

8:00 p.m.

MATT was smart enough to know when to stop talking. There was too much on the table to work through in one evening. Darian needed time, and so did he. Matt was already angry with Jamie for leaving him. Now he was angry with Jamie for not mentioning Darian! How much harder was it for Darian? Matt was Jamie's best friend; Darian *knew* this. Matt had to believe that, whatever he was feeling, Darian was feeling a hundred times worse.

On top of it all, Matt felt the most bizarre emotions he'd ever experienced in his life. He didn't get why he felt so strongly connected to Darian. Sure, there was their mutual link to Jamie, but his "connection" started long before he knew who Darian was. He wished he knew how to hold onto Darian long enough to sort it out.

When it was obvious that Darian was done talking, he'd brushed his teeth and asked to go back to his car. He was silent the whole way back. Matt wanted to hold him but knew it was not the time. Jamie had told Darian all kinds of things, apparently, about his past. He'd have to prove his sincerity, or this was not going to develop into anything, even friendship. Matt could easily lose his last bit of Jamie! So when Darian hopped out of his truck after he parked it and started walking up the street, Matt quickly followed.

"Darian, wait up." Darian didn't look at him, but he did slow his pace. Matt stepped in alongside him and went with him to his car. "Will you at least give me your phone number?" Matt asked. "I don't want to push, and I know you have a lot to think about, but please don't push me away. I really like you, Darian. I want to get to know you. I want to hear about the side of Jamie *you* knew." Which was true! He desperately wanted to know who Jamie loved enough to marry.

Darian looked up. Matt felt the flutter of desire flow through him. Those brown eyes were just so darn beautiful! Matt loved his long lashes and the curve of his cheekbones and the way his lips begged for Matt to touch them with his fingers. Matt realized how difficult it was going to be, keeping his prick in his pants. He seriously wanted to fuck him again! But Matt could not bear the thought of losing Darian because he took him to bed every time they were together. He had to force himself to *talk*—like normal people.

Darian's words were barely audible. "Just give me time. Okay? I'll be here tomorrow at seven and for the funeral."

Matt ached for him. The sorrow in his voice was too much to bear. "Space. Got it. Will you at least give me your number? I won't call and bug you, but I might text."

"Okay." Darian gave in. After Matt took out his phone, Darian proceeded to tell him his number.

"Thanks. No pressure, I promise."

Darian nodded. Matt leaned in, and Darian moved back, eyeing him suspiciously.

Matt looked around, "What? There's no one here."

"I thought you didn't kiss."

"Did I say that?" Matt smirked. Leave it to Darian to remind him of his own rules. "Maybe I just never met someone worth kissing. Did Jamie like to kiss?" An odd question but it popped into his head all the same.

Darian nodded.

Matt wanted to ask if he kissed better than Jamie, but that would have been rude and inappropriate. Thankfully he didn't blurt out his thoughts. Instead he asked, "Just one kiss? Please." Darian stared at him as Matt pleaded with his eyes. He slowly responded with a thin smile, emboldening Matt to lean in again and kiss him. Soft, yet unwavering, Matt conveyed in one kiss all the emotion he felt gurgling up inside him. He held his tongue in check—there was no need to be overzealous—and moved his lips over Darian's like he was making love to Darian's soul. He moved his arms around him securely and threaded his fingers in Darian's hair, sighing against his lips. Darian was the sweetest candy dipped in the strongest liqueur. Matt felt himself falling, yearning, becoming victim to all the reasons he gave before as to why he never kissed. It was too intimate. But with Darian, he yearned for intimacy. He just didn't understand why. Darian's lips tugged at his heart, and Matt knew in that moment he was helpless to resist. His entire body tingled, from his lips down to his toes.

When he finally let go, he plopped a kiss on Darian's nose. "I have a feeling my life is never going to be the same."

"Mine either." Darian blushed.

His reply gave Matt hope. "Go." Matt stepped back, motioning toward Darian's car. "I'll text you. We'll get through the next few days and then think about what happens next. Okay?"

Darian nodded and Matt left.

INSIDE the funeral home, things had not changed. Family and friends gathered, talked, and sobbed. The weight of it all fell on Matt again.

What the hell happened? Why did Jamie do this?

Matt took a deep breath, hoping it would steady his nerves. It didn't. Suddenly he felt like Darian was not the only one with a rebellious stomach. He inched forward. He had to look into the casket tonight. He had to! Darian would be here tomorrow, and he didn't want him to see him weak like this. Matt *had* to say his goodbyes now.

Everything looked the same. The polished wood, the baby-blue satin, the spray of roses over the casket. Matt took the last step and peered in.

Jamie looked ghastly. His skin was pasty from the embalming process, and he looked as if he was wearing makeup to artificially give him color. *Jamie didn't need color when he was alive,* Matt thought. *He had great skin. Although not as clear as Darian's.* Jamie's cheeks would get red for no reason at all, and his freckles added character. He even had great lips. Pink enough to kiss but not red enough to look like he was wearing lipstick.

"Shit, Jamie. Now I'm thinking about your lips! What the fuck?" He spoke to Jimmy like he was listening. "Must be all the kissing I've done lately."

This situation was so surreal, as if he'd been transported into another dimension. Truly this couldn't be his life? Matt's life did not exist without his best friend. "I can't do this without you, ya know?" Matt whispered. "I don't know what to do without you telling me. You're my rock, Jamie. My safe house. I need you."

Tears leaked from his eyes.

"I have something to tell you." Matt swallowed and looked around nervously, hoping no one was listening in. Of course no one was. "I… I slept with Darian. I'm sorry. I didn't know who he was beforehand, I swear. I didn't know you had a fiancé. I didn't know you'd been with him for six years. Why, Jamie? Why couldn't you tell me?"

Matt stepped closer, as close as he could, and looked at the closed-eyed body. It was still and morbidly unsettling. Even though the body looked fake and made up like a wax dummy from Ripley's Believe It or Not Wax Museum, Matt felt surrounded by an eerie foreboding that Jamie would open his eyes any second and tell him it was just the worst nightmare he'd ever had. That it wasn't real.

Silent seconds passed, and Jamie didn't move.

Matt glanced around. No one was looking. He reached in and touched Jamie's hand. It was hard and cold. Still, he could not pull his fingers away.

"I knew you were lying that time. You know? Years back when you told me you were straight. I knew you were gay. I don't know why I couldn't bring myself to tell you. I was glad you were like me on some level and scared for you on another. It hasn't been easy for me, and I guess I didn't want you to go through the same things.

"My parents have no idea. My coworkers have no idea. My church has no idea. People treat me like just one of the guys. Like any other guy. I like that, but at the same time it kills me to know who I am inside. I wish I could be straight on the inside or gay on the outside.

You know what I mean? Not flamboyant and shit, that's not me, but someone who isn't afraid of being ridiculed and shunned, or looked at like a hedonistic sinner. But Jamie, I don't know what else to do. They don't make a 'straight pill' or I'd take one! Maybe. I guess. Oh, hell, I don't know!

"I've pretended to be the guy I am for so many years. I don't know how to change. The guys I… the ones I… *date*…." Matt leaned in closer and whispered. "You know, *date?* The one-night stand dating? Anyway… none of them live nearby. At least, I haven't run into anyone. So far, living two separate lives has been just that—separate. And now…."

Matt ran his fingers over Jamie's, up and down, thinking. "I'm so confused. Darian is…." He hung his head in shame. "Darian's amazing. How the hell could you leave him like that?" It was wrong to reprimand his friend now, but if felt so natural to argue. "Fuck, Jamie! Why'd you do this? Now I'm stuck here without you. What do I do? You need to tell me what to do. I'm feeling all kinds of things I never felt before, and I'm scared as hell."

He heard noise close enough behind him to make him pull away. No way did he want to get caught touching a corpse.

"He was like a son to me, ya know?" Matt's dad gave him a forced smile. "He's been coming and going through our front door just as often as you over the years."

Matt nodded. "I know." He looked at his dad's feet, unable to lift his gaze because he knew meeting his dad's eyes would force the tears to fall. "He loved you."

"Why, Matt? Why'd he do it?"

The crack in his dad's voice pulled his attention back up where he didn't want it to be. As soon as he saw the tears welling in his dad's eyes, his own started pouring out. "I don't know, Dad," Matt sobbed.

He sank into his dad's arms, and they both cried together. "I miss him so much, Dad. He was my best friend. More than that, he was like a brother, and now I don't know who I can talk to."

Mr. Dixon clutched his son fiercely. "Oh, Matt. I'm so sorry. I know you were close. He stood by you in everything. Jimmy cheered you on the loudest at track meets. He mowed lawns for you that summer when you broke your ankle, remember?"

Matt eased out of the hug and smiled at his dad, wiping his eyes. "Yeah, I remember. Jamie was always there for me." He turned back to the still, almost plastic version of Jamie. "I look at him, and I still can't believe this is happening."

"Me neither. Your mom said she can't get Joan to stop crying and come to the viewing. She's gonna come tomorrow, whether Joan does or not. She said she needs to say goodbye to her other son."

"I know Mom loved him. Whenever she and I had a disagreement, she'd call Jamie and ask him to straighten me out. She knew he'd convince me she was right."

They both chuckled.

"I'm gonna go. I have a shift tomorrow before the viewing."

"Okay. I'll see you tomorrow. I love you, son."

"You too, Dad."

Matt trudged out of the funeral home, feeling lost and alone. His best friend was truly gone. He was on his own to figure out his problems and he hadn't a clue where to start.

September 23, 2010
10:00 a.m.

MATT crossed September 22nd off the wall calendar with a red Sharpie and then sat across the table from his friend Jason. His shift at the fire station started at seven this morning, but nothing was going on, so the two of them decided to play cards. Matt was grateful for some downtime. It came so sporadically. Normally he would study for another certification or brush up on the latest revised guidelines for search and rescue, but he was drained.

Jason dealt the cards, and Matt picked up his hand.

"Jason, can I ask you something?"

His friend of several years looked up. "Sure, ask away."

Matt knew he was going to come off gay asking a stupid, girly question, but he hoped Jason would not read into it. Jason was a levelheaded guy. He was solid. Matt needed advice, and he trusted Jason more than anyone else he worked with. He took a deep breath. *Here it goes.* "Have you ever done something spontaneous that was totally out of character and then wondered why?"

Jason discarded a four and scratched his head. "Uh, yeah, I guess."

"Like what?"

"Like… I bought my Toyota on a whim. My dad always told me to buy American. I went out that day fully set on a Ford. Then, for some unknown reason, I stopped at the Toyota dealership instead. It was weird."

Matt frowned. *Not what I had in mind.* He laid down three kings and discarded.

As if reading his facial expression, Jason said, "I can tell that's not what you meant. Sorry. It was the best I could come up with on a spur of the moment. So what did you do so radical it's got you coming to me? We normally talk cars, politics, or religion. You didn't switch sides on me, did you?"

Matt shook his head. "No." He was sure hoping Jason meant political sides.

"Then what?"

Matt liked how interested Jason seemed. He didn't look bothered at all. "Jason, you're in a relationship, right?" Matt asked as he arranged his cards after drawing two. Two sixes and a four, and a king of hearts….

"Yup. We've been married six years last Wednesday." He drew two cards and discarded an eight.

"Wow. Congratulations."

"Thanks."

How do I start? Jason doesn't know I'm gay. Can I ask things without being specific? "I met someone. Last night. We went back to my place—which I never do! We fucked like rabbits. Also, something I never do. I'm more of a hit-and-run kind of guy. So last night, when I couldn't get enough, it was freaking me out! Everything we did, I just wanted more. I literally had my mouth tongue deep in ass last night, and all I keep thinking about is how much I want to do it again!" Matt looked up when Jason didn't respond. Suddenly embarrassed by his crudeness and Jason's gaping mouth, Matt felt heat flush his neck. "Sorry, was that too much?"

Jason rubbed his eyes and forehead. "Well, it was a lot, that's for sure. We've never talked about our sex lives before, and then you start with that! Wow."

"I'm sorry. We can stick to cards."

Jason laid his hand down. "No. It's okay. I can handle it. So... last night's experience was... different?"

Matt sat up straight. "Yes. Very. Mind blowing. I've never felt so energized."

"Okay. But why does one sexual encounter—no matter how great—have you coming to me?"

"I've never stuck around for seconds before. Or thirds... or fourths. I even kissed this one!"

"So?"

"I don't kiss!" he stressed.

"What?" Jason's voice went up. "How can you date without kissing?"

"Dude, I don't date."

"I got that part. In fact, I'm glad you said something. The guys and I were starting to wonder if you were...."

Matt's eyes narrowed. "Were what? I'm not doing anything."

"That's the point. None of us has seen you with a woman. We all thought you were one of those guys who—"

"Who what?" Matt interrupted rudely. It was making him sick to think he played right into their assumptions. Did they think he was gay?

"Who fuck and run. You know? A guy who hits the bars only long enough to snag a hot blond and get her into bed. You don't talk about girlfriends. The guys and I assumed there wasn't one. No hard feelings."

Rather than being offended, Matt was relieved. "No, it's okay. I've had plenty of one-night stands. You're right about that."

"But not this time," Jason smirked.

Matt shook his head. "No. This one is… different."

"They always are, that *one* that gets you. I remember John talkin' about his woman when they met. He said she spilled a Coke across the table and ate half his fries, but he couldn't stop smiling. She had that *somethin'* that got him right here." Jason thumped his fist against his chest.

Matt nodded. "I heard him talk about her. I think she was at the fire hall picnic last year."

"Yup. Geena. She's real sweet. So, tell me about your little honey. Cute?"

"Oh, yeah!" Matt beamed. "Fucking adorable!"

"Blue eyes?"

"Brown. Shoulder length black hair, thin waist, and an ass I could kill for."

"Niiice. So what's the problem?"

Matt sighed. "Well, now I'm feeling all tingly, and I don't know why?"

"Love does that to a guy."

Matt jumped back. "Love! What? I'm not talkin' love. I'm talking 'second date'. Dude! Don't chain me down yet."

Jason smirked but held his tongue. "Oh. Matt." He shook his head. "Fine. Not love. But something beyond lust."

"Yeah. I think so. I don't know—that's why I came to you!"

"Settle down." Jason gestured with his hands in front of him. "No need to get feisty. I'm trying to help you. So you're considering dating this girl, right?"

"Yes. Possibly. That depends on how tonight goes. See, I got this reputation of being… well… a pig. And I don't have a clue about proving history wrong."

"She knows about the past?"

"Yup."

"Ooooh, messy. Well, I suggest you do everything different from whatever you did in the past."

"Like what?"

"Well...." Jason sat up straight and slapped his hands together. The wild look in his eyes was like he'd struck gold! Matt could tell he was really enjoying this. "Like, be romantic. Assuming you aren't normally romantic on these one-night stands."

"No. Never."

"Well, start now. Light candles. Play soft music."

"Like what kind?"

"Classical. Chicks dig classical."

"Then what?" Matt was thoroughly interested, leaning forward, hanging onto Jason's every word.

"Make the night about her."

"What do you mean?"

"About her." He raised his eyebrows.

Matt stared.

"You really are bad at this."

"I told you!"

"What I'm saying is that you need to show her you can be with her without thinking of your own orgasm first. Give her one. Better yet, make her cum a few times before you even *think* of getting your willy wet."

"I guess I can do that."

"Show some finesse. Slow things down. You said you fucked like rabbits last night, so let her know you can switch things up tonight. I'm telling you, there's no better way to gain a woman's trust in bed than to show her how long you can go without fucking her blind. Use your imagination, and see how many new sounds you can provoke from her. It can be fun."

Matt grinned. "Sounds like it."

Jason smirked again. "It is. Sex is important in marriage… or dating…." he quickly corrected himself, "but boring sex, or sex that's all about you, gets old. You gotta mix it up."

"Good to know."

"And by all means kiss her! Women love to kiss. It creates an intimate connection that your dick can't. Kissing will make her melt in ways you can't imagine and heat her up to the point of begging. Trust me. You seein' her tonight?"

"I hope so." Matt knew Darian would be at the viewing, but he wasn't sure about seeing him for any length of time afterward. His body was aching for Darian.

"And hey, I hope you figure it all out. Whether it's a date or true love. I'm pullin' for ya. Just seeing you flustered gives me hope." Jason winked. "You know where I stand on monogamy."

"Ha, ha, yeah. I know." Matt reached across the table and pulled the cards into one pile. They were done. Jason stood up and walked over beside his chair.

"What time you off?" he asked.

"Two. Billy switched my last five hours."

"Going back to the funeral home?"

Matt nodded.

Jason placed his hand on Matt's shoulder. "If I didn't say so yesterday, I'm sorry about Jimmy. He was a great guy."

"Thanks."

MATT left the Fire Hall grateful for the lack of fires or emergencies. He was glad for his conversation with Jason but still confused over his feelings. Was it love? How could he know? What did love feel like? And how could he love someone he just met? Jason was a dreamer. This wasn't love. It was extreme lust with complications.

He stood in the funeral home and waited. He hoped no one would try and talk to him. Not yet. He needed to wait for Darian. Darian would come. He knew it. He had to wait.

His mom walked through the door and thankfully right into Dan Miller's arms. They hugged, and Dan seemed grateful for her presence. Matt was glad. He fingered the petals of a carnation in the arrangement next to him and tried not to text Darian to see where he was. He had his number but had not found the courage to use it. He wanted to tell Darian that he was thinking of him this morning but thought it might have sounded desperate or oafish.

"I'm a grown man. I can wait patiently. Maybe. Sometimes," he mumbled to himself.

Movement in the doorway caused him to look up.

It was Darian. He looked awful. Pale. Gaunt eyes.

Matt's first impulse was to rush over and pull him into a long, secure embrace, but he knew better than to do something so blatant. People would talk. People would question. People might think things that were better left unthought. Matt hung back by the flower arrangements.

Then Darian's eyes caught his, and all hope of remaining stalwart fled.

16

August, 2006

I can't believe what just happened, and I was there. When I woke up this morning, Matt was curled around me. His pelvis was crushed against my ass, and he held me tightly as he slept with his left arm under my neck, pulling my shoulders to his chest, and the other arm over my hip, cupping my balls with his right hand INSIDE my underwear. Holy shit! I didn't dare move. I've been thinking about this moment for so long, wanting this, and yet having what I wished for only reminded me of how wrong it was. Sure, I wanted Matt, but not like this.

He was vulnerable, and I knew it.

Last night I saw something I'd never seen in him before, and it scared me. Matt is the strong one. He can leap buildings in a single bound and stop freight trains in their tracks. Matt is invincible... was invincible.

Even though that image was forever altered in my eyes, I'm still glad his mom called me...

"... Jimmy?" Mrs. Dixon's voice sounded shaky on the other end of the phone.

"Yes, Mrs. Dixon, it's me. What's wrong?" Jimmy asked, concerned.

"What makes you think something is wrong?"

Her sudden defensiveness was odd. Jimmy scrunched up his eyes and took the phone away from his ear. He looked at the receiver briefly, like he'd answered the wrong call. Reluctantly, he put the phone back to his ear and answered. "Um, your voice? I've never heard you sound so shook up before. I didn't mean to ask the wrong thing."

Jimmy heard her exhale. "I'm sorry. I am just very… I need to talk to you. Could you possibly come over to our house?"

"Sure. I just need to finish scrubbing the toilets, and I'm free to go. Say… twenty minutes?"

"That long?" she pleaded.

Now Jimmy was really concerned. "All right, I'll do the fastest job I can get away with. I'll be over in ten."

"Thank you."

When Jimmy got there, Mrs. Dixon ushered him into the house faster than he could say "Hello." As soon as the door closed behind him, Jimmy found himself in a crushing embrace. "Um, Mrs. Dixon, I can't breathe."

She immediately let him go and turned her face to the side. Jimmy heard her sniffles. Dread swept into his gut and pulled his stomach down into his shoes. He forced the words from between his lips. "What happened?"

She was on the verge of crying, but she held her composure long enough to get out the basics. "Matt went out last night. You know he likes to go out, and we never question where he goes or what he does. Most of the time he says he's with you. He's nineteen and we trust him. We know most of his friends, and he has a great job and has always been responsible with everything."

Jimmy noticed she wasn't looking him in the eyes like she normally would. Mrs. Dixon was a very friendly person, overly friendly. Matt got his disregard for personal space from her. When she spoke to you, she did it real close. Like on that Seinfeld show, she was a "close talker." Consequently, as Mrs. Dixon spoke to him yet kept her eyes averted, Jimmy knew this conversation was taking them somewhere he probably didn't want to go.

She paused long enough the grab a tissue and wipe her nose. "I never thought about it when he came in last night. I heard the door. I glanced at the clock. One thirty was a little earlier than usual, but it didn't keep me awake. I closed my eyes and drifted back to sleep."

"Mrs. Dixon, I don't want to seem rude, but this doesn't sound unusual to me."

"I'm sorry. You're right. I'm rambling. Come with me." She took Jimmy by the wrist and led him up the steps. Her voice softened to a whisper. "When I woke up, Matt was still asleep. He normally sleeps in until about nine and then goes out for a run."

"I know. I go with him most of the time."

"This morning he didn't go. Also not alarming, I know." She answered Jimmy's roll of his eyes before he could even gripe. "I went into his bathroom, and this is what I found."

She led Jimmy into the bathroom with her and turned on the light. In the sink was a pile of hair. Matt's hair. There were enough clippings to construct a yappy little Pomeranian. Jimmy was confused. Matt's hair grew like a weed; everyone knew that. It was curly and unruly and normally grew quite long before he decided to cut it back. Even when he'd started his job with the Fire Department, he had a hard time keeping it regulation length, so he resorted to pulling it back into a short, fuzzy ponytail. His nickname was "afro-man", for crying out loud! Why would a little hair in the sink cause this much concern?

"So he cut his hair? I don't get why—"

"He trimmed his hair two days ago. *This* time he used a razor." Mrs. Dixon held up a used razor, still clogged with hair and shaving cream.

"Is that blood?" Jimmy inspected the razor.

"I think so. I knocked on his door, but he didn't answer. I tried the knob and it's locked."

"Don't you have the key?"

She nodded. "I didn't want to intrude if he didn't want me there, but I thought maybe he'd let you in. Matt trusts you."

"He trusts you too."

She smiled slightly at his affirmation. "Thank you, but you know what I mean. I'm his mother. Matt isn't a child anymore, and if I press for answers he's not ready to give, then he may shut me out entirely. I know he has secrets, everyone does, but I thought maybe he would share some of those with you." She placed her hand on Jimmy's shoulder and squeezed, and then handed him a key. "Here. I'm going for a walk. I'll give you some time alone. If you need me to call your mother...."

"No, I'm due at my dad's today. I'll call him later or text him. It's fine."

"Let me know if you need anything."

When Mrs. Dixon left him alone, Jimmy knocked on the door. Silence. He used the key and cracked the door. When he peeked inside, he found the bed empty. Jimmy opened the door further and stepped into the room. "Matt?" Jimmy heard a sniffle, and his eyes searched frantically to find where his friend was hiding. He was huddled in the corner of the room, in the dark, rocking, with his knees pulled up to his chest. His hair was gone—shaved bald for the most part—and Jimmy noticed a couple of spots of congealed blood.

He approached his friend with caution, got down on his hands and knees and crawled over to the corner where he sat. "Matt?" he said his name very softly and reached out to touch his hand.

Matt swatted him away and turned his face into the corner. He started thumping his forehead against the wall, murmuring, "No, no, no, no, no...."

Jimmy sat, dumbfounded. *What the hell happened to him?* He watched as Matt continued to thump his head on the wall and rock more urgently. There were red marks and torn skin around his wrists. *Handcuffs?* He figured Matt liked being the dominant one in any given sexual situation, but never in a million years would Jimmy imagine him in handcuffs by choice.

As his eyes adjusted to the lighting in this corner of the room, Jimmy also noticed bruises on Matt's scalp, bruises and a couple spots where the hair was obviously yanked out. No way a razor did that! A cold shiver went through his body. *Poor Matt.*

Jimmy scooted closer. Matt's repetitious protestations got louder as Jimmy tried to put his arms around his best friend. Jimmy would not take "no" for an answer and kept moving back in every time Matt shoved him away.

"No, no, no, *no, no, no!*" Matt protested loudly before he broke down and cried. His shoulders bobbed, and he leaned weakly into Jimmy.

Jimmy pulled him to his chest and held him.

HOURS turned morning into evening. Jimmy managed to get Matt to drink some water and crawl into bed. His phone buzzed several times, but he ignored it. He knew it was Darian. He felt bad ignoring his boyfriend, but he had no choice. Matt needed him. He would just have to text Darian tomorrow and explain he was not in a position to talk *or* text. Darian would understand. And if he got mad, Jimmy would just have to use the tactics of "makeup" sex to convince him he shouldn't be. (Although they would have to be having sex to have makeup sex, but that was a stupid technicality.)

Jimmy crawled into the bed beside Matt and held him, stroking his arm and softly humming, anything to soothe his friend.

THE morning light shining through the drapes told Jimmy it was Sunday. He really needed to talk to Matt, so he could go make up with Darian. He hoped Matt was up for it. *Up* for it? Yes, he was definitely *up!* Jimmy could feel Matt's morning wood, wedged between his cheeks. And come to think of it, Jimmy's balls were nice and warm and being massaged by a hand that was not his own.

"Oh, fuck!" Jimmy was torn between wanting to bolt out of the room and wanting to carefully pull his briefs out of Matt's way. It would only take a little lube, and that bulge Jimmy was feeling would slip right inside.

Matt inside of me? Damn. I've wanted that so long.

But he couldn't. He didn't know what had happened to Matt last night, but these were not the right circumstances to have sex.

Jimmy tried to move away, but Matt started thrusting against his backside. "Shit! Matt!" Jimmy rasped. He wanted to get Matt's attention, sure, but he did *not* want to call attention to what was going on in the room if Matt's mom was close enough to hear. "Matt!" Jimmy said between gritted teeth.

The feel of Matt's erection rubbing up and down his crack was enough to make him hard. Jimmy swallowed and tried to breathe evenly, but then Matt's hand moved from Jimmy's balls up to his shaft and Jimmy whimpered. He was trapped. *Trapped in a porn star's nightmare.* Why would he possibly want to get out of this situation?

Darian. I'm with Darian. I can't let Matt dry hump my back.

It was a logical argument, except for the fact that his brain was on vacation. The warm hand on his dick was logic's substitute, and its voice was *way* louder. Matt started grunting in his sleep. Jimmy hoped he was asleep. If Matt was awake, this situation was going to get even further out of hand. Jimmy turned his neck as far as he could but couldn't see Matt's face. It was nestled into the back of Jimmy's hair.

Then Matt whispered, "Yeah, baby. That's it. Cum for me."

Oh, yeah, he's asleep. Jimmy was glad but wondered who was in his dream image. Suddenly Jimmy felt like a cheap whore. Matt was getting off in his sleep, and Jimmy was just a body to thrust against. His dick softened, despite Matt's stroking.

Matt grunted louder and thrust one last time. Jimmy figured he was finished when his friend let go of his penis and rolled onto his back. Jimmy waited a few seconds and then dared to look at Matt. He appeared very content and placid as he slept.

Fucker! "I can't believe you just did that," Jimmy hissed. He was upset but not ready to wake Matt up.

Jimmy slipped from the bed and showered before he entered the kitchen. He'd borrowed some of Matt's clothes. They were almost the same size, though Jimmy was shorter. He could tell Mrs. Dixon was eager to talk, but he wanted to wait until Mr. Dixon finished breakfast. Matt's dad stood up and addressed Jimmy like he always did.

"Mornin', Jim. Nice to see you up early. I didn't hear you guys come in last night. You must have gotten in after midnight?"

Jimmy glanced at Mrs. Dixon but answered without hesitation. "Yup. Sorry. Once a partier, always a partier. What can I say?"

"As long as you're being smart about it. No drinking and driving, no fooling around without protection, right?" His stern gaze answered the question for Jimmy.

"Of course, sir. Always."

"Good. I don't want to hear about my sons, my oldest one or my adopted one,"—he winked—"getting some poor girl pregnant because they were too drunk and too stupid." He folded his Sunday paper and walked his coffee cup to the sink. "Now, if you'll excuse me, I'm going to get ready for church. We have to leave in thirty-five minutes. Are you coming with us, Jim?"

"Yes, sir. I mean, no, sir. I mean… no girls are going to get pregnant, sir, and I'll see if Matt's up yet. He mentioned something about going to Jason Riley's church today," Jimmy lied as fast as he could. A pretty darn convincing one, if he did say so himself.

"That Baptist at the Fire Department? Oh well, I guess that's okay. As long as you haul Matt's *be*-hind into church. You coming up, Linda?"

"In a minute. I just want to get Jimmy something to eat."

"Okay. Have a good day, Jimmy."

"Thanks. You too, sir." Jimmy watched him leave the room. As soon as Mr. Dixon was out of earshot, Linda asked, "Is Matt all right? I couldn't sleep a wink last night."

"I think he's fine. Or he will be. He got into a fight with someone at work over something, and the guy took a swing at Matt." One lie had worked, so Jimmy thought he'd try one more. He was getting good at it. "I think the guy grabbed a hunk of his hair and yanked some out. Matt'll be fine. His hair grows so fast, no one will even notice in a week or two."

"So… he's okay?"

"Yup." Lie number three.

Mrs. Dixon breathed a sigh of relief. "I was so worried when he wouldn't talk to me or let me in."

"You know Matt, he always wins. Maybe the other guy got the best of him, and he was embarrassed. He's a man! We men don't like to admit when someone beats us." Sounded logical to Jimmy.

"That sounds logical."

And apparently to Mrs. Dixon too.

She took a deep breath. "Okay. I'm going to get ready for church. If you get Matt up and out, do try to leave me a note. I am going to be worried about him, even if you tell me he's all right."

"Got it." Jimmy winked.

No sooner did she leave the room through one door than Matt entered it through another. He was fresh out of the shower, clean clothes, a baseball hat, and terrycloth wristbands. "Morning, Jamie. You sleep okay?"

It was disturbing how well Matt could act like nothing was amiss. "Fine. You?"

"Good. Slept real good." Matt poured himself some coffee. "You want to go running this morning? We could go now and eat when we get back?"

"Not unless you want to talk about what happened last night."

"Nothing. I just got into a fight with one of the guys at work, and he pulled some of my hair out like a sissy girl. So, I came home and shaved it off. End of story."

Jimmy slumped back into his chair. "You heard."

"I heard." He took a seat next to Jimmy. "Great lie. I'll use it if you don't mind."

"Go right ahead. You gonna tell me what really happened?"

Matt looked into his cup for the answers. "No. But you could probably figure it out."

Jimmy didn't want to *figure it out*. He didn't want to think about someone hurting his best friend. He tried to be vague. "You met some guy in a bar. He was older. He tied you up and did things that you didn't like. When you tried to leave, he grabbed your ample amount of hair and forced you to… do things. Close enough?"

Matt still eyeballed his coffee as he swirled it around the rim. "Close enough."

Matt's silence went on for several minutes. Jimmy didn't know what he should do. Stay? Leave? He should text Darian, but he hadn't come up with a reason for not seeing him this weekend. He certainly could not tell him the truth. He might tell Darian some of Matt's little secrets, but this was not going to be one of them. This was way too personal. This was going to be locked away in Jimmy's mind for good.

Jimmy stood up. "I guess I should call my dad and tell him—" Matt's hand on his wrist stopped him mid-thought. He looked at Matt.

Matt still held his head low. He wouldn't look Jimmy in the eyes. "I think I was raped."

Jimmy's eyes popped wide, but he held his tongue.

"I think so. I mean… I know guys who are into kinky sex, bondage and stuff like that, but this was different. He… he h-hurt me. Maybe he was a s-sadist. I don't know. All I remember is that I said *no,* and he still did whatever he wanted. I've never felt so scared. I thought I was going to die. I thought: this guy is going to kill me when he's done humiliating me, and no one will know where I am or who I'm with."

Jimmy's heart pounded. He could not imagine what Matt had gone through the night before. "You should talk to someone. A counselor."

"A shrink?" Matt asked, as if the notion was absurd. "No thanks. I got you." He clutched Jimmy's hand, and Jimmy sat back down. "You've been telling me for years I need to be more careful. You were right. I need to be more careful who I hook up with. I will be, I promise. No more random guys are taking me home. I'll make sure I talk to them first or at least ask what they're into. Maybe I'll come up with some basic questions to screen out the weirdoes."

"Matt, don't you see that you're still setting yourself up for danger? For an empty life? Why can't you *date* someone? Get to know them on a deeper level *before* you fuck them?"

"One bad experience isn't going to make me look for Mr. Right. I'm not ready to settle down and buy a ranch and a dog with my life partner. Jamie! Get a grip."

"Me?" Jimmy couldn't believe what he was hearing. "Matt, you were raped. Don't you think that is a serious wake-up call? You're the religious one. Don't you think God is trying to tell you something about the way you live your life?"

Matt glared at him. "And now you're lecturing me? I know I was raped, thank you very much. I was the one with a fourteen-inch dildo shoved up his ass, Jamie, which is not something I can forget right away. Especially when I was blindfolded and handcuffed to a bed with a spreader between my ankles. I had no idea who was pouring wax on my nipples, or who the hell was fucking me, or how many! One sick bastard in a sea of willing sex bunnies doesn't set the standard for all the rest. I'm not changing my lifestyle because of *that guy*. If I do, he wins. I'm not going into hiding because of what he did to me."

"Then what was last night?"

"Me working through it, and you being there for me like you always are."

Jimmy couldn't refute that. He *was* always there for Matt. Only, this was the *worst* thing to come up. Jimmy would still be there for Matt in whatever way he needed. "Fine. I'm here for you. But will you talk to someone, please? I think being raped is a bigger deal than you realize. See someone for me. Will you?"

Matt reluctantly nodded.

17

November 2006

It's been months. I HAVE to make this up to Darian. I feel like I just dropped him cold, right out of my life. I can't believe I've been so distant from him. Darian is the nicest guy in the world, and here I am making excuses for why I can't be with him. I am an asshole.

Darian bounced back great from the broken ribs. He said they hurt from time to time, but ibuprofen is all it takes to feel better. He said he told Jerry off for giving him drugs and shit. I believe him. Darian's no good at lying to me.

It's been a year since Darian and I fooled around, and he sucked me into oblivion. One year, and not a day goes by when I don't think about it. Not that it wasn't the most amazing blowjob I'd ever had, which it was, and not that I didn't want to reciprocate, which I did. My constant obsession over that day is due to the fact that, when he blew me, I closed my eyes and saw Matt. I wanted it to be Matt sinking his mouth around my erection and massaging my thighs with his strong hands.

I can almost feel it now. The way Darian's lips sucked my head and moved in such a sweet, slow delivery of gentle kisses along my rigid cock was amazing. I can close my eyes here at my desk and feel him growing more urgent with each bob of his head. I can even feel him pressing his tongue piercing against my flesh. How could I not *want that again?*

Except I don't. Not from him.

I've denied how I feel about Matt for forever. Even when I tried to tell Darian I was sorry, I still saw Matt when I went home that night.

Everything inside me felt like it was Matt between my legs. My best friend. The one person I'd known and loved all my life was suddenly the focus of my desire and lust. Maybe that's why it's been so easy to blow Darian off these few months and stay with Matt as much as he needs.

Do I really want Matt like that? YES! Yes, I do. Matt with his hard, muscular body and broad shoulders, Matt with his hunting rifle and camos, I want to wrestle a sweaty Matt Dixon to the ground and feel him fuck me so hard I won't be able to move for hours.

But that's not going to happen, not in my lifetime. I'm not his type—at least I don't think I am. I'd have to probe his brain to figure that one out! His only comment so far was about not settling down.

I don't want to be just another fuck. I want Matt—all of Matt. I want his kisses, his caresses, I want to wake up in bed and still find his arms wrapped around me. Just like that Sunday morning, when his boner was thrusting into my crack.

I am such a fucking dreamer.

That's going to be my undoing right there! Wanting a prince when the man I love treats those he's with like trash. I don't want to be that to him. I need what we have between us now. Trust. We talk way more than we ever did, about anything and everything. He tells me where he's going and who he's with and what he does. I couldn't risk losing my best friend by asking for more than he is capable of giving.

That's why I've decided to try and shove my feelings for Matt aside and give Darian what he needs from me. A real boyfriend. A lover. He's been so patient. He hasn't tried to do anything to me, which I appreciate, but I wonder if he thinks I've lost interest? Or maybe he knows I'm fantasizing about Matt? I can't have Matt like that. I HAVE to make it work with Darian. I love him. I do. I love both of them.

Today is Darian's birthday. Now he's the one turning eighteen and stepping into "adulthood," so to say. I'm thinking you're not really a man until you're not a virgin any longer. Am I right? I'm sick of being a virgin. So... my birthday present to Darian is gonna be me. I just need to make sure I scream out the correct name!

"HEY. I got your text." Darian let himself in the front door of Dan Miller's house and walked up to Jimmy in the living room.

Jimmy closed his notebook and smiled up at him.

"What?" Darian grinned. "You got a weird look in your face, man."

"Nothing." Jimmy shrugged, standing up and looking into Darian's eyes. *He really does have beautiful eyes.* Jimmy didn't mind the eyeliner so much anymore, or the bar through his eyebrow, or the lip ring Darian had insisted on getting as a birthday present to himself a week ago. Darian Weston was really hot, and Jimmy definitely wanted to fuck him. No, not fuck him. That phrase made it sound like Matt and his hook-ups. Jimmy wanted to make love to Darian and hear him moan his name when he came. "Come on." He motioned for Darian to follow.

"What's up?" he asked, dutifully following Jimmy up the steps to his room.

Jimmy stopped at the door and smiled. "It's your birthday, right?"

"Yeah. Did you make me a cake?"

"No. Better."

"Chocolate chip cookies?"

"Better."

Darian still had no clue what was going on, and Jimmy patted his own back for coming up with the perfect surprise.

"Turn around and wait here a second." Jimmy held up a hand to make sure Darian was staying put. He returned to the hall moments later, after preparing his surprise, and touched Darian's back.

Darian turned around with an inquisitive look in his eyes. "What are you doing, Jamie? Are you burning candles in there?"

"Yup." Jimmy took his hand and laced their fingers together. "Come on," he urged, tugging him gently into his room. Jimmy closed the door and leaned in to kiss him.

Darian pulled back before Jimmy's lips touched his, which made Jimmy's eyes pop open.

"What about your dad? Isn't he—"

"Gone. Out with Cheryl for a while. No one is home for the next two hours. I have two hours," Jimmy whispered the last bit as seductively as he could, "of you all to myself."

Then Jimmy got his kiss.

He slanted his mouth over Darian's and sent his tongue out exploring. Darian's tongue was just as needy as his, and the two of them stood in the middle of the floor for several minutes, engaged in a serpentine wrestling competition, before Jimmy's brain registered what the rest of his body was doing. Darian was groaning into his mouth and Jimmy into his. The heat of his groin sent alarms off in his head. This was not what he had in mind!

"Dare," Jimmy panted as he broke their kiss. "I'm gonna cum."

Darian nipped at his earlobe and panted back, "Me too."

Their lower bodies were frantically grinding against one another. The friction sent Jimmy right to the edge, faster than he realized it would. Had he known from that first kiss he'd be dry humping Darian's thigh like a desperate hound dog in heat, he would have laid him back on the bed first and at least undressed him. This was so juvenile. Jimmy wasn't twelve any longer, but he might as well have been by the way he couldn't help from thrusting against Darian's hip.

Jimmy could also feel his boyfriend's erection through his jeans. It was like sliding his little woody next to a Maglite. Not that he'd ever done that before! It was basically the first metaphor to pop into his mind while thinking about how hard and thick Darian's dick seemed through the denim. Jimmy couldn't wait to get his hands on it, or his mouth.

Wow! Did I really think that? I guess I did.

Jimmy wanted his mouth on Darian Weston, *not* Matthias Dixon... and the admission felt *freeing.*

He clung to Darian as he came, his hips bucking slowly. Darian was done too, and holding him just as tight. Jimmy felt his hands gliding over his back. He heard Darian sigh before kissing his neck. One of his hands moved lower, cupping Jimmy's ass.

"That is not what I had in mind, just so you know." Jimmy felt the need to make that clear.

Darian chuckled and stepped back enough to look into Jimmy's eyes. "Well, we have,"—he peered over Jimmy's shoulder for a second—"one hour and fifty-two minutes to do whatever it is you had in mind."

After Jimmy got a wet washcloth from the bathroom, he and Darian stripped down and wiped off. The two of them paused there for a moment, taking each other in. No words were needed, and Jimmy was glad he didn't feel the need to fill the silence with humor, as Matt was apt to do.

Darian's body was lovely. Yeah, he was skinny, and he had nowhere *near* the amount of muscle that Matt had, but looking at the way his hips curved made Jimmy desperate to glide his fingers over the shape of his bones. He'd always had a thing for hips. Seeing a guy's penis was nice, sure. What's not to like about an oozing head that makes your mouth water and your throat contract with the thought of swallowing it? But hips….

He really liked the pictures on the Internet that showed a guy's hips, and maybe a smidgeon of pubic hair. The mystery of what was beneath the denim made him hard. Darian had great hips. Jimmy reached out and slid his palms over them on each side. His eyes followed his thumbs as they caressed the arches of his bones. He squeezed and moved his hands forward and lower, toward Darian's groin. The curly hair tickled Jimmy's thumbs and knuckles. He moved one hand back up and over his hip, the other lower to cup Darian's balls.

Darian sucked in air and placed his hands on Jimmy's shoulders as if to steady himself. "Jamie…."

Jimmy reveled in the sound of Darian breathless from such a small move. His fingers dug into Jimmy's shoulders, and Jimmy glanced up to see his eyes were closed. Jimmy smirked. *Darian likes how I'm touching him.*

Darian's Adam's apple moved up and down as he swallowed. He spread his legs more as Jimmy's fingers drifted over the skin behind his testicles. "Oh, Jamie," he breathed.

Jimmy nudged him backward. "Get on the bed. This is not going to be a hand job. I want to try everything."

Darian scooted back on the pillow, and Jimmy bent his head forward to lap at Darian's nipple. That ring had held such fascination for way too long. He swirled his tongue over the hoop and nipped. Darian whimpered and opened his legs wider, allowing Jimmy to settle between them. The sensation of his bare body lying on top of Darian's naked flesh was heavenly.

He rocked his hips into Darian's and could feel the heat of his asshole pucker against the sensitive skin of his head. Jimmy's dick wanted in! He reached down and rubbed his helmet over Darian's entrance. "I need to be in you, Dare." He tried in vain not to sound desperate.

"You gotta prepare me first," Darian replied. "You got lube? You can't just push in. It'll hurt. I haven't been fucked in a long time."

"I got lube." Jimmy reached under the adjacent pillow and grabbed the bottle he'd stashed. He sat back on his haunches and lubed up his fingers. "Now what do I do?"

"Stick them in me. First one, then two, and try to work slowly up to three. That should loosen the muscle up enough to take in your dick without too much pain."

"Okay."

Jimmy crouched down between Darian's thighs. It was a curious thing to be staring at an asshole. It really did pucker. Tight and wrinkled, the hole pulsated with each move Darian made. Weird. *And I'm gonna stick my fingers in there. And then my dick!*

Jimmy stopped overanalyzing and touched his index finger to Darian's opening. Slowly, he pushed inside. It was squishy. Would he find poop in there? That would be gross. *Jamie, stop thinking like a fucking prude!*

Darian didn't squirm, but he did shut his eyes. Jimmy moved his finger in and out, twisting his wrist and picking up rhythm. Watching Darian's face was priceless. This whole experience made his dick throb. He put two fingers in that pink little pucker, two fingers jutting as deep as he could get them. This was hot! Three made Darian grunt and writhe.

"You like that?"

"Yes," Darian breathed.

"And it doesn't hurt?"

"No."

"Looks like it would hurt."

Darian's eyes snapped open. "Jamie. Stop talking and fuck me." He tilted his hips up.

"Geez, testy." He pulled his fingers out and grabbed a condom. He positioned the head of his sheathed cock and entered cautiously. "Let me know if I hurt you."

"You won't."

"Well, if I do… just say and I'll stop."

"Jamie! Stop talking and get in me already."

"Okay, okay!" Jimmy kept going until his balls were resting against the bed. They were locked together, and Jimmy could feel the muscles of Darian's canal embracing him. "Shit, Dare, this feels incredible."

Jimmy let his body fall forward over Darian. He leaned on one arm and held Darian's left knee with the other. Then he started to move. He pulled out and pushed back in. "Oh, fuck, this feels good." Out and back in.

"Harder."

Jimmy searched Darian's face to make sure he'd heard him right. "Harder? Are you sure? I don't want to hur—"

Darian's eyes blazed. "You're *not* going to hurt me, Jamie. Stop talking and fuck me like you mean it." As if to make a point, he lifted his hips to meet Jimmy's thrusts.

"I was just trying to make sure you were okay, Darian, you don't gotta get mad at me."

Darian groaned. "I'm not mad, I'm just… distracted. I want to feel you thrusting, not hear your commentary."

"Oh, sorry. I didn't mean to…."

Darian grabbed his shoulders and pulled Jimmy down into a deep kiss. That got his attention. Darian's tongue made Jimmy's adrenaline rush, and his hips moved without any conscious thought. He was thrusting hard and deep and groaning into Darian's throat.

"Dare… not… gonna… last…," Jimmy grunted.

Darian answered by wrapping his legs around Jimmy's hips and tilting his pelvis. Suddenly their sweaty bodies felt way more than sweaty.

"You came?"

"Yup," Darian gasped.

Jimmy stopped pumping. "I didn't even touch you."

"I'm a teenager. It doesn't take much. I'm surprised you haven't."

"I did."

"You did?"

Jimmy pinched the base of the condom and pulled out. "Yeah. But I was too embarrassed to say something. I figured since I was still stiff enough to stay inside, I'd keep going. Then I felt myself getting hard again."

"We can go again if you want."

"You sure?"

"Hell yeah! I've been waiting for two years, Jamie. And this was not exactly the way I envisioned it happening. For one, in *my* fantasy, we fought less."

Jimmy's eyes drooped. "Sorry."

"We can fuck as long and hard as you like. Come here." He reached out, and Jimmy fell on top of him again.

Jimmy kissed Darian's throat. "If you're sure." He licked the sweat off Darian's neck. "I think I can get it up again."

Darian chuckled as Jimmy nudged him with a very definitely erect penis.

Things were fine until Darian suggested we switch. "His ass was getting sore, and I needed to feel how awesome it was to have a dick pounding me." End quote. It sounded great until he sunk into me, and I closed my eyes.

The whole time I was making sweet love to my Darian, he was all I could see.

Darian's brown eyes.

Darian biting his pierced lip.

Darian writhing beneath me as I took him from several positions.

But when he entered ME, my fucked-up brain took over. I pictured Matt. Matt with his fucking unbelievable chest and kissable lips. HE was the one holding my knees apart, thrusting into my ass for all it was worth. It was HIS grunting I heard and his cry of ecstasy when he came. Shit!

I was so fucking worried I'd scream the wrong name!

I didn't.

But then we heard my dad downstairs and rushed to get decent in case he came right upstairs. Thank God he didn't.

I was so worried Darian knew I wasn't thinking about him during our last session that I forgot to question the bruise on his arm. It looked like he'd had blood drawn and the nurse missed the vein a few times. Not sure what it was from, but I know I need to ask. Right now I am trying to let my hard-on cool down on its own. If I jack off I KNOW I'll see Matt's face, and that is not good.

I'm with Darian.

I love Darian.

I ~~fucked~~ made love to Darian.

Matt needs to get the fuck out of my head!

18

September 22, 2010
8:32 p.m.

DARIAN drove home from Matt's in a daze, but when he neared Dan's house he just kept on going. "I can't go home."

He found a Super 8 Hotel and checked in for the night.

A shower and a clean bed did nothing for his mood or his mental state. His thoughts were scattered all over the place. Darian was in pain; he wanted to cry, to scream, to run. Darian wanted Matt. He wanted to feel his cock thrusting deeply into his ass, nailing his prostate and assaulting his nerve endings before rocking him into orgasmic rapture. Darian wanted sleep. Darian wanted all those things but would trade everything to get the thing he most needed: Jamie. Darian wanted his Jamie back in his arms, safe and alive.

Instead, he had nothing but a hole the size of the Grand Canyon opening in his heart and devouring every last piece of his soul.

Darian scoffed at his own musings. "That's not completely true, and you know it, Dare." He rolled over and moaned into the pillow.

"Why'd you have to leave me, Jamie? Why?" he cried. Tears wet the pillowcase, and mucus dripped from his nose. "Lovely," he muttered. He wiped his nose on the spare pillow and tossed it off the side of the bed. It was a hotel. He was sure worse things had gotten on the sheets before.

The nightstand conveniently had a box of tissues. He blew his nose and lugged himself into the bathroom to splash water on his face.

His reflection looked wretched. The dark circles under his eyes made him look terribly similar to a zombie from *Shaun of the Dead*. He had to get some food into him, or his ribs would start showing. They were already showing.

Back to the bed and his inability to sleep. Darian could not stop his brain from working, thinking. He thought of Jamie, and oddly, he could not stop images of Matt from popping in. *Why?* He'd only just met him. A couple of hours with the guy did not prove anything. From years of listening to Jamie, he knew Matt! Matt was a sleep-around kind of guy, a lack-of-commitment guy, a cum-and-run sort who was not worth Darian's time.

Right?

Except, his inner voice kept whispering: "Remember how he's always doing stuff for his mom? Remember how Jamie talked about his charming personality and how wonderful he is? Remember all the nice things Jamie told you over the years?"

Darian answered audibly, "Yes. I know. Matt's great. I just don't know if I can trust him." He groaned and punched the pillow. "I don't want to be used."

He reached for his phone on the nightstand and looked at the pictures stored in memory.

Jamie. Jamie smiling. Jamie crossing his eyes. Jamie's hand—that was an accidental shot. Jamie's dick. Jamie's dick. Another one of Jamie holding his dick.

Darian groaned. He felt things stirring in his lower body as he looked back through the pictures on his camera phone. The one of Darian's mouth on Jamie pushed him over the edge.

Darian tossed the phone aside and quickly shed his boxers.

Erection in hand, he closed his eyes and willed up more mental images of their times together. New York! Jamie loved New York…

… Jamie and Darian walked through Central Park, enjoying the sights and sounds that only seemed to come with being in New York. The noise of the streets, filled with as many people as cars, faded into the background with each step they took further into the park. Soon, only birds could be heard overhead. It was amazing! Less than one hundred feet behind them was the hustle and bustle of city life, but here it was as if none of that existed.

Darian felt Jamie take his hand as they walked. He grinned and felt his heart swell.

"Here we can just be us!" Jamie said, bringing their clasped fingers to his mouth and kissing the back of Darian's hand.

They walked on, meandering the paved paths that wound through the park. An open field on their left looked enticing, as they spied many couples lying out on blankets, sharing a picnic or simply some cuddle time. Jamie led them to a shady spot and sat down. Darian sat next to him.

"No, not there," Jamie said. He scooted back against a tree and spread his legs. "Like at home, on Dad's comfy chair. I want to hold you."

Darian did not hesitate to seat himself between Jamie's legs with his back against Jamie's chest. He tilted his head back on Jamie's shoulder.

"Now *this* is what I call a vacation!" Jamie declared.

Darian hugged Jamie's arms, which were wrapped around his chest. "Me too."

"Look," Jamie pointed discreetly.

Darian followed Jamie's instruction and noticed another gay couple enjoying much the same arrangement. One boy had his back leaning on one of the large boulders that were scattered throughout the park, and the other boy was lying back in his arms, between his legs. The only difference was these boys were taking pleasure in sharing a lingering kiss.

"No one even cares," Jamie pointed out. "People walk by like it's normal."

"I think it's normal here, Jamie. Or at the very least, 'normal' that New Yorkers don't care. I've already seen loads of couples walking down the street arm in arm or kissing on the sidewalk, and no one bats an eye. We just live in the wrong town."

"Then maybe we should move here!"

Darian cocked his head so he could look at Jamie in the eyes. "Are you serious? Could you really live here and move away from your dad?"

Jamie made a face. "I guess not. I don't know. Maybe we could live in DC for a while, and I could get used to living away from him first."

"Or we could start by living in an apartment in Hanover," Darian suggested. "Start slower, Jamie. I know how much you love your dad. We'll move out of his house, find an apartment, live there a while and then move gradually further away. How's that?"

"Sounds like the perfect plan. Unless… unless my dad agrees to move to New York with Cheryl. Then all my problems are solved!"

Darian smiled and rested his head back in its favored position. He felt Jamie rubbing his chin on the side of his head, like he enjoyed doing most of the time they sat this way. He was glad Jamie had decided to shave this morning. His stubble had a habit of teasing Darian's hair into a royal mess when he nuzzled this way.

"As much as I normally like this position, I think I'd rather be doing what that couple is doing," Jamie declared.

He shifted his leg and moved Darian's shoulders to the side. Now Darian was literally lying in his arms, and Jamie could lean down and kiss his lips.

Darian was surprised by his boldness. Jamie would never do something like this at home. He was so afraid of getting caught by someone he knew. But by the way his tongue languidly mapped out the contours of Darian's mouth, no one would guess how reticent he normally was. Darian decided they needed to come to New York more often!

When Jamie reached down and started rubbing the front of his shorts, Darian jumped and pulled away from his lips. "Jamie! We're in a public park."

"Sorry. I forgot."

Darian shook his head. *How could he forget?* "You're crazy."

"About you." Jamie smiled and leaned in, resuming the lazy lovemaking he was applying to Darian's lips.

"One more year, and I'll be finished with school." Jamie caressed Darian's cheek and gazed into his eyes. "Mom said four years is all I had to commit to at McDaniel College. Kevin's free ride only goes so far." Jamie kissed his nose. "I'll have a Bachelor's Degree in Accounting. I'm sure I can do something with that. I can provide for you." He winked.

"I'm sure I can get used to that."

"I hope so."

Jamie started moving away, and Darian asked, "What's wrong?" as he followed suit and sat up.

"Nothing." Jamie situated his body so he was sitting back on his legs and looked very seriously into Darian's eyes. Darian felt his insides quiver. "I didn't plan on doing this now, but it just feels right." He took Darian's hand in his and breathed in deeply. "Darian Andrew Weston.... Would you do me the honor of... becoming my bride?" Darian's eyebrow shot up, and Jamie scrambled to correct his question. "My husband...? My life partner? Yeah, 'life partner' sounds better." He smiled. "Would you be my life partner?"

Darian felt the tears coming. "Fuck, why'd you do this in public?" He swiped his eyes. "Oh, Jamie...." He sniffled and tried desperately to keep himself composed when there were so many people in the park who might notice him crying like the sentimental sap that he was.

"So is that a 'yes'? Because I didn't hear anything."

"Yes! Of course it's a 'yes'. I love you. I want to be with you forever."

Jamie smiled and leaned in, kissing Darian again.

Darian whimpered into his mouth and moved onto his knees as he brought his body closer to Jamie's. His hands went to the sides of Jamie's neck, and he felt Jamie's hands slide over his hips. The kiss was becoming more passionate by the second. Tongues clashing and hands caressing, Darian moved his hips forward. Jamie's hand moved from his hip to grope his butt.

Someone wolf-whistled.

The two of them broke apart instantly, each one looking guilty as they surveyed the area to see who may have done the whistling. Darian saw the gay couple they'd spotted earlier looking their way, pointing and smiling. One of them winked at Darian, who blushed and averted his eyes. "It was those guys, Jamie." He pointed without making eye contact.

Jamie shook his head and called over, "Hey, thanks. Now he's gone all shy on me!"

"Sorry," the guy yelled back. "I couldn't help myself."

Jimmy turned his attention back to Darian. "I wish I planned this better," he said. "I didn't want to ask you until I graduated. I was going to buy a ring and everything."

Darian shrugged. "It's okay. I'm thrilled no matter what. I was surprised, which makes it more fun."

"Well, I may not have a ring, but I can give you this." Jimmy reached behind his neck and undid his necklace. "Here, I want you to have it." He clasped the chain behind Darian's neck.

Darian looked down at the Russian cross. "This is the one Matt gave you. You've been wearing it since we met."

"Longer. I think he was thirteen when he went on the mission trip to St. Petersburg. I've worn it for eight years."

"But Matt? Are you sure he'd—" His words were stopped by Jamie's lips. Darian went with the kiss. Surely Jamie would know if Matt would be upset or not? Matt was his best childhood friend. Matt was the person he talked most about…

… Matt was the one whose mouth could suck a cantaloupe through a straw. *Matt's lips tugging Darian's nipple ring as his fingers rubbed his….* Cum coated his fingers. Darian's eyes shot open. His hand stopped moving. He lay stock-still until it hit him what just happened. "Fuck!"

He leapt off the bed and started shaking. "This can't be happening," he argued with himself. "I *did not* just destroy the memory of the happiest day of my life. I *did not* just think about Matt when I was trying to imagine Jamie. I *did not* lose what I had with Jamie because of one stinking night with Matt. Not even a night, a few hours!" He paced like a caged animal and shook as if on the verge of a mental breakdown. "This can't be happening. I love Jamie. I need Jamie. I miss Jamie."

He paced and tore at his hair with gripping fists. The room was spinning. He wanted to run but didn't know where to go. "I can't do this. I can't do this." He stood in the middle of the room, rocking his head between his arms on both sides. Desperate, he dove for his pants, draped over the motel-room chair. "I have to have some. There have to be a few left!"

Darian grabbed his wallet and unzipped the change compartment. Coins fell into his hand, and he tossed them onto the dresser in front of him. He dug into the change pocket with his finger. Lint. Then, along the side where the stitching was unraveling and creating a tiny pocket inside the pocket, Darian found two pills.

He stared at them as they sat in his palm.

Dilaudid.

Two milligrams each.

Relief.

He popped them into his mouth and tilted back his head.

DARIAN entered the funeral home Thursday evening with a pounding headache. He'd woken up three minutes before checkout and dashed down just in time to avoid the cost of another night's stay. Luckily he still had a few things at his mom's house, so he could safely take a shower and avoid going to Dan's house. He couldn't bear the thought. He'd stood under the hot water until it ran cold.

He'd made it to the viewing like he'd said he would, but standing in the hallway did nothing to give him the courage he needed to walk up to the casket. He was still shaking like he had the day before.

Standing in the doorway, he caught sight of Matt over by some flowers, touching them like he was making sure they were real. When their eyes locked, Darian all but sobbed his heart out. The spark he saw in Matt's eyes was unmistakable. *He wants me.*

It wasn't a look of lust. It wasn't a look of simple recognition. It wasn't even a look of relief because Darian had made it to the viewing. When Matt looked up, Darian saw *longing*.

His heart stopped for a second, and he forgot to breathe. Matt wanted him, and Darian could have melted.

But this was not the place. It was a funeral home.

Fuck!

His mind whirled with more confusion. He didn't want to feel desperate for Matt, but logic and reality were at odds. He struggled to remain still.

Darian's eyes moved from Matt to the casket. He had to go over and say goodbye. His stomach flipped. Darian clutched his mouth and ran from the room.

He made it into the stall before heaving. There wasn't much more than bile. Darian hadn't eaten since he upchucked the tea last night. He sat back and panted when he heard the restroom door open.

"Darian?"

"Matt?"

Matt opened the stall door and crouched down. "Darian, are you okay?"

"I'm vomiting air. Does it sound like I'm fine?"

"Hey, I'm just asking." He reached out and tucked Darian's hair behind his ear. "Can I get you some water?"

Darian reconsidered his previous snap. "Yeah, thanks." He stood up and allowed Matt to take his hand. He watched as Matt wet a few napkins and thoughtfully wiped his face. "That feels nice."

Matt smiled. "My mom always did it for me when I was sick. Wait here and I'll get you something to drink."

He watched Matt disappear and return a minute later with a cup of water in hand. He took the offering and drank it all down.

"Hey, hey, slowly. I don't want you chucking it right back up."

Darian could not suppress a smirk.

Matt caressed his cheek. "I like that smile."

"Thanks. I'm rather fond of yours too." The truth slipped from his lips.

"Really?"

"Really." Darian stood there in silence, relishing the gentleness of Matt's touch. But then it dawned on him where they were, and he had to ask, "Aren't you afraid someone might come in?"

Matt shrugged. "No. Mr. Miller saw you bolt, and he asked if I'd go see if you were all right. I think he assumes we know each other."

Matt stepped closer, and Darian felt all aflutter. Matt tilted his head, and Darian closed his eyes. Matt's warm lips easily coaxed a whimper from his throat. He could feel that large body stepping closer and Matt's arms pulling him in tight. Matt didn't overwhelm him. He kissed him just enough to cause his body to relax. Then he held Darian tenderly and rubbed his back.

Darian sighed. "Thank you."

"Don't mention it. I'm just glad you stopped throwing up for five minutes. Although I do find it interesting how twice I've kissed you afterward, and I don't even find it gross."

Darian covered his face with his hand. "Oh, God. I'm sorry."

"No. It's okay, really. I don't care. As long as you're in my arms."

Darian was hesitant to say anything. Matt sounded so sincere. Maybe all the nice things Jamie said about him were true. Maybe Matt wasn't all about self-gratification. Maybe Matt wanted more this time? Part of Darian wanted to confess he felt the same way, and the other part of him said he should wait. He felt so conflicted that he didn't know what to say. He needed Matt's strength so badly.

"I think I'm ready to say goodbye to Jamie, but you have to go with me." He saw Matt's eyes go wide. "You don't have to do or say anything. Just stand near me, okay? If I know you're there, I think I can do it. I have to do it."

"You got it."

Darian felt cold when Matt let go of him, but he knew he had to make it through the next few minutes unassisted. "I can do this." He chanted his mantra one more time.

He made it down the hall. He made it into the room. Darian even made it all the way up to the casket without feeling his knees buckle. When he saw the whiteness of Jamie's surrealistic face, all the air was sucked from the room. He stood there frozen in his tracks. "Jamie," he whispered.

He could not pull his eyes away. He was glued to the morbidity of embalmment. Here was the body of his lover and friend, made up to look as though he was sleeping. It was sick. Jamie didn't look like that in his sleep. Jamie smirked in his sleep, most of the time. He dreamed a lot and talked gibberish, but he definitely didn't look serene in his sleep. He looked amused.

This was gross.

Darian shook his head and took a step closer. "Oh, Jamie, what did they do to you?" He reached out and touched Jamie's fingers. They were hard and cold. Darian shivered. "This isn't you. It's just a shell. It isn't you." He backed away and glanced at Matt before running from the room.

DARIAN sat in his mom's house, fingering the syringe on his desk. This world was too much! How could he get through one more day? He'd thought he could say goodbye, but that corpse was not Jamie. It was a shell. Now he'd have to say goodbye during the funeral… or even worse, days later by Jamie's tombstone. He couldn't do it. It was too much. The pain was too much.

Darian picked up the syringe and flicked the housing. A bubble floated to the tip, and he squeezed just enough fluid from the needle to allow the air to escape.

"Escape. I need to escape."

Darian held the tip to the inside of his elbow. The vein bulged as if it knew what was coming. He broke the skin and felt his heart rush with anticipation. But before he pushed the plunger and injected his veins with liquid bliss, Darian heard Jamie's voice whisper, *"Please don't."*

Violently he ripped the needle from his skin and threw the syringe across the room. He heard the glass break, and he started to sob uncontrollably. "I can't do this, Jamie!" he yelled. "I can't do this alone!" He rocked his body in the chair, holding his head. "I can't do this." His strength was all but gone.

Jumping up, he grabbed his coat and headed for the only place he knew he could escape the pain.

Matt's.

19

March 17, 2007

JIMMY loved the feel of Darian in his arms. It was a lovely way to wake up. He was very warm, despite the fact that it was March and the two of them slept with only a sheet covering them. He squeezed Darian, who responded by moving his leg higher over Jimmy's torso. Darian's knee was resting across Jimmy's dick. Hmmm... he rather liked that.

Jimmy took a deep, contented breath and smelled coffee. His dad was up! He rolled Darian to his side, and luckily the sleepyhead barely registered the shift. He hugged the pillow and sighed.

Jimmy got out of bed and slipped on a pair of jeans he snagged off the floor. He headed down the steps and greeted his dad with a hug from behind.

"Whoa, morning, Jimbo." He tried to move and hug his son back. "To what do I owe the honor of such a sappy 'good morning'?"

Jimmy heaved a sigh. "Nothing. I'm just happy." Jimmy finally let go, and his dad turned around.

Dan ran his hand over the top of Jimmy's head and smiled. "I noticed. You've been happy for a while now. I don't suppose a certain person sleeping in your bed has something to do with that?"

Jimmy leaned back in for another hug. "Oh, Dad. I love him."

Dan squeezed Jimmy. "I know, son. I know."

Jimmy sighed again and let go of his father. He took a mug out of the cabinet and filled it. "You're really cool to let him stay here overnight. I mean… I know you know that we… do stuff." As nervous as he felt in saying it, Jimmy could not stop his mouth from forming the words.

"Well, Jimbo, let me tell you something. When I was your age, I remember… doing stuff." He grinned and sat down at the kitchen table. "I remember taking my girlfriend at the time into the basement when my parents were doing who knows what. They had no idea we were… doing stuff. My parents were very naive. Anyway… whether my parents were home or not, or whether they 'allowed' it or not, didn't matter; we did what we wanted to do anyway.

"Point is…. You and I have this 'thing' between us. Call it *sincerity, trust, honesty,* or whatever… I gave you the talk already. I have to trust that you'll make the right decisions. Having you under my roof, instead of gallivanting around in an alley somewhere or in the back seat of your car, I feel is safer. I like Darian. He's sweet and funny, and he's completely head over heels for you. I told you before: I want you to be happy. Be happy, but be careful."

Jimmy's chest swelled. "Thanks, Dad. I will."

"Now, I would like to ask you something." Dan stood up and went to the counter. He reached up and took something off the window ledge and held it out to Jimmy. It was a small pill. "Is this yours? Cheryl found it on the living room floor the other day."

Jimmy took it and studied the shape. White. Round. Had a number three on one side. "No. Maybe it's Darian's? I know his ribs still hurt from time to time, and he has some Percocet in my room."

"It's not Percocet."

"Maybe it's Dilaudid? I think he had a few of those left over from last year." Jimmy didn't like the serious look his dad gave him.

"Jim, I looked it up online. It took me a while to research the shape, but I found it. This is fentanyl. It normally comes in patch form and is used with cancer patients. Jimmy… Wikipedia says it's one hundred times more potent than morphine."

"What? You don't think…. But Darian wouldn't…."

"Jimmy. I love you and I trust you, but there's no way Darian's in enough pain to be taking fentanyl. And if Darian has a drug problem, he needs to see someone about it. This is serious stuff. An overdose is lethal. And if he's careless enough to lose one in our living room, then…."

"Dad, it's not him. It can't be. He told me he was off drugs."

"When?"

"Last year. When I was grounded for fighting. He told me over the phone that he quit."

"Over the phone? So you knew he was taking pain meds?"

"He had broken ribs, dad. That kid at Winter's Mill kicked his ass. He was taking Percocet, and Jerry, his mom's boyfriend, gave him something stronger. He didn't say what. I asked him to stop taking it, and he said he would."

"And you believed him."

"Yeah. Darian can't lie. His face blushes. It's so cute. I think it's adorable how he—"

Dan interrupted, "But you said this was over the phone."

Jimmy stopped smiling. "Yeah, but he…." Jimmy let his thoughts trail off. Had he ever asked Darian face to face? He couldn't remember. They talked on the phone a lot. Or texted. And last summer was a mess, with Matt and all. Jimmy could not remember if the discussion ever came up.

"I guess I just assumed that he… Dad, what if Darian's addicted to painkillers?"

"It could be worse, but I think we should... *you* should ask him." He squeezed Jimmy's shoulder. "I gotta go to work. Ask him when he wakes up. If it's true, then we'll deal with it. Just remember, he loves you. That much is very evident."

"I know. Thanks."

AN HOUR went by before the sleeping dead showed up in the kitchen. "Good morning," Darian grinned as he entered the room. "Did you sleep well?"

Jimmy looked up from his journal. "Yeah. I always do when you're in my arms."

"You better watch it; you're sounding more and more like me." He opened the refrigerator.

Jimmy laughed. "Well, you know what they say: after a while couples start to talk and act like each other."

Darian stopped moving and placed the milk on the counter. He remained still and asked Jimmy, "Is that what we are? A couple?"

"Don't you think so?"

"I was hoping so."

Jimmy got up and walked over to the cutest boy in the room. "Stop wondering. We *are* a couple." He slid his arms around Darian's hips and kissed the side of his neck. "I love you."

"I love you too, Jamie."

Jimmy kissed Darian and nuzzled his nose over his ear, which made Darian giggle. "Can I ask you something?" Jimmy asked between kissing and nuzzling.

"Ah huh."

"Promise not to get mad."

"How can I get mad at you?" Darian asked as he squirmed in Jimmy's arms. "Stop sucking so hard. Jamie. Stop. You're gonna give me another hickey."

Jimmy stopped assaulting Darian's neck. "See, you're mad now."

"I'm not mad." He pointed to his expression. "This is frustration. You know I've got an interview with American Eagle. I can't have a hickey! It's unprofessional."

"Oh, yeah. Sorry." Jimmy let go and sat back down while Darian poured a glass of milk.

"So what did you want to ask me?"

"Ummm…. Is this yours?" Jimmy asked as he pushed the little pill across the table toward Darian.

Darian walked over and picked up the pill. He took a drink of his milk and then studied it. "Where'd you find this?"

"Is it yours?"

"Yes. Where was it? Were you looking through my things? I can't believe you did that! Besides, you don't know what this is. I've been in pain. I needed—"

"It's fentanyl," Jimmy replied calmly. He didn't like Darian's defensiveness, but he allowed his attitude for now. He was obviously surprised to be confronted like this. People under confrontation often got defensive. Jimmy held his cool.

Darian hung his head.

Jimmy waited.

"I don't know what you want me to say," Darian said very quietly.

"Just the truth," Jimmy answered. "Have you been taking drugs when you told me you'd stop?"

There was a long, silent pause before Darian nodded.

Jimmy closed his eyes. Disappointed, he took a deep breath. "Have you been taking painkillers all year?"

"Yes. But not all the time. It's not what you think. I'm not addicted. I can stop. I just hurt sometimes. Like when it's going to rain. I can feel it in my ribs, and I ache all over, so I take one. Really, Jimmy, you gotta believe me."

Jimmy understood the strain in Darian's voice. He could also see the anxiety in his beautiful eyes. Jimmy wanted to forgive him and believe he would stop, but hearing the name "Jimmy" kept him from giving in. "Darian, I say this because I love you. You need help."

"No, I don't." Darian stood abruptly, sending the chair crashing backward. "You don't know what you're talking about. I'm fine." He left the room.

Jimmy rushed after him. In the living room he grabbed his arm, spinning him around. "Don't walk away from this. Painkillers are no small thing. You have to stop. You have to talk to someone. I don't know, like a drug counselor or something."

"That's a bunch of bullshit! I don't need this." Darian yanked himself from Jimmy's grip and stormed out the front door.

Jimmy chided himself. "Oh, that went well."

JIMMY was watching television when his dad came home.

"Hey, buddy. How'd your little talk go?" Mr. Miller hung his coat in the closet and took a seat next to Jimmy.

Jimmy flicked off the TV and exhaled noisily. "Not good. He stormed out. No shirt, bare feet in the beginning of March, Darian slammed the door and walked home. I'm glad he doesn't live far, and that it isn't snowing."

"I take it that pill was his?"

"Yeah. He said he doesn't have a problem. He says he can stop anytime. He mainly got ticked when I suggested a drug counselor."

"Oh, Jimbo.... It's not easy admitting when you're wrong. Darian needs to work through this. Give him some time. Then go over and talk to him again. If you push too hard too soon, he may cut you off. Don't risk it. He needs to feel like he can trust you."

"I know. Believe me. Mom had me seeing a counselor, and it was awful. That guy didn't give a shit about me. He just wanted to make himself feel better by helping some poor, lost soul."

His dad leaned forward. "She had you talk to a counselor? When? About what?"

"Oh, last year," Jimmy shrugged. "You know, when I accidentally hit the teacher."

"Oh. When Joey said something about *me* being gay?"

"Yeah. Don't worry. I kept my answers as short as I possibly could. He has no idea I'm gay or that any of this happened because of it. I think he believed it was all about my anger over the divorce." When his dad's cheek flinched at the words, Jimmy jumped in and qualified his statement. "Not that it is! It's not. I am totally fine with the divorce. Really. You are so happy with Cheryl, and I don't blame you for splitting up with Mom."

"Are you sure? I don't want my mistakes to be the cause of your emotional problems." He looked relieved.

"They're not, Dad. I promise. I was angry at first, but I realized that it didn't matter if you were married to Mom or not. You were still my dad. And... Mom would still be Mom, with or without you in the house. I can't change her. I'm just trying to be the best I can be and hope she loves me."

"She does love you."

"Are you sure? Sometimes I can't tell. And I'm not so sure she'll treat me the same when I tell her I'm gay. She hates gays. I know it. She'll probably call me a hedonistic sinner. You know she goes to church now, right?"

"Yeah, I heard. Doesn't seem to have changed her much."

"No. It has. Like when I lost my scholarship to Strayer University because of the two suspensions. I thought she'd kill me. She didn't. She was mad and said some really mean things, but she didn't hit me like I expected. It's actually been years since she slapped me across the face or took a belt to my ass."

Mr. Miller tried to chuckle, but Jimmy could tell he was still miffed. "Your mother is…," he huffed, "… difficult. Let's just leave it at that."

"I know what you mean."

Jimmy's phone buzzed. "It's a text from Darian. He says, *'I'm sorry I got mad. You're right. I'll think about counseling'*."

"See. I told you he just needed time."

April 28, 2007

Darian's doing well, I think. The drug counselor saw him a few times and even talked to me once. She gave me some pamphlets to read, explaining what to look for in Darian's behavior in case his addiction gets worse. She recommended he see a psychotherapist; seems Darian has worse problems than drugs.

I drove him there tonight.

The drug counselor told me the first session would be the worst, and she wasn't joking. He was shaking. I'm not sure why. I normally like the way he can't stop touching me, but this was different. He wouldn't talk about what they discussed. When he left her office and entered the waiting room where I sat, I overheard the words "deep-

seated issues" and something about taking time to work through them. Whatever the hell that means. Darian clung to me the whole way home.

I didn't want to leave him. It was hard enough getting out of the house to drive Darian to see the therapist. I had to get home before Mom flipped. Well... flipped more.

May 16th

I spoke too soon. Walmart called my dad's house looking for Darian. Seems he missed a few days. They told me to tell him not to bother coming in. I need to find him. I texted and he responded, "I'm sleeping."

What the hell?

Then the drug counselor called because he missed two appointments.

If I wasn't so busy trying to watch over Matt and make my mom think I'm perfect and keep the pastor off my ass about being gay AND get through finals this week, I'd be driving all over town right now!

Please God, if you're there, keep Darian out of trouble.

May 24th

I guess I didn't pray hard enough.

"DARIAN?" Jimmy looked in Darian's room, but he wasn't there. They were supposed to meet by the pond and fish—a.k.a. "make love under the trees and hope to catch a fish without trying"—so when Darian didn't show, Jimmy went looking for him.

I don't think he mentioned having to start at American Eagle yet.

Jimmy scratched his head and headed to the bathroom. *Maybe he's in there?* The door was closed, so he knocked. "Darian? Are you in there? Darian?" Jimmy turned the knob and cracked the door when no one answered. He peeked in and gasped at the sight of Darian passed out on the floor. "Dare!" Jimmy immediately fell to his knees beside Darian and felt for a pulse. He found one.

Jimmy untied the strap around Darian's bicep and pulled the needle out of his arm. "Yuck!" He tossed it toward the trash. Jimmy then looked Darian over for any injuries, in case he'd hit his head on the tub when he passed out. Nothing.

"Darian. Darian, can you hear me?" He tapped Darian's cheeks. "Darian." He slapped him again, harder. Darian moaned. Jimmy felt relieved, even from this slight response. He pulled on Darian's arms in an attempt to get his body far enough away from the toilet bowl so he could lift him up and carry him to his room.

For once, Jimmy was glad Matt liked to work out all the time and felt the need to drag Jimmy to the gym with him. His arms were strong, and he easily lifted Darian's slender frame. He carried his limp body to the bed and laid him down, sitting on the mattress next to him. He lifted his eyelids. Darian's pupils were constricted, as if the room was bright—which it wasn't—and his eyes were bloodshot.

"What the fuck?" Jimmy murmured. He tenderly stroked the side of Darian's neck. He'd caught him with a needle in his arm. *Drugs, definitely!* But what kind? Jimmy noticed more than one needle mark on Darian's arm. This was not something he could blow off by claiming the doctor took some blood for a test. These were the track marks of someone doing intravenous drugs on a regular basis.

Heroin? "God, I hope not."

Darian moaned again and lifted his hand to his face, rubbing his eyes. "Ohhh, I am soooo fucking tired."

"Darian. Are you okay?"

Darian stopped rubbing his eyes at the sound of Jimmy's voice. "Jimmy? Hey. What are you doing here?" He could barely keep his eyes open.

Jimmy was not happy to be questioned about why he was there. "Um, we were going fishing? Don't you remember?"

"Oh, yeah… fishing… I remember. Sure. Fishing. Like with a pole." He sat up, leaning on his elbow, and reached over to Jimmy's crotch. "I'll hold your pole anytime," he said with wink and a grope.

"Quit it." Jimmy shoved his hand away. "I can't believe you forgot. And what's this?" Jimmy asked as he grabbed Darian's arm and held it open, pointing to the marks on his arms.

"Nothing." Darian tried to pull away, but his attempt was not as strong as Jimmy's grip. Jimmy glared at him.

"Is this from heroin? Did you get it from Jerry? Don't tell me your mom's boyfriend is responsible. How many times have you done this? Is this why you missed work a couple weeks ago? Is this why you were fired?"

"So many questions." Darian fell back onto the pillow. "Can't think right now. I need a cigarette." He fumbled for the pack off his nightstand and lit up, right there in his bed.

"Darian, this is serious. You can't stay here if Jerry is giving you drugs. I won't let you get roped into that. You need help."

"I told you. I'm fine." He took a long, hard draw on the cigarette. Darian could barely keep his head from rolling sideways. He was so out of it.

"You are not! I'm calling my dad. We're taking you to a rehab place or something." Jimmy reached into his pocket and started to dial.

"I don't need rehab, Jimmy. I did a little to help me think straight. Big deal. I'll be fine." He grabbed for Jimmy's phone.

Jimmy held the phone out of his reach. "Stop fuckin' calling me Jimmy! This isn't you, Darian. This is the drug addict who thinks he's you. I'm getting you help. I'm not letting you destroy yourself, your life or mine."

JIMMY waited nervously at the end of the hall. His dad had been talking to the doctor for a really long time. He hated being here. The walls were a putrid taupe color. It was meant to be soothing, but it just made Jimmy hyperaware of the sterilized environment he was leaving Darian in. He didn't want to leave. He wanted to break into his room and sleep next to him in the hospital bed.

Finally, his dad came out.

"Well? What'd he say?" Jimmy grabbed his dad's arm anxiously.

His dad looked around before answering. "Let's go outside, first. 'K?"

Jimmy gave his dad a look but followed without another word. When they got to the car he let go of his control. "Well? What did the doctor tell you? You can't keep me in the dark, you know."

"I know. I'm not going to try. The doctor I was chatting with is a friend of mine. We used to hang out and smoke pot in the back of his father's pickup truck."

"Dad!"

"I know, more things about me you don't need to hear. Anyway… Roger and I were talking about a lot of things that he could get fired for, which is why I asked you to come outside first."

"Okay, so, spill."

"First of all, I'm not supposed to know any of this since I'm not a family member. Roger made an exception because we're friends and because you and Darian are involved."

"Got it. Secret safe with me."

"Second… Darian's not a minor. He can't be forced to stay here. If he wants to leave, no one can stop him."

"But, Dad, he's so full of drugs most of the time, how can he make a logical decision like that?"

"Calm down. Roger's going to talk to him. He's been helping rehab patients for years, and I'm confident he will know how to handle it. Roger said there was heroin in his system, as well as traces of some other things. He's actually lucky to be alive. Often times, mixing drugs can kill you."

"Fuck! And I thought finding the fentanyl was bad!"

"I wish it was only painkillers, really I do. Heroin is one of the worst drugs to quit."

"Oh, Dad, what if Dare—"

His dad cupped the side of Jimmy's face. "You have to trust Roger, Jimmy."

Jimmy didn't like the feeling of helplessness that came with trusting a doctor he didn't know with one of the most precious people in his life. It was heart wrenching. "Okay."

"Third…. When Darian gets through this, I want him to move in with me."

Jimmy's eyes popped. "What?"

His dad grinned. "He practically lives there anyway. I think that if I can watch over him when you're not home, it would help. Plus, he really shouldn't be living with his mom if her boyfriend is the cause of all this. I talked to her."

"You did?"

"Yup. She was stoned. Denied all of it. Got a little mean. I figured I'd back off and go with my gut. Darian doesn't need to be around her, and he's old enough to go where he pleases. We'll just make sure he wants to stay with me."

Jimmy smiled with gratitude. "He will. He really digs you. He said you're like the dad he never had."

20

August 31, 2006

"YOUR hair looks good. It's growing fast," Jimmy casually commented. Matt had worn a baseball cap for weeks, so Jimmy hadn't gotten the chance to see how his hair was coming back in. As the two of them started jogging down the road, Jimmy decided to bring up the events of Matt's recent past.

"Yeah. I buzzed it once already this week." Matt held a steady pace.

"Buzzed, eh? You going for a new look? No curly mess any longer?" Jimmy was curious but somehow knew the answer he'd get.

"Yup. No fuckin' way a guy's gonna grab a hold of my hair again. No fuckin' way!"

Jimmy felt sick at the reminder of what Matt had been through but wasn't about to ask Matt to stop running for a minute. Stopping would give him away for sure, and Matt would end up getting angry or defensive. Jimmy didn't need that. Jimmy had witnessed a flux of emotional outbursts in the last few weeks. It was almost comforting to be running and feel something normal between them.

Matt was a strong-willed son-of-a-bitch.

Jimmy had seen him through that first weekend, even gave him a logical story to tack onto it all, but then the days went by, and it became apparent that Matt was not as strong as he thought he was. He'd texted Jimmy on several occasions, asking him to come over. Each time, Jimmy found him in his room, sitting silently in the dark. Somehow,

Mrs. Dixon was blissfully unaware, which made Jimmy happy that she wouldn't worry but angry at the same time for not realizing her son was in pain. Each time, Jimmy would sit with him and listen.

Jimmy urged Matt again to see a therapist.

Matt told him more about his exploits in these last few weeks. Jimmy had no idea guys went cruising for other guys all the time. He had no idea there were designated parks and *ways* of looking for the right guy. He was so naive about underground parties and sex clubs. Matt seemed to know way more than he was letting on. Jimmy had been glad when some of those conversations ended. It was too much.

Jimmy liked the romantic ideal of falling in love with a cute boy at school and living happily ever after. He didn't want to think about guys getting HIV because they forgot to wear a condom, and their fuck-buddy was *positive* but didn't say beforehand. He didn't like thinking about what the term "chocolate or vanilla" meant. He was perfectly happy only thinking of that question with reference to ice cream.

And who in their right mind would *want* to be flogged?

Jimmy didn't. It scared him to think that Matt had been a part of that world in some small way. Matt referenced a spreader, but Jimmy didn't even know what that was. He was afraid to ask, afraid to even look it up on the Internet for fear of what kinds of images would pop up.

Jimmy was not into porn. He used to look a little bit, but that was before he had a boyfriend. Now it felt wrong to even consider looking at another male body if it wasn't Darian's.

Or Matt's.

Jimmy felt guilty enough over his fantasies about Matt. He didn't need Internet porn to add to his shame. If only he could look at Darian's body once, then maybe he wouldn't keep thinking about Matt's.

Darian had forgiven him over the phone, but he still sounded lonely. Jimmy could not make him understand how much Matt needed him unless he came clean about all Matt's secrets. He couldn't. Matt trusted him, and he had to try and keep as much as he could to himself.

"You want to go shoot pool later?" Matt asked as they jogged.

"Well, I was kinda planning to go to my dad's. I've been spending so much time with you, I've hardly had any time for him." *Or Darian!*

"Oh, okay. Fine. What do you do over there? Are you still rebuilding the place? I thought the drywall and flooring was done?"

"It is."

"Then what is so exciting? You get this look in your eyes whenever you mention going there."

"I don't know. I like my dad's new girlfriend." Jimmy was kicking himself again for lying. Lying by avoidance, that is. He had it programmed in as an automatic response.

"Does this new girlfriend have a daughter you're interested in?"

"*No!*" *Please don't start with this again. Please don't start with this again.*

"Well, maybe you can help me and my dad tear the carpet out this fall. He wants to refinish the hardwood underneath."

Jimmy inwardly sighed with relief when the conversation jumped to home improvement. He in no way wanted to talk about himself. "Sure. I can do that! Me and my dad did the kitchen floor. It was fun."

"Redoing the floor was fun? Dude, you need to get out more!"

Jimmy shoved him, and Matt stumbled a few steps before recovering. The two of them laughed as they kept running, and Jimmy felt the comfort of the years between them warm him like a cup of hot chocolate on a cold winter's day.

November 25, 2006

I was with my dad over Thanksgiving this year! Oh, what a lot I have to be thankful for. He let Darian have dinner with us. I was so happy I couldn't stop smiling long enough to greet Cheryl when she got there. Darian kept touching me under the table. I know Dad knows what he was doing. How could he not? Darian is no good at keeping a poker face. He even licked his teeth a few times when he thought no one was looking. I caught my dad fighting back a laugh. I know I did!

After dinner he was helping me clear the table and practically attacked me in the kitchen. I think my dad was dead-on about "wanting to tear each other's clothes off!" Ever since we did it, I can't stop thinking about having sex again. Maybe this is why Matt is such a pig. The feeling is indescribable.

Darian makes my body explode. I don't know what it is about him, but I feel like I'm buzzing with electricity every time he has his mouth on me. His tongue sends shivers through every appendage. And I mean EVERY appendage. I seriously don't understand how I resisted his magnetic pull for two long years. I must be a moron.

I was to the point of freaking out when he dropped to the floor in front of me. I could hear my dad in the other room, and here Darian was unzipping my dress pants. He had my swelling cock practically in his mouth before I could wrestle the lower half of my body away from him.

Then my phone buzzed and killed his gusto of lusto. (Sorry, I felt the need to rhyme that!)

It was Matt. He texted: I need you.

Darian got huffy.

I don't know why I showed him the message, except that I'd told him on more than one occasion that I wanted to be completely honest with him. I did. Except for the frequency with which I thought about Matt. He didn't need to know that. It would just hurt him. I'm trying to be honest as often as I can.

"YOU are not going over to your father's again this week."

"Mom, I have to."

Joan glared at her son. "Excuse me?"

Jimmy dropped his gaze. "I mean, please, Mom, can I go to Dad's tonight? We were going to change the brakes on the Malibu." *Yeah, I know it's a lie. I only hope you buy it.*

"Since when do you want to work on cars? Auto mechanics have subservient jobs, James. You're better than that."

"Mom," he tried his darnedest not to sound argumentative, "mechanics have a respected profession, and some make really decent money."

"James, I don't care what people say about mechanics. They are lower-class citizens, workers, serfs in the greater scheme of things. *You* are not destined to be a serf. After your ridiculous outbursts cost you your scholarship, I was reluctant to even let you attend McDaniel College. It is an inferior school."

"Mom, it's not a—"

She stepped frighteningly close. Jimmy flinched. "Don't you dare interrupt me! McDaniel is not Harvard!"

He could have laughed. "There's no way I would have gotten a scholarship to Harvard. I'm not that smart. I only have straight A's because I'm afraid of what you'll do to me if I get a B." Jimmy wasn't sure where his need to defend mechanics came from, or his sudden desire to talk back to his mother, but the words were out.

He barely had a second to think before his mother came at him. She picked up the first thing her hand could grab and swung it at Jimmy. The silver candlestick connected with his upper arm. "Mom!" he screamed. "Stop!" She swung three more times, making contact with his bicep, before the phone rang and jarred her from her frenzied attack.

Jimmy sank to the floor and leaned his head against the wall. He could hear his mom's chirping laughter in the other room. He panted for a few minutes and then tried to move. His arm throbbed, and Jimmy started laughing. He wasn't amused, but he couldn't bring himself to cry. "This is my life," he whispered.

Upon inspection, there were knots forming under the skin. His bicep was turning purple. He couldn't work out with Matt until it healed. He straightened his arm out. It hurt like hell moving the muscles, but he at least knew it wasn't broken.

He spoke to his reflection in the bathroom mirror. "So much for telling Dad she'd changed. I'd rather have a belt on my ass." He hung his head. Jimmy didn't understand why his mother couldn't just be proud of him for what he was.

It was more to think about than he really had time for. He was leaving. Darian had an appointment with his psychotherapist, and

Jimmy was not going to let him down. He said he'd be there, and he would. Jimmy hoped he would get to talk to the therapist but didn't know for sure. He grabbed his keys and walked out the door.

April 28, 2007

Darian's therapist noticed my arm. I think. I tried to hide it, but she handed me a cup of water, and I think she caught a glimpse when I reached for it and winced. Stupid me for forgetting I had a bruised arm! Fuck!

I know Matt is seeing a therapist too, but I'll be damned if I need to see one. My mother is the one who needs to go. This is my therapy—writing. The school's counselor was right after all. I write what I feel, and somehow it helps.

I left Darian at Dad's and drove home. I wanted to make sure I got home before Mom flipped out again. Mom isn't here.

Hold that thought....

There was a knock on Jimmy's door. "Yeah," he answered.

"Hey, it's me." Matt poked his head in. "I stopped by earlier, and your mom didn't know where you were."

Jimmy closed his notebook. "I had to go… I went out."

Matt pointed to Jimmy's notebook as he neared the desk. "You think you might ever read me something out of that?"

Jimmy tried to grin. "Yeah, maybe, if you're a good little boy."

"Someone once told me never to write anything down you didn't want someone else to read."

"Yeah, well, we'll see. I told you maybe, if you're good."

Matt sat on the edge of the bed. "You okay? You didn't answer my texts."

Jimmy looked confused. He reached into his pocket and retrieved his phone. "Battery died. I forgot to plug it in last night."

"What the fuck?" Matt exclaimed. He reached for Jimmy's arm and pulled up the shirtsleeve. Jimmy winced. "What happened to you?"

"My sadistic, schizophrenic mother." Jimmy waved off the seriousness.

"Jamie… you need to put ice on that!" Matt headed to the door.

"Matt, I don't…." He stopped protesting when it was clear Matt wasn't listening. He left the room and returned moments later with a Baggie full of ice.

"Come here." He waved Jimmy over to the bed. "Lie down."

"Matt, I don't need—"

"Shut up and listen to me!"

When Jimmy complied, Matt had him lie on his side. He propped his wounded arm up with a pillow and placed the bag of ice on the welts.

"Ow, shit, be careful!"

"It wouldn't be so painful if you put ice on it right away and didn't let the welts get so large. Dumbass." Matt fussed and smacked him on the top of his head. Once the bag of ice was sitting so it wouldn't slide back off, Matt sat on the bed next to Jimmy. He didn't say anything. He simply feathered his fingers through Jimmy's hair.

Jimmy closed his eyes. He loved the tenderness Matt possessed. He longed for each moment like this where Matt would touch him. It didn't have to be sexual. Jimmy liked the affection.

"I've been worried about you," Matt whispered.

Jimmy's eyes shot open. "Me?" he asked, as if the whole notion was absurd.

"Yeah, you've been so distracted lately. Like with your phone." Matt continued to touch his hair as he talked. Jimmy closed his eyes again. "It's not like you to forget to charge it. It's our link. I've known you to text me at two in the morning."

"Hey, you do it too," Jimmy grumbled.

"Exactly. Where've you been, lately? You're hardly around, and even when you are it's like your mind is somewhere else. Are you okay, Jamie? Is something wrong with your dad? Or—"

"James?"

Jimmy jumped. "Shit!" He mouthed. "She can't find you in here," he whispered to Matt.

Matt knew the drill. Jimmy wasn't allowed company unless he asked first. Matt flipped off the bed and landed flat on the floor.

"Yeah, Mom?" Jimmy answered back.

Matt was successfully hidden under the bed by the time the door opened.

"I was wondering if you were hungry, dear?" She entered the room and sat next to him on the bed. Jimmy tried not to flinch when she reached toward his face. Her fingers caressed his jaw. "Oh, James, you're not fighting again, are you?"

Jimmy shook his head. "No, mom. I, um, fell. There was a stump, and I landed on it. I'll be fine." He forced a smile.

"If you're sure. I'll be in the kitchen if you need anything." She patted his head and left the room without another word.

Jimmy waited another minute and then signaled to Matt all was clear. "Pst! You can come out."

"Dude, I haven't been under your bed in years. I don't think I can do that again. I was so squished I could barely breathe." Matt flopped onto the bed, huffing for air.

"I hope you won't have to. Thanks."

Matt smiled. "Anything for you, buddy. So, your mom really doesn't remember, does she?"

"Either that or she really is schizo. I know something's wrong with her. I've known for a while." Jimmy lay back down and resituated the ice.

Matt pivoted around so he was lying facing Jimmy. "I never believed you until now. But she's all nice one moment and flipping out the next. I guess there'd have to be something wrong. Can't you tell your stepdad?"

"I thought about it. I'm not sure he'd believe me. He knows I fight. Mom has never done something this bad before. I don't want to cause problems. My mom already had one divorce. I can't make waves and cause another."

"But Jamie, she hit you with a blunt object. That's physical abuse. She shouldn't be allowed to hurt you."

"Matt, think about it. If I say something, they may take her away. What would Kevin do? Little kids and a baby? And *me*, the outcast son who condemned her to jail time."

"They wouldn't put her in jail, Jamie. She'd probably have to go…"

They looked at each other. "… *See a therapist*…." Jimmy and Matt finished the sentence at the same time and then started laughing.

"I think the whole fuckin' world needs therapy," Jimmy said when the giggle fit subsided.

"Probably," Matt agreed.

They fell asleep together, thinking about how fucked up the population of the world really was.

April 29

Matt was here last night. Where was I?

I wish I knew what the therapist talked to Darian about—other than his addiction to prescription drugs. He was really shaken up, but he didn't want to talk about it. I'll wait. I know how much a therapist helped Matt. I only hope it can have the same positive effect on Darian.

Last night was the first time I was thankful my mom came home. I KNOW Matt wanted to talk more about what was going on with ME, and I could not very well tell him about Darian and his problems. I feel like I've been so fractured lately. I keep everything in neat little boxes, and spilling my world with Darian into Matt's box would somehow make it harder to deal with. Him not knowing is easier right now. Matt has enough on his mind than finding out the truth about me.

In some ways my lies have become routine. When I leave my dad's, that world stays there, and I shift back to the me I am with Matt. Same thing happens when I leave my mom's and visit Darian. I guess my dad is the link in the middle because he knows about both sides. That doesn't matter. I trust him. I know he won't tell anyone I'm gay until I agree, and I also know he wants nothing to do with my mom and her craziness.

Worlds are safely separate. I like it like that. I need that.

21

September 23, 2010

10:15 p.m.

"DARIAN." Matt opened the door like he'd fully expected to see Darian show up after the viewing ended, and Darian did not disappoint as he practically fell through the open door into Matt's arms. Matt pulled him close and held him.

Darian started sobbing. Again. Matt allowed him the time he needed and tried to soothe him as best he could with hushed tones in his ear as he slowly rubbed his back. "Shhh, it's okay. I'm here. You'll be all right." It hurt like hell to hear him crying, but Matt was not going to rush to do anything that Darian didn't want or need. He was going to be the anti-Matt. Like Jason said. *Not* the sleaze ball who only thought of sex. Darian's heart was obviously broken, and he didn't need any more pressure from Matt.

Without warning, Darian stepped back and pleaded, "Please, fuck me."

"W-what?" Matt sputtered. *Yes,* he wanted sex, but not like this.

"Fuck me. I need you, Matt. I need you to make the pain go away. I need to feel… something. Anything. You know how to make me feel so good. You blow my mind. I need you inside me. I need this feeling to end. Please? Fuck me so hard I can't think straight."

For a second, Matt thought the offer sounded great. What more did he need for his ego? *I blow his mind?* There was nothing better to hear than how great you were in bed. But after the second passed, Matt realized it was something the *old* Matt would go for. The sex-pig, pig-in-the-making really, could easily fuck Darian into next Sunday and not have to think twice about it. But that was the old Matt.

Darian was worth way more. Even if Matt wasn't sure of his own feelings, he was very sure that Darian was not a guy he should screw over. If for no other reason than out of respect for Jamie!

"No," Matt said quietly.

Darian's shoulders slumped, and his arms started quaking. His eyes conveyed to Matt his slim grip on sanity. Matt could plainly see his pain was deep and his desperation was escalating by the second. He grabbed Matt's shirt in his fists and begged. "Matt, please? You don't understand how much this hurts. I need you to fuck me, please."

Matt took a hold of his fists and looked into his red-rimmed eyes. "No, Darian. I'm not going to fuck you. I know what you need, and that's not it."

"But, I...." Darian was at a loss for words.

"Do you trust me?"

"Yes."

Darian's quiet affirmation was all Matt needed. He smiled warmly and lifted his hands to Darian's chin, pulling it gently to guide him into a kiss. Darian tried to jump at him, but Matt held him in place and only gave a small taste of his lips. "Shhh, stop. If you trust me, then do as I say. Okay?"

Darian nodded, breathing hard and shaking in Matt's hands.

Matt caressed his cheek. Now was the moment to put everything he'd read into motion. His talk with Jason, his exploration of the topic of "romance" on the web, everything he'd researched in scant hours was about to be put to the test. Darian didn't need a *fix* like a drug addict; he needed healing. Matt also knew healing would take much longer than what he could do tonight, but this was a start.

"Come with me," he beckoned, taking Darian's hand and leading him to the bedroom. After they entered the room, he closed the door. He unbuttoned Darian's shirt and leaned in to kiss his neck.

"I thought you said we weren't going to fuck." He was confused but also on the verge of whimpering. Darian sucked in a breath and tilted his head back, giving Matt more access.

"No, I said I wasn't going to fuck you," Matt replied, between kisses. "I'm not." He pushed Darian's shirt over his shoulders and down Darian's arms. Matt caressed Darian's bare chest and looked at him seductively. "I'm going to make love to you." He went back to kissing Darian's neck.

Darian sighed. His moved his hands up to grip Matt's arms. "There's a difference?"

Matt nibbled on Darian's ear. "Oh, there's a difference. Especially if you know me like I think you do, like I think Jamie did. I'm not treating you like somebody to use and discard." He kissed his way down Darian's neck and lapped his pierced nipple. "The potential of this relationship means more to me than a quick fuck, and I am going to prove it to you." He stopped licking and stepped back. "Take off your pants and lay on the bed…. Please." He winked, lightening the mood.

Suddenly things were getting very serious, and Matt didn't want Darian to think he didn't have any choice in the matter. This wasn't an S&M parlor. Matt didn't have a whip, and he wasn't about to go all Dom on poor Darian. Matt walked over to the dresser and lit the candles he'd bought on the way home. He wasn't sure what scent they were supposed to be, but he hoped they wouldn't stink up the place. He pushed play on his iPod and adjusted the speakers.

Perfect.

He turned around.

Correction, perfection was lying in his bed. Darian was beautiful in the candlelight, and Matt gasped. Golden shadows splayed across his milky white skin and danced as the flames flickered. Matt pulled his T-shirt off over his head. *Slow, take this slow*, he reminded himself. *It's not a race.* Then he shed his sweats.

Once undressed, he crawled onto the bed like a hunting cat admiring the prey he was going to devour after hours of play. Only, this wasn't play, this was a personal test to see if he could change for someone he was starting to care about. He started by lying next to

Darian and leaning against his side, kissing his neck. He caressed his chest and ribs, trying very hard not to tickle him, and then pinched his nipple. Just the feel of Darian's nipple getting hard between his finger and thumb was enough to make his own dick scream for some attention. He ignored it. For now. This was for Darian, not him. Well, it *was* for him too, but this time he was not going to think of his own pleasure over his lover's. The anti-Matt needed to make sure Darian was satisfied first. More than satisfied: satiated, quenched, and fully gratified. He moved his mouth to the small gold hoop.

Darian moaned and arched his back, lifting his chest toward Matt's mouth. Matt could not hold back a chuckle. He sucked on the ring and swirled his tongue around until he made Darian moan louder. Darian groaned deeply and reached for his erection. Matt stopped his hand. "No. Not yet. Just relax and let me take care of you."

"I'm so hard, Matt. I need to cum so bad. Pleeeease...."

Matt felt bad because he sounded so pitiful, and the sound of Darian's begging also made it nearly impossible for Matt to keep his dick in check. He took Darian's wrist and placed it above his head. "Relax. I promise to take care of you." He glanced down at Darian's swelled cock and then back up to his eyes. "*All* of you." He winked.

Darian made all sorts of guttural sounds.

Matt knew he had to make good on his promise. He moved over Darian and straddled his waist. Slowly, he kissed and licked his way down Darian's body. He nibbled his nipples and sucked the skin of his stomach. He dipped his tongue into Darian's belly button and licked his piercing. All the while, his body slid further down Darian's, pressing his abs and chest against Darian's very hard, pulsing shaft. Darian squirmed.

As he moved lower, Matt lapped up the pre-cum that gathered at the edge of Darian's neatly trimmed pubic hair. Matt noticed how nice Darian smelled and how his balls were cleanly shaven. *Did Darian plan this ahead of time?* Maybe that's why he took so long to get to Matt's house after the viewing. Did Darian plan a fuck marathon? Did he plan to be used? Or did he always shave his balls?

Matt would not give in. He was more determined than ever to show *this* boy, *this* young man, just how much pleasure he could bestow *without* ramming him like a jackhammer. Darian already knew he was a talented jackhammer! What Darian didn't know was that Matt could also slow things down and simply enjoy the taste of Darian's skin. (Granted, Matt was new to this experience too, but he was trying to make it *seem* like he had talents Darian knew nothing about.)

Matt nuzzled Darian's ball sack and slipped his tongue underneath, flicking it teasingly. Darian squirmed more and moaned louder.

"Oh, Matt, yes," he rasped.

With his hands, Matt massaged Darian's hips and upper thighs. With his nose, he pushed Darian's balls up so he could lick the tender skin beneath. He breathed in deeply. Darian smelled so good. Matt could smell his manly musk, just beneath the lingering scent of soap. He licked more aggressively with the flat of his tongue, from just above Darian's anus to as much of his sack as he could swipe with one lick.

Darian's impatient grunting told him he should stop teasing.

Matt took Darian's testicles into his mouth and suckled while he gripped Darian's shaft in one hand and pumped slowly. Matt felt Darian curl one leg around him. He rubbed Matt's backside with his foot. Matt shivered with enjoyment. Then Darian started tilting his groin up to meet Matt's pumping fist. Going slow was proving very difficult.

Letting Darian's balls slide back out of his mouth, Matt decided it was time to move this along. He could get Darian off and then keep giving him a thorough loving until he was hard again. No one said making love meant you only got to cum once! This was going to be a multiple-orgasm extravaganza.

Matt lifted Darian's oozing head to his lips and tasted. The salty sweetness made him groan with his own need. Suddenly *slow* was too slow. He engulfed Darian in one plunge, the head hitting the back of Matt's throat. Darian's hips bucked. Matt maneuvered himself so he had a better angle, shifting to the side and allowing the natural curve of Darian's cock to slide in without hitting his teeth. He worked his tongue and sucked hard, causing Darian to cry out his name. Matt reveled in that! Darian's fingers found the short, buzzed hair of his scalp and tugged.

For a second, Matt's brain flashed to the past. He squeezed his eyes shut, forcing the images away. Darian's labored breathing aided Matt in holding to the present. Darian's hands were on him. Darian's legs were around him. Darian's taste was on his tongue. Matt clung to the lover in his arms, and the past floated away from his mind as quickly as it appeared.

Matt knew Darian was close. Darian's quick gasps for breath intermixed with whimpers of delight had Matt on the verge of coming as well. He sucked hard as he wet his fingers with the ample amounts of saliva gathering at the base of Darian's cock and worked them toward Darian's crack. Intuitively, Darian spread his legs wider, allowing Matt all the access he needed. As soon as Matt's two fingers eased into Darian's body, he came. Matt swallowed while he ground his hips into the bed, assisting him over the edge and all over the sheets.

Darian panted and relaxed, his body liquid bones on the mattress.

Matt lifted his head to gaze at his beautifully sated lover. He grinned, knowing this was only the beginning.

"That was amazing," Darian said lazily, barely able to keep his eyes open.

"Don't get sleepy on me yet, I'm not done." Matt kissed across his stomach and urged Darian to roll over.

Matt knelt over him, kissing and licking his back and neck. He rubbed his groin over Darian's rounded cheeks before easing his way down to engage in their next activity. Rimming. Matt massaged Darian's ass and thighs while he kissed and nibbled his lower back. Once he was nestled again between Darian's legs, he spread his cheeks and dipped his tongue in for a taste. Darian's pucker was slightly salty and slightly soapy, as well as cleanly shaven. He lapped again. The ring of muscle relaxed for him, which made him grin and urged him on.

Yesterday's rim-job is gonna be like a tease compared to this one. I'm givin' it to you good this time!

Matt kissed it, fully engaging his lips and tongue, as if he would make love to this orifice with his mouth alone. His thumbs opened Darian wider, and Matt pushed his tongue in as far as it would go.

"Oh, Matt," Darian groaned, pushing himself back, beckoning Matt for more.

Matt fucked that hole with his tongue for as long as his body could stand. Every time Darian twitched, the muscle under Matt's tongue pulsed. *God, I love this.* The skin was so smooth and tender, and extremely sensitive, if Darian's moaning was any indication. As he'd confessed earlier to Darian, he'd never done this to a guy before. He'd watched a few times. He'd been offered a rim-job, but never accepted.

For once I'm glad to have a first experience. One that Darian and I can explore together. He's making this just as much fun for me.

Matt squeezed and rubbed the back of Darian's thighs. He swirled his tongue and sucked Darian's salty essence until his cock ached for attention. He had to stop. As much as he loved making Darian come unglued by lapping at his anus, Matt's need was beyond the breaking point. He seriously was not about to cum on the sheets *again*. He needed Darian's sweet ass—that taut, beautiful ass—milking the cum out of him! He took one last long lick and moved back, grasping Darian's hip and tugging gently.

"Up on your knees, baby."

Darian complied without hesitation.

Matt was knocking on his back door before he had the chance to say a word. Darian's entrance was well lubed with saliva and well prepped. Matt slid home easily. He held himself there, fully embedded, gripping Darian's hips, and concentrated. A few deep breaths helped him steady himself.

"Matt, please," Darian begged. "I need to feel you move."

Matt cherished his begging. He rubbed Darian's back and buttocks lovingly. "I know, baby, I know. I need a minute. I don't want to cum in one thrust." When the surging in his balls subsided, he began to move. He slid his dick almost fully out and then back in. Darian's hole squeezing him made it difficult to go slow. He loved the feel of this ass. This luscious, perfect ass that he still tasted on his tongue. He threw his head back and went with his passion, gripping Darian's hips tightly and ramming him with all he had.

Darian's deep grunts of pleasure told Matt this was what they both wanted. His balls slapped wildly against Darian's thighs, and the bed squeaked. Matt was ruthless in those last few strokes, diving deep and pushing hard. He slapped Darian's cheek with a loud *thwack!* just before he came, growling his immense pleasure from deep within his throat, loud and long, drowning out his exceptionally vocal lover.

Matt held onto Darian as he slumped forward and rolled them to their sides. Still inside him, Matt wrapped his arms around Darian and breathed heavily into his ear. "Was that good for you, baby?"

"God, yes," Darian panted, holding the arms that held him.

Matt kissed his neck. "I told you I'd take care of you."

"You did."

He licked and nibbled Darian, satisfied with himself for successfully loving this young man with every ounce of passion he had, and still wanting to lie here with him afterward. He was truly a different Matthias Dixon. Darian was the motive for change, and this night proved to Matt he was able to be a different man. If he only had the omniscience to know if this "new self" would stick around for a while!

"Are you going to trust me now?"

"I'll try."

"Good." Matt had expected a "yes" in reply but appreciated the honesty in "I'll try."

When his dick softened enough to slide out of Darian's body, Matt reached down to remove the condom. Suddenly realizing his cock was bare, he swore, "Shit."

"What?" Darian asked, craning his neck to look at Matt.

Matt rolled onto his back and covered his face briefly with one hand, rubbing his eyes out of frustration. "I can't believe I did that. I never do that."

"What?" Darian sounded more concerned and rolled over. "What's wrong?"

Matt looked at Darian. "I... I wasn't wearing a condom." He tried to look sorry. He was. He sincerely tried to convey to Darian in his voice and expression that he was not giving him a line when he said, "I completely forgot. I was so caught up in how good it felt to make love with you that I didn't even reach for one. I swear I never do that. I *always* play it safe."

Darian didn't say anything. He lay on his back and stared at the ceiling.

"Darian, I swear, I have not had unprotected sex." That would have been a great way to leave it but Matt had to add, "That I can remember."

Darian looked at him. "That you can remember? That's not very reassuring."

Matt leaned over him and laid his hand on Darian's stomach. "I swear, baby, I didn't mean to screw up. I was so into loving on you, it never crossed my mind to grab a condom. I wanted just to feel you. Skin on skin. Heat on heat." He moved in for a kiss. "Please forgive me?"

Darian didn't return the kiss. He lay there, unblinking and quiet. "When were you last tested?"

Matt continued to caress his skin. "July 18th. I was clean."

"And when was your last hook-up?"

"Two weeks ago."

"Was he the only one?"

Matt hung his head. He couldn't look at Darian with his next reply. "No. I've had four different guys since July."

"Great." He started to roll off the bed. "I guess I'll be the fifth and leave now before—"

Matt grabbed him. "Please don't go. Darian. Please."

Darian didn't try to get away. He allowed Matt to pull him back into an embrace.

"Please believe me, I didn't mean to endanger you in any way. I'm sure I'm clean. I have to be. I'll get tested again."

"Promise?"

Matt was relieved Darian wasn't fuming—*he* sure would be—but he was obviously not thrilled either. "Promise. And I'll make sure I wear a condom every time until then."

"Every time? I thought Matt Dixon didn't do guys more than once," Darian jibed.

"This is the new me." He smiled down at his lover, their bodies pressed together. "And if you're looking for monogamy, I guess I can give it a shot. If I know Jamie, he only gave himself to you."

Darian nodded.

"And I did pretty good with the romantic stuff, right?"

Darian grinned. "Uh-huh. Real nice. Very romantic."

"I was, wasn't I?" *I owe Jason big time for that one!* He rubbed his nose over Darian's before he kissed him. Then he kissed him again, and again. How could he have avoided kissing for so long? It was amazing! Their tongues dueled. "Darian, I am so sorry. I've never had to think so much before."

"How hard is it to wear a condom?"

Matt moved back and rubbed his head, ashamed. "I know, I know. I wasn't thinking. I was all caught up in how I feel about you and how *new* everything is that I simply didn't think about a condom." He rolled over and got out of bed. Once he turned on the lights, Matt pleaded, "I have no excuses. I lost my head when I fell in love with you." Matt froze. *Did I just say that?* "I mean, when we hooked up the other day and…."

First Jamie gets in my head, and now fuckin' Jason. Damn! I'm screwed.

There was no use finishing his sentence when it was clear as day Darian heard what he'd just said. His face was extremely serious.

Matt paused before back-pedaling. "Darian, I don't know why I just said—"

"You love me?"

Matt shrugged. "I guess so. Maybe." He knew that sounded weak. "I mean… I've never felt like this before, so…." He tried not to look at Darian. He studied the dingy carpet instead. When Darian's feet stepped into his field of vision, Matt looked back up into Darian's waiting eyes.

"What do you feel?" Curiosity hung in the air.

Matt was thankful Darian didn't walk out, except now he had to explain himself. "I feel jittery."

"Oh, then it's gotta be love." Darian shook his head and turned away.

Matt knew sarcasm when he heard it. He grabbed Darian's elbow and pulled him into his arms. Darian's hands were smashed to his chest, and his face was very close to Matt's. "I'm not letting you walk out," he asserted. "You make me feel sick."

"Oh, that's so much better."

"Let. Me. Finish." He was getting angry at this point. Didn't Darian understand how hard it was to put his feelings into words? "From the first moment I kissed you yesterday, next to that house, I've felt all mixed up. My insides are jumping, and I can't eat. You're all I think about. And that was *before* I knew who you were. It was all in that first kiss. Everything inside of me scrambled to figure out what was going on, but my heart just kept falling. I don't understand what it is about you, but I bet Jamie did. I bet he felt the same magnetic energy pulling him into an abyss of full-on helplessness, and he just gave in because he had no choice but to love you.

"It's the way you touch me, Darian, and the way you look at me, and the way my body can't get enough of you. So, yeah... I'm jittery and I feel sick, but it's because everything inside of me is screaming when not I'm holding you in my arms. I've never felt so out of control in my life. It scares the hell out of me that, if I let go, you'll disappear forever and take my last link to Jamie with you."

Darian listened, but Matt could not read his face. Then he was leaning in and resting his face on the side of Matt's neck. He wasn't crying. He wasn't talking. Darian was merely resting his body against Matt's. Perhaps he was thinking about everything Matt said? Perhaps he was considering the possibilities? Perhaps?

Matt touched his face to Darian's hair and held him for what seemed like hours.

Darian finally pulled away and suggested sleep. Matt complied without question. In the night their bodies wound together, arms and legs entangled.

Comfortable. Content. Quiet.

22

May 19, 2008

"ARE you sure you want *me* to go with you?" Jimmy asked. He juggled the cell phone on his shoulder while he rinsed the fish off in his dad's sink. Darian would be home from work soon, and Jimmy wanted to surprise him with one of his favorite meals.

"Yeah, Jamie. I don't have a woman. I am sure as fuck not taking a *guy*. You can be my date," Matt answered.

"Oh, because I'm not a woman *or* a guy." He placed the fish in a pan.

Matt chuckled on the other end. "You know what I mean. The guys at the station will like you. You're funny, smart, and normal. *Normal* being the pertinent term. I want them to know I have friends they can hang with. It's important to me."

"Fine, I'll go. When is it?"

"The last Sunday of the month."

"Oh, wait, I can't. That's my dad's family reunion cookout thingy."

"I thought you said that was next weekend?"

"It is."

"Oh, wait a minute. What month is this? I meant the last Sunday of June. They're having a sort of pre-celebration for the Fourth. A warm up. You should like it. They're shooting off illegal fireworks."

Jimmy was relieved. Even though he was slightly intimidated at having to meet a bunch of firefighters, he really wanted to go. "Cool. I'll be there!"

"Awesome! Thanks, buddy."

June 29, 2008

If I get hard being around a bunch of hot firefighters, I will die. Fingers crossed I make it through today!

JIMMY met Matt at the end of the driveway. "Nice truck! New?"

Matt smiled. "Yup! Just got it yesterday. I wanted to surprise you."

"Nice! I like the color," Jimmy got in.

"I was *going* to choose red but thought it'd be too flashy. Silver seemed perfect." Matt put it in drive and pulled away from Jimmy's house.

"I got something too," Jimmy said, holding out his wrist.

Matt glanced and did a double take. "No shit! You finally got a tattoo! You've been talking about doing it for years. I thought you'd never go through with it. When'd you get it?"

"A month ago."

"What? Where have I been?"

"Duh, working. I ran by myself more times in the past few weeks than I care to mention."

"Yeah, sorry, it sucks. Crappy shifts for new guys. Fires happen at all times of the night, somebody has to stand ready. I'll be switched to day shift soon. Sorry about not being around much."

"I worry sometimes, but it's okay as long as you're fine. When we don't text and call continuously, it makes me feel like things are back to normal. Ya know? We used to do that in high school, but now that you work all the time and I have college, time slips by."

"I know what you mean." Matt paused. He made the next turn and looked over at Jimmy. "I've been good, Jamie. No nightmares. No freaking out when people touch me. I'm good."

"You sure?"

He grinned at his friend. "Yeah. You've seen to that. I don't know what I would do without you."

"Have you been out lately? I've missed hearing stories."

"No. Nightshifts don't work well with clubbing. It's fine. Gives me time to think. Who needs to go out anyway?"

Jimmy nodded. He followed Matt's logic but also read between the lines. "You're looking at Internet porn, aren't you?"

Matt smiled. "I can't fool you a bit, can I?"

They shared a laugh and soon ended up at the party.

They walked across the front yard of the house and around the back, through a gate in the chain-link fence. Matt led Jimmy up to a thin gentleman flipping burgers on a grill. "Jason, this is Jimmy."

Jason extended his hand and shook Jimmy's. "Ah-ha! The best friend. Great to meet you. Matt talks about you all the time."

"Good things, I hope."

Jason's eyes twinkled. "Let's just say, if Mother Teresa didn't have the market on saintliness, you could take her job."

Jimmy's jaw went slack, and he rolled his head in Matt's direction. "I'm gonna kill you."

Matt just grinned. "Hey, I call 'em like I see 'em!"

"Listen, can you watch the burgers?" Jason asked. "I need to go get the cheese from the fridge and another beer."

Matt shrugged. "Sure." He took the spatula from Jason and watched him walk away.

"You like him, don't you?" Jimmy keenly observed Matt's careful study of his friend's posterior.

"He's fuckin' hot!" Matt spoke quietly but did not refute Jimmy's observation. "And married."

"And black."

"So?" Matt snapped.

Jimmy wasn't sure why Matt would cop an attitude. "Ah, your dad… remember? He used to have this thing against bla—"

"Ohhh!" Matt waved the spatula at Jimmy when the lights went on. "Yeah, dude, that was *years* ago! Dad got over his prejudices when he met a black guy at work. Dude was a self-made… well, not millionaire, but close. Dad said his opinions were from growing up in the city. This guy was different. Made Dad think about being closed-minded. Not every black guy sponges off the government, just like not every white guy is an intolerant bigot."

Jimmy laughed. "I can't see your dad as an intolerant bigot."

"Me neither, but I'm not about to test the theory."

"Oh, well, I wasn't suggesting you come out or anything."

Matt put his hand on Jimmy's shoulder. "I know, Jamie. I've been thinking a lot lately. The therapist really knows how to throw things at you that you don't want to face. She said I should talk to my folks. She said it would free up the tension I have over being gay and not sharing it with anyone." He heaved a sigh. "I really hate my therapist."

"No you don't."

"No, I don't."

Jason returned, cheese in hand. "Thanks. They're throwing horseshoes on the other side of the house. I'll take over flipping burgers. You go and have some fun!"

Matt looked at Jimmy. "You still a ringer?"

Jimmy raised an eyebrow. "Are you fuckin' kidding me? Let's go kick some ass."

Jimmy and Matt won two out of three rounds before someone's wife came up with another game she wanted to try. Somewhere between eating three hamburgers and drinking four Dr Peppers, Jimmy was buzzing with enthusiasm and willing to try anything. "Anything" turned out to be Pin the Tail on the Donkey, only with tiny paper fire hoses, and the "donkey" was Tim's sleazy girlfriend's behind.

Jimmy laughed as he removed the blindfold and found he'd pinned the fire hose on her lower back.

"Who's next?" Anna asked. "Jason?"

"No, Sugar. The only ass I plan on getting near is yours." Jason winked and put his arms around his wife.

"Okay. How about you, Matt?" she asked, holding out a paper fire hose.

"No. That's okay. I'll pass." Matt waved her off.

"Oh, come on, Matt," Jason urged. "You're one of the last guys left."

"I don't want to."

Another coworker, Bob, stepped up to Matt and slapped him on the back. Jimmy saw him flinch. "Come on. It's just a silly game."

"I don't bite," the willing target teased.

Matt looked from her to Jason to Bob and shook his head nervously.

His gut told Jimmy this was not something Matt felt comfortable doing. "He doesn't want to, guys," Jimmy said.

Another guy shouted, "Come on Matt, hose her ass!"

The comment spurred on chanting from the group. "Hose her ass! Hose her ass! Hose her ass!"

Some woman, whose name Jimmy could not remember, came up behind Matt and slid a blindfold over his eyes. She'd tied it beforehand, and it fit his head perfectly, if not a little snug.

Suddenly, Matt swatted his hands around his head like bees were attacking him. "Get it off! Get it off!" he shouted. When one finger finally hooked under the edge of the fabric, he tugged the blindfold off and flung it away.

He glanced frantically around the shocked onlookers. Jimmy could see the growing panic in Matt's eyes at his inexplicable outburst. Matt started breathing harder and then bolted. Jimmy exchanged looks with Jason and then took off after Matt. He rounded the corner of the house to see Matt speed off in his truck.

Jimmy watched him disappear and turned back to see Jason following him to the street. "I guess I need to catch a ride with someone."

Jason reached into his pocket. He tossed Jimmy a set of keys. "Mine's the black Corolla, right over there. Make sure he's okay."

Jimmy caught the keys. "Thanks." He ran off and jumped in the car. He wasn't sure where Matt might be going, but he hoped if he drove fast enough, he'd catch up. He caught taillights through some trees, which meant Matt had turned right. He heard the distinct sound of a V-8 and looked left just as Matt's truck made another turn through the development's winding streets. *He's not heading home.*

Jimmy didn't even stop at the next few signs. He did a quick check to see if cars were around but barely bothered to slow down. If a cop was anywhere in sight, he'd be ticketed for sure! He didn't care; he needed to catch up to his friend.

Finally, they came to a major road, and Jimmy could put the pedal to the floor. In no time he was right behind Matt's truck and following it into the parking lot of the community pond.

"What?" This was a peculiar destination, but he followed nonetheless. Matt was already out of his vehicle and walking over to some picnic tables when Jimmy pulled up. He turned off the engine and jogged over to his friend. Matt was sitting facing the trees along the edge of the park, not the scenic pond and gardens like most folks would. Jimmy approached cautiously. "Matt?" No response. He knew Matt could hear him. He reached out and touched Matt's shoulder. Matt flinched away from Jimmy's touch.

"I thought I was over this," Matt mumbled. "I thought I'd dealt with all the shit that guy did to me, but I was wrong. Way wrong." Matt bent forward and supported his face with his elbows perched on his knees.

Jimmy walked around and took a seat next to him. He wasn't sure what he could say to make this any easier on Matt, so he waited quietly.

After several minutes, Matt spoke toward the ground in front of him without changing his position. "That blindfold brought everything flooding back. The spreader bar, the wrist restraints, and whatever the hell the guy clamped onto my scrotum; it all flashed through my mind like it was yesterday." He looked up and pleaded with his eyes. "I could feel it all, Jamie. I could fuckin' feel every twinge of pleasure and pain and remember how fuckin' scared I was. I've seen some kinky shit.

I've tried a few things before, and it was all fun. I didn't know some guys got off on doing stuff that the other guy didn't want. I didn't think when I said, 'No, I don't want to,' that my hook-up would see it as a turn-on and force me."

Jimmy could not think of anything to say. He couldn't make it better with a word or two. It was a painful realization that Matt suffered this way, and Jimmy couldn't remove his pain. He scooted closer and draped his arm over Matt's shoulders.

Matt leaned in. Matt took his other hand between his, and Jimmy squeezed his fingers. They sat in silence until Matt pulled back and rubbed the side of his neck. "Sorry, that position was killing me."

Jimmy returned a smile.

"I don't know what I'd do without you," Matt said.

"Don't worry, I'm not going anywhere."

"Really? I thought you were moving out?"

Matt's question caught Jimmy off guard. "What? Where'd you hear that?"

"Your mom talked to my mom."

"You should know by now never to take what she says for real."

"I figured, but my mom seemed convinced."

Jimmy shook his head. "No. I said I wanted to stay at Dad's more, and she accused me of moving out. She said I was an ungrateful little brat and I was taking advantage of Kevin's generosity in paying for college."

"But I thought you went for free because he's the history professor?"

"I do."

"Your mom's a freak."

"Don't I know it! I'm not moving out. I'm not that stupid. But I also don't see the point of visiting my dad *only* on weekends. I won't be a teenager much longer. I should be able to sleep wherever I want."

Matt smirked.

"What?" Jimmy felt inexplicably defensive.

"Your mom still pay all your bills?"

"Yeah."

"And feed you and buy your clothes and shit?"

Jimmy saw the direction Matt was headed. He narrowed his eyes. "Yeeaaahhh."

"And you don't have a job."

"Okay, okay, I get your point."

Matt held up his hands. "I'm just trying to point out that you haven't exactly moved forward in the 'independent adult' department. You've been a suck-up for years, Jamie. I don't see her letting go of you easily. She pays for everything, so she probably feels like you owe her."

Jimmy felt attacked. "Hey! When did this conversation suddenly become about me? I can't help that my mom offers to pay for things. I can't help that she'd rather me not work so I can help with my siblings and do stuff around the house."

"No. But you also think you should be able to do what you want, like stay at your dad's. You can't. She's seen to that. Jamie, your mom plays victim with everyone she knows. My mom has a hard time with it, but luckily she can blame my dad for her not always following along with Joan, and Joan believes it. Your mom's an A-class manipulator."

Jimmy huffed, but he couldn't argue. "She is, isn't she? Shit. Well… like it or not, I'm sleeping at my dad's a couple times a week. She's just going to have to get used to it."

"I hope it's that easy for you. After college, are you moving out of her house?"

"Yeah. I can't take living there."

"Then why do you put up with it now?" Matt asked. "How do you take her shit and follow her rules? Does an accounting degree really make that much of a difference?"

"It's not the degree."

"Then what? What keeps you there under the rule of Hitler's wife?"

Jimmy closed his eyes. He'd never come clean before on his reasons for trying to please her all these years. He took a deep breath and got it off his chest. "I want her to be proud of me."

Matt nodded. He patted Jimmy's knee. "I get that. I'm here for you, man. Anytime." He turned his hand over on Jimmy's leg and Jimmy took it, clamping his hand onto Matt's.

"Thanks."

"But seriously, you're gonna have to face this shit sooner or later. She's got rage issues. When you move out, you have to talk to her."

He nodded. "I know."

Matt stretched. "I feel better. How about you?"

Jimmy grinned. "I think I'll be all right. I got you."

Matt held up his fist, aiming his knuckles at Jimmy. "Bestest friends?"

Jimmy beamed. "Bestest friends!" They bumped knuckles right before hugging. It was the longest hug they'd shared in years.

23

May 24, 2008

"HEY boys, where have you been? We need to leave in fifteen minutes." Dan Miller placed the foldable chairs by the door just as Jimmy and Darian were coming in.

"Sorry, Dad," Jimmy replied. "We were having a hard time deciding on what to get."

"Get?" He placed a small cooler next to the chairs.

"Yeah, to celebrate," Darian said.

Mr. Miller scratched his head. "Did I miss something?"

Jimmy shook his head and chuckled. "Dad, Darian's been clean for one year. No drugs. So we got matching tattoos." He held out his arm. "See?"

Darian held his out next to Jimmy's, and Mr. Miller inspected their freshly inked skin. "Oh, nice—spiders."

"Black widows, Dad," Jimmy chided. "See this bit on its back? We go back next week to have the red filled in."

"I can't say I'm thrilled about you boys getting tattoos. You know they're permanent. What happens if a future employer doesn't approve? Especially you, Jimmy; accountants don't tend to sport tattoos."

"Ah, but here's the beauty!" Jimmy reached in his pocket and took out his watch. He laid it over his wrist and threaded the leather band through the clasp. "Ta-da!" He flipped his wrist back over. "The spider is small enough to fit under my watchband! We did that on purpose. Darian normally wears a really wide band anyway, so no one would see his if he wore it on that wrist. We decided to go with a small black widow—since they're my favorite spider—and position it where it can be hidden if it needs to be."

"Thinking ahead, I like that." His dad patted Jimmy on the shoulder.

Darian added, "I figured I already had to lose the eyeliner for work, and I have to remove my lip ring when the assistant manager is on duty. I didn't need any more flack about my 'unprofessional' appearance."

Dan reached over and squeezed Darian's shoulder. "Sometimes these small sacrifices are worth it, especially when you get a raise."

Darian's eyes lit up. "Then Jamie told you?"

"About the raise? Yes. Congratulations."

"Thanks, Mr. Miller."

"I told you, call me Dad."

"Okay… Dad." Darian grinned sheepishly and dipped his head.

"But that sounds like we're brothers, which we're not," Jimmy argued.

"No, no, no…. Not in the incestuous way where 'Dad' implies that you're sleeping with your brother, more like… a father-in-law."

Jimmy swiped his forehead. "Whew, you had me worried there for a second. I thought you were adopting him."

"Only in the sense that he's like my son-in-law because he's in a committed relationship with you, Jim."

Darian laid his head on Jimmy's shoulder. "I can get used to that."

Jimmy put his arm around Darian and grinned.

"Okay," Mr. Miller changed the subject, "who's ready to go to a Memorial Day cookout?"

"Me." Jimmy raised his hand.

"Me." Darian did the same. "Are you sure your family will like me?" he asked.

"Of course we're sure!" Dan replied. He then looked to Jimmy. "Are *you* sure you want to come out to my side of the family? That's a big step."

Jimmy nodded. "I'm sure. Besides, everyone on your side hates my mom for what she did. If I ask them to be quiet about it, I'm sure they'd do that for me. And Maggie is going to be there. I have to have her meet Darian!"

"Okay, Tiger. Let's go eat hotdogs and go swimming!"

"I'M NERVOUS," Darian quietly admitted as he and Jimmy rode in the back seat of the car.

Jimmy squeezed his hand. "You don't have to be. *I'm* the one who should be nervous. I'm about to come out to my family. I thought I'd be freaking out, but I'm not."

"I just meant… I'm nervous about them liking me."

Jimmy would have said "*awww,*" but that seemed too girly. Matt would disapprove. Instead, he turned in the seat, hooked Darian's chin with his index finger, and planted a sloppy kiss on Darian's worried mouth. "It will all be fine. They'll love you. Besides, my dad's family is not all stuck up and prudish like my mom's. My cousin Maggie will probably be there. I haven't seen her in years. She's neat. She's got this really cool dragon tattoo on her back. She spent years traveling the world and always has great stories of places she's been and people she's met. You'll like her."

"If you're sure."

He squeezed Darian's hand one more time. "I'm sure."

THEY arrived at the cookout and smoke already filled the yard from the barbeque grill. "Looks like my brother Ted's burning *something* again."

Jimmy chuckled. The boys followed Mr. Miller and Cheryl up to the front door. It opened before Dan even knocked.

"Danny!" a blond woman in an apron cried. "I haven't seen you in ages!" She hugged him tight. "Come on in!" She waved to Dan, and the boys followed. "It seems like every time there's a family get-together I'm giving birth or having surgery or visiting my sister in California. I'm so glad we could host the reunion at our house this year."

"Reunion?" Darian whispered into Jimmy's ear. "I thought you said it would be a *small* gathering?"

"I thought it would be," Jimmy whispered back. "I haven't been to one of these in two years. The last time it was small!"

Dan smiled and presented his girlfriend. "Donna, this is Cheryl, my girlfriend."

"Hello. Welcome to our home." Donna reached out and shook her hand.

"Thank you," Cheryl replied. "I'm glad to be here."

Then he gestured to Jimmy. "And you remember my son, Jim?"

"Jimmy!" She cried with the same enthusiasm he always remembered. She squeezed the life out of him before she let go.

"Hi, Aunt Donna."

"You are getting so big! I can't believe it. How old are you now? Seventeen? Eighteen?"

"Twenty."

"*Almost* twenty," Dan corrected. "He's still got a couple months to go."

"And who is your friend?" She eyed Darian.

Jimmy beamed proudly. "This is Dar—"

"Where's the bathroom?" Darian blurted as Jimmy started to introduce him.

Donna looked startled but answered anyway. "Um, down the hall, first door on the right." She pointed.

"Thanks."

Jimmy watched Darian hurry off. "Um, I'm just gonna check on him." Jimmy raised an eyebrow. "He's not normally like this."

"So, who's Jimmy's friend?" he heard his aunt Donna ask his dad. He slowed his steps to eavesdrop on what might be said next.

"His name is Darian."

"He's a real cutie. I could just eat him right up!" Her comment made Jimmy grin.

"Don't let Jimmy hear you say that." Jimmy inwardly groaned.

"What? Why?"

"I'll let him explain when he comes back out. Let me help you get this watermelon out to the picnic table."

"Okay. Thanks."

Jimmy thought about growling at his dad later. He was coming out, but he wanted to do it himself!

Jimmy slowly went down the hall to find Darian. The hall was dark. The bathroom door was at the end of the hallway, and it was left open a crack. Something prompted him to peek in before knocking.

On the sink sat a plastic bag of what looked like a mixed bunch of pills. His stomach churned. Darian was running the water in the sink. He splashed some on his face and then dried it. When Darian seemed to be leaning his hands on the edge of the sink, resting or thinking or something, Jimmy backed up a few steps and tried to sound normal on his approach to the door. He took a few steps and then knocked. "Darian? Are you okay in there?" He caught a glimpse of Darian's hand swiping the bag off the sink before he nudged the door open.

"I'm fine," Darian answered quickly.

The nervous look on his face did not sit well with Jimmy. "You bolted from the kitchen before I could introduce you to my Aunt Donna."

"I'm sorry. We can go back in and...."

"Yeah, we can." Jimmy willed his body to remain calm. He stepped up to Darian and gazed into his eyes. Such lovely eyes, so full of anxiety! *I guess so. I'd be anxious too if I was taking pills and lying to my boyfriend.* Jimmy lifted his hand and caressed Darian's cheek. "It's okay. You don't have to be nervous. I'm here. You'll be fine."

"Yeah, I know. I'm fine."

Jimmy nodded. Jimmy's hand left Darian's cheek. "Fine? Is that why you need these?" As he asked, he reached for Darian's front pocket.

Darian did not fight off Jimmy's probing hand. He merely closed his eyes, knowing he'd been caught.

Jimmy pulled the bag out and held it up. Darian's eyes acknowledged the evidence and swiftly looked away. Jimmy turned and walked over to the bathroom door, shutting it. "Why?" he asked when he turned around. He was actually quite surprised with himself for being so calm.

"I told you, I'm nervous."

Jimmy walked back up to him and held out his wrist, exposing his spider tattoo. "What happened with this? Was it all a lie? We were celebrating together, Darian. One year clean, remember?"

"It wasn't a lie, Jamie. I have been clean… well, sort of. I haven't taken any illegal drugs. No heroin, I swear! All year I've been good."

Jimmy didn't buy it. "Then what's with these?" He shook the bag in front of Darian's face.

"It's just Percocet."

"Just Percocet?" He sneered. "Dare, last year started because of 'just Percocet'. This simple little painkiller was prescribed because you had broken ribs, and it didn't take long to convince yourself you needed more of a fix."

"I only needed it to relax, Jamie. I'm nervous about meeting your family."

"You keep saying that. Why the hell are you so nervous? I told you my family isn't scary."

Darian rubbed his face and turned his back. "I just am."

Jimmy didn't understand his behavior. Darian was normally very sure of himself. Whenever they went anywhere, clubs, dinner, movies, etc., Darian was very confident and had no problems holding Jimmy's hand or kissing him in public. Right now he looked the complete opposite. "Darian, what's wrong? You aren't normally like this. Are you embarrassed to be with me?"

"No! I just… I can't…."

He was trying to get it out, but Jimmy could see he was losing it. His eyes were darting around, and he looked as if he'd cry any second. Jimmy stepped closer and took him into his arms. Darian was shaking. "Shhh, it's okay. I'm here. You can trust me."

"I don't do *families*," he whispered.

Jimmy pulled back enough to look him in the eyes. He moved Darian's hair out of his eyes and gently cupped his cheek. "What do you mean, you don't do families?"

Darian shook his head. "I don't know how."

"But Dare, you're great with my dad."

"I know, but it's so difficult."

"I don't understand."

Darian heaved an exasperated breath. "Jamie… living with your dad this last year has been the greatest thing ever and the scariest at the same time." Darian's eyes kept darting away, but at least he was talking. Jimmy held his tongue and let him explain. "Did you know your dad practically tucks me in bed every night?"

"I'd think that'd be annoying. You're practically a grown-up! I kind of like my privacy more than anything now. Not really into Dad kissing my forehead every night, like when I was a little kid."

Darian's eyes stopped darting. "But I've never had a father."

His serious answer was like a sock to Jimmy's thick skull. How could he have been so stupid? And even though he still needed some explanation for Darian's need for painkillers, he was starting to understand where Darian was coming from.

Darian continued, "Every morning I wake up, and I wait to open my eyes because I'm scared that's it's all been a dream. Then I smell the coffee, and my chest tightens, and I take a few minutes to remember how to breathe. I go down to the kitchen, and there he is… making breakfast… for me." A tear streaked Darian's cheek. "He pats my shoulder and tells me what shift he has that day. Says he'll be home later to make dinner. He asks if I need a ride to work. He drops me off and picks me up. He's there when he says he'll be." Darian sniffled. "I've never had that, Jamie. Never. It scares me that it'll all go away."

"Oh, God, Darian...." Jimmy pulled him into a comforting hug and tried not to cry.

Darian whimpered and cried on Jimmy's shoulder. "Living at my mom's was depressing. She was always stoned. She takes almost all my money. I lived there, but I felt like I was dying at the same time. The drugs happened like you said: I needed something stronger for the pain, and then something stronger, and stronger, and Jerry had some heroin downstairs one night. I told myself it would just be the one time, but that's not easy to do with heroin. Once wasn't enough. I started needing it to keep from hurting." He pulled out of Jimmy's embrace and snagged some toilet paper to blow his nose.

"Why didn't you say something?"

"I didn't know how. You had your own problems. School, your mom, and Matt, I didn't want to burden you."

Jimmy grabbed his upper arm. "Burden me. Please. I don't want you thinking you have to go through anything alone."

Darian lifted the side of his mouth in a half smile. "I'll try. I've been struggling not to take anything stronger than Percocet. It doesn't really do much anymore. I keep upping the dosage. I've been down to my last six fentanyl for three weeks now, but I've tried really hard not to give in."

"Oh, Darian." He was saddened to hear this confession. "How long have you been taking painkillers?"

"Four months... I think. I kind of lost track of time."

Jimmy's heart sunk, like the expression on his face. "I guess I can see why you started. Your home life was not the best. But why now? I thought you liked living with my dad?"

"I do. He's the best. And that's what scares me the most. You guys are the closest thing to family I've ever had. If you slept there more often, it would be like living together. I love that, but I'm also afraid of it all disappearing one day, when I least expect it. I don't think I could live without you, Jamie. So... when the fear gets too much, I escape. Painkillers are easy to get."

Jimmy could not stop the tears from seeping from his eyes. Darian's confessions and Jimmy's own deep love for him were swirling around in his heart and mind. He wasn't happy about the drugs, but he understood the reason. He grabbed Darian to his chest. "Oh, Darian. I love you. You don't need to be afraid. I'm here. I'm not going anywhere." He pulled back and kissed him. "You don't need an escape." He kissed him again, and again. "I'll keep you safe. I promise."

Darian clutched Jimmy. "I love you too."

After a few quiet moments of hugging and when the crying seemed to dissipate, they let go of each other. "You don't need these." Jimmy shoved bag of mixed pills into his pocket. "And if you ever feel the need to do painkillers again, or God forbid—heroin, please don't. For me."

Darian wiped his eyes. "Okay. I'll try."

Satisfied with Darian's answer, Jimmy smiled. "All right. Are you ready to meet my family? I've got some *coming out* to do!" He winked.

Darian took a deep breath and nodded.

Jimmy reached out and took his hand.

OUTSIDE, there were more people than when they first arrived. Small groups gathered together by the grill, the horseshoe pits, and the swing set. Jimmy gripped Darian's hand reassuringly. He pointed. "That group over there is my dad's sister Helen and her family. My little cousins Johnny, Jordan, and Janey. Johnny is twelve now, I think."

"Johnny, Jordan, and Janey…. Got it!"

Jimmy pointed to their left. "Over by the horseshoes are my older cousins, Ronnie and his wife Kim, and Brandon and his girlfriend Melissa. They are *huge* horseshoe fanatics and *always* challenge people to play."

"I'll play."

Jimmy gave him a skeptical look. "I'm afraid of you tossing a horseshoe."

"I might surprise you."

"Surprise me by hitting the house?"

"Nooooo, I bet I can throw that thing and hit the little pole."

Jimmy giggled. "Toss, not throw. You toss a horseshoe." He was jibing Darian on purpose to try and alleviate the tension that had gotten so thick in the bathroom. Obviously he'd succeeded. Darian was rolling his eyes and grinning. Jimmy reached up and touched the side of Darian's face as he leaned in and kissed him sweetly on the lips.

They both jumped when someone cleared their throat.

"I was about to ask who your friend might be, but now I'm taking a stab that he's *more* than just a study-buddy."

Jimmy smiled. "Darian, this is my dad's cousin, Maggie. Maggie, this is my boyfriend Darian."

The bemused woman put her arms on Darian's shoulders and leaned in for a hug. She even kissed his cheek. "I'm so glad to meet you, Darian." She cocked an eyebrow toward Jimmy. "So... a boyfriend? You been out long? Because I'll be highly offended if I'm the last to know!"

Jimmy shook his head. Finally the nervousness was catching up to him. "No Maggie. This is actually the first time I've openly admitted it in front of family. I mean... we've been out on dates before, dinner and clubs, but never around family. My mom doesn't know."

"Well, your mom is a bitch... if you pardon my French. I can't blame you for not telling her. You been together long?"

Jimmy liked her casual tone. It made him relax considerably. "Um, in August it'll be four years since we met. I asked him to be my boyfriend maybe a year after that."

Darian piped in with certainty, "May 13, 2005! Three years and sixteen days, including today."

"Well, I'd say he's got a good memory." Maggie smiled and took Jimmy's hand. "Come on, I want you to meet my partner."

Jimmy stopped short. "Partner?"

Maggie grinned back at him. "Yup! Her name is Lisel. We met in Germany."

Jimmy could not believe his ears. "What? You're a...."

Maggie giggled. "I think the term you're searching for is *lesbian.*"

"But how come…. Why didn't Dad…. Does everyone know but me?" He felt slighted and couldn't help the little whine that escaped his throat.

"No, honey. Like you, this is a first time deal. I've been in Europe for the last couple years, so I haven't had the chance to show her off. Plus, it took some years to come to grips with it myself. Being in the Air Force for so many years, I was forced to hide who I was. *Don't ask, don't tell.* It's a bunch of bullshit. Anyway, Lisel and I have been together for six years but have only been telling friends and family recently."

"Wow." Jimmy started walking again and followed her.

"She's the blond in the sundress."

"Again I say 'wow'. She's pretty hot, Maggie." Jimmy might not be into girls, but he knew a hot babe when he saw one. Lisel was thin, buxom, and had the loveliest long, blond curls he ever did see. She was *stunning*!

Maggie grinned. "Thanks. But I shouldn't have to point out that your man is quite the looker. He's down right delicious."

Darian ducked his face into Jimmy's neck.

She laughed. "He's even more endearing when he blushes."

"Stop it!" Jimmy playfully smacked her shoulder. "You're gonna make him hide in the house!"

"Oh, Jimmy, it's all in good fun! Right, Darian? You're not going to hide from me, are you?"

Darian quickly shook his head as he slipped his arms around Jimmy.

Jimmy held him and rolled his eyes. "Thanks a lot, Maggie."

She smiled wide and hollered across the yard. "Hey, darlin', come on over here a second so I can show you off to my favorite cousin!"

Lisel looked up and smiled. She said something to Jimmy's dad and the group of relatives she was speaking with and came right over. "Hello, you must be Jimmy. I've heard so much about you." She extended her hand.

Jimmy shook her hand and smiled back. "Yeah, I'm Jimmy. And this is Darian."

"Hello, Darian." She kindly shook Darian's hand. "Your father has been telling me stories about you, Jimmy. He says you are doing exceedingly well in school and that you have turned into a very compassionate young man. He's very proud of you."

Jimmy straightened his shoulders. "He did? He is?"

"Why do you look so surprised?" Maggie asked. "He's been bragging on you since you were born."

"Really? I didn't know." He suddenly felt warm and gushy inside.

"If you will excuse me, I need to use the powder room." Lisel smiled and slipped away.

Maggie watched her retreat into the house.

"She's really sweet, Maggie," Jimmy said. "I love her accent. Where's she from?"

"La Garenne-Colombes, France. Her mother is French and her father is German. And yeah, she *can* be sweet, when she wants to be."

"*Can be?*" He asked, because Maggie didn't sound like she believed her own words.

Maggie leaned closer to answer. "She's a real take-charge kind of gal. If you know what I mean? Get her in the bedroom and she goes all *dominatrix*!"

"TMI, Maggie, TMI!" Jimmy shook his head but chuckled at the same time.

"Hey, Jimmy," his dad yelled. "Come over here. Stop yapping with Maggie and speak to the rest of the family!"

Jimmy shrugged. "Duty calls."

"No problem. I don't mind sharing. But you and me and that horseshoe pit later, okay? That is, if we can wrestle the horseshoes away from Ronnie long enough to play."

"We could do teams. Take them on?" He offered.

"Definitely!" Maggie and Jimmy high-fived.

Jimmy walked toward his dad, still wrapped in Darian's arms. He hugged him close to his side. "Still nervous?"

Darian shook his head bashfully. "No, I guess not. But don't let go of me yet, I might not be able to stand on my own."

"I'm not letting go. Ever."

May 24, 2008

Today was a blast. Darian is the best boyfriend ever. He can't play horseshoes worth a darn, but we still beat Ronnie and Brandon!

I can't believe Maggie is a lesbian. Besides being a huge relief that she accepts me even though I'm gay, it is nice to know I am not alone in the whole lifestyle choice. If I ever need support, I know Maggie will truly understand.

The incident with the drugs is disconcerting. Darian is more insecure than I realized. I never, ever thought about what it would be like for him growing up. I guess I just thought about how my family was and never imagined that things could be worse. Of course, when I met him I KNEW things were worse; he described them that way, but I never really thought about it until he said something today. He never had a dad. Fuck! I can't imagine what that would be like. And then here we are barging into his world and offering him a place to stay without batting an eye. I never considered it might be more difficult than giving up drugs.

I really need to think about his feelings more. Darian has had too much hurt in his life, and I definitely don't need to add to it!!!

24

September 24, 2010

9:00 a.m.

DARIAN opened his eyes. He looked across the room and wondered where he was. This wasn't his and Jamie's room. It was neater and darker, and the carpet was the wrong color. The arm around his waist tightened its hold and then he knew… this was Matt's room.

Jamie would get tired of sleeping so close. He said it was too hot and made him sweaty.

Somewhere in the middle of the night they'd shifted positions for the fourth time and Matt ended up spooned around Darian's back. He held Darian snug against his hard body as he breathed steadily onto the back of Darian's neck. Matt sighed in his sleep and whispered the first half of Darian's name as he caressed Darian's collarbone with his thumb. Darian felt a lump form in his throat. He liked hearing his name whispered. It was unexpectedly thrilling.

Jamie never whispered my name in his sleep.

Darian was caught in a whirlpool of emotion for this big guy. It was frightening to consider what he felt. Did he want whatever they had to last, once the trauma in their lives was over? Was it just a matter of needing Matt to get over the pain of losing Jamie, or was there something more? It couldn't be all about sex, could it? He clutched Matt's arm to his chest. This *had* to last! He couldn't be alone.

He pulled Matt's fingers to his mouth and kissed them. He loved the things that these fingers could do. He tongued Matt's index finger, and the body against his back shifted. Darian grinned. He took two fingers into his mouth and licked them. Matt grunted. Darian folded all but Matt's index finger down and inserted it between his lips. He moved it in and out, all the while swirling his tongue around it. Matt's moaning grew louder. Then Darian could feel Matt's erection against his butt. Matt's hips were rocking gently.

"Mmmm, Dare…," Matt sighed heavily.

Darian giggled. *My name. He's saying* my *name.* Darian's heart pounded in his chest.

He let go of Matt's hand and rolled over carefully. He knew Matt's face was very close to the back of his head, and he didn't want to accidently clonk him. He was grateful that they'd slept naked, since it made morning sex much easier. *Jamie had a habit of slipping his briefs back on.* Darian could feel Matt's erection touching his as he repositioned himself to face his lover. He tilted his hips. Skin on skin was undoubtedly a most marvelous feeling. He could see how Matt so easily forgot to grab a condom last night. Now, in the light of morning, his anger was defused. What was done was done. They'd both have to get an HIV screening before he could logically worry anymore. Right now, all that mattered was his seeping, flared head rubbing over the tip of Matt's, and the need that was bubbling up inside his aching groin.

He reached between them and took both erections in his fist and stroked. It took literally four seconds for Matt's eyes to pop open.

"Oh, Darian." He closed his eyes and moaned. "I like how you think." He reopened his eyes and grinned, then kissed Darian and swept his warm hands over Darian's back.

Darian let go and nudged Matt onto his back. The sheet pooled around him as he moved over Matt's hips and straddled him. He scooted far enough down Matt's thighs to lean over and engulf Matt's erection.

"Oh, fuck!" Matt hissed. "Are you always this horny in the morning?" He arched his back and fisted the sheets.

Darian chuckled as he swiftly bobbed his head. He held onto the base of Matt's shaft and glided his tongue around the sensitive ridge of its crown. Pre-cum oozed from the slit, and Darian lapped it up. "Where's the lube?" he asked between sucking and tonguing.

"Huh?" Matt grunted.

"Lube. I need some."

"I… um… it's under… oh, God, I can't think."

Darian was really enjoying Matt's loss of control. Although Darian *liked* being submissive, there was still a part of him—especially in the mornings—that liked taking what he wanted. Right now, he wanted Matt screaming his name.

Somehow, Matt pointed, and Darian retrieved the bottle of lube off the floor without losing much rhythm from his oral onslaught. He popped the top and squirted some Astroglide into his palm. He slicked Matt's erection, right before rubbing the rest over his own needy hole. He reached over to the nightstand and tore open a condom packet. Calmly waited as Darian rolled it down Matt's cock, readied himself, moved up, and positioned them. Their eyes locked as Darian lowered himself onto Matt and back up, then back down.

"Oh fuck!" Matt closed his eyes again. "Dare! Fuck!"

"It doesn't take much to please you, does it?" Darian asked as he rode Matt's cock. He leaned forward, placing his palms on Matt's ribs and balancing himself by leaning his weight on Matt and using his thighs to pump. His muscles were burning in minutes, but it was a small price to pay for the pleasure that ignited inside him. He tilted his pelvis on the next downstroke and Matt's cock hit his prostate. Darian groaned loudly. "Oh… fuck! Yes!" He picked up the pace, becoming a jackhammer in reverse.

Matt reached for Darian's bobbing shaft and started pumping. "Come with me, baby."

Darian growled. He slammed himself brutally onto Matt's rock-hard rod and rode the waves of orgasm all the way to their sated end. Panting, Darian sagged forward and looked at Matt briefly before collapsing entirely.

"Fuckin' hell, Darian." Matt held him to his chest. "That was fuckin' astounding." His breath was less labored than Darian's. "I can't feel my fuckin' toes."

Darian wiped the sweat-drenched bangs from his eyes. "Ah, ever the articulate genius," Darian mused, still unable to move or even disconnect their bodies.

"Fuck you."

Matt's voice did not convey anger, only amusement. That, coupled with the fact that Matt's hands were rubbing all over Darian's ass and lower back, helped Darian to understand that Matt was just messing with him. Darian mewed and nibbled Matt's neck.

"I guess you're not mad about last night. I'm glad," said Matt. "But if you're gonna suck me off, you should use a condom. I normally do."

"You didn't with me."

"I didn't blow you until *after* I knew about Jamie. I'm not worried about *your* health, I'm worried about *mine* affecting yours. Jamie was clean. I'm sure of it. He'd never think of group sex, multiple partners, *or* doing intravenous drugs."

Darian stopped licking Matt's throat. *Intravenous drugs? Does he know about that?* Darian didn't know when to bring up his life. Apparently Jamie only shared in one direction, and Matt was left in the dark. Perhaps they could have that talk next week? He'd have to get tested anyway. Darian propped his face on crossed arms to look at him. "Maybe I'll wait until I can do it without a condom. I like the feel of your skin on my tongue and the taste of you in my mouth."

"Fuck yeah! Me too."

"I never really thought about before. Jamie and I hardly used condoms. Plus, I was too intent on riding you. I wanted you hard fast. It felt so damn good."

"Yeah, it did! You are a real animal when you want to be, aren't you?"

Darian nodded and blushed.

"You are too adorable for words. You know that?" Matt asked and grabbed Darian to him. He plunged his tongue into Darian's mouth and rolled them over as they kissed.

Darian felt Matt's dick slip from his ass. He would normally have whimpered at the feeling of separation, but Matt was devouring him so completely that Darian could not be bothered to complain. He knew they would be joined again soon enough.

Matt rocked into him and pulled away suddenly. "Don't fret, baby, I'll be right back." He stroked the side of Darian's sad face. Matt got off the bed and returned with a towel. "The condom was dripping. You made me cum so hard." He wiped his leg and balls and tossed the towel on the nightstand.

"Sex is messy business."

"Yup." Matt crawled over Darian. "But I'm willing to get all sloppy with you again." He winked.

Darian yanked him into another kiss.

When they were spent, sweaty, and seeping cum onto the sheets again, Matt suggested a shower. Darian pictured other positions he thought they'd try, but Matt was all about the washing. He washed Darian's hair for him. He washed Darian's back and chest. He even bent down and washed his feet. Darian thought it was going to be a complete disappointment, but Matt did manage to plant a kiss on the head of his penis when he was done washing his feet.

"Sorry. I know you wanted more, but we're running out of time," Matt said, turning off the water.

Time! It finally dawned on Darian that this was Friday. The funeral. Jamie. His enjoyment of the morning followed the bubbles right down the drain. Darian was suddenly lifeless. He'd been trying to avoid this moment and bury himself in the pleasure Matt gave him. Still, the moment was here, and he had to face the reality of Jamie's absence. Jamie was dead.

"Darian?"

He heard Matt's voice but couldn't answer. Guilt had reared its ugly head again. Jamie was dead, and Darian couldn't stay away from Matt long enough to bury him. He willingly gave his body to another in exchange for a few hours free from the pain of loss. *How could I treat my promises to him so callously?*

Zombie-like, he felt Matt assist him from the tub and towel him dry.

"Darian, I know this is going to be super hard for you, but you have to help me. I can't do everything, you have to move."

It was as though Matt knew exactly what he needed. He dried him off and guided him into the bedroom and helped him get dressed without making any comments on his sudden mood change. As awful as he felt for cheating on Jamie, Darian was grateful for Matt, but he couldn't make the words come out. He felt Matt's hands on his face.

"Oh, baby, look at you." Matt's words were so full of compassion. He felt Matt's lips on his forehead. "It'll be okay. I promise. We'll make it through this." He tenderly kissed Darian's eyelids and cheeks. Matt pulled him into a hug and rubbed his back. Darian melted into him. His affection was so soothing, and Darian needed every bit of it.

Matt's strong concern and care was a healing presence to his dying soul.

"Come on," Matt urged. "You need to eat something."

Darian made a face. "No," he said weakly.

"Look at you, Darian. You look like a waif. You could fall over any second. You need something to build up your strength." He took Darian by the arm and walked him out to the kitchen. "Here, sit down and I'll make you a bagel. A nice, warm, toasty bagel with cream cheese."

Darian sat at the breakfast bar, and the bagel was placed before him before he even knew that Matt took it out of the bag. Darian took a bite. After washing it down with some water and not feeling like it would come back up, he took another bite.

Matt stood next to him and stroked his back. The bar stool brought his height close to Matt's even though Darian was sitting. "We need to leave in about twenty minutes," Matt said. He fingered the edges of Darian's hair and smoothed it back over his ear. Then he touched the back and played with the long strands. Darian liked the feel of his fingers in his hair. "I hope you don't mind me touching your hair? I like it. It's soft," Matt quietly observed as he continued to touch Darian. "I can't seem to stop touching you."

Darian put the bagel down and leaned into Matt's chest. Matt held him silently until they had to leave.

MATT drove them to the funeral home, but once they arrived he was no longer touching Darian's hair, arm, or hands. Darian felt the separation like a chill on his skin. He needed Matt's warmth, but they were back in the public eye, and he knew better than to expect anything more. They walked without speaking to the door. Not in a bad way, more of a silence bred from knowing what was going to come next.

Darian hated this day more than any other in his life. It felt like an end. It felt like burying Jamie would snuff out all hope of joy. Darian longed for an escape but had no such luck. Matt drove. This meant there were no pills stashed under the seat. This meant he could not bolt from the room and go seek out one of his dealers. He was left high and dry with his sorrow. Darian was a breath away from considering joining his fiancé in the placid stillness of death. It would be easier than this.

People were seated in rows of chairs, awaiting the service. Darian saw a few of his friends present, but their sympathetic gestures could not pull him up from the depths of gloom that clutched him. He was empty, and nothing could coax emotion from his zombie-like state.

Dan was at his side, introducing him to someone in the family whom Darian had not met. He nodded in greeting but truly did not hear the name or anything else that was said. His mind had shut down. He felt Dan guiding him to a chair, and there was some piped-in organ music before the pastor started speaking. The words around him entered his ears distorted and stretched, like a record played at half the speed. Nothing was real.

Darian sat staring at the floor as the pastor spoke about death and the resurrection of the body through hope in Jesus Christ. Jamie went to church with his mom; Darian knew that. Sometimes he'd talk about things he learned about the Bible, but Jamie was not overly religious, as religious people went. He said he believed in Jesus as his Savior, but Jamie didn't think it was up to him to push his beliefs on others. He thought it was all about relationships. More poignantly, the relationship each person had with God.

After the pastor, other people stepped up to the podium and spoke about Jamie. How they met, fun times shared, or something funny Jamie had done. Darian was aware of many of these events but could not bring himself to join in the muffled laughs that were scattered about the room. When his ears caught Matt's voice, he looked up.

Matt was standing behind the podium. He looked so fine in his suit. He stumbled on his words and took a sip of water, then cleared his throat. "Okay, let me try this again." He looked nervous, and Darian wished he would make eye contact, just for a second. He wanted to give Matt strength, but he didn't know how.

"Jim Miller and I have been best friends since birth. Well, practically. I've known him all my life, and he's always been there for me. I knew him as Jamie. I remember when we were young. I gave him the silly nickname because of the Van Halen song, 'Jamie's Crying'. He laughed and told me to shut up, but the nickname stuck.

"We did everything together, from boating to fishing to camping, even deer hunting, and let me tell you, there is no one else in the world I'd rather have spent my childhood with than Jamie. He cheered me on in the stands when I won All County track. He was there at my graduation and at my induction ceremony when I became a firefighter. Jamie was the kind of guy who did anything for you and asked for nothing in return. He loved everyone and hated no one."

Matt pinched the bridge of his nose and paused for breath. Darian felt heat filling his body and knew, just knew, he would cry at any moment. Seeing Matt fighting the tears was prompting his own emotions to break forth. But if the tears started, would he be able to stop?

Matt's voice cracked, "Jamie... I'm sorry." He took another deep breath. "Jamie was the kindest person... I ever knew. I loved him like a brother." His tears came harder, and Matt was struggling to make it through his tribute. "I will never forget everything he's done for me, and I hope that each of you will remember that Jamie Miller loved all of you just as you are. He never judged; he only loved."

Matt stepped down, and the room fell silent. No one moved to follow his speech.

Darian's eyes were blurred from tears. He struggled to keep from sobbing loud enough for people to notice. Something was said, and people started to stand up and leave the room. Dan placed his arm around Darian.

"Darian, we are going to the gravesite. Do you want to ride in the limo with me?"

Darian managed a nod.

His grief increased as the limo ride continued on to Lakeview Memorial Park.

People gathered around the grave. The casket was set on the pulleys. The pastor said a few words about ashes to ashes and dust to dust. Family and friends stepped up and placed flowers on the casket and stepped away.

Darian clung to Dan Miller at this point and sobbed into his shirt. He knew people could hear him, but he could not stop. His Jamie was gone. Gone! No more hugs, no more kisses from his soft lips. Darian felt the weight of the last few days pressing on him and forcing him to face the fact that his lover and friend would never again wipe away his tears or kiss away his pain. He was empty and completely and utterly alone.

He collapsed to the ground and fisted the fresh dirt, sobbing uncontrollably. "I can't say goodbye. I won't say goodbye. My Jamie." The words were uttered through tears and gasps for air. People were whispering, but he could not care less. He had nothing left. His life was in the wooden box, embalmed: a waxy representation of the person who once breathed life into his heart and saved him in so many ways.

How could he possibly go on?

Darian wept unabashedly and faintly heard someone curse. *"Oh, fuck!"* He felt a sudden presence at his side and a stroking hand on his back. He knew that hand. He lifted his head and felt it pulled to a strong chest. *Matt.* His heart cried.

"Shhh, baby, it'll be okay. I'm here." Matt whispered into his ear and helped him to his feet.

Darian reached around his waist and buried his face in the crook of Matt's neck. Matt held him tight and guided him away from the casket and to a car nearby. He heard people whispering, but Darian was clinging to Matt's warmth and had no desire to address their inquiries or insinuations.

25

June 2009

We just got back from New York. I know, I know… amazing that Mom let me go. She didn't. She thought I was on a camping trip with my dad and almost changed her mind twice. Well, in New York, I asked Darian to marry me. I'm not sure why, because I planned to wait. Wait until I was done with school. I guess I got caught up in the moment, and the words just fell out. He was so cute, and New York is such an awesome place. I lost myself there and forgot about the problems surrounding my real life if I was going to plan a gay wedding. Fuck!

Now I'm scared.

Darian needs me to love him wholeheartedly, unconditionally, and be fully committed to our relationship. Which I am. Sort of. Oh, God… I don't know if I am or not. Now that I've asked him, I'm having doubts. Doubts about my own commitment. I can't really love him wholeheartedly. Half of my heart belongs to Matt. It always will. Can I love Darian and still be in love with Matt?

We were in New York for a week. I texted Matt every day. I saw things I wished I could share with Matt. I even almost blurted out that we should bring Matt next time. I'm so glad I didn't! Thoughts of him follow me around everywhere.

Why am I like this? Darian is all I could ever want in a boyfriend. He's cute, kind, loving, gives one hell of a blowjob, he's talented, he's thoughtful, and he is 100 percent in this relationship for the long haul. What more could I want?

I hate asking that question, because it always answers itself: Matt. I want him to be Matt. Why, is the only question I can't answer.

Because I can't have him?

Because I feel perfect when I'm with him?

Because he knows me better than I know myself sometimes?

I don't know. I just can't stop wondering what would happen if he ever changed his mind. What if Matt asked me out? Would I go? Would I cheat on Darian if I had the chance to date Matt?

I'M SCARED THAT MY ANSWER WOULD BE YES....

Jimmy closed his notebook when Darian entered the room. "Hey, you." He smiled.

Darian's face lit up like it always did. "Good morning." He walked over to Jimmy at the kitchen table and kissed him. "Are you leaving for your mom's soon?"

"Yeah. Grass needs mowed and I have to fix the clog in the bathroom sink." *All before she returns! Grrr.* Jimmy kept his irritation to himself. Darian never appreciated him complaining about his mom when *Jimmy's* mom was actually around. Darian's was not.

"Um, it's 'the grass needs to *be* mowed' if you want to stick with correct grammar. And why can't she hire a plumber?" Darian took the milk out of the fridge and headed to the counter to get a glass from the dish drain.

"She could, but she's cheap when it comes to repairs. She figures I learned all these handyman skills from working with my dad, so she should be able to use them."

"And not pay you," he pointed out. "Makes sense. You gonna talk to her about moving in with me… I mean, your dad?"

"Um, yeah, I guess. She wasn't happy the last time I brought it up." Jimmy dreaded this conversation.

"But Jamie, you brought it up a year ago! You have one year left in college. After graduation, you said we'd move to DC, or New York, or wherever I wanted. Remember?" Darian put the milk away and sat at the table across from Jimmy.

"I know. You're right. I just… I guess I need more time."

"More time?" Darian screeched.

Jimmy jumped. Darian rarely got agitated, but this conversation always stirred him up. He did nothing to disguise his frustration over a matter they had discussed time and time again. Jimmy braced himself.

"How could you say that?" Darian asked disbelievingly. "You've had years!"

"No, I haven't."

"*Yes*, you have. We've been together for *years*. You've been gay for *years*. Your father has known for *years*. Your family has known for, well, *a* year! When are you going to tell your mom? When are you going to tell Matt? When are you going to own up to who you are and not be afraid of what people think?"

Darian was so alive with conviction that his face was turning red. Jimmy knew he was right. He knew he should have faced these things years ago, but it wasn't that simple. Jimmy liked the way things were. He liked his straight world and his gay world separate. Why did he have to change?

Because it's time you grew up, you moron!

Jimmy hung his head. "I'll take you to my house," he mumbled.

"What?"

Jimmy looked up and repeated himself. "I'll take you to my house. You can see my room. And meet my mom. We can even drive by Matt's and see if he's home."

Darian looked shocked. "Oh, okay."

JIMMY drove them to his mom's house. Relief surged as large as a tidal wave when no cars were in the driveway. He was 90 percent sure everyone was somewhere else, but it was the other 10 percent that would kill him. He'd prayed the whole way over that they would indeed be out. He parked the car and led Darian up to the door.

"Nice house," Darian commented as he looked over the stone two-story contemporary, complete with professional landscaping.

"Thanks. My mom is a banker, and my stepdad's a professor. They do well."

Jimmy led them inside and closed the door.

"Wow," Darian said, gaping. "Your house is like an art museum. I can't believe you haven't brought me here before."

Jimmy watched as Darian walked up to the suit of armor and studied the filigree on the helmet. He then walked to the Monet on the wall next to it, and the Bouguereau next to that. His eyes were wide, and his jaw was dragging on the floor as he stepped from one painting to the next. He looked over the Elizabethan sword collection on the wall and then the Ming vase replica on the podium next to the bookcase.

"I'll be right back." Jimmy quickly excused himself and left Darian in the living room.

He shut the bathroom door and sat on the toilet seat, burying his face in his hands as the tears of guilt were too strong to hold at bay. "I can't believe I did this," he chastised himself. "Darian is an artist, for Christ's sake! He's the best artist I've ever seen, and I didn't even want to share this stuff with him. I never even gave it a thought! My mom has a fucking art gallery in there, and yet I never once thought to bring Darian here! I am such a fucking asshole!"

He punched the tile wall. Pain cascaded over his knuckles and radiated through his hand into his arm. He clutched it to his chest.

Jimmy sat there for a few minutes, thinking about how *unthinking* he had been toward Darian. Here he'd gone to New York and thought about every little thing he wanted to share with Matt. A truck Matt would like. A store Matt would like. Even a few guys Matt would probably like. But here, in his everyday world, he'd never even thought once that Darian would probably like to see the art his mom had collected over the years. He'd never even considered that maybe his mom would actually like Darian because they had some things in common. He shook his head and got up before Darian knocked on the door. He rinsed his face off and hoped his eyes were not pink enough to reveal he'd been crying. Then he let the cold water run over the back of his hand to quell the throbbing. Nothing broken, swelling controlled, he turned off the water and left.

He found Darian still looking over the art collection, but he had wandered into the dining room and was standing in front of the Van Gogh. "So, you like it?"

"Yes!" Darian said. "Are these real?" He stroked the frame of a painting by Pierre-Auguste Cot.

"Half of them are. I forget which ones. I'm not allowed to touch any of them."

Darian took his hand away. "That's amazing. They must be worth a fortune."

"I think so. I heard my mom talking to the insurance agent once about coverage. It was a lot."

"Millions?"

"Maybe. I don't really remember. Come up and see my room."

"All right."

Darian followed him up the steps. In Jimmy's room, he still walked around studying the pictures on the wall and the trinkets on Jimmy's desk.

Jimmy was embarrassed that his walls still sported *Lord of the Rings* posters and *Star Wars* and soccer players. It was a little kid's room in so many ways. He had a corkboard with old pictures of him and Matt. They were so outdated! Nothing of them in the last seven years! Jimmy had rolls and rolls of undeveloped film in a drawer somewhere. Matt told him repeatedly to use digital, but Jimmy hadn't asked his mom for a new camera yet.

"I know… my room makes it look like I'm twelve."

Darian grinned. "I think it's cute. I'm seeing a side of you I haven't seen. You when you were young. Ya know? I like it." He crossed the room and slipped his arms around Jimmy's waist.

"I was such a sci-fi nerd. Matt and I role-played sometimes. Had sword fights. Recited lines from *Star Wars* and shit."

"Which character were you?" Darian nipped Jimmy's jaw and kissed his neck.

"Well, I wanted to be Legolas. Everyone wants to be Legolas. Matt usually pretended to be him, so I was Gimli."

"Not Aragorn?"

"No. I never wanted to be King. I liked the idea of fighting for the King, protecting the King, and following Legolas into battle. He has a nice ass."

Darian laughed. "True. Speaking of nice asses…." Darian groped Jimmy and gave him a suggestive flicker of his eyebrows. "We could make love in *this* bed. Christen your room?"

Jimmy was unsure. "Um, my mom could come home at any moment. I'm not sure that would be a great idea."

"Oh, come on. If I suck you first, it won't take you as long."

"Ouch. Not exactly a compliment."

"Hey, we're young. It comes with the territory. Cum fast and fuck often. Right? Or I could fuck you?" He palmed Jimmy. "Would you like that?" Darian unbuttoned Jimmy's jeans and reached into his briefs. "Do you want me to fuck you, Jamie?"

Darian fucking me? No! Can't do that. He always turns into Matt. "No. I'll do you."

"Yeah?" Darian did not seem convinced.

"Yeah," Jimmy asserted, undoing Darian's jeans. "I want you from behind." He stripped Darian's pants off and turned him around.

Darian crawled onto the bed and readied himself on all fours. He stroked his dick and turned his head to face Jimmy as he finished undressing. "Do you have lube here?"

"Ah, yeah, I think so." He left the room and returned with Vaseline. "Sorry. This is all I have."

"It'll do. Good thing we already ditched condoms, or you'd be using Glad Wrap."

"Ha, ha!" He rolled his eyes. "Do you want me to fuck you, or are you going to try and irritate me as much as possible?"

"Fuck me. Please."

Jimmy got on the bed behind Darian and rubbed his ass cheeks. He looked at his hole as he scooped out a glob of Vaseline to coat it. The hair around his ass was growing back in. Had it really been that long since Darian shaved? He usually kept his body free of hair in this area because Jimmy liked him smooth. He'd have to mention it later.

He eased two fingers into Darian's body and enjoyed the moan he was rewarded with. Darian rocked back onto his fingers. He twisted his wrist and Darian moaned louder. He brushed over his prostate and Darian jerked. Jimmy grinned.

"Fuck... Jamie.... Fuck me. Damn...."

Jimmy loved how easy it was to make Darian plead. "Is this what you want?" he asked, as he swatted Darian's butt with his cock. He slapped him with it, teasing him by caressing Darian's thighs and ass with its oozing head.

"Yes! Please. I want it."

Jimmy lubed up and pushed in.

"Oh, yes." Darian groaned with satisfaction. He rocked back. "Harder."

Jimmy thrust forward. He wasn't sure how much harder it could get. He grabbed Darian's hips on both sides and pulled him back as he pushed forward.

"Oh! Fuck!" Darian growled. "Yes!"

Jimmy was alarmed at how vocal Darian was becoming over the years. Darian seemed to like it hard and rough. *But how rough?* What could Jimmy get away with, and when was a good time to bring up things they could try? He'd looked online at kinky things, but he was afraid to bring it up. It seemed so naughty. Would Darian be up for role-playing? He'd have to think about it some more.

Jimmy grunted as he jutted his hips forward and back, moving in and out of Darian. His balls swung wildly between his parted legs. Jimmy lifted his hand and slapped Darian's ass.

"Ah!" Darian cried. "Do that... again."

Again? Jimmy was shocked at his own behavior, let alone that his boyfriend wanted more. He complied.

"Harder!"

Jimmy slapped again. His hand stung, and Darian's ass cheek was red. *Very naughty.*

"Oh, yes," Darian growled.

Jimmy saw Darian take himself in hand and jerk. His eyes drifted from Darian's arm motions to the corkboard. Pictures. Matt's pictures.

Matt in a football uniform in tenth grade, getting ready to hike a football between his legs. It was a posed shot. Jimmy laughed when he did it. But right now, Jimmy could not shake the vision of Matt's ass taking his dick deep and hard. In his football uniform and everything! Jimmy was fucking Matt.

Again.

Cum shot into Darian's hole, and Jimmy groaned. He slapped him one more time and gripped those hipbones until every bit of seed was spilled. They both collapsed forward, together. Jimmy panted in Darian's ear. "Oh, fuck, that was good!"

Darian didn't answer. He was out of breath.

"Sorry.... Sorry about your hips." Jimmy was winded himself. "I might have left some marks. I was… gripping really hard."

"It's okay."

"So you… liked that?"

"Yeah," Darian responded weakly.

Jimmy slipped out and moved off Darian's back. He kissed Darian's shoulder blade. "Okay. Just as long as you don't mind me being a little rough. I don't want to push too far."

Darian rolled over. "I don't mind." His eyes were glassy. Jimmy loved that look!

"Well, I think we can safely say that the bed was christened."

"Yup!"

"What do you say to going over to Matt's?"

"Do we have to? Your mom isn't home yet."

"And I am not letting her catch us like this. She'd have a heart attack!"

Darian laughed. "All right. We can go. But you will bring me back again, right?"

"Yeah, promise!" Jimmy crossed his fingers over his heart.

The boys got dressed and straightened the bed and then headed over to Matt's house.

I know I'm a coward. I admit it. I purposefully took Darian to my mom's when I knew she was on a ladies' retreat with Matt's mom. My siblings were with my other grandparents, and Kevin was in Chicago for a conference. I've turned into a really good liar. I think I could tell Darian anything, and he would believe me. I set out in this relationship with the complete intention of being honest with him… funny how it didn't turn out that way. I didn't mean to lie, this time or any other time, but like I said, I've gotten really good at it, and it's easier than the truth.

I like my world the way it is. I like the control I have. And I'm afraid of change.

And that slapping thing I did… it felt dirty. Darian liked me slapping his ass red, but I don't think I liked it. My hand hurt. But then I looked at Matt's picture and everything got blurry again. I could give it to Matt's ass brutally and slap him a few times, I'm sure of it. Why is it that I feel naughty about being rough with Darian but at the same time feel turned on thinking about Matt in the same context? That's just not right.

February 2010

It's fucking cold outside, but Darian is like sleeping with an electric blanket. He makes me sweaty. I cuddle until he falls asleep and then roll him away from me. I don't like sweating when I sleep. I've even opened the window a few times.

JIMMY finished brushing his teeth and joined Darian in their bed. "Scoot over, bed hog!" he jibed. "It's frickin' cold in here."

Darian rolled his eyes and moved over to let Jimmy in. "You're the one who keeps opening the window."

"I don't like sweating in my sleep."

"Then don't complain about the cold."

Jimmy ignored him and got situated. He looked over at Darian, who was sitting against the headrest with an open book in his lap. "What'ya reading?"

"A book."

"Gee, Snarky, I'm glad it's not the back of a soup can. What book?"

"You wouldn't like it." Darian flipped the page.

"Try me."

Darian closed the cover and showed Jimmy: two men on the front, one in a tight, black T-shirt holding a tulip and looking over his shoulder in a very smoldering way. Jimmy compulsively licked his lips. "*Sculpting Clay*…. What's it about?"

"A gay faery who finds his true love in New York City." He opened back to the page he was reading.

"That sounds weird." He reached over and took the book. He perused the back blurb. "It doesn't say that here."

Darian stuck out his hand, silently asking for the book back. When Jimmy gave it to him, he flipped to a section and started reading. "Taran could sense it was morning. Something about the sound of the quiet differed from the black-of-night quiet to the morning-sunshine quiet. He thought he heard birds chirping and the smell of the air was perfumed with… *Clay?*

"*Hmmm*, he was in Clay's bed, where he always wanted to be. And he was having the most wonderful dream. His body felt like he was floating. It started tingling in a way that made him pant for breath. Taran whimpered in his sleepy state and tilted his hips upward toward the incredible sensations that radiated from that spot. The tingling intensified into jolts of electricity and waves of heat."

Jimmy grabbed Darian's arm and interrupted him. "Wait… is this like a dirty book?"

Darian grinned. "Depends on your definition of *dirty*. It's somewhat erotic. Although I read online that the sex scenes get hotter as the author goes along."

"It's got sex in it?" Jimmy could not believe what he was hearing. Darian… reading a *sex* novel?

Darian found where he left off and kept reading. "His body quaked, every muscle in his stomach pulled tight. The vibrations were building so fast and so strong Taran wasn't sure how long he could stand it; still, he could not help but open himself up to it and welcome the pleasure in. His hands gripped the sheets tight enough to tear the fabric as he pulled his legs up and bent his knees, allowing his legs to fall open as wide as possible. Then he tilted his hips upward again. The wet heat that surrounded him begged him to give into its call. He allowed himself to explode as the need demanded and rode the waves of ecstasy until his body quivered and quieted into sated bliss." Darian turned a satisfied expression Jimmy's way. "What do you think?"

"I think...." Jimmy was still trying to process what was read to him. "I think the writer was describing a blowjob."

Darian started laughing. "Great deduction, Sherlock. I can't imagine what your English teachers went through, grading your research papers!"

Jimmy shoved his shoulder. "Shut up!" He really wasn't annoyed. "Why are you reading that, anyway? I never knew you liked that kind of book."

He shrugged. "I read lots of stuff. I was on goodreads.com and came across a comment. It said something like: 'Oh my God, what a great book! I laughed, I cried, I got hot flashes! How in the world were you able to write men so well? Gay men, that is? Holy shit! I couldn't read the pages fast enough. Brava! By cowboyromance.' I liked the sound of that, so I bought the book the next day."

"Huh." Jimmy couldn't think of another response. "Sooo, you like it?"

"Yeah, it's a cute story. I like Taran. He's a really sweet character." Darian leaned over and fiddled by the nightstand. He turned back to Jimmy and tossed him a different book. "Here, you can read that."

It looked like a cowboy book, judging from the cowboy on the cover with a farm in the background. *Love Means... No Shame* by Andrew Grey. Is it good?"

Darian grinned. "Oh yeah! I read that one twice."

Jimmy opened the book. It was inscribed. Jimmy read, "'Darian, find out what love means… to you. All the best, Andrew.' He signed the book to you?"

"Yup. I met him at a book fair. Real nice guy."

Jimmy looked at the book. "Huh. A dirty gay sex book. I can't believe I'm gonna read this." He flipped to the first page.

Darian leaned over again. He covered the page with his hand. "If you're gonna keep calling it 'a dirty sex book', then I'm not letting you read it. It's not dirty. It's artistic erotica. There is nothing disgusting or *dirty* about it. All the sex is consensual between adults… cowboys *or faeries*. I'm not going to let you insult the author. It's a very good book, with some deep thoughts about being gay and overcoming shame that can be associated with coming out when your family may be less than receptive. Just read it. I think you'll see some insight into your situation with your mom."

"Really?" Now he was interested. He removed Darian's hand from his book.

"Really. Just think about the title as you go. *Love Means… No Shame*. You could learn something." Darian opened his book again.

He's not being very subtle. Jimmy sat there staring at the page. *Do I feel ashamed? I don't think I'm ashamed. What is he getting at? Humph!*

May 23, 2010

"GOOD morning, Mom." Jimmy walked up to his mother in the kitchen and kissed her cheek.

"There's my graduate! Are you all ready for the ceremonies today?" she asked happily.

"Yeah, I guess." Jimmy walked over to the fridge and took out the juice.

"This is a big deal, James. Finally you'll be qualified to make something with your life. Start your own business or maybe sign with

J.P. Doughtery and Sons," Mrs. Smithers said proudly as she finished wiping food off the highchair. "Maybe you can cross-examine criminals!"

"Mom, they're lawyers. I have an accounting degree. I'm not going to go up against criminals unless it's over tax evasion. And even then, it's not me they'd fight, but the IRS." Jimmy wondered where his mom got her wild ideas.

"Whatever, dear. You'll be graduating in a few hours, and then you can start paying rent."

Jimmy spewed juice across the table. It even came out his nose. "What? Rent? Mom, since when do I have to pay rent?"

"Since today," she insisted. "You're a college graduate and should not be allowed to go through life sucking off your parents."

"I'm not. In fact, I was… I was thinking I'd move in with Dad." There! He'd said it. He told her.

His mom's eyes got wide. "You'll do no such thing! If I have ever heard of anything more ungrateful in my life! We clothe you, feed you, and pay for your education, and you reward your father…"

Stepfather…

"… by moving out and living with an uneducated, shiftless lowlife like… that man… I cannot believe you would do such a thing to your mother!" She turned away, and Jimmy heard sniveling. "After all I've done for you." She seriously sounded like she was crying.

Jimmy stood up and moved behind her. He touched her shoulder. "Mom. Mom, I never meant to disrespect Kevin. I'm grateful for all you've done for me. I just think it's time for me to move out, is all. You said yourself I'm going to have to pay rent. Dad and I have talked about me moving in for a while now."

She abruptly turned around. "You spoke to him behind my back? You schemed and planned this all along, didn't you?" Her sadness from moments ago disappeared behind the eyes of inexplicable rage. "You did this on purpose! You let us pay for everything, and then you were just going to leave without even a 'thank you'!" Intentional or not, she was spitting on his face as she screamed.

Jimmy felt the spittle but dared not wipe it away. "Mom. I tried to talk about moving out last year, but you freaked." *Oh shit, freaked was not the wisest word to use.*

"Freaked?"

Without warning, Joan moved like lightning and shoved Jimmy's head against the refrigerator. She grabbed his skull on the left side, gripping his hair, and rammed it against the stainless steel. As his body slid down the hard surface, she walked away, muttering, "Stupid little ingrate. I don't know why I bother. He's just like his father."

Jimmy slumped on the floor, stunned. He knew she was angry. He knew she was irrational. He knew she was capable of doing any number of things, but Jimmy did not foresee getting his head crushed against the fridge. His vision blurred and his head throbbed, but at least he didn't pass out. He reached up and touched his ear, since most of the pain was in that region. His fingers came away with blood on them. A ruptured eardrum, or maybe just a cut? Jimmy hoped it was only a cut.

He struggled to stand, and when he finally got his footing, Jimmy took some ice out of the freezer and put a bag full to his ear. He had to lie down. Graduation was in a few hours, and he had to make it seem like everything was normal.

He could fake this one. Everything would be fine.

AT THE Decker Auditorium, everything was far from fine. Jimmy's mom had just excused herself to go to the bathroom when Jimmy caught sight of his dad and Darian walking through the crowd. *Oh, shit!*

"Kev—I mean, Dad, I'm going to talk with some friends for a minute. I'll be right back." He didn't wait for an answer. Jimmy slipped between three chatty gals and weaved away through the crowd before his stepfather had a chance to respond.

Lucky for him, Darian hadn't seen him yet, so he was not trying to shuffle through in Jimmy's direction. The place was a madhouse, and Jimmy was thankful. He walked up behind them.

"Hey, what are you doing here?" He masked the fear and dread he really felt and put forth his best cheery hello.

Darian turned around. He smiled and tilted forward as if he might kiss Jimmy right there for all to see, but then the smile faded and he looked down instead. It hurt Jimmy to see how disappointed he was that he could not act on instinct.

"I know you said I didn't have to come, but I did. I wanted to see you graduate." Darian lifted his eyes and smiled. "I'm proud of you."

Jimmy got a lump in his throat. If ever he wanted to pull Darian into his arms and kiss him, it was now!

"I second that," his dad added.

Jimmy opted to hug his dad. "Thanks, Dad." He eyed Darian. "Thanks, Darian." He stuck his hand out and they shook. Jimmy held his hand and moved his index finger across Darian's wrist—stroking it. Darian's face softened, and he blushed. Jimmy knew everything was fine, even though he didn't hug him openly.

"When does this thing start?" Darian asked.

"In about fifteen minutes."

"How are they going to get all these people inside and seated by then?" his dad asked.

"I have no idea. Listen, I need to go and find my seat. Mom is over in that direction. She's wearing that dark blue dress you bought her on Mother's Day that time in Colorado. You may want to avoid eye contact. She was in a rare form this morning."

"Got it. She still wears that dress?"

"Yes. Only she thinks Kevin gave it to her. He even said he didn't, twice, but she doesn't believe him."

"Is everything okay with your mom?" Dan asked.

"Yeah," Jimmy nodded quickly. "She's the same as she always is."

"All right. Darian, let's go find some seats in this horde."

Before Darian stepped away, he asked, "Jimmy? Is Matt going to be here?"

Jimmy's gut clenched. *Matt? Fuck!* "Matt? Yeah, he said he'd be here. I haven't seen him yet."

Darian nodded solemnly. "I was just wondering."

"Normally he would text if..."—he reached into his pocket and retrieved his phone and then finished his thought—"... if he was here somewhere." He looked at the screen. "I have a text. Matt's says he's...." *Not coming. There's a fire, and I can't make it.* His heart sunk. He wanted Matt to be here.

"He's... where?" Darian asked. "Jimmy? Are you okay?"

"Um, yeah, I'm fine. Matt had an emergency. A fire somewhere. He can't make it."

Dan spoke up and touched his shoulder. "Oh, Jimbo, I'm sorry. I know it meant a lot to have him here."

"Yeah, well, he can't. It's okay." He grinned at Darian and squeezed his arm. "I have you two. What more do I need?" He hoped he sounded sincere. The pink hue that touched Darian's cheeks suggested the lie went over perfectly. "Now, I really gotta go. Talk to you after."

As Jimmy walked away, he felt the threat of tears. Of course he didn't cry, but he wanted to. Matt was going to miss his graduation from college! Four years of grueling tests which had challenged his capability to stay awake during lectures on statistics and number grouping. It was one of the most important things in his life, and Matt would miss it. He couldn't believe it.

But Darian is here, a voice in his mind whispered. *Yeah, Darian.* "And he said he's proud of me." His lips curved. "Darian is proud of me." He said it again. Not to convince himself, but rather to reaffirm himself. The tears that threatened before instantly fled when his heart puffed up. Surely he could not discount Darian's praise? "My Darian is proud of me." Jimmy said it out loud one more time as he pulled his shoulders back and stepped into his spot next to Paul Mason.

"Who's Darian?" Paul asked.

Jimmy really didn't know Paul. They took a couple of classes together but rarely spoke about anything but accounting. "Nobody," Jimmy said quickly and then took his seat.

Nobody you need to know.

August 7, 2010

"YA KNOW, you're not really moved out unless all your stuff is gone." Darian pointed out the flaw in Jimmy's reasoning.

"It's gone. Mostly. Why would I need my old CDs and childhood papers and stuff? They can stay at my mom's. And I don't need another bed or a desk. So what do you suggest I do with it all?" Jimmy didn't like to be questioned all the time for his actions.

"Jamie, you've been sleeping here for two weeks. I believe you when you say you moved out. I do. Really. But normally when someone says they moved out of their parent's house, they *actually moved out!* You could step back in there tomorrow and be right where you were before."

"No, I couldn't."

"Do you still have clothes there?"

"Yeah. What if I—"

"Nope. Not moved out. You're just on an extended leave of absence."

"Are you going to argue this point all night?" Jimmy asked Darian as he rolled over on top of him in their bed. "Because I seem to recall a certain someone suggesting that we skip the dessert my dad offered tonight in favor of making dessert of our own."

"I did say that, didn't I?"

"You did." Jimmy kissed Darian's throat and felt him spread his legs. "Now that's more like it." Jimmy kissed his way down Darian's chest, and the argument over "technicalities" was forgotten.

September 19, 2010

"YOU'RE serious?" Darian asked, eyeing Jimmy and the envelope in his hand.

"Yup. I booked reservations in a hotel and everything."

"Seriously?" Darian's eyes went wide, and he jumped at the envelope.

Jimmy pulled it back and held it out of Darian's reach, causing him to hop around to try and grab it. "Ah, ah, ah! Not yet. There is still something I need to do."

"What?"

Jimmy got down on one knee, right there in the kitchen. He placed the envelope on the floor and pulled a small velvet box out of his pocket. He opened it and held it up to Darian. "Darian, will you do me the honor of becoming my life partner?"

Darian gasped and reached for the box. He took it from Jimmy's hand and pulled out the shiny platinum band. "It's beautiful."

"You helped pick it out."

"I know, but it's different when you're on your knees, proposing again." He slipped it on his finger and admired it.

"You're not supposed to wear it before the wedding. And you're also supposed to say 'yes' when I ask you to marry me."

Darian looked back at Jimmy's waiting eyes. "Yes. Yes, I'll marry you!"

Jimmy smiled and got off the hard floor. He hugged Darian. "Good. I was hoping you didn't change your mind in the last year."

"I didn't." Darian rolled his eyes.

"Good. Like I said, I made reservations in a hotel. We leave on a bus for DC at 11:30 tomorrow morning."

"What? Tomorrow? But I have to pack! I have to get off work!" Darian tried to pull away, but Jimmy kept his hold around his hips. "Jamie, let go."

"Nope! All done. I packed for you. I called the last week of August and saved the dates and worked it out. We get married tomorrow night and have the whole week to look around Washington. See the Smithsonian and the Air and Space Museum...."

"And the National Art Gallery?"

"Yup! Speaking of which… now that I'm done with school, I think you should go back." Jimmy caressed his cheek and ran his thumb along his jaw.

"What do you mean?"

"I mean, I'm making good money now. I want you to go back to college. I want you to study art."

"You do?"

"Yeah. I think you'd make a great teacher."

Darian leaned into Jimmy's loving hand. "I'd like that."

"Good. Then it's settled. We'll go get married and enjoy our honeymoon, and when we get back, you enroll in whatever college you want. Well, that we can afford."

"Cool!" Darian squeezed Jimmy tightly around the neck. "Thank you."

"You're welcome. I love you."

Darian eased back. "I love you too." He kissed Jimmy softly.

Jimmy let him go and took a deep breath. "Now, I am off to my mom's for a long overdue conversation."

"Now? You're going now? What made you decide to do this now?" Darian was clearly shocked.

"You. I finished reading that book you gave me. And then you said you were proud of me at graduation. You make me dinner, you do my laundry, you call me at work just to tell me you love me. Darian, I'd be a fool to let this pass by. I *am* a fool for letting this go this long! You're wonderful, and it's about time I let the world know, *and my mother know,* just how much I love and appreciate you. I'm going to tell her today. She should be back from church any minute."

"I'll tell my mom too, then."

"Okay. I'll see you tonight." Jimmy started to walk away but turned back. Darian was admiring the rings again but left them in the box. *I do love him. He's great.* He stepped back next to Darian and gave him one last bear hug. This was the hardest time he'd ever had pulling away from those big brown eyes and Darian's soft, kissable lips.

26

February, 2009

Crapola. Mom says I have to go to church.

JIMMY sat next to Matt in the pew. He didn't like going to church, but
it was hard to avoid it when his mother insisted. At least she allowed
him to sit with Matt sometimes. Like now. The songs were good. He
liked "Shine Jesus Shine" and "Be Thou My Vision" and a few other
songs. Or hymns or whatever they were termed. He liked the whole
idea of Christianity in general. This wasn't a bad religion. In fact,
Christians did a lot of good in the world. Matt's church was actively
helping Samaritan's Purse and their pursuit of reaching out to orphans
around the world. Matt's church went to soup kitchens and cold
shelters around the state, volunteering and giving of their time and
resources to help the poor.

Jimmy liked that.

What he didn't like were the occasions where the pastor gave a
sermon on homosexuality. Of course, he didn't do it blatantly.
Everything was subtle and sneaky and in-between the lines. That irked
him! *Why doesn't Pastor Dennis just come out and say, "Hey, Jimmy,
are you gay? Are you and Matt gay together? I've been watching you."*
Jimmy got paranoid every time they had one of their "meetings" and he
brought up homosexuality. Jimmy thought the pastor knew, but so far
their talks had been about his dad and the divorce and his fighting in
school. Even after he graduated high school, his mom insisted he see

Pastor Dennis a few times, just to make sure his fighting tendencies didn't continue.

Jimmy tried to pay attention, but the sermon was too hard to follow. They kept flipping text and looking up more verses. *Where the hell were they?* He looked at Matt's Bible. It was open to Romans, chapter one.

The pastor recited, "For this reason God gave them up to dishonorable passions. For their women exchanged natural relations for those that are contrary to nature; and the men likewise gave up natural relations with women and were consumed with passion for one another, men committing shameless acts with men and receiving in themselves the due penalty for their error."

Due penalty? What does that mean? Jimmy didn't know. He'd thought the last twenty minutes was about adultery, which he did not condone. Now it seemed like the pastor was moving into homosexuality. Again! Every time he came to church, there was something in the sermon pointing to that subject! Was this a coincidence or a conspiracy? Jimmy shifted uncomfortably.

He leaned over and whispered to Matt, "I gotta pee." He scooted out of the pew and headed to the men's restroom. While standing at the urinal, he got a text.

Dude? U ok?

He texted Matt back: *Yeah. Fine. I don't like how he talks about gay stuff every time I come to church. How do you stand it?*

I've gotten used 2 it. He says lots of things I don't agree with.

Well, I don't like it. It makes me want to punch him.

Please don't. LOL.... The way I see it, church is full of sinful people who all make mistakes. Not everyone agrees. Not everyone believes in everything the Bible teaches in exactly the same ways. We all gotta work it out on our own. After all, the Bible also says to work out your own salvation with fear and trembling. My opinion is that it is an individual thing. Just God and me.

Feeling belligerent, Jimmy had to ask the question: *Then why are you still in the closet?*

Because I'm good with me & God, it's the "between me & the parents" part I still have problems with. Get done peeing already & get back in here. I'm all alone!

Jimmy washed his hands and headed back into the sanctuary. He might not fully agree, or understand, but he didn't want Matt to be alone. They were in this thing together!

June 2009

Just like I said, I'm always thinking of Matt. I bought him a present in New York, and now I'm headed over to give it to him.

JIMMY walked into the kitchen. His mom was sitting at the table, writing in her checkbook. "The bathrooms are clean, the ironing is put away. I'm going to Matt's. I'll be back later," he said.

She looked up. "Matt's? You just got back from New York, and you have to go over there already?"

"He's not there often, since he moved in with his aunt." She was silent, and Jimmy scratched his head. Should he stay or should he go? He opted to go. Lingering in the doorway, he added, "I had fun in New York, by the way. Thanks for letting me go."

"That's nice, dear." She scribbled something else and finally looked up. "Did you have a nice time?"

Jimmy inwardly groaned. "Yes, Mom."

"Your father said it was just okay."

"You asked Dad?" *Don't panic, don't panic.*

"Of course. I called a couple of times to make sure you were with him and not off traipsing around with a bunch of punk kids. He told me you saw the Empire State Building and Times Square."

"Yeah. Times Square was insane. Like Ocean City boardwalk without the beach."

"I expect to see pictures."

"Pictures?"

"Yes. Pictures." The look she gave was unwavering, even more so when she crossed her arms over her chest.

"Sure. Pictures. I'll show you." Jimmy stepped into the hall, one leg out of the kitchen, one to go. "See ya, Mom." He turned before panic attacked. He could produce pictures. *No problem. Maybe Darian could Photoshop one in of my dad?* He was good with computers. Darian could do it! He talked himself into relaxing as he headed over to Matt's.

MATT was in his parents' garage when Jimmy arrived. "Hey, at it again, I see." Jimmy pointed to the open hood of the Jetta.

Matt nodded, "Yeah, it's making a weird sound. Mom wanted me to look at it. Somebody in the family always has a weird sound for me to listen to, or oil to change, or tires to rotate. I feel like a fucking Jiffy Lube attendant."

Jimmy laughed and handed Matt a paper bag. "Here, I bought this for you."

Matt took the bag and pulled out a red, guitar-shaped Hard Rock Café keychain. "Wow, thanks. Where'd you get this?"

"Duh! New York. I thought you'd like it. The guitar spins around and everything."

"I do like it." He turned his head to look at Jimmy in the yellow light of the garage. "When did you go to New York? How did your mother ever agree to that?"

Nervous tension gripped his innards. *I should really plan out these moments better.* "I went with some guys in my class. A guy named Paul and his girlfriend. Somebody mentioned their stepdad had a condo or something and invited some of us up for a few days." *That is the worst lie I've ever told. Way to be vague, Jamie!*

"How come you didn't tell me? Maybe I could've gone?"

At least Matt sounded like he believed him. "I texted, and when you didn't reply I figured you were out on a call or something." Jimmy looked back inside the engine.

Matt wiped off his oil-covered hands on a rag. "Yeah, I guess. I'm out on calls often, but we also tend to sit around a lot, playing cards, cleaning the fire truck and stuff. I feel like I live there. Maybe another time?"

"For sure!" Jimmy smiled, lie successfully taken. "You need a hand with this?

Matt nodded. "Always."

July 2009

> *I am sick of mowing grass!!!!*

September 2009

> *I am sick of doing oil changes!*

December 2009

> *I love Matt, but I am tired of working on cars with him. I like the money, I guess. I'm saving up, so when I move out of my mom's house I will have some.*

April 2010

MATT and Jimmy sat in Matt's parents' kitchen after they finished changing the spark plugs on Jimmy's Taurus and Matt's uncle's Camaro. Jimmy had nearly cried when Matt called and asked if he could swing by. Over the winter they practically opened their very own Jiffy Lube! They rotated tires over Thanksgiving and changed oil in three cars over Christmas. It was hot and greasy work, cooped up in the garage, but Jimmy liked the time he spent with Matt. It was like old times. With Matt working lots of hours and living far away, Jimmy had forgotten what it felt like to be around him for hours. He missed it. He hardly ever made time to see him. Jimmy spent his free time studying for exams. Months just flew by, and now it was April, the year two thousand and ten. How the heck did that happen? Jimmy blinked and suddenly a year went by!

One of these months I need to bring Darian, Jimmy thought. *Maybe.*

After a few hours of lubing and cranking, Mrs. Dixon kindly offered them ice cream. *One was never too old for ice cream,* she said. Jimmy was glad—he loved mint chocolate chip.

Mrs. Dixon was busily checking e-mails on her MacBook Pro next to them, so Matt doled out another helping, complete with whipped cream and hot fudge. When she gave a small sigh, Matt and Jimmy glanced over. "What's wrong, Mrs. D.?" Jimmy asked.

"Oh, nothing."

Another sigh meant it was more than nothing. Jimmy and Matt both knew that. They exchanged glances. "Mom, you can talk if you want. We'll listen," Matt offered politely.

She gave him a weak smile. "Thanks, honey. I'm just disappointed, is all."

"About what?" Jimmy asked.

"I just got an e-mail from my friend Eleanor. She sent me a link to USA Today's page," she explained. "It's an article on Jennifer Knapp."

Matt placed the Breyers back into the freezer. "That Christian guitarist you dragged me to see at King's Dominion in '02?"

She looked surprised. "You remember that?"

Matt arched his brow. "Yeah, Mom. It rained. You made me wait in line with you to get your CD autographed by Sonicflood. Remember? We both had head colds the next day."

"I thought you said it was Jennifer Knapp?" asked Jimmy.

"It was. Sonicflood and Jennifer Knapp opened for Third Day." Matt filled in the missing details for Jimmy. "It was a great concert. Really. They jammed way louder than I ever imagined from listening to their CDs. Mom looked like a groupie. It was funny. She danced and screamed and whistled so loud I thought my eardrums would ring for a week."

"Now I remember," Jimmy grinned. "You definitely told me about your mom!" He laughed. "But how come you went and not your dad?"

"He's not into Christian Rock music. My mom only has a few friends who like Christian Rock as much as she does. She didn't want to go alone, so I offered. Plus, it was at King's Dominion, dude! We rode roller coasters all day and listened to a rock concert all night. It was awesome!" Matt sat down and ate another bite. "Yeah, man, good times. So what's the news about, Mom?"

Mrs. Dixon sighed again. "Seems she came out."

Jimmy asked, "Came out of where?" Matt kicked him under the table. Jimmy glared. "What?"

Matt rolled his eyes. "Out, dude. Like *out.*"

"She says she's a lesbian, Jimmy," Mrs. Dixon clarified.

Now he felt like a twat. "Oh." Then the weight of it rested on his shoulders, and he repeated, "Ohhhh. *Out.* Got it."

Matt patted his mother's hand. "Are you okay?"

"Yes, I guess so. It's so disappointing. She was such a fine artist."

"She still is. I heard she has another album coming out in May." Matt tried to be positive.

"I know, but a *lesbian*? This, on top of what I heard last week about Ray Boltz and Ricky Martin, is just too much to grasp all at once. I need to go for a walk." She abruptly grabbed her jacket from the back of the kitchen door and went out without another word.

Jimmy looked confused. "Who's Ray Boltz?"

"Another Christian singer who came out. She has his autograph." Matt cleaned the bowl of the last bit of melted ice cream with his spoon.

"And why Ricky Martin? That's not something I've heard her listening to."

"No, but she used to listen to Menudo when she was a kid, and Ricky Martin was on a poster she had on her bedroom wall."

"What's Menudo?"

Matt shrugged and snorted. "No way to explain that one, man. You better Google it."

"Okaayyy. So, she's pretty bummed over Jennifer Knapp, eh?" Jimmy wasn't sure what to say.

"Yup."

"How do you feel about it?"

"Dude, it rocks! For her to stand up to the Christian community and say 'I'm gay' and take some hits for it, I think she's got some balls! It takes way more courage than I have, but in a way it gives me some inspiration. I think she's really great for taking a stand!"

"You gonna tell your mom you're gay?"

"Not now, I'm not! She'd keel over and die of shock. Naw, maybe sometime if I have a boyfriend. You know? Like it would be easier to face if I wasn't alone." Matt put their bowls in the sink and wiped off the table.

"I thought you didn't do boyfriends?" Jimmy's hope grew.

"I don't."

Hope shriveled back down.

"I meant later. When I'm old, remember? I'm not hitchin' myself to anyone now."

They headed back out to the garage.

June 17, 2010

JIMMY kissed Darian right before he headed off to work. The door closed, and Jimmy went into the kitchen to clean up before he had his interview. The door opened a few minutes later, and Jimmy grinned. "Did you forget somethi—" He froze mid-sentence when he discovered it was not Darian in the room. It was Matt.

"Surprise!" Matt held his hands out to the sides.

"Matt, what are you doing here?" Jimmy was shocked and anxious and slightly panicky.

"I came to apologize for not being at your graduation. Will you forgive me?" Matt gave Jimmy his puppy-dog eyes.

"Stop!" Jimmy giggled. "We're not little kids anymore."

"I brought presents." He revealed a hidden package from behind his back. "Well, one present."

Jimmy smiled and took it. "You wrapped it in a paper bag? Classy."

"Hey, I'm not Martha Stewart."

Jimmy opened it. "A calculator."

"Yeah. I remembered you had that interview today."

"I didn't get the job yet."

"You will. You're the smartest guy I know. That accounting firm would be foolish not to take you."

Matt's compliment made Jimmy blush. "Thanks."

Matt popped him on the shoulder. "Come on, show me your room. I don't think I've been here for the last few years. Come to think of it, I don't think I've ever been here." He pursed his lips as if the thought was absurd. "So how come I haven't been here?"

Don't panic, don't panic. "Dude, you work all the time. Remember? You work and you live like an hour south now; when do you have time?" Jimmy played it off effortlessly.

"I know, but I can't believe I've never been to your dad's. It's pretty nice." He looked around and wandered into the other room.

Jimmy quickly snatched the picture of him and Darian off the fridge and hustled into the living room. He turned over the picture on the end table while Matt was looking in the other direction.

"Did you take up drawing?" Matt pointed to the open sketchpad on the coffee table.

"No. Um, my dad's girlfriend draws." *Quick thinking!*

"She's good!" Matt lingered in the living room, and things were growing abnormally weird. "Soooo? You showing me your room, or what?"

"I would, but I really have to go. Interview. Yup, interview in twenty minutes. You walked in just as I was about to leave."

"Really? Okay. Are you going dressed like that?" He pointed dubiously at Jimmy's casual attire.

"Um, yeah, they said casual was fine." He hoped his cheeks didn't flush with his distress.

Matt tilted his head. "Okay. If you say so. But I would still have gone with a suit and tie. At least a tie. You're an accountant, not a fry cook."

Jimmy grabbed his keys and headed to the door. "It's fine. But as I said, I really have to go. You'll have to come over again sometime. Maybe tomorrow." He opened the front door, and they both walked out.

"I can't. I have a twelve-hour shift."

"Oh, too bad. Maybe another time." Jimmy patted Matt on the back. "Thanks for the calculator."

Matt smiled. "Anytime. Good luck today! Call me when you get the job."

"You got it! Later." Jimmy gave Matt a quick hug and jumped in his car. "That was a close call," he said to himself. He didn't wait for Matt to get into his truck before he pulled away. He needed to get far ahead. No way did he want Matt following him halfway down the road! If he did, Jimmy would have to drive miles out of his way in order to circle back around and go back to the house. His interview was in three hours. Somehow he'd have to text Matt before then and say he got the job and then hope to God he did get it!

This lying business was getting harder and harder to keep straight in his head. Eventually, everything was going to explode. Jimmy hoped he could work up the nerve to come clean before everyone in his life found out how often he embellished.

27

September 24, 2010

1:08 p.m.

MATT drove Darian to his parents' house. His mom and dad had volunteered to have the reception after the funeral, to alleviate any burdens on the Smithers family. Unlike the other day when he'd driven Darian to his aunt's and allowed him his silence, this time Matt was not about to let Darian suffer across the seat. He drove one-handed and kept his other arm firmly around the sobbing mess that was Darian Weston.

He'd never seen another human being so torn up before. Matt had seen death. Several family members had died while he was growing up. He'd seen people cry and even shed his own tears over losing a loved one. He'd loved Jamie, and he'd cried for that loss. It hurt so much seeing the casket lowered into the ground. It hurt to do a eulogy for his best friend when Jamie was only twenty-two years old! He'd thought he and Jamie had years ahead of them to laugh, and suddenly those years were gone. *Why?*

Matt didn't know why.

He didn't understand how all this happened. He didn't understand how someone who seemed so happy could do something like this. He didn't understand why Jamie would kill himself and leave behind his dad, his best friend, and his fiancé.

His fiancé! Why would Jamie do this to Darian?

Matt was feeling angry again. *Fuckin' Jamie!* How could he do this to someone as fragile and sweet as Darian? Surely he would have known that Darian would be devastated? Surely Jamie would have thought *something* about Darian before he killed himself? But that was just it—Matt had no idea why or what Jamie was thinking when he did it. It was all a blank.

He pulled up to the curb and parked his truck.

They sat a few minutes before Matt tried to move Darian from his plastered presence at his side. "Dare…. We need to go in."

Darian lifted his face.

Matt nearly snorted a laugh but managed to muffle it. Not really a time to laugh, but it was hard not to. He reached for a napkin in the side pocket of his door. "Here, you need to wipe your nose. You have mucus hanging there, longer than the spittle stream that hangs from my dog's jowls."

Matt was relieved to see a faint hint of a smile touch Darian's lips. He tried to go for more humor and find out if he could coax a chuckle. "And my shirt is officially yuckified. I think my dog makes less of a mess when she drinks and lets the water run back out of her mouth all over the floor. I feel drenched." He exaggerated his fake irritation by pulling the wet parts of his shirt away from his shoulder. He pinched the fabric, extending the unused other fingers as if he was afraid to touch the mucus-covered areas.

Darian smirked.

Matt smiled. "Hey, at least I got a half a smile." He cupped Darian's cheek and gazed into Darian's tired eyes before kissing his lips. After a half a dozen soft kisses, he suggested they head inside. "I'll show you to the bathroom. You can cool your face off and try to gather yourself together. Okay?"

Darian weakly nodded.

In the bathroom, Matt turned to leave. Darian blurted, "Don't leave me."

Matt lingered by the door. *Guys don't hang in the bathroom with other guys.* He knew people would talk if they noticed them in here together. *Fuck!* Matt peeked out. No one was in the hall. Maybe he could risk a few minutes. He closed the door and turned around.

"Thank you," Darian said.

Darian looked pitiful. He was a lost puppy, and Matt was the old curmudgeon who'd found him on the roadside. Could he seriously turn away? Could Matt step back for fear of what people might say? Darian needed him.

Fuck everyone else!

Matt crossed the floor and opened his arms. "Come here."

Darian molded to his body like a missing puzzle piece. He fit. Holding the young man in his arms was right. He knew it with every fiber of his being. When he held Darian, it was as if everything else in his life had led him to this point. Darian was the absent answer to all his questions. How could he possibly let go because he feared what his family would say?

He couldn't.

But when they left the safety of the bathroom, and their private intimacy was out for all to witness, Matt fully dreaded the confrontation that was sure to come.

He kissed him. Gently. He licked Darian's lips and made him whimper as he teased him with his tongue. Darian pinched his nipples and Matt suppressed a growl. His little lover knew just how to push his buttons, and Matt reveled in it. "Oh, baby." He kissed and nibbled his way across Darian's throat. "I'm gonna love on you so good when we get back to my place."

"I need you."

"I know, baby. I need you too." Matt kissed his lips and wrestled with his tongue.

"Please don't leave me."

"I won't, baby, I won't." He snagged Darian's lower lip between his teeth.

There was a knock at the door, and Matt jumped back. His hands were still on Darian's hips, but he could see the disappointment in Darian's eyes. "I'll be right out," he called to whoever was in the hall. To Darian he explained quietly, "I won't leave you, Darian. I promise. No matter what people say, no matter what looks my mom gives me, I won't let go. Okay? But I need something from you too." He searched Darian's eyes.

"What?"

"You gotta tell me if what I feel is worth it. When we walk out that door, together, I can't just jump back in. Once I'm out, I'm out. I can't do that if you're gonna step away when the pain of Jamie's death is past. I gotta know that you're gonna be there for me, too."

The hesitation before Darian's answer was longer than Matt would have liked, but at least he got one. Darian nodded.

"Yeah?" Matt asked in disbelief. "You're in this with me? Together?"

"Yes."

Matt grabbed him up and lifted Darian off his feet. "Oh, Darian. I promise to do everything I can to make you happy. I swear." He squeezed him tight and heard him grunt.

"Can't... breathe...."

Matt chuckled and set him back on his feet. "Sorry. I'm just really happy you're giving us a chance. I know I'm not Jamie. I know you loved him more than anything. So did I, but I think we could have something special too."

Darian smiled. "Me too."

"Really? 'Cause you look like you're about to throw up."

The corner of Darian's mouth lifted. "Maybe."

Matt widened his smile. "This is not going to be easy for either one of us, but I'm willing to go for it. Just... let's take it slow, okay? No one knows I'm gay. I don't know how to tell them, but I really don't want it to be obvious because I have you suckin' on my neck or grabbin' my crotch and shit."

Darian gave him a look. "Matt, I *can* control myself, ya know."

"Okay," he sighed with relief. "Sorry. I'm new at this."

Another knock. Matt took a deep breath and walked to the door to open it. The raised eyebrow of Mr. Miller's cousin Maggie greeted him. "Hey, Maggie."

She looked at him and then to Darian. "Are you all right, Darian? I was worried."

"You know him?" Matt asked.

"Yes, Matt. We met at the family reunion, a few summers ago, before I returned to Germany." She reached out and touched the side of Darian's face. "Jimmy called me to tell me he proposed."

Darian ducked his head as he blushed. "He was so happy. His dad even opened some champagne when we got back from New York."

Matt could see he was fighting back tears.

"Did Jimmy ever tell his mom?"

Darian shook his head. "We were…." He choked up. "We were… going to… go get married in DC last Monday."

His pain just about did Matt in. He reached around Darian's back and guided him into a hug. Darian cried into the other side of Matt's shirt.

Maggie eyed Matt curiously. "Is there something going on?" Her eyes flicked to Darian and back to Matt. "You seem a little too cuddly to me."

Matt gulped. This was the first of many questions, he was sure. "I, uh, we… Darian and I are…."

Darian sniveled and wiped his nose on his cuff. "I'll e-mail you, Maggie. I don't want to talk about it now. Matt and I are… together. We need each other."

She nodded. "Okay. It's unexpected, but I think I can see the reasons. I just didn't know Matt was gay."

"Nobody else does either," Matt confessed.

"Oh, then this should be an interesting wake."

"To say the least."

"Well, I'd love to keep chatting, but I have to pee."

Matt and Darian left Maggie and ended up on the sofa in the family room. Darian said he felt sick again and dizzy, so Matt advised him to lie across the cushions. It would have been easy to avoid questioning glances if Darian chose to prop his head on a pillow at the opposite end of the couch, but oh no! As Darian started get situated,

Matt insisted—without thinking—that he lie at this end in order to allow Matt to rest his arm around him. So Darian placed a pillow against Matt's thigh and got comfortable.

As soon as Matt settled his arm on Darian's outstretched side, he felt the gaze of everyone in the house upon him. *They know. They know and they are judging me!*

"Thank you for saying such nice things about my son."

Matt jumped as Mr. Miller sat in the recliner next to him and offered a cube of cheese off his plate.

Matt took it. "Thanks." He nervously waited to see what Jamie's dad would say about him, or more importantly, about him and Darian making themselves so comfortable on the couch.

"This is the hardest thing I've ever had to do," he confessed to Matt.

"Me too."

They sat, uncomfortable with the silence yet unable to make conversation. People walked in and out of adjoining rooms, but for the most part they were left alone. Matt was thankful. He needed to take this one person at a time.

"Is he asleep?"

Matt jumped again. "Huh?"

Mr. Miller pointed to Darian. "I said, is he asleep?"

Matt peered down at Darian's serene expression. His slack jaw and the slight drool dripping from the corner of his mouth answered the question. Matt grinned. "Oh, yeah, he's out." Matt gently smoothed back the hair from the front of Darian's face.

Mr. Miller nodded. He looked as shattered as Darian did. Matt felt for him, but he had no idea what to say. The man just lost his son. What did one say? *"I'm sorry?"* That phrase sounded so inadequate.

"Ya know... I've been worried about Darian," Mr. Miller said. "I texted him a few times in the last two days, but he didn't reply." He paused and wiped the newly forming tears from his eyes. "I thought... I thought... shit, I'm sorry." He covered his face with his hand.

Grief loomed about them like an ominous grey cloud in the dead of winter. Matt's hairs stood up on his forearms. "Mr. Miller, I… you don't need to apologize to me. I've shed more tears in the last few days than I have in my life."

A few deep breaths and he looked back to Matt. "I wasn't sure what Darian would do. Jamie has seen him though so much, I didn't know if…." He paused again, pinching the tears back. "I couldn't face losing another son."

Matt furrowed his brow. *Son?* He knew Jamie had proposed to Darian, but he didn't realize that Mr. Miller thought of Darian so fondly. "He was with me, Mr. Miller. If I'd known you were worried, I would've called. I didn't realize you were close."

Mr. Miller looked at him like he'd said something completely bizarre. "He's lived with me for three years, Matt. I love him. After seeing him run out of the funeral home last night, and then when he didn't respond to my texts, I thought he'd done something awful."

Matt realized what Mr. Miller was trying to say. "Oh, shit, Mr. Miller, I swear, if I thought for a second you were worried about him ending his life like Jamie… oh, God…." Matt squeezed Darian's upper arm. "He was fine. Really. I kept Darian safe."

Dan gave him a weak smile. "Thank you. You're a good friend. I'm glad he has you." He stood up. "Will you let me know how he is, from time to time? I understand if he doesn't want to come home. I haven't been able to face Jim's room either. I just want to know Darian's safe."

"I will. I promise."

Jamie's dad left, and Matt looked at the sleeping angel next to him. "I should take you up to my bed and let you sleep in peace," he whispered, stroking Darian's hair. "Darian? Darian?"

He didn't move. Matt eased his thigh from under the pillow. He slipped from the couch and knelt down, caressed Darian's cheek and kissed his forehead. "What is it about you, baby? I'm scared as hell about people finding out, yet when I look at you… when I look at you, baby, I can't stop myself from touching you." He leaned his face against Darian's hair and took a deep breath. Caring for him felt so right.

MATT left Darian to sleep and moved into another room. His mom had done a great job of clearing out the dining room, and the family room, and the library, and the game room, so that all of the guests from the funeral had plenty of space to mill about and chat. He overheard several conversations that nagged at him. People were saying stupid stuff, like blaming Jamie's death on bad friends and rock music. People were idiots! He seriously wanted to get Darian and leave.

He stopped abruptly from entering the kitchen when he heard his name mentioned.

"The one with Matt? You know, that boy who collapsed at the cemetery. Who is he?" Matt thought the question came from Miss Carrie from church. He didn't dare peer in and get caught eavesdropping.

"I don't know." That was his mom's voice.

"I was wondering the same thing." That voice was definitely Ms. Joan. Matt would know her condescending tone anywhere. "The way he completely made a fool of himself like that. Blubbering like an idiot! Where does he come off acting like that when I just lost my son? He should know how to be respectful." He heard her sniffle. "I was…" *sniff* "… beside myself." *sniff* "It's been awful."

"There, there, dear."

Joan continued seeking sympathy. "No one cared about me. They all seemed to focus on him!" *sniff* "I needed comfort, and they all looked at that blubbering boy!"

Matt could not take another word. He burst around the corner, fueled to set them straight. "How dare you say such things about Darian!"

The startled woman stood gape-mouthed.

"Darian is the name of the boy you are so quick to ridicule for his unabashed display of emotion."

"Well, he was being absurd." Joan Smithers recovered surprisingly well from her crying fit and served him back an attitude. "Where does he get off, acting like that?"

Matt walked right up to her and ignored his mother's disapproving scowl. "You are so self-centered. Can't you believe for one second that someone besides you might be hurting too? Mr. Miller can barely hold himself together. Maggie keeps her chin up, but really she's sick with grief. You should have seen her in the funeral home. And Darian… Darian was Jamie's fiancé, for goodness sake. I'll have you know, he's hurting worse than any of us right now. They were supposed to get married last Monday!"

"No!" Joan's eyes burned fire. "My son was *not* gay."

"Matt, please don't—"

He ignored his mom's plea, puffed out his chest, and cocked his head. "Yes, he was, Joan. Your beloved James was gay, and he was in love with Darian Weston."

Jamie's mother slapped him across the face. "How dare you? You don't know anything, you smartass kid!"

Matt was shocked but held his cool. He heard his mom and the other ladies gasp, but he was not about to let Joan Smithers get the best of him. He locked eyes with her and let her rant.

"I'll have you know my son was in counseling for *years* over this," Joan sneered, "and Pastor Dennis was convinced James was normal! It's that boy in there,"—she pointed frantically—"that Darian Weston, he's the one that's perverted my son with his *practices*. *He* is the… *homosexual* who should be condemned for his sins." She then turned her accusatory finger on Matt. "And you… you call yourself a Christian, and yet you associate with such people. I saw you! I saw you in there consoling him and… *touching* him. You should be ashamed."

When she paused, Matt took a step forward, glaring with as much fire in his eyes as she had. "And true to your reputation, you still can't say the word homosexual above a whisper. Pathetic." His hands shook with pent-up aggression for all the years he'd sat back and watched other gays take a hit. Not today! He got right in her face. "You can believe whatever you like, but I knew your son better than most. I know for damn sure Jamie was a… *homosexual*." Matt mocked her disdain for the word. "And that *boy* in there—who is a man, by the way—is one of the sweetest people you'll ever meet, and for you to disregard his love and suffering over the loss of his fiancé sickens me. I may be a Christian, but at least I'm not a hypocrite like you. Maybe you'd be a little more compassionate if you stopped judging for once and learned to take Kevin's dick up *your* ass!"

She gasped. So did his mother.

"Matt!" Maggie gasped from the doorway.

Matt's adrenaline burst was draining away, and he was left feeling the weight of what he'd just said. It was completely uncalled for and vulgar. He closed his eyes briefly before looking at his mom. "I'm sorry."

He turned and left the women to their horror. *This is not good.* "If I'd only kept my stupid mouth shut. I shouldn't have said that. It wasn't fair to my mom or Joan. It certainly wasn't very Christian-like." He went back to Darian and knelt down. "Darian." He touched his face.

Darian's eyes fluttered open.

"We need to go, baby. I can't be here anymore. Can you walk, or do you want me to carry you?"

"I can walk." Darian sat up and took Matt's offered hand.

Matt heard the argument in the kitchen escalating.

"My son was not gay!" he heard Joan shout.

"Joan, calm down."

He almost grinned. Leave it to his mom to always jump in and play mediator. He led Darian to the door.

"Where do you think you're going with that sodomite?"

He glanced back and saw Joan charging through the dining room after him. "Oh, fuck!"

"What did you do, Matt?" Darian asked.

"Something stupid. Let's get out of here." He ushered Darian through the door and practically let it slam in Joan Smithers's face.

MATT'S brain was on overload. "What have I done?" he asked Darian as he emerged from the bathroom.

"I think you outed me." Darian lifted the covers for Matt.

"I'm serious." Matt crawled in and lay back on the pillow, lifting his arm automatically, allowing Darian to snuggle against his chest. It felt like the most natural thing in the world. Matt held Darian close and caressed his skin as he continued thinking out loud. "I can't believe I was arguing with Jamie's mom. What the fuck is wrong with me? I could have let it go. I could have walked away, but something inside wouldn't let me. They dissed you, and I snapped. I said some pretty rude things."

"Me? They said something mean about me? But they don't even know me."

"Exactly! Joan said something about the way you were acting, and I lost it. You had every right to act the way you did. You were closer to Jamie than anyone besides his dad. I don't blame you for letting your emotions out. I probably would have acted the same way. Well, maybe. I tend to get angry; you seem to cry."

"I do. I think I've cried enough for years. I feel so wasted."

Matt heard the weight in his voice. "You sound exhausted. You've been through so much."

Darian yawned. "I am. I can't even think. I'm so tired." He sighed and stretched his arm across Matt's chest.

"Close your eyes." Matt held him protectively. "I just can't believe the things I said. I wasn't thinking. I just went off. My mom's got to be disappointed in me. I know it. How am I going to face people in church on Sunday?"

Matt heard Darian's faint snore. He smiled and caressed Darian's arm. Somehow, he knew everything would work itself out. He had Darian.

Matt would apologize for the rude comment about Kevin's dick, but not for anything else. He couldn't. Joan was out of line. He may have just met Darian, but deep in his bones Matt knew that what he'd said to her was true: Darian was one of the sweetest men ever. She could not be allowed to treat him like that.

Matt would protect him.

His eyes fluttered. Darian's steady breathing lulled him. Matt fought to stay awake and think about what would come next, but he was helpless. He nuzzled his nose into Darian's hair and took one last lungful of his scent before he gave in to the call of sleep.

28

September 25, 2010

MATT carefully separated his body from the tangled heap of sheets and Darian's limbs. He got a kick out of how cute Darian was in his sleep and how very *asleep* he could be! Matt almost laughed out loud, but didn't want to chance waking Darian up. He really needed his sleep. Matt did too, but he also knew he wasn't going to get it.

His mind was working way too hard. He kept thinking about Jamie. What had happened? Why? He wandered into the kitchen and turned on the coffee pot. He stood there, hands on the counter, thinking. Always thinking. Too much thinking in the last few days. He wanted to go back to the way things were before Jimmy's death. He liked his life then.

His racing mind paused.

Matt looked up from his current position of blankly studying the crumbs on the linoleum floor while the coffee perked. "The way life was before?" he muttered, looking toward the hallway. In his bed lay what life promised now. Darian. What good would it do to play the "what-if" game? Matt couldn't change anything. He couldn't turn back time. What was done was done. He had to press on. But overcoming this tragedy was not going to be easy, and he needed some answers. *God, please give me some answers.*

Movement caught his attention.

"Good morning," he greeted Darian with a smile.

Darian grunted and trudged over to his waiting arms.

Matt hugged him. *In spite of all the pain, this is what the future holds, and I want to keep it!* Darian let go, and Matt kissed him before he took out a mug and poured his coffee. "Coffee?"

Darian shook his head. "Milk."

"Not a coffee drinker? I live on the stuff. Coffee and Gatorade!"

"I like it sometimes. I prefer milk or juice. I never liked Gatorade. Or soda." Darian found Rice Krispies in the cabinet. "Bowls?"

Matt pointed. "Door to the left. Braving some food, eh? It's about time!"

Darian shrugged. "We'll see if it stays down. Got any bananas left?"

Matt looked on the counter by the toaster. "Yup. One. It's all yours." He handed him the banana.

"Does your aunt ever come home?" Darian asked.

Matt chuckled, "Yeah. She's away on business for a couple weeks." His chuckle faded as he worked up the nerve to say what he had to say. "Um, Dare, I'm going to go to Jamie's house today."

Darian's head snapped back in his direction. "What?" One slice of banana hit the floor.

Matt could not avoid this conversation. He knew what he had to do, and he knew it was going to be hard on both of them. "I need to find some answers. I need to know why. I need to figure out what happened that pushed him over the edge. The answers are in his room. I know it."

"I can't go in there."

Matt heard the panic in his voice. He stepped closer, avoiding the banana slice on the floor. He touched Darian's cheek. "I know. I don't expect you to. For one thing, Joan might be home, and no one in his or her right mind should have to deal with her shit. I'll go. I'll find out what everybody wants to know, and I'll come back here. Will you stay?"

"Yeah, I guess so. I don't have any pressing engagements. Unless Trevor Wright calls and asks me out on a date, I'll be here."

Matt enjoyed his almost-playful tone in suggesting such a hot actor might call him up, out of the blue. Darian had been such a mess in the last few days. It was nice to see a different side of him. "I may have to deck Mr. Wright if he calls. I'm keeping you." He winked. Matt kissed his lips. He stepped closer, threading his fingers through Darian's hair and caressing the bare skin of his lower back. Matt could seriously get used to mornings like this.

Darian whimpered and clutched Matt's hips.

Matt loved those sounds. "I hope to be back in a few hours. I'm not sure how long it'll take. Try not to worry."

"I'll try."

"Try not to obsess and work yourself into a weeping mess?"

Darian blushed. "I'll try."

Matt brushed his thumb over Darian's jaw. "I know it's hard. I do. We'll get through this together. I'm only leaving for a little while. I'll be back. I promise."

"Okay."

"Okay?"

"Yeah." Darian nodded.

Matt slipped into the bedroom, got dressed, and kissed him goodbye.

THE whole way over, Matt obsessed over what he *might* find. He worried that Joan and Kevin would be home. They could be. Even if Jamie's body was found in their bathroom, a week had gone by. People had to return to their normal routine. Would they move because of this? Who knew?

The driveway was empty. Matt sighed in relief. He parked his truck by the curb he'd parked by for years and turned off the engine. He had a key to the front door. Jamie had given it to him. The house smelled like disinfectant. Matt climbed the stairs and went right to Jamie's room. Part of him wanted to look into the bathroom, but this was not a TV show. The blood stains in there would be from his best friend. *That* he couldn't look at.

He poked around Jamie's sterilized room, wondering where to begin his search for clues. All Jamie's things had been tidied. He knew who'd done that. Why Jamie's mother thought his death would be made easier by straightening up the piles of papers and CDs and photographs that cluttered his dresser and desk was beyond him. Jamie had *just* died; couldn't she leave his fucking things alone for more than six days?

He looked in a few drawers before his brain clicked. Behind Jamie's bed! The stash hole held all Jamie's secret things. He pulled the bed away from the wall and reached in. He found his journals and some pictures of Darian.

"Darian…. He even had to hide you in there."

Matt set the pictures on the floor and read the letter that fell out of Jamie's journal. It pained him to feel Jamie's sadness in just a few simple words. Jamie loved him. Matt choked back his tears.

IN THE next few hours, he relived the events of Jamie's life. Many of the things that happened, he knew about. They were about him, and yet the perspective made his memories come across differently. Jamie wrote about him with mixed emotions. Lust and love and friendship. Matt felt cheated. What could have happened if Jamie had only come clean about his feelings? How much different would their lives have been?

Jamie clearly loved Darian as well, but it was his desire for Matt that Jamie wanted hidden—burned. If the journals were read by Darian, he would be crushed. Matt knew he could never let that happen.

Matt's hand trembled. Reading these last entries made it clear that the end was coming soon.

August 14, 2010

Our anniversary of sorts. I'm making his favorite dessert. Lucky for me chocolate chip cookies are my specialty!

Matt chuckled. "Darian's easy to please, isn't he?"

September 16, 2010

I ordered our bus tickets and made the hotel reservations. Darian has no idea. I can't wait to give him the ring.

September 18, 2010

I went running with Matt. I almost told him. I should have. I chickened out. Why is this so hard? He'll be happy for me; I know he will. Maybe it's that final door I fear closing? Once I tell him I'm getting married, there's no room for "me and Matt." Maybe I like leaving that door cracked slightly instead of fully closed.

September 19

Can I be any more happy? Darian is so excited. I'm excited. I'm gonna go talk to my mom. Darian just left to walk over to his mom's. I don't know if I'll get the nerve up or not, but I'm gonna try. I figure, if I can't tell her today, I'll try again next week, when we get back from DC.

Matt saw the letters change. They weren't simple script. Jamie's handwriting shifted, and his emotions were coming through, even in the lettering—bigger, messier, and scrawled, as if he held the pencil in a balled fist. There were marks that looked like tear stains on the page.

I can t do this anymore.

Matt's intestines squirmed as he read the next lines. He was fixated on the horror in knowing he was reading the last moments of his friend's life. No matter how scared he was to read it, he could not look away. The scene played out before him. Matt could not imagine it being any more vivid than if he had been in the room…

... Jimmy opened the door to his mom's house. He set his notebook and keys on the table by the door. "Mom?" he called through the house. He got no reply, so he walked into the kitchen. His mom sat at the kitchen table, looking at something. A letter? "Hey, Mom. I wanted to come by before I left for the week. Me and Dad are going camping for a few days." She continued to stare and ignore her son. "Mom?" He neared her chair. "Are you okay?"

"Tell me it's not true," she whispered.

"What? Tell you what's not true?"

"Tell me I don't have a gay son." Her voice was no longer a whisper but something bordering on disgust.

"Gay?" He chuckled uncomfortably. Jimmy felt the fear of this moment gripping his throat. "Why would you ask that?" Jimmy had come here to tell his mom that very thing, but being confronted before he spoke the words was not the plan.

"Tell me I'm not seeing things right. Tell me this is someone's idea of a sick and twisted joke." His mom's voice was growing more strained and harsh. It scared Jimmy to hear it any huskier.

"Mom, I'm not sure what you're talking about." Truly he wasn't. What was whose sick joke? He didn't know.

To answer him, she thrust the picture she'd been holding across the table so he could get a good look. Dread seized him. This was no longer fear but full-on terror. *She knows!*

The picture was of him at a New Year's Eve party two years back. Jimmy remembered a girl was taking pictures, although he hadn't seen this one. Jimmy had been sitting on the couch that night, with Darian straddling his lap. Jimmy could see in the picture his hands clearly up the back of Darian's shirt as Darian leaned in, kissing him. Darian's face was tilted away, and it was hard to make out who was in his lap, but he knew it would only have been Darian. Jimmy could also clearly see his tongue reaching out to invade Darian's mouth. Terror shot through him. His mother had a photo of him kissing Darian. There was no refuting his gayness now.

"Mom... I...."

She abruptly pushed the chair back and stood. The chair tumbled and hit the kitchen floor. "Do. Not. Tell. Me. You're. Gay." She was livid.

Jimmy quaked in his shoes. Where could he run? And should he? She might throw something and hit him from behind.

She closed the gap between them, glaring into his eyes and uttering her words like a sharp piece of glass ripping skin. "I will not have a dirty homosexual living in my house. You hear me? I'd rather find you dead in a gutter, overdosed on narcotics—like heroin or PCP or something—than bring such shame to this family by touching another man, or kissing one. It's disgusting."

Jimmy was not sure he heard her right. Dead? On heroin? How could she say that? He felt the bile building in his throat. It burned his esophagus. His stomach acid churned and threatened to explode from both ends. Jimmy was ill and wanted to bolt from the room, but something more sickening held him where he stood: his own mother's burning hate. How could anyone hate something so much as to wish something so awful as a heroin overdose on him?

Darian had a heroin problem. It was terrible to see him go through it. He'd never wish that on another human being. He'd watched him go through withdrawal. He'd heard him crying out in pain. His mother hated homosexuals so much that she would rather see them suffer from heroin addiction and die from it. Jimmy was a homosexual. She'd rather see him die.

"I'm gay, Mom." He no longer had the power to hide the truth.

She slapped him across the face. "No!"

Jimmy held his ground and turned back to face her. "I'm gay, and I love a man named D—" He received another slap.

"I will not have you talking like that in my house! That is a lie." She snatched the picture off the table and held it out. "This picture is a lie! Someone Photoshopped it and made a mockery of us. My son is not gay!" She proceeded to tear the picture to shreds.

Jimmy repeated, "I am." Joan slapped him again and this time broke the skin of his lip. Jimmy tasted blood.

"I will not have that kind of talk from you," she hissed. "You are not a *homosexual*. It's an abomination. A sin! My son is normal. And if it takes electroshock therapy to convince you, or mind-altering drugs, so be it." She walked over to the kitchen counter and picked up her keys. She straightened her skirt and smoothed back her hair. "I have to pick up your sister from her friend's house right now. When I come back, I expect you to have a different answer waiting for me."

Joan walked from the room, and Jimmy collapsed. His breathing came in short pants, and his vision blurred. The room distorted. Everything he'd ever known crumbled around him.

I can t do this anymore.

There was nothing left. Jimmy's hope of feeling love from the woman who birthed him had stabbed him in the back. Clinging to that dream suddenly laughed in his face.

I m so pathetic!

There was nothing in him she would love. Jimmy was the very thing his mother would never accept. He crawled on his hands and knees to the steps. He instinctively reached for the notebook on the table and pulled himself upright. He clambered up the steps.

He closed his door and stared blankly at the back of it. Nothing he could do would change time, would change his life. He lurched and released the bile that built up in his churning gut. He spit the remnants on the floor. "Who cares?" He spit again, this time at the back of the door. The glob slid down Aragorn's face, and Jimmy began to laugh. It was the laughter of a madman. When the laughter was no longer funny, he violently ripped the poster from the door and balled it up. He threw it across the room and grabbed his desk chair. He flung it at his wall mirror, smashing it. Shards of glass littered the carpet. He laughed some more.

He grabbed his porcelain piggy bank from his nightstand and threw it at another wall. Coins flew in every direction. He stumbled and knocked books off his desk. His jewelry box also fell. Jimmy didn't own jewelry. He stuck odds and ends inside. The box landed sideways and the top opened, spilling the contents.

Jimmy's eyes locked on the small bag that lay on the carpet.

He remembered that bag. He'd taken it from Darian years ago. He'd stuck it in his jewelry box under a picture Darian drew and forgot all about it.

Jimmy knelt down and picked it up. It contained all sorts of pretty pills. Some white, some green, some oval, but all containing the same wonderful result: painlessness, ecstasy, and—as Darian put it—escape. He poured the pills into his hand. *It's what she wanted.*

He tilted his head back and let them all fall in. Jimmy chewed them and bit back the gagging desire to puke the bitterness back out. There was a reason pills were designed to be swallowed! One, they tasted horrible. Two, they often contained a time-release coating. Jimmy ran to the bathroom and stuck his head under the faucet. Water did little for the flavor, but it rid his mouth of the awful chalky paste. He glimpsed his gaunt reflection. Pathetic.

He shoved things off his desk and picked up his chair. Jimmy grabbed his notebook. He tore out a page.

> *Dearest Matt,*
>
> > *Don't let Darian read this book. Burn it. Burn all of them. Take my secrets to the grave and let my pain end here. I couldn't be the person I wanted to be, the person that you would want. I'm sorry. Know that I loved you more than the stars have power to kiss the night sky.*
> >
> > *~Jamie*

He folded it neatly and placed it in an envelope.

I don't know why I tried. So many years, yet it amounted to nothing. She'll never love me. No matter how much I try to love her and be whoever it is she wants, my mother will never love me for who I am. My love was not enough.

Jimmy sat at his desk, feeling a strange trembling in his stomach. It was not long, maybe ten minutes since he'd swallowed whatever Darian had in that bag. He felt odd. Jimmy had never taken drugs before. He'd never even had a beer. Was this what it was like? He couldn't focus. He started to write, but the pen was hard to hold. He dropped it. Jimmy picked up a pencil and put his whole fist around it. *I won't drop it now.*

The room tilted. He felt a rush of heat and queasiness overcome his senses. *This is taking too fucking long. I need it to end.*

She'd rather have me dead than gay. Okay, mom, you get your wish.

Before his incoherence escalated, Jimmy pushed his bed aside and deposited his notebook into his stash hole. Jimmy then stumbled to his dressing bureau. Inside the top drawer, under his leftover odd socks, was Matt's hunting knife. He'd needed to return it five years ago and never took the time. He held it to his wrist. "Will this hurt?" Somehow the question came out weird. "I just took a handful of painkillers, you moron!" He started laughing again. It sounded like the maniacal laughter of Vincent Price in some creepy old horror flick, and it made Jimmy laugh more maniacally.

He staggered into the bathroom. "I shouldn't do this. I can hardly hold the knife." He felt the bile in his throat again. He spit into the sink. It was blood. He looked into the mirror and saw the blood in his mouth, down his chin, and on his shirt.

Blood.

Jimmy sank to the floor and sliced across his wrist as fast and deep as he could in one swipe. More blood. But not enough to wash him clean from the sin of homosexuality....

… Matt leaned over and got sick. He could see everything so clearly. He'd grown up watching horror shows. His dad loved anything bloody. Hack 'em, slash 'em, eat 'em, blow 'em up; anything that had guns or knives and someone dying made him laugh. Normally those movies involved monsters, but even serial killers had their moments. Matt was not afraid of blood. He'd gutted plenty of deer in his day. But seeing Jimmy's final moments played out in 3-D was more than he wanted his mind to conjure up. Sure, it may *not* have gone that way, but more than likely it had. He'd heard his mom and dad talking. He knew what the coroner told Joan. He knew Jimmy had OD'ed on something and dragged a heavy blade over his wrist.

Now he knew why.

29

September 25, 2010
10:30 a.m.

DARIAN felt the silence as soon as Matt closed the door. The apartment was empty and deafeningly quiet. He could hear himself swallow. He could hear his blood rushing like thunder in his ears. His short breaths sounded like a panting dog, left outside in mid-July to swelter. The walls were closing in. A siren blared outside, and Darian jumped four feet. He grabbed for the wall to steady himself.

"Pull yourself together, Dare!" He shook his head, hoping against all hope to clear his mind of anxiety and paranoia. "It's just a panic attack. I'm fine. I can do this. Matt's only been gone for two minutes. I can be left by myself. I can do this."

His breathing slowed. He swallowed and stepped away from the wall. The apartment was still quiet, and it bothered him more than a little. He needed something to distract him and fill the time. He sat on the couch and turned on the television.

Ferris Bueller's Day Off was playing, and Darian started sobbing.

2:15 p.m.

DARIAN felt the silence gnawing away at him. At first, it was overwhelming. Then, when he'd seen Matthew Broderick on the television screen, Darian found the silence more comforting, compared to hearing those classic lines and reliving his and Jamie's first date. He'd turned the television off hours ago. He was back to silence equals bad, noise equals good. What he really wanted was for Matt to return. He was scared to know what he'd find in Jamie's room. Scared and anxious happened to be the coinciding themes for the day. At least he'd stopped puking! Darian had eaten an entire bowl of cereal before Matt left, and he'd kept it down. Progress.

He took a shower and put the ring back through his lip. He'd have to explain later to Matt how he took it out because puke was gathering under it and he'd feared losing it down the commode. He sighed.

Matt.

"Where's Matt? I don't know. Have you seen him? Nope. I hear he should be by any minute now. Okay, thanks." Was it saner to hold a two-way conversation with himself than to sit quietly and add to the quiet, therefore ushering in his own death by utter madness? Or perhaps he was already mad? He swore he could hear the neighbor's clock *through* the wall! This was killing him!

Darian stood abruptly and paced the floor. "How can Matt be taking this long? He's been gone for four hours. I can't take this anymore. I'm going to go insane if he doesn't come back soon." Darian pulled at his hair. "No. No, no, no… I'm fine. I can do this. It's just for a few hours. Matt had to go. I couldn't go in there. Not yet. I *chose* to stay behind. Matt will be back soon."

Darian took several cleansing breaths. Deep. Inhale. Exhale. Cleansing. He did feel better. "I can draw. Maybe." He shook his head. "I don't have any supplies over here." Pause. Thinking. "No drawing. I guess I could write."

Darian was not a wordsmith. He opted to paint pictures with his feelings as opposed to writing poetry or prose. Jamie used to write a lot. Did Jamie write poetry?

Darian was disappointed that he never got to say anything at the funeral. Of course, what could he say? There was no way he'd be able to get through a eulogy like Matt. Darian would choke up on the first few words. Perhaps now was the time to write a tribute to how he felt about Jamie? A poem would be short. He could do that.

5:45 p.m.

BALLS of crinkled paper littered the floor. It was hard writing a poem. Perhaps that was why he drew! He could capture the shine in a person's eyes, but he often had difficulty voicing feelings and emotions. He tried several times, and each poem came out dismal and the next one morose. He had nothing sweet to say, and therefore nothing lovely touched his pages. Even this last one was tiresome. He hated rhyming poems. Why did they have to rhyme? And why did he start a rhyming poem in the first place? What words rhyme with "letters"?

"Arrgh!" Darian balled up the piece of paper and threw it across the room.

The door opened. *Matt!* He jumped to his feet and flew over to greet him.

Darian stopped before he touched Matt. He could feel the tension around him like a blast of cold air. Something wasn't right. "Matt?" He spoke softly.

Matt brought his eyes off the carpet long enough to inaudibly convey that he was not in the mood to talk. Darian reached for him, and Matt lifted his hand to hold him at bay. *What? Why?*

"Give me a few minutes." Matt mumbled the words, but Darian understood them fine. He was not ready for this type of behavior, but he could surely understand the kind of emotional trauma that Matt had faced, going into his dead best friend's room. Darian would not have been able to make one sentence, let alone drive home beforehand.

"Okay. I'll be right here."

Matt disappeared down the short hall and closed the bedroom door.

Now Darian was alone again. Alone with the silence and the neighbor's damn clock ticking its way through the damn wall!

He sat down and started another sheet of paper. "What do I feel?" It seemed like the most logical place to start. Writers write about what they know. "I feel like shit! I don't want to write about shit. I feel cold. Empty. Gray." Suddenly he knew what he wanted to say.

9:25 p.m.

DARIAN drifted off to sleep on the couch but jumped with a start when the door to the bedroom creaked. He got up and padded to the bathroom door. He placed his ear against the wood. Darian was itching to hold Matt, talk to Matt, but he knew enough to leave Matt alone. Men needed their space.

The door opened, and Darian jumped back.

"What are you doing?" Matt questioned skeptically.

"Um, listening by the door?" He couldn't lie. Jamie had always told him he couldn't lie worth crap. He knew he'd blush.

"Why?" Matt headed toward the kitchen. Darian followed.

"I wanted to see if you were all right. I've never seen you look like this before. It worries me."

Matt took a sticky pad from the junk drawer and wrote on it. He then hung his head.

Darian waited. He glanced at the sticky note. It read, "Get toilet paper." Darian waited and heard the neighbor's clock ticking again. Silence was going to kill him for sure. Matt needed to talk, or Darian would slip into insanity, without any hope of returning to the ordinary world.

Just when his hands started shaking, Matt looked up. His eyes were full of tears. Darian's heart palpitated. He reached for him, and Matt melted against his thin frame.

It was Matt's turn to weep, and amazingly enough, Darian held together. Matt was taller and broader of chest, but at least his large body did not snap Darian like a pencil. Matt's warmth and muscle surrounded him with just the right amount of completeness, and Matt held him with just the right amount of pressure. His hands gripped Darian's shoulder blades and lower back, and Darian felt Matt shaking against him as he sobbed.

Minutes later, Matt let go. "I need to sit down."

Darian followed him to the couch. He waited for Matt to make the first move. Just because Darian desired to be held, it didn't mean Matt still felt the same need. He smiled inwardly when Matt reached out. Matt reclined and pulled Darian to lie on top of him. He held Darian tightly and cried until the tissue box next to him was empty. "I guess I need to put those on the list too." Matt sniffled.

Darian lifted his face and could see that Matt's grief had run its course. His eyes were swollen and red, but he was regaining his composure. They both sat up.

Matt took a deep breath. "I don't know how I'm going to handle tomorrow."

"Tomorrow? What happens tomorrow?" Darian was genuinely confused.

"Church."

Matt said it like Darian should automatically know the answer, which he didn't. "And? What happens there?"

"I'm sorry. I forgot you don't go to my church. The pastor will probably say something about Jamie. More than likely the sermon will include hope from despair and some message on Jesus's triumph over death and hell. People might even be encouraged to say a few words. You could say something if you like."

Darian was a deer in headlights. He shook his head frantically. "Too much pressure."

"I could say it for you. Write down something, a story or a memory…."

"Or a poem?"

Matt nodded. "Yeah, a poem would be nice."

"I wrote one while you were out. It's not a happy poem. I wasn't feeling happy when I wrote it."

"It doesn't have to be happy." Matt tucked Darian's hair behind his ear and chuckled when it fell back in his face. "I think you need a haircut. Have you always worn it long?"

"It was longer a few years ago. I tied it back in a ponytail, and Jamie squawked."

Matt's smile broadened. "Jamie hated it when I had a ponytail."

The humor faded from the moment. Matt leaned back again and reached for Darian. Automatically, Darian sank into his arms. He felt safe there in ways he could not describe. Matt was his shelter and sanctuary. In his arms, silence was soothing.

30

September 26, 2010
10:29 a.m.

ONCE again, Matt felt all eyes focused on him. He walked into church, mind-numbingly aware of how his fingers ached to touch Darian. He had to repeat over and over to himself that this was not the time and place to put his arm around Darian, no matter how much instinct told him to do so! They were just two guys walking into church. Emphasize two *guys*.

Matt saw Ms. Carrie eyeing them from across the sanctuary. She was at Matt's parents' house the other night. She knew who Darian was. Matt waved like he normally would, and she looked away. *Great!*

"You made it. I'm glad." Matt turned to his mom and grinned. He gave her a hug. "And this is Darian, correct?" She turned with a smile and held out her hand.

Darian shook it. "Yes, ma'am."

"You're Jim's...." Her hesitation pained Matt. *Can't she say it?* "You're Jim's... friend. I'm glad to meet you."

"He's Jamie's boyfriend, Mom. You don't need to pretend the other night didn't happen."

She looked shocked. Matt felt bad for being too direct. "Please don't do this here," she said.

"I'm sorry. I didn't mean to snap."

She touched Matt's arm. "It's okay. Everyone's been under a lot of pressure lately. It's been a very hard week."

Darian looked down. Matt forgot himself briefly and brushed Darian's lower back in a gesture of comfort. Darian smiled at him. Luckily the music started, and Matt could avoid talking to his mom and everyone else. They took their seats in the pew.

Darian sang along with the hymns, and Matt found it very pleasing to hear his voice. He could sing well. He surreptitiously touched Darian's fingers as they shared a hymnal. Matt smiled and winked, hoping no one saw the look of joy on his face.

When he walked in to church, he was sure everyone could see the bags under his eyes from lack of sleep as well as the emotional outpouring he went through after finding the journals. But singing hymns with this wonderfully sweet young man, Matt's burden seemed lighter. Darian made everything easier to bear. He had to smile. Even with all the pain he felt inside.

The pastor stepped up to the podium when all the singing was over. He cleared his throat and looked out into the congregation. He spoke slowly, deliberately, using each word to soothe those who listened. Sometimes it irked Matt when he talked that way. *Didn't he know it came off haughty?* "Today is a day of reflection. As we ponder the loss of our dear friend James Miller…"

Matt rolled his eyes. *Jamie didn't like you, and you know it!*

"… each one of us must answer the question of our own mortality. Are we ready to face the end? Will we know it when it comes? Or will we meet our maker unprepared and covered with our own shame? These are the things we need to consider as we grieve with our sister Joan and bring to her family comfort and encouragement.

"Does the Lord know of our suffering? Does he care about the pain we feel when one of our own takes it upon himself to usurp the Lord's control and end his life? My answer is yes. Yes, the Lord knows of our grief and pain, and I propose that He grieves along with us. His love for James was no less because he ended his life."

Pastor Dennis paused and took a sip of water from the cup sitting on the edge of the podium.

Matt glanced down at Darian's hand. It was resting on his thigh. Matt so wanted to reach over and touch it. He liked the feeling of Darian's fingers laced through his. His hand was small and delicate compared to Matt's. Darian's hands were still manly, but Matt liked the contrast. His hands were beefy and callused from years of hard work. Darian's hands were graceful. Matt felt a knot in his throat. *Holy crap, I'm getting choked up in church thinking about his fucking hands! That has to take the cake for the sappiest sentimentality ever.* Matt was almost glad for the pastor's continuation of his sermon.

"Now, as I have heard through the grapevine, there seem to be rumors going around about James that Joan and Kevin would like put to rest."

Correction, Matt was *not* glad he continued.

"James was in my counsel on several occasions. We discussed some of his difficulties in school and his anger over his parents' unexpected divorce."

Unexpected? What the—? Jamie knew looong before they got a divorce that there were problems. Matt was not going to be able to sit here if Pastor Dennis kept coloring the facts.

Darian shifted in his seat.

See? Darian can't take the embellishments either!

"James was a troubled soul. He, like so many of us, needed the love of our Lord Jesus Christ to fill the void in his heart and cleanse him of his sins. I believe he would not want to be whispered about and accused of some unseemly acts...."

Unseemly? What the hell does that mean?

"He has left us, and I ask all in the congregation to respect his passing and ease his parents' burden by abstaining from gossip." He heaved a sigh. "That said... I would like to open the microphone to any and all who would like to share an anecdote or remembrance of our dear friend James Miller."

Miss Deana took it upon herself to step up and smile at everyone. "Hello. I remember Jimmy a couple of Christmases ago when he helped to salt the driveway so people could get into the church for Wednesday prayer meeting. He was kind and polite, and I will always remember his smile and willingness to help out whenever asked." She smiled and stepped down.

"Thank you, Miss Deana. Is there anyone else?" Pastor Dennis asked.

Matt watched and listened. Mostly what people said was true. Jamie was a helpful person and did have a great smile. He never complained, and he volunteered as often as he could. Matt heard a sniffle. He knew Darian was trying not to cry, but hearing all the good things that Jamie did in his life made it very difficult not to miss him all the more. He reached into his pocket and handed Darian a tissue. He'd come prepared.

After several people in the congregation shared stories, Pastor Dennis stood before everyone again. "Thank you. I am sure James is smiling down on all of us right now. And that is what I want everyone to remember now. The good times with James. What is done is done. We need to concentrate our efforts on not letting something this tragic happen to any other youth in the church. How can we do this? I propose stricter regulation on the music we allow our children to listen to…."

What? Matt was bothered again.

"We as parents need to be careful whom our children hang out with, so that they are only influenced by the most righteous. The Internet needs to be monitored and the movies they watch; these are windows the Devil uses to ensnare."

Oh, my God…. Matt shifted in his seat.

"I also challenge you men out there to set a good example for our children to follow. If we can't hold jobs, if we are not leading our family, if we are not showing our sons what it means to be men, then we are the ones to blame when they choose idleness and shameful lifestyles."

This has to fucking stop! Matt had heard about all he could take. He leaned over to Darian and whispered, "I'm going up there. Do you want to sit here or stand up there with me?"

Darian's eyes went wide. "Up there?"

A woman in a pew in front of them turned her head and shushed them. Matt glared and she turned her "well-I-never" look back around.

"Staying or going?" he asked Darian again, holding out an open palm.

Darian looked down at his offered hand and took it. "Going."

"Where are you going?" Matt's mom asked as they got up and filed past her.

"I have something to say. Right or wrong, I can't sit here and listen to Pastor Dennis. Jamie doesn't deserve this. And Mom, I'm sorry. I didn't plan on letting you find out this way. I have no choice."

"Find out what?"

Matt leaned in and whispered in her ear. She blanched. "Tell Dad when he gets back from the bathroom."

"Matt...." Her eyes pleaded.

"Mom, I have to."

"I can't watch this." His mother stood up and started up the side aisle.

"Mom?"

More shushing ensued from other parishioners.

She looked down. Matt knew she was looking at their clasped hands. She looked back up and shook her head. She walked away, and Matt felt very alone. Still, he had to do this. For Jamie.

He led Darian up to the front and stepped up to the podium. Pastor Dennis looked bewildered. "Matt? This is not the time to—"

"Pastor Dennis, with all due respect, I have something to say to everyone." He let go of Darian's hand and reached into his pocket. He pulled out a piece of paper. "You can object all you want, but what I have to say *will* be said."

"Matt, I—"

"I'm not giving you an option." Matt restrained his intended threat, but he knew he needed to be stern.

The pastor turned to the audience. "It seems that we have one more person who would like to say something today." He smiled uncomfortably but allowed Matt to take the podium.

Matt looked at everyone. Some looked shocked, some whispered, and one little girl in the second row waved. Matt grinned and waved back. It was her happy face that gave him courage.

"Hello. I'm Matt Dixon. Most of you know me. My parents have been going to this church for a really long time. I've shoveled your driveways, mowed your lawns, and gave rides to church when cars were broken down. Most of you also know that Jim Miller, or as I called him, Jamie, was my best friend. Many of you were at the funeral and heard what I had to say then, but that was only part of the story. Not everything is sweet and pleasant. And not everyone can fixate on the good times to get us through since Jamie's death."

Joan Smithers stood up from her seat on the right and muttered loud enough for Matt to hear, "I am not going to stand for this."

"Miss Joan. Please sit. You'll hear what I have to say right now, or I'll do an article for the paper."

She clamped her hand over her gaping mouth and immediately sat back down.

"Thank you. I'd like to start with a poem. It's a tribute to Jamie that I think speaks to how we should all feel." Matt opened the paper.

Darian leaned in. "That's my poem."

"You want to read it?" Matt quietly conferred.

Darian adamantly refused. "You go ahead."

Matt cleared his throat and read:

> *"I see the color of the sky today,*
> *It's gray; all the orange has seeped away.*
> *The birds are hushed and the wind stilled,*
> *Too many sorrows leave the autumn air chilled.*
> *I long for a sound of joy on my open page—*
> *Only dry words echo across this empty stage.*
> *Where were your smiles among the letters?*
> *Did happiness become harsh fetters?*
> *—Or did the rain fall and steal that kiss*
> *Sucking the brilliance from those eyes I miss.*
> *The water is placid on the lake of my heart,*

Its deep chasm of imagination won't start.
The key in my hand, I can't find the door,
I close my eyes and cry loneliness once more."

When he was done, he folded the paper and placed it back in his pocket. "To me, this is what death is like: a harsh separation that heralds in emptiness for those who are left behind. Death sucks! At Jamie's funeral, I listened to all the good things people had to say about him, and I myself paid tribute to the wonderful person that he was. Are we glad to have known Jamie? Yes, of course we are. But I think the emptiness and sorrow of his absence is not something we should forget. His absence affects us all, especially for one individual." Matt looked into Darian's tear-streaked face. He placed his arm around his shoulders. "This is Darian Weston. He is the author of the poem I read. He was also Jamie's fiancé." Matt heard gasps and watched people whispering back and forth. He also noticed Pastor Dennis rising and headed his way. He held up his hand. "Don't. I can do this peaceably, or I can do this the messy way." Pastor Dennis reconsidered and sat back down. Matt nodded. "Good choice."

He looked back out to the people who were now restless. "Why am I telling you all this? Simple. Jamie was my best friend, and he was also gay. That's the rumor Pastor Dennis tried to warn you about spreading. I'm the one who started it, and I'm the one who's going to finish it. It's not malicious gossip; it's the truth. I feel I need to tell you straight out, because Jamie didn't kill himself because of the people he hung with or because of the music he listened to. Censoring the Internet and the movies your children watch is not going to prevent suicide from happening. Jamie killed himself because he was a coward."

The murmuring of the crowd grew louder. People looked from one to another.

Darian gripped Matt's arm. "Matt, don't."

"Trust me," he whispered back.

"I don't say this to be hurtful, especially to my best friend. I say this to blame all of you. Not just those in this church, but to people all over this county and state and around the world. Jamie died because of *hate*. He took his life because his fear of intolerance was greater than he could bear. His blood is on all our hands."

He saw his father and mother standing by the doors. They hadn't left. He took a deep breath and continued before he lost his nerve. "Gandhi once said to 'be the change you want to see in your world.' I think that Jamie was on his way to becoming that. He loved everyone. Do you know that? Jamie loved people just as they are. He was a peacekeeper and a counselor and a comforter to all who needed it. He never judged. He loved unconditionally, and I think that is what did him in. He wanted to see the good in all people, but it was the bad that killed him. Some people have more hate and judgment and ridicule than any of us will ever be able to overcome with love. I think that's why God allows it. To show us mere humans that only God's love is greater than our bitterness. I called Jamie a coward, not because he was too afraid to stand up for who and what he was. I called him a coward because he could not admit his own inability to change the hatred in other people. We as individuals cannot change another person's heart; only God can. What we can do is show them love. God's love. Gandhi also said, 'I like your Christ; I do not like your Christians. Your Christians are so unlike your Christ.'" Matt shook his head in disgust. "How can anyone show God's love when they do not display the love that God has shown us? I am a Christian. I will not deny that. I believe in Jesus Christ as my Savior. I follow the teachings of Jesus Christ. That is what makes me Christian and not some other religion in the world. There are other religions; do you know that? So what are we to do as Christians if we do not shine as a light for the Christ we claim to follow? It will be your neighbor, not Mahatma Gandhi, who says 'I do not like your Christians'."

Matt's voice was getting louder as he went along. His anger was flaring. His disgust for the self-righteous rose within his veins, and he was taking this moment to let loose all his pent-up irritation. "I read somewhere that the best and worst things about Christianity are Christians. Don't let that be our legacy! Jesus loved people. All people. Saints and sinners. He said he was here to save the unrighteous. Then why do Christians go around hating people when they are different? Jamie was in love with another man. This young man. Does that mean Jesus loved him less? Some of you would say yes. Some of you would call homosexuality an abomination. You sicken me. You are the same ones who divorce your husband or cheat on your wife, the ones who steal pens from work, cheat on your taxes, and pass by the homeless on the street without even a thought to their suffering. And you are the same ones who would proclaim that these things are not the same as homosexuality! I've read the Bible. The God of the Bible calls all sin equal. Is being gay a sin? No. I believe God made us who we are, and He did so for a reason. And what it all comes down to is each of us coming to terms with the God whom we believe in. It comes down to *my* heart and *my* God. So don't any of you go around thinking you are so much better off because at least you're not one of those... *homosexuals*." He whispered the last word for Joan's benefit. "We are just like you. We laugh, we hate, we hurt, and yes, we fall in love. I can say all these things because I am a Christian, *and* I'm a homosexual."

Matt heard more than one person question, "We? What? How? Did he just say...?"

"Thank you for your time." He stepped down with his hand firmly gripping Darian's. Pastor Dennis stepped in front of him. His face was stern. Matt automatically tensed up for what might come. Then, just as swiftly as he stepped in front of Matt, his expression changed. He now wore a pleasant smile as he reached out and patted Matt's arm.

"Very interesting speech you gave there," he commented. The pastor was now abnormally calm, which made Matt grow abnormally cautious. "You know why he did it, don't you? The real reason Jimmy killed himself."

Matt looked him straight in the eye. "Yes. I do."

The man hesitated and waved off a few people who were approaching. He gently coaxed Matt over near a wall while outraged congregates milled in groups voicing their discontent. Pastor Dennis placed his arm over Matt's shoulder. "I respect you for holding your tongue, even if I do not agree with your theological exposition."

Matt kept up his guard; there was no need to argue anything now, not here where he was outnumbered. He opted for the expected response. "Thank you." He smiled back to the pastor.

"We'll talk. I think you've brought up a lot of good points. There are many things the church could learn about loving. James—Jamie— was definitely a prime example of what a Christian should be. I got the feeling from our talks that he carried far more burdens than any of us should carry alone."

He is so fake! "Thank you for saying that." Matt nodded, though he did not believe his sincerity. "And you would be right. He carried a lot."

Pastor Dennis held out his hand. "Darian, it is good to meet you." He shook Darian's hand. "I'm sorry for your loss. That poem was very… symbolic. Thank you for sharing it."

Darian nodded shyly.

Matt picked up on his discomfort. "We gotta jet. There are too many people here, and I really don't feel like fielding all the questions at once."

"I can understand that. Go. Use the back stairs if you like."

"I plan to."

Matt turned and exited quickly. People were already in the parking lot, but luckily he got Darian to the truck and out unscathed.

MATT did it. He'd confronted his fears and told everyone the truth—most of the truth, anyway. But now he was scared of what would come next. He was *out* and there was no going back. What would people say? How fast would the news get around? Would it affect him at work? He had no way of knowing how the news from the church would travel through the gossip chain.

He turned the light off in the bathroom and walked over to his very quiet lover, who was already in bed. Darian was on his stomach facing away from Matt, clutching his pillow. Matt heard Darian make a little squeak.

"Dare?" He questioned as he kneeled on the bed and reached for him. "Baby, what's wrong?" Of course he knew what was wrong. Jamie was gone. But what else does one say in a situation such as this? He stretched out his legs and reclined as close to Darian as he could. He touched Darian's bare back. His fingers ghosted over his shoulder and traced the curves of his scapula. He curled his fingers and ran his knuckles down Darian's spine and all his vertebrae, one after another after another. Matt had never touched anyone like this before. Feeling the smoothness of Darian's skin and watching goose bumps form from his slight touch held more fascination for Matt than any faceless orgasm he'd had in his life. Living for the next piece of ass suddenly became for Matt "the folly of youth." Quietly he thanked Jamie for all those times he'd questioned Matt and planted those seeds of maturity that took so many years to sprout. He was sure now that he could truly love this man in his bed, and he would do anything and everything to prove that love to him in the years to come.

He leaned down and kissed his skin. He massaged Darian's shoulder and kissed him again. He scooted his body closer. He pressed his groin alongside Darian's hip and enfolded him in his arms. Matt nuzzled his face against his hair and nibbled and kissed the ridge of his ear.

Darian still did not respond, verbally or otherwise. He only sniffled.

Matt moved closer still, practically lying on top of Darian. He was covering him with himself like a blanket of security, squeezing him tight as he rested his head on the back of Darian's neck. He whispered, "I'm sorry. I wish I could take this pain from you."

"I can't avoid it, Matt." Darian's voice was barely audible, but Matt was relieved he was talking. Darian continued weakly, "I lost him. I have to let Jamie go. What hurts is not knowing how to let him go."

"I know, baby. I know."

Darian spoke softly. "I keep reliving the things we shared. I close my eyes, and I can almost hear his voice."

"Me, too."

"I wish we'd spent more time together over the years. Jamie was always running off to do something for his mom. He visited his dad as much as she allowed, but she had such control over him. I never understood that. He always seemed distracted. Even when he made love to me, I felt like his mind was elsewhere."

Matt didn't comment. He wasn't sure how much Darian knew about Jamie's burdens. He kissed Darian's shoulder and caressed his upper arm.

Darian continued quietly. "I guess I didn't know him as well as I thought I did. I didn't know he wanted to kill himself. I didn't know he suffered so much. What if I... what if it was me who...?" He started sniveling again and his body quaked.

Matt squeezed him. "Don't. Don't you dare blame yourself. No one knew. No one could have known. Jamie shut us all out. Jamie hid everything. It wasn't anything you did or said. He loved you."

"I guess a part of me didn't want to believe this was real. All week I kept thinking I would wake up from this horrible nightmare and find him sleeping next to me. Then when they put him in the ground, I felt everything just crashing on top of me."

Darian tried to move, so Matt scooted far enough back to allow him the space to roll over. Darian reached for him, and Matt covered his body again.

"He felt like everything to me," Darian said. "Jamie was the first person to show me what life and loving could be like. Until him, I was just going through the motions of existing. You know? Now he's gone. My tether is gone. I thought I'd have no reason to live, once they buried him. But you were there." Darian lifted his hand and ran it over Matt's buzzed hair. "You don't know how grateful I am to have found you. I need you."

Matt tilted his face sideways and kissed Darian's wrist. He leaned down and kissed his chest. He didn't know what to say, so he acted out his affection. He kissed from Darian's ribs up to his neck. He kissed over his chin and kissed his cheeks and forehead. He finished with a kiss on his nose. He tenderly smiled. "I need you too."

Darian smiled back.

"If I had this to do all over, I think I'd opt for it to be exactly the same. Although, I'd have Jamie be alive and maybe make it a threesome." He winked. Humor had always helped with Jamie; he hoped it would be equally effective with Darian.

Darian started to chuckle. "Oh, God!" He rubbed Matt between his bare shoulders. "You, me, and Jamie? I don't know if that would have worked. But in some ways, I feel like it was the three of us all along. He talked about you all the time. He even said your name in his sleep. He thought you were Superman. I think he idolized you. Even when you had that incident in '06, he still thought you were incredibly strong."

Matt's expression fell. "He told you about that?" He knew what he'd read in the journal but had to ask. It was suddenly very frightening to consider that Jamie didn't record the truth.

Darian shook his head. "No. Not specifically. He said you had something serious going on, but it wasn't his place to tell me. I respected him for that."

Matt was relieved. Jamie wrote that he didn't tell Darian. Matt was glad. "I'll tell you my life's story. Eventually. It's not a pretty picture to paint all at once."

Darian touched the back of Matt's head, and then over the top of his scalp as if he was enjoying the feel of Matt's buzzed hair. "Matt, the point of getting to know someone is just that—*getting to know someone.* I don't expect it to be a one-day thing, like cramming for an exam."

"Okay, okay, I guess that makes sense." Matt moved his body, rubbing Darian's in subtle ways that were not meant to be erotic. He liked feeling Darian beneath him, and he liked rubbing his stomach against Darian's and his thighs against Darian's. He leaned down and kissed his chest. He could feel Darian's breastbone beneath his lips. *He needs to gain some weight,* Matt thought.

Darian kept rubbing his head with one hand while the other was stroking his neck.

"You like my hair?"

Darian giggled. "I do." He rubbed Matt's head some more. "It's soft and kind of fuzzy. I like it."

Matt was pleased to see a shine back in Darian's eyes. He kissed across to Darian's nipple ring. He pinched it between his lips and tugged, and licked, and nibbled. "I'm glad. It feels nice having your hands running over my head. It sends shivers down my spine."

Darian groaned. "Speaking of shivers… oh, God, keep doing that." He arched his back and tilted back his head.

Matt was amused. He sucked Darian's nipple into his mouth.

Darian's whimpers and soft moans filled his ears. He could listen to those sounds for hours, if not days. Darian was very vocal, and Matt delighted in it. The coos from Darian's throat made his skin buzz, not to mention made his dick throb. His cock wanted attention, and he ignored it in favor of teasing Darian closer and closer to the edge.

Jamie would laugh at you now, Matt! You've done a one-eighty, and he's looking down, shaking his head. Years of fast fucks and instant gratification faded from the forefront. He'd become a new man, all because of opening his mind to the possibility of a relationship.

He licked and pulled on Darian's piercing with his teeth. Darian gasped and cried out. Matt reached down and palmed Darian's crotch and was rewarded with more delightful sounds from Darian's throat. *Damn, this is fucking good!*

"Matt… please… I want… oh, fuck…." Darian panted and wiggled beneath him.

Matt chuckled. "You are so easy to turn on."

Darian bucked, pushing his groin into Matt's hand. "I want you. I need you inside me. Please."

Matt loved his begging, but he had to make his intentions clear. Matt stopped rubbing Darian below the waist and caressed his chest. "Shh, shh, shh… don't rush this. I've done my share of wham, bam, thank you ma'am, I want to enjoy every bit of you tonight." He kissed down his chest and kept going. "I'm through with getting off in the first three minutes. I want to taste you, Darian. I want to hear how much you like it and how bad you want it, but I'm not giving in just yet." He licked across Darian's stomach and tugged on Darian's sweats.

"Matt… shit." He lifted his hips.

Matt chuckled wickedly. He was truly loving this! Matt slid Darian's pants off and got rid of his own boxers. He kissed his way up and down Darian's legs. It thrilled him to no end, watching Darian clutching the sheets and biting his lip. And he loved the lip ring! He could mention now how glad he was that Darian put it back in, but that might distract them from the current mood. No way he was going to interrupt this!

Matt licked the back of Darian's knee, making him convulse. He giggled, "Ticklish?"

"Ye—yes."

Matt did it again and then nipped his way up to where he truly wanted to be. Darian's thick cock was pulsing on its own in anticipation of Matt's next move, and his testicles moved. Matt's friend Jenny often mused about the wonders of the male anatomy, and he'd never thought about it before. It was pretty weird how those little guys squirmed inside the scrotum with no apparent connection to the conscious mind. They moved when they wanted to. Weird. Matt watched—fascinated—as he nuzzled his way closer.

He nudged the sack with his nose and flicked out his tongue. Darian's testicles disappeared, drawing up inside his body and pulling the sack as tight against him as it would go. Matt opened wide and descended. They would not be hiding for long! He swirled his tongue over the wrinkled sack and felt it relax in his mouth. Darian groaned. Matt gently sucked and coaxed one ball free of its hiding place.

"Matt… please…." One corner of the fitted sheet sprang free of the mattress as Darian pulled. He let it go and slammed the side of his fist down several times as if Matt's behavior was torturing him. Matt loved it!

Darian is so impatient. Hee, hee, hee.

Matt lapped and pulled on the scrotum in his mouth. This was so much fun. Darian was dying with need, and Matt just wanted to tease him more and more. Darian gave up resisting and reached for his cock. Matt reached up and swatted Darian's hand away. "Don't even think about it." He hated letting go long enough to talk, but it had to be done.

Darian's fist thumped back down on the mattress. "You're killing me."

"I know." Matt was having fun, but torturing your lover needed to have limits. He gave in to Darian's need. He licked slowly up Darian's waiting cock and scooted over the side of his leg to get a better position. He lay next to him with his back curved over Darian's stomach so he could suck that member in as far as possible.

"It's not going to take long. I'm gonna cum."

Matt cupped Darian's balls with one hand and massaged. With the other hand, he pinched the base of Darian's dick. That should buy him a few minutes. Darian moaned but didn't cum. Matt felt his hand on his back. Darian was digging his fingers into his flesh. The pinching sensation was nice. Matt liked the idea of being marked by Darian. Maybe Darian would get wild enough to bite him someday? Matt could sense his feisty nature. The first few hours they'd spent together Wednesday night revealed Darian to be a very lively lover indeed. The thought excited Matt. He wanted to try so many things. He hardly knew where to begin.

Time. All in good time!

Matt heard his lover's breathing change and knew Darian was going to blow. He pulled back to allow enough room in his mouth to gather the semen. He knew he was breaking another one of his rules, but he let it go. He didn't want to suck Darian off with a condom. If Jamie's journals were correct, Darian was tested two years ago. Supposedly he'd been off heroin since 2007. He had to trust his gut. Darian was clean. He had to be.

Matt licked under the ridge of Darian's crown right before he felt liquid squirting into his mouth. He didn't swallow. He resisted the urge as the amount of cum grew. Darian jerked a few times before his body finally relaxed.

Matt pulled off, careful not to spill a drop. He turned to Darian and leaned over him knowingly. He grinned.

Darian looked sated. He touched Matt's cheek and searched his eyes. "What?"

Matt answered with a deep chuckle. He leaned in and opened his mouth over Darian's when he felt Darian's tongue probing for entrance. Darian's tangy fluid enveloped their kiss, coating their tongues and overpowering every other taste. Matt groaned this time. He pushed his tongue so deep into Darian he could have sworn he felt Darian's Adam's apple.

Matt moved his arm firmly around Darian's ribs and pulled him tight against his chest. He felt Darian's hand gripping his neck and pinching fingers dig into his back. Darian's throat vibrated with his mewls. Matt kissed him until they were both so breathless they could hardly stand it. He pulled back, practically wheezing. Darian was in the same state.

Matt grinned. "You like that?"

Darian nodded.

Matt smiled wider before settling down next to him. He laid his head on Darian's shoulder and tangled his leg over Darian's. He kissed his throat where his lips could reach. "I'm glad." He squeezed him tightly in his arms. "I can't get enough of you, Darian." Matt nestled under Darian's chin. "I want this to last."

Darian cooed.

Matt fell asleep, hoping that when he woke up, Darian would still be in his arms and that the events of the day had not been just a horrible dream.

September 27, 2010

MATT awoke with a start. The bed was empty. He looked around the room as panic gripped him. Where was Darian? Was this all real? Did he really tell his church he was gay? Did he dream everything? Was Jamie still alive?

His suit coat with the wilted carnation in the buttonhole lying on the chair by the wall told him the funeral was real. He got out of bed and slipped on some underwear. Matt wandered out into the apartment and felt a huge amount of relief when he spied Darian on the sofa.

Darian looked up and smiled. "Good morning."

Matt rubbed his eyes. "What time is it?" He walked into the kitchen and filled the coffee pot with three cups of water.

"About ten thirty," Darian answered, getting off the couch and stepping up behind Matt.

Matt felt Darian pressing against his back. He stroked the arms that held his waist. It was a wonderful feeling to have him here. It was comforting and reassuring. He turned in his arms and hugged Darian back. "I panicked when you weren't in bed this morning." He rubbed Darian's back and rubbed his face on Darian's soft hair.

"I tried to wake you up, but you wouldn't budge."

Matt released him and resumed making his coffee.

"I even left for a while and came back with doughnuts." Darian pointed to a bag on the counter.

"Gee, then I'm glad I didn't wake up sooner. I *really* would have panicked."

Darian smoothed his hand over Matt's chest. "I wrote a note. I wouldn't leave without making sure you knew I'd be back."

Matt breathed a sigh. "Thanks. I'm not sure I could have made it through today if you walked out."

Darian shook his head. "Not walking out."

Matt hugged him again while the coffee brewed. He noticed some things in the living room that had not been there the night before. "What'dya buy?"

Darian answered without questioning. "Art supplies. I like to draw when I'm stressed."

Matt nodded. "Draw, right! Because you're an artist." Jamie's journal entries popped into mind. Darian was an artist and Jamie thought he was a damn good one at that! Matt should encourage it. Jamie would have liked that. "So, what did you get? Show me." He let go and walked into the living room, Darian in tow. "Chalk?"

Darian hurriedly picked up his sketchpad. "Yeah, but this isn't done." He held it protectively away from Matt's view.

Matt smirked. "Are you sure I can't take a peek?"

Darian shook his head.

"Please? Even if I promise to blow your mind after breakfast?" Matt's grin widened.

Darian bashfully ducked his face. "You drive a hard bargain."

"Oh, I can drive you as hard as you like." He winked.

Darian smiled and blushed. Matt loved when he blushed! Then Darian flipped open the pad. "All right. But don't laugh." He turned the picture around.

Matt stared at his own reflection—practically. It was only half colored in, but the rendering was Matt lying in his bed, eyes smoldering. Darian drew him naked but only included his chest and arms. Matt was glad. An X-rated masterpiece would have been embarrassing to display. "That's amazing," he quietly admitted. He walked closer and gently took the sketchpad from Darian's hand to study the details. Darian had captured the very ocean-blue color of his eyes, and every stray hair that grew around his pink nipples. And the cords of muscle in his chest really did look like that! Darian was truly gifted, just as Jamie described. Matt was taken with a sudden wave of pride for his lover. *Darian is really good!* "Can we hang it in our apartment?" he asked.

Darian looked up sharply, "Our?"

Matt smirked. "Yeah. If you want? I figured we could find a place together. I don't think I could stand living apart. You?"

Darian hesitated before shaking his head. "I don't think I could take it either. And I seriously can't go back in Dan's house and see all Jamie's stuff in our room. I can't do it."

Matt caressed Darian's face. "You don't have to. I'll pack your stuff."

"Really? You'd do that for me?" Darian had tears in his eyes.

"I'd do anything for you."

Matt was sure of it. As sure as he would die if he stopped breathing, and sure as he'd stop breathing if Darian were not with him, wherever he went. He needed him. Matt needed Darian as much as air and water and sunshine. Darian was life. And Matt knew he loved him more than the stars had the power to kiss the night sky.

Epilogue

September 27, 2010

I NEVER thought life could be so harsh until my best friend died last week!

I never expected to feel so much pain. Not after everything I'd been through these last few years.

I think a huge part of me died along with him.

But half my soul died last week and was buried in the casket alongside Jamie Miller.

Somehow, I found a new beginning.

Somehow, I found a new beginning.

I didn't expect to fall in love in the aftermath of life-shattering sorrow, but I met Darian and my heart could not resist his warm lips and beautiful brown eyes.

Matt swept into my life like a hurricane on AMP, and suddenly I was freefalling… away from the paralyzing anguish of my loss and into the warm shelter of unexpected tenderness.

Darian made me feel complete, for the first time in my life.

Matt makes me feel so safe.

Will things between us change? As the days and weeks go by, will I revert back to who I was and forget how amazing I feel right now in his arms? It scares me. I don't know what tomorrow holds.

Matt's my comfort. Matt's my security. Matt's my solace. I've never felt so protected in all my life and it scares me. Jamie loved me, I have no doubt, but in six years he never put my needs first in one tenth of the way Matt did this week. Will that change?

I held my eyes shut tonight after we made love and pretended to sleep so I could listen to Darian breathe and take in as much of his wonderful scent as I could. I feel drunk on him, and I never want the feeling to go away.

I clamped my eyes closed tonight after we made love and pretended to sleep so I could listen to him breathing. I inhaled as much of his intoxicating scent as I could. I feel high on Matthias Dixon, and I never want the feeling to fade.

The morning holds what comes next.

The morning holds what comes next.

Will this all fade into nothing?

Will this all fade into nothing?

Or will Darian and I take the first steps into a new life together, clinging to one another, facing the world and finding out that our love is strong enough to endure even our own chasm of doubt? I guess I'll open my eyes in the morning and see.

WADE KELLY lives and writes in conservative, small-town America where it is not easy to live free and open in one's beliefs. Wade writes passionately about the controversial issues witnessed in real life and strives to make a difference by making people think. Wade does not have a background in writing or philosophy but still draws from personal experience to ponder contentious subjects on paper. When not writing, Wade is thinking about writing and more than likely scribbling notes on old napkins in the car.

Visit Wade Kelly at http://wadekelly.weebly.com/index.html. You can contact Wade at writerwadekelly@gmail.com.

Also from DREAMSPINNER PRESS

http://www.dreamspinnerpress.com

www.ingramcontent.com/pod-product-compliance
Lightning Source LLC
Chambersburg PA
CBHW050020070726
47506CB00015B/399